U0101777

中級美語 下

序

這本書是《英語從頭學》系列叢書的第五本。

《英語從頭學》系列叢書共分六本，分別是：

《會話入門》：內容全為基礎會話，教您如何用簡易而實用的字開口說英語。

《初級美語》：分上、下冊，內容有會話及簡易閱讀文章，培養您會話及閱讀的基礎。

《中級美語》：亦分上、下冊，是初級美語的延讀。

《高級閱讀》：培養看懂 *Time* 及 *Newsweek* 的閱讀能力。

這六本書均由本人及外籍編輯按國人英語學習的環境構思情境會話及閱讀文章，內容由淺入深。特別值得一提的是，所有課文均附完全解析，舉凡單字、片語、句型及文法均有實用的例句解說，每課後面均附練習及解答。這也就是為何每本書均厚達 300 頁以上的原因。

讀者拿到本書時，千萬不要嫌它厚重。紮實的內容正是本書的特色。若按部就班，一定可學好英語。

其實，這六本書同時也在**大陸中央人民廣播電台及地方台播出**，由本人親自在空中講解，數年來在整個大陸地區培養了萬千的英語愛好者。其中令我印象最深刻的就是**大連市的王馨穎小妹妹**，她七歲之前沒學過英語，只會唸 ABC 廿六個字母，

在爸爸的鼓勵下，以七個半月的時間，學完會話入門及初級美語上、下冊，竟然在二〇〇二年就**勇奪全中國青少年英語演講比賽冠軍**。如今她九歲了，已成了當地電台及電視台的小小英文老師，爸爸也因此開了一家英語補習班。學習英語改變了他們一家的命運！

吉林省長春市的初中二年級鄭陽同學，也唸這套系列叢書學了兩年英文，於二〇〇三年**勇奪吉林省青少年英文演講大賽冠軍**。**上海一位高中輟學的空調裝配員**則使用本系列業書配合我在中央台的廣播教學學了五年英文，竟然也唸完了**《高級閱讀》**，練就一口流利的美語及精湛的閱讀能力，**如今已是某外商公司的副總經理**。

這些大陸學子的成功全靠著讀本系列叢書。他們能如此，難道您也不能如此嗎？！但願這套《英語從頭學》系列叢書為所有想從頭學好英語的讀者重拾學習英語的信心、開拓光明的前程！

賴世雄

于台北寓書房

目錄 CONTENTS

Lesson 65
Italian Culture
義大利文化

Reading
閱 讀

Italy is a land of history and culture. And as we all know, the ancient architecture there is breathtaking. Just as we Chinese are proud of our history and culture, so are the Italians. One of their traditions is to enjoy a long midday meal. This lengthy lunch can last up to four hours! As you can imagine, after all the eating, drinking and chatting, they need to take a nap.

Well, this custom may be great for the stomach, but it's not so great for getting things done. If you happen to be in Italy, don't be surprised if you have to wait for a long time for the banks and post offices to open.

義大利是個富有歷史和文化的國家。我們都知道，那兒的古代建築令人驚嘆不已。就如同我們中國人對我們的歷史文化感到驕傲，義大利人也是一樣。享受漫長的中餐是他們的傳統之一。這頓漫長的午餐可以持續到四個小時之久呢！你可以想像得到，在這番吃喝閒聊之後，他們需要小睡片刻。

嗯，這種習慣對胃來說可能很棒，但對辦事可就不怎麼好了。如果你正好在義大利，那麼等銀行和郵局開門要等上老半天也不必太驚訝。

Vocabulary & Idioms 單字 & 片語註解

1. **Italian** [ɪ'tæljən] a. 義大利 (語) 的, 義大利人的 & n. 義大利語/人
   Italy ['ɪtəlɪ] n. 義大利

2. **culture** ['kʌltʃɚ] n. 文化
   cultural ['kʌltʃərəl] a. 文化 (上) 的
   例: China has at least 4,000 years of culture.
   (中國至少有四千年的文化。)
   Modernization is bringing about a cultural change in our society.
   (現代化正帶給我們社會文化上的改變。)

3. **land** [lænd] n. 國家 (可數); 土地 (不可數)
   例: America is said to be the land of the free.
   (有人說美國是自由人士的國度。)
   My dad owns some land in the country.
   (我爸在鄉下擁有一些土地。)

4. **ancient** ['enʃənt] a. 古代的; 古老的
   例: There is an ancient statue in the middle of the city.
   (市中央有座古老的雕像。)

5. **architecture** [ˈɑrkəˌtɛktʃɚ] n. 建築

architect [ˈɑrkəˌtɛkt] n. 建築師

例: The tourists admired the architecture of the buildings in Chicago.
(那些觀光客欣賞了芝加哥的大樓建築。)

A good architect must also be artistic.
(好的建築師也必須具有藝術眼光。)

6. **breathtaking** [ˈbrɛθˌtekɪŋ] a. 令人驚嘆的

例: The view of the city is breathtaking.
(城市的景觀令人驚嘆。)

7. **proud** [praʊd] a. 驕傲的

be proud of...　　以……為傲/為榮

例: Mrs. Chen is very proud of her successful children.
(陳太太非常以她兒女的成功為榮。)

8. **midday** [ˈmɪdˌde] n. & a. 正中午 (的)

例: The sun is hottest at midday.
(太陽正午時最熱。)

9. **lengthy** [ˈlɛŋθɪ] a. 冗長的

例: My parents and I had a lengthy discussion about my future.
(關於我的未來，爸媽和我有過冗長的討論。)

10. **last** [læst] vi. 持續

例: This pair of shoes has lasted five years and they're still good.
(這雙鞋子已穿了五年而仍然很好沒有損壞。)

11. **up to + 數字**　　多達……

例: The one-year-old boy can count up to ten.
(那個一歲大的男孩會數到十。)

12. **imagine** [ɪ'mædʒɪn] vt. 想像

例: Can you imagine how it feels to be an astronaut?
(你能想像當一名太空人的感覺嗎？)
＊ astronaut ['æstrəˌnɔt] n. 太空人

13. **chatting** ['tʃætɪŋ] n. 閒談, 聊天

chat [tʃæt] vi. & n. 閒談, 聊天

例: He chats with his girlfriend on the phone for hours every day.
(他每天和女朋友都會在電話上聊好幾個鐘頭。)

Let's go over to our neighbors for a chat.
(咱們去找鄰居聊聊天。)

14. **take a nap** 小睡, 打盹兒

nap [næp] n. 小睡

例: Ron took a nap and felt refreshed.
(朗恩小睡後便覺得精神恢復過來了。)

15. **custom** ['kʌstəm] n. 習慣, 習俗

例: The African tribe has many strange customs.
(那個非洲部落有許多奇怪的習俗。)

16. **stomach** ['stʌmək] n. 胃

17. **get things done** 將事情做完

例: I'm the type of person who likes to get things done quickly.
(我是那種喜歡將事情快快做完的人。)

18. **surprised** [sɚ'praɪzd] a. 感到驚訝的

be surprised at... 對……感到驚訝

例: When I was traveling, I was surprised at people's friendliness.
(在我旅行時，人們的友善讓我感到驚訝。)

Grammar Notes
文法重點

本課介紹 as 作關係代名詞的用法, 並介紹"Just as..., so + 倒裝句"的用法。

1. **And as we all know, the ancient architecture there is breathtaking.**

我們都知道, 那兒的古代建築令人驚嘆不已。

As you can imagine, after all the eating, drinking and chatting, they need to take a nap.

你可以想像得到, 在這番吃喝閒聊之後, 他們需要小睡片刻。

在上列句中, as 作關係代名詞用, 分別代替句中"the ancient architecture there is breathtaking"和"after all the eating, drinking and chatting, they need to take a nap"這兩個主要子句。

as 作關係代名詞時, 即等於 which, 用以代替句中整個主要子句, as 在其引導的形容詞子句中可作主詞或受詞。

例: He is a man of his word, as is known to all of us.
主詞

= He is a man of his word, as we all know.
受詞

= He is a man of his word, which is known to all of us.
= He is a man of his word, which we all know.
(他是個言而有信的人，這點我們都知道。)

注意:

使用 as 取代 which 時, 要注意下列要點:

a. as 引導的形容詞子句可置於主要子句之前或之後, 而 which 引導的形容詞子句則只能置於主要子句之後。故上列例句亦可改為:

As is known to all of us, he is a man of his word.

= As we all know, he is a man of his word.

例: The sun rises in the east, which everybody knows.
主要子句

= The sun rises in the east, as everybody knows.

= As everybody knows, the sun rises in the east.
(太陽從東方升起，此事人人皆知。)

但: Which everybody knows, the sun rises in the east. (×)

b. as 所引導的形容詞子句其句構為"as + be 動詞 + 過去分詞"時, be 動詞可以省略。

例: He is a man of his word, which was mentioned before.

= He is a man of his word, as was mentioned before.
be 動詞　過去分詞

= He is a man of his word, as mentioned before.
(如前如述，他是個言而有信的人。)

由上述可知, 本文亦可寫成:

And the ancient architecture there is breathtaking, as/which we all know.

After all the eating, drinking and chatting, they need to take a nap, as/which we can imagine.

2. **Just as we Chinese are proud of our history and culture, so are the Italians.**

= Just as we Chinese are proud of our history and culture, so are the Italians proud of their history and culture.

就如同我們中國人對我們的歷史文化感到驕傲, 義大利人也是一樣。

上列句中的 Italians 後本有與其前相同的詞類"proud of their history and culture", 為避免重覆, 故予以省略。

本句使用了"Just as..., so + 倒裝句" (就如同…一樣, ……也是……) 的句構, 其中的 just 為強調用法的副詞, 亦可予以省略。

so 之後的句子要採倒裝句構, 倒裝原則如下:

a. 句中有 be 動詞時:

例: Just as most men are ambitious, so are women nowadays.
(就像大部分的男人都懷有雄心大志，現在的婦女也是如此。)

b. 句中有助動詞時:

例: Just as you will protect your children, so will I protect mine.
(就像你會保護自己的子女一樣，我也是如此。)

c. 句中只有一般動詞時, 則按主詞人稱及動詞的時態作變化, 借用助動詞 do、does 或 did:

例: Just as humans need love, so do dogs.
(就像人類需要愛一樣，狗狗也是如此。)

1. **And as we all know, the ancient architecture there is breathtaking.**

As you can see, there are always two sides to an argument.

As we all know, nobody's perfect.

我們都知道, 那兒的古代建築令人驚嘆不已。
如你所知, 每個爭論總有兩面之辭。
我們都知道, 沒有人是完美的。

2. **Just as we Chinese are proud of our history and culture, so are the Italians.**

Just as man needs water to survive, so do plants.

Just as the Chinese are frugal, so are the Jews.

就如同我們中國人對我們的歷史文化感到驕傲, 義大利人也是一樣。
就如同人類需要水才能生存, 植物也是一樣。
就如同中國人很節省, 猶太人也是一樣。

Lesson 66

It's Nap Time

現在是午睡時間

Dialogue
實用會話

Mr. Mishima, a Japanese tourist, enters a bank in Milan, Italy.

(M=Mishima; T=bank teller)

M: Uh, excuse me...

T: Zzzzzz...

M: EXCUSE ME!

T: Aggghhh! What do you want? You scared the life out of me!

M: I'd like to cash a traveler's check, please.

T: At this hour? You must be kidding!

M: But it's two in the afternoon.

T: That's right—and as usual, it's nap time. Come back at three or four. We don't work the same hours as you do in your country.

M: But I have to cash this check. I have no cash!

T: Don't worry. You won't need any cash. All of Italy is asleep at this moment. Zzzzzz...

來自日本的觀光客三島先生走進義大利米蘭市的一家銀行。
三島：嗯，對不起……
行員：(打呼聲)
三島：(大叫)對不起！
行員：啊……！你想幹什麼？嚇死我了！
三島：我想麻煩你兌現一張旅行支票。
行員：現在這個時間嗎？您一定在開玩笑！
三島：可是現在已經下午兩點了。
行員：沒錯——老樣子，現在是午睡時間。三、四點再來吧。我們和你們國家工作的時間不一樣。
三島：可是我得把這張支票兌現。我身上沒錢了！
行員：放心。你用不著現金。現在全義大利都在睡覺。(打呼聲)

Vocabulary & Idioms 單字 & 片語註解

1. **tourist** [ˈtʊrɪst] n. 觀光客

   例: The poor tourist looks as if he's lost.
   (那個可憐的觀光客看起來好像迷路了。)

2. **Milan** [mɪˈlæn] n. 米蘭 (位於義大利北部的都市, 以時裝著稱)

3. **bank teller** [ˈbæŋk ˌtɛlɚ] n. 銀行行員

4. **scare** [skɛr] vt. 驚嚇

   scared [skɛrd] a. 驚嚇的
   scare the life out of + 人　嚇死某人
   be scared of...　害怕……(= be afraid of...)

   例: The old man's ghostly face in the dark scared the life out of me.
   (在黑暗中那老人鬼魅般的臉孔嚇死我了。)

   My little sister is scared of being at home alone at night.
   (我小妹害怕晚上一個人在家。)

5. **cash** [kæʃ] vt. 兌現, 兌付 & n. 現金

例: Do you think we can cash these gift coupons?
(你認為我們可以將這些禮券兌換成現金嗎？)
＊ coupon [ˈkupɑn] n. 優惠券

You don't need cash if you have a credit card.
(你若有張信用卡就不需要現金。)

6. **traveler's check** [ˈtrævlɚz ˌtʃɛk] n. 旅行支票

7. **as usual** 如以往一樣

注意:

as usual 為副詞片語, 作副詞用, 修飾全句, 可置於句首或句尾。

例: <u>As usual</u>, James was the last to leave the office.
= James was the last to leave the office <u>as usual</u>.
(詹姆士如往常一樣是最後一個離開辦公室的。)

8. 本文:

We don't work the same hours as you <u>do</u> in your country.

= We don't work <u>at</u> the same hours as you <u>work</u> in your country.
我們和你們國家工作的時間不一樣。

注意:

a. the same hours 之前, 按理應有介系詞 at, 但 at 可予以省略。

b. 助動詞 do 代替前句的動詞 work。

9. **asleep** [əˈslip] a. 睡著的

fall asleep 入睡

例: When you can't fall asleep, try counting sheep.
(你無法入睡時，試試數羊吧。)

請選出下列各句中正確的一項

1. We have the same fast-food restaurants ______ you do in America.
(A) that (B) so (C) as (D) which

2. The ______ who designed this magnificient building became very famous.
(A) architecture (B) building
(C) architect (D) build

3. As ______, the gambler lost a lot of money in the casino.
(A) usual (B) usually (C) always (D) often

4. I'm so tired, I need to ______ a nap.
(A) make (B) get (C) do (D) take

5. ______ we all know, when autumn comes, leaves turn brown.
(A) Which (B) That (C) As (D) Such

解答:

1. (C) 2. (C) 3. (A) 4. (D) 5. (C)

Lesson 67

Mean What You Say

說話算話

Some people say that promises are made to be broken. That certainly seems to be true in this cutthroat society that we live in. But if you break your promise, you will ruin your reputation and no one will trust you anymore. So whenever we say, "I give you my word," we should mean it. There is nothing worse than to be let down by others because they have not kept their promises.

In fact, it isn't so difficult to keep promises. Just remember never to promise anything we are not sure we can live up to. In

short, therefore, to be trustworthy, we should always say what we mean and mean what we say.

有些人說承諾就是許下來違背的。這種情形在我們所處這個競爭激烈的社會裡似乎是真話。但是如果你違背諾言，就會損毀名譽，而且沒有人會再相信你了。所以每當我們說：『我向你保證，』我們應該是真心誠意。再也沒有比因為別人未能遵守諾言而讓你失望更糟的事了。

事實上，守信並不是那麼困難的事。只要記住絕對不要許下任何你沒把握遵守的諾言。總之，要成為一個值得信賴的人，我們應該時時說內心話和說話算話。

Vocabulary & Idioms 單字 & 片語註解

1. **mean** [min] vt. 意味

人 + mean what + 人 + say　　某人說話算話/心口如一

例: A trustworthy person always means what he says.
(值得信賴的人總是說話算話。)

＊ trustworthy [ˈtrʌstˌwɝðɪ] a. 值得信賴的

2. **promise** [ˈprɑmɪs] n. 承諾, 諾言 & vt. 承諾

make a/one's promise　　許下承諾

keep a/one's promise　　遵守諾言

break a/one's promise　　打破諾言, 食言

promise (人) to + 原形動詞　　答應 (某人) 做……

promise (人) + that 子句　　答應 (某人)……

例: Bobby made a promise to his parents to study harder in the future.
(鮑比對父母許下承諾說以後會更用功。)

Dad kept his promise and took us to Europe on vacation.
(老爸遵守諾言帶我們到歐洲度假。)

Ian promised to repay me the loan in a week.
(伊恩答應一個禮拜後還我錢。)

* repay [rɪˈpe] vt. 付還, 償還

3. **cutthroat** [ˈkʌtˌθrot] a. 競爭激烈的

throat [θrot] n. 喉嚨

例: In this cutthroat society, we must all be careful when doing business.
(在這個競爭激烈的社會裡，做生意時我們都得小心。)

4. **ruin** [ˈruɪn] vt. 毀滅; 破壞

例: The bad weather ruined our holiday.
(壞天氣破壞了我們的假期。)

5. **reputation** [ˌrɛpjəˈteʃən] n. 名譽, 名聲

例: Nick has a reputation as a fair person.
(尼克為人公正是出了名的。)

6. **trust** [trʌst] vt. & n. 信賴

例: If you can't trust your parents, who(m) can you trust?
(如果你連父母都不信賴，還會信賴誰呢？)

My honesty has earned me everybody's trust.
(誠實已為我贏得每個人的信賴。)

7. 本文:

...<u>no</u> one will trust you <u>anymore</u>.

= ...<u>no</u> one will trust you <u>any longer</u>.
……沒有人會再相信你了。

8. **I give you my word.** 我給你我的承諾/我向你保證。

* word [wɝd] n. 諾言; 字眼, 話語; 爭論

注意:

word 表『諾言』時為不可數名詞; 但若表『字眼、話語、爭論』時則為可數名詞, 且常用複數。

keep/break one's word　　信守/不守諾言

have words with...　　與……爭論/口角

例: He is a man of his word.
(他是個信守承諾的人。)

Kent broke his <u>words</u> when... (×)

→ Kent broke his word when he failed to show up at the meeting. (○)
(肯特不守諾言，因為他沒有在會議上出現。)

The principal had words with the naughty student's parents.
(校長和那名頑皮學生的家長發生口角。)

9. **let + 人 + down**　　讓某人失望

= disappoint + 人

＊ disappoint [ˌdɪsəˈpɔɪnt] vt. 使失望

例: My friend let me down when I was in trouble.
= My friend disappointed me when I was in trouble.
(朋友在我有麻煩時令我失望。)

10. **be sure + (that) 子句**　　確信/定……

例: Be sure that the door is locked before you leave the house.
(在你離開屋子前，要確定門鎖上了。)

11. **live up to...**　　符合/遵守……

例: Pete lived up to his father's expectations.
(彼特達到了他父親的期望。)

12. 句型分析:

<u>Just remember</u> <u>never to promise anything</u> <u>we are</u> <u>not sure we can live up to.</u>
(1)　(2)　(3)

(1) 原形及物動詞形成的命令句, 其前省略了 You should。

(2) 否定副詞 never 加不定詞片語形成的否定不定詞片語，作(1)中及物動詞 remember 的受詞。

(3) 關係代名詞 that (已省略) 引導的形容詞子句，代替(2)中的 anything，並作 live up to 的受詞；其中 sure 之後省略了 that，其所引導的子句修飾其前的 sure，故此子句視為副詞子句。

13. **in short** 簡言之

例: In short, that was the best concert that I've ever been to.
(簡言之，那是我曾去過最好的一場音樂會。)

14. **trustworthy** [ˈtrʌstˌwɝðɪ] a. 值得信賴的，可靠的

例: A trustworthy person usually has many friends.
(一個值得信賴的人通常會有許多朋友。)

Grammar Notes 文法重點

本課介紹不定詞片語與否定副詞 never、not 並用形成否定句構的用法。

Just remember <u>never to</u> promise anything we are not sure we can live up to.
只要記住絕對不要許下任何你沒把握遵守的諾言。

注意:

不定詞片語 (to + 原形動詞) 與否定副詞 never、not 並用形成否定句構時，要將 never 或 not 置於 to 之前，而不可置於其後。

例: Mother told me <u>to never speak</u> to strangers. (×)
→ Mother told me <u>never to speak</u> to strangers. (○)
(媽媽告訴我絕不可和陌生人說話。)

The doctor advised me <u>to not eat</u> fatty foods. (×)

→ The doctor advised me not to eat fatty foods. (○)
(醫生建議我不要吃油膩的食物。)

Substitution 代換

Just remember never to promise anything we are not sure we can live up to.

My dad told me not to trust anyone.

Remember not to be late for the meeting.

只要記住絕對不要許下任何你沒把握遵守的諾言。

我爸爸告訴我不要信任任何人。

記住開會不要遲到了。

Lesson 68

A Promise Is a Promise

君子一言，駟馬難追

Dialogue
實用會話

Larry is talking to his classmate, Hedy.

(L= Larry; H=Hedy)

L: Hi, Hedy! What seems to be bothering you?

H: I don't understand why my boyfriend finds it so hard to keep his word.

L: What has he done this time?

H: Well, he made a date with me to see a movie last night, but he stood me up.

L: What a lousy guy!

H: I know. And there's nothing worse than to be in love with such a guy.

L: Why don't you just dump him?

H: I can't.

L: Why not?

H: I promised I'd never leave him. And a promise is a promise.

L: Oh, boy.

賴瑞正在和他的同學海蒂談話。
賴瑞：嗨，海蒂！好像有什麼事情煩著妳？
海蒂：我不懂為什麼我的男朋友會覺得說話算話那麼難。
賴瑞：他這次幹了什麼好事？
海蒂：嗯，他昨晚約我去看電影但是他放我鴿子。
賴瑞：真是個差勁的傢伙！
海蒂：我知道。而且沒有比愛上這種傢伙更糟的事了。
賴瑞：妳何不就把他給甩了？
海蒂：我做不到。
賴瑞：為什麼？
海蒂：我答應過他我絕不會離開他的。君子一言，駟馬難追。
賴瑞：哦，天啊！

Key Points 重點提示

1. **A promise is a promise.** 君子一言, 駟馬難追。

例: You must keep your word; a promise is a promise.
(你必須信守承諾；君子一言，駟馬難追。)

2. **bother** [ˈbɑðɚ] vt. 困擾, 煩擾

例: Don't bother me with all your trivial problems.
(不要拿你所有的瑣事來煩我。)
* trivial [ˈtrɪvɪəl] a. 瑣碎的; 微不足道的

3. **date** [det] n. 約會

make a date with + 人　約某人約定見面
go on a date with + 人　和某人約會

例: Can I make a date with you to take in a movie tomorrow?
(我可以約你明天去看一場電影嗎？)
* take in...　觀賞 (電影、演唱會等)

Do you believe that I once went on a date with that actress?
(你相不相信我曾經和那名女演員約會過？)

4. **stand + 人 + up** 放某人鴿子

例: If I stand my girlfriend up just once, she'll dump me right away.
(如果我放我女朋友一次鴿子，她會立刻甩了我。)

5. **lousy** [ˈlaʊzɪ] a. 差勁的

例: What a lousy movie that was!
(那真是一部爛片！)

6. **there is nothing worse than...** 沒有比……更糟的事了

there is nothing better than... 沒有比……更好的事了

例: There is nothing worse than being (或 to be) addicted to drugs.
(沒有比沈溺於毒品更糟的事了。)

There is nothing better than taking (或 to take) a bath after a busy day.
(沒有比忙了一天後洗個澡更好的事了。)

7. **dump** [dʌmp] vt. (俚) 甩掉 (本意為『傾倒』)

例: The woman dumped her husband and ran off with a rich old man.
(那個婦人甩了她老公和一個有錢的老頭跑了。)

請選出下列各句中正確的一項

1. Little Johnny promised ______ lies again.
(A) never to tell (B) to never tell
(C) never tell (D) to tell never

2. If you ______ a promise, you won't be believed the next time you make one.
(A) make (B) take (C) break (D) keep

3. Frank ______ last night because he suddenly got sick.
(A) stood us by (B) stood by us
(C) stood us up (D) stood up us

4. Andy finds ______ to visit the zoo.
(A) exciting (B) it exciting (C) excited (D) it excited

5. ______ short, I think this is quite a good book.
(A) At (B) In (C) Of (D) By

解答:

1. (A) 2. (C) 3. (C) 4. (B) 5. (B)

Lesson 69

Earth in Danger

地球危機

Seeing is believing. But seeing a huge rock half the size of Earth smash into Jupiter in July 1996 was incredible. Can you imagine what would happen if Earth collided with a huge space rock? It would be disastrous. In fact, it is thought that a meteor killed the dinosaurs millions of years ago.

A rock like the one that hit Jupiter could split Earth in two. Doing nothing about it is like waiting for the end of the world. So scientists plan to start a project to identify all space rocks that could hit Earth.

眼見為憑，但目睹一顆有地球一半大的巨大石塊在西元一九九六年七月撞向木星卻令人無法置信。你能夠想像地球如果撞上太空中的一顆巨大石塊會怎麼樣嗎？那後果將不堪設想。事實上，有人認為在數百萬年前就是一塊隕石造成所有的恐龍滅絕。

一顆像撞到木星那樣的岩石便可把地球撞成兩半。如果不提出對策就無異於等待地球末日的來臨。因此科學家打算展開一項計畫來辨識所有可能擊中地球的隕石。

Vocabulary & Idioms 單字 & 片語註解

1. **be in danger** 陷入危險中

例: Mr. Wang is in danger of going bankrupt.
(王先生有破產之虞。)

2. **Seeing is believing.** 眼見為憑。(諺語)

= To see is to believe.

例: Maggie: I can eat three bowls of noodles in one minute.
Frank: Seeing is believing.
(梅　姬：我可以在一分鐘內吃三碗麵。)
(法蘭克：眼見為憑。)

3. **huge** [hjudʒ] a. 巨大的

例: There's a huge swelling on my right foot.
(我的右腳上有個大腫塊。)

4. **rock** [rɑk] n. 石塊, 岩石

5. **smash** [smæʃ] vi. 猛衝; 碰撞

smash into... 撞及……

例: The truck smashed into a tree.
(那輛卡車撞到了一棵樹。)

6. **Jupiter** [ˈdʒupətɚ] n. 木星

7. **incredible** [ɪnˈkrɛdəbl̩] a. 令人難相信的, 難以置信的

例: Anita has an incredible voice.
(安妮塔有著令人難以相信的美妙嗓音。)

8. **imagine** [ɪˈmædʒɪn] vt. 想像, 推測

例: It's hard to imagine what it would be like to be an astronaut.
(很難想像成為一名太空人會是什麼樣子。)

9. **collide** [kəˈlaɪd] vi. 互撞, 碰撞

collide with...　　和……互撞/相撞

例: The jeep collided with a truck on the highway.
(那輛吉普車在高速公路上和一輛卡車相撞。)

10. **disastrous** [dɪˈzæstrəs] a. 悲慘的, 不幸的; 災害的

disaster [dɪˈzæstɚ] n. 災難

例: The disastrous earthquake destroyed many houses.
(那場災難性的地震摧毀了許多房屋。)

The pilot's quick reaction avoided a disaster.
(那名飛行員快速的反應避免了一場災難。)

11. **meteor** [ˈmitɪɚ] n. 流星

meteorite [ˈmitɪəˌraɪt] n. 隕石

例: When a meteor enters the earth's atmosphere, it burns up leaving a streak of light.
(當流星進入地球大氣時，它會燒毀而遺留下一道亮光。)

Scientists estimate the meteorite to be at least ten thousand years old.
(科學家們估計那顆隕石至少已有一萬年了。)

12. **dinosaur** [ˈdaɪnəˌsɔr] n. 恐龍

例: *Jurassic Park* is a movie about dinosaurs.
(『侏羅紀公園』是一部關於恐龍的電影。)

13. **split** [splɪt] vt. & vi. (使) 分裂

動詞三態均為 split。

split...in two　　把……分成兩半

split into...　　分成……

例: The vendor can split apples in two with his hands.
(那個攤販可以用手把蘋果分成兩半。)

Let's split into two groups and try to look for the lost child.
(咱們分成兩組想辦法尋找那名走失的小孩。)

14. **do nothing about...**　　不對……採取行動

do something about...　　對……採取行動

例: If you do nothing about your cold, it will only get worse.
(如果你對感冒置之不理，它將只會更糟。)

Ben promised to do something about the broken computer.
(班承諾要處理這台壞掉的電腦。)

15. **scientist** [ˈsaɪəntɪst] n. 科學家

例: Some scientists have gone into jungles to look for a cure for AIDS.
(有些科學家已經進入叢林去尋找治療愛滋病的方法。)

16. **project** [ˈprɑdʒɛkt] n. 計畫

例: How is your project to build your own house coming along?
(你建造自己房子的計畫進展得如何？)

17. **identify** [aɪˈdɛntəˌfaɪ] vt. 辨識, 確認

例: The bodies were burnt so badly in the fire, no one could identify them.
(那些屍體在火場中燒毀得很嚴重，以致於沒有人能夠辨識它們。)

Grammar Notes
文法重點

本課介紹"倍數詞 + the size of..." (是……的幾倍大小) 的用法。

1. **But seeing a huge rock half the size of Earth smash into Jupiter in July 1996 was incredible.**

= But seeing a huge rock (which was) half as large as Earth smash into Jupiter in July 1996 was incredible.
但目睹一顆有地球一半大的巨大石塊在西元一九九六年七月撞向木星卻令人無法置信。

be + 倍數詞 (one-third、half、twice、three times...) + the size of...
= be + 倍數詞 (one-third、half、twice、three times...) + as large as...
是……的三分之一、一半、兩倍、三倍……大

例: My bedroom is half the size of my living room.
= My bedroom is half as large as my living room.
(我的臥室是我家客廳的一半大。)

The boss's desk is three times the size of his employees' desks.
= The boss's desk is three times as large as his employee's desks.
(老闆的辦公桌是他員工的三倍大。)

2. **A rock like the one that hit Jupiter could split Earth in two.**
(1) A rock (2) like the one (3) that hit Jupiter (4) could split Earth in two.
一顆像撞到木星那樣的岩石便可把地球撞成兩半。
句型分析:
(1) 主詞
(2) 介詞片語, 作形容詞用, 修飾 (1); 此處的 like 是介詞, 譯成『像……』, the one 則為代名詞, 等於 the rock。
(3) 關係代名詞 that 引導的形容詞子句, 修飾(2)中的 the one。
(4) 述部

Substitution 代換

Seeing a huge rock half the size of Earth smash into Jupiter in July 1996 was incredible.

My new office is twice the size of my old one.

The child's hand is only one-third the size of his mother's.

目睹一顆有地球一半大的巨大石塊在西元一九九六年七月撞向木星卻令人無法置信。

我的新辦公室是舊辦公室的兩倍大。

那小孩的手只有他媽媽的三分之一大。

Lesson 70

Saving the World

拯救世界

Dialogue 實用會話

A student is talking to her teacher.

(S=student; T=teacher)

S: I hear that scientists are planning to study asteroids and meteors, right?

T: Yes. They want to determine whether Earth is in danger of being struck by such a rock.

S: What if they discover that a big one is coming straight for us?

T: In that case, there are two things they can do. They can launch rockets to push the rock off its course.

S: So that it will miss Earth, right?

T: Right. And if that fails, we can try destroying the rock with nuclear missiles.

S: Wow! I never thought that nuclear weapons could save the world instead of ending it!

一位學生正在和她的老師說話。
學生：我聽說科學家正計畫研究小行星和隕石，對不對？
老師：對。他們要判定地球是否會有被那種石頭撞上的危險。
學生：如果他們發現有一顆大石頭直接朝我們來怎麼辦？
老師：那樣的話，他們能做的有兩件事。他們可以發射火箭將石頭推離軌道。
學生：這麼一來石頭便撞不著地球了，對不對？
老師：對。這個方法不成功的話，我們還可以嘗試用核子飛彈來摧毀石塊。
學生：哇！我從來沒有想到核子武器可以拯救世界而不是毀了它！

1. **asteroid** [ˈæstəˌrɔɪd] n. 小行星

例: There are many asteroids that revolve round the sun.
(有許多小行星繞著太陽運轉。)

2. **determine** [dɪˈtɝmɪn] vt. 判定; 決定

determined [dɪˈtɝmɪnd] a. 下定決心的

determine + that 子句　　判定/決定……

be determined to + 原形動詞　　決心……

例: The jury determined that the man was innocent.
(陪審團判定那名男子無罪。)

Nick is determined to play in the NBA one day.
(尼克決心有一天要打美國職籃。)

3. **be in danger of...**　　面臨……的危險

例: This type of animal is in danger of being extinct.
(這類動物有瀕臨絕種的危險。)

4. **strike** [straɪk] vt. 敲, 擊; 擊中, 撞

動詞三態: strike、struck [strʌk]、struck。

＊ 本文 struck 為過去分詞形態。

例: The monk struck the gong every hour.
(那個和尚每個鐘頭敲一次鑼。)
＊ gong [gɔŋ] n. 鑼

The tree was struck by lightning.
(那棵樹被閃電擊中了。)

5. **discover** [dɪˈskʌvɚ] vt. 發現

discovery [dɪˈskʌvərɪ] n. 發現 (物)

make a/the discovery　　完成一項發現

例: Fortunately, the secretary discovered the mistake before the letter was sent.
(幸好，那位秘書在該信函寄出前就發現了這個錯誤。)

Scientists have made wonderful discoveries in the last decade.
(過去十年來，科學家已經完成了多項驚人的發現。)

6. **straight** [stret] adv. 筆直地

例: The drunkard couldn't walk straight.
(那個醉漢無法直線而行。)

7. **launch** [lɔntʃ] vt. 發射

例: The terrorists launched a rocket bomb at the Pentagon.
(恐怖份子向美國的五角大廈發射了一枚火箭飛彈。)
＊ the Pentagon [ˈpɛntəˌgɑn] n. 五角大廈, 美國國防部

8. **rocket** [ˈrɑkɪt] n. 火箭

9. **course** [kɔrs] n. 所經之路, 軌道

off (one's) course　　偏離軌道/航線

on (one's) course　　沿著軌道/航線

in due course　　假以時日, 在適當的時候

例: The boat went off course during the storm.
(那艘船在暴風雨中偏離了航線。)

If you work hard, you'll be successful in due course.
(你若用功的話，假以時日必會成功。)

10. **miss** [mɪs] vt. 錯過; 想念

例: I overslept and missed the train this morning.
(今早我睡過頭而錯過了火車。)

Christina misses her friends in Canada.
(克莉絲汀娜想念她在加拿大的朋友。)

11. 本文:

So that it will miss Earth, right?

= <u>They can launch rockets to push the rock off its course</u> so that it will miss Earth, right?
他們可以發射火箭將石塊推離軌道, 這樣一來它就不會撞到地球了, 對不對？

＊ 此處 so that 為副詞連接詞, 表『這樣一來』。

12. **destroy** [dɪˈstrɔɪ] vt. 摧毀

例: The fire destroyed everything he owned.
(那場大火摧毀了他擁有的一切。)

13. **nuclear** [ˈnjuklɪɚ] a. 核子的

例: If there's a nuclear war, that will be the end of the world.
(如果發生核戰，那將會是世界末日。)

14. **missile** [ˈmɪsḷ] n. 飛彈

15. **weapon** [ˈwɛpən] n. 武器

16. **instead of + 動名詞/名詞**　　代替……, 而非……

例: We stayed at home instead of going out in the stormy weather.
(在暴風雨天裡我們留在家中不出門。)

請選出下列各句中正確的一項

1. As the taxi turned the corner, it ______ a bus.
   (A) collided (B) collided with
   (C) collided into (D) collided by

2. The basketball player's hands are ______ mine.
   (A) as large as twice (B) as twice large as
   (C) as large twice as (D) twice as large as

3. ______ complaining, you should try to solve the problem.
   (A) Instead (B) Beside (C) Instead of (D) Condition

4. Although they're behind schedule now, they'll finish the project ______ due course.
   (A) in (B) on (C) off (D) above

5. This is the most interesting novel ______ I have ever read.
   (A) which (B) who (C) that (D) as

解答:

1. (B) 2. (D) 3. (C) 4. (A) 5. (C)

Lesson 71

Don't Be a Fish Out of Water

不要覺得彆扭

Reading 閱讀

Do you sometimes have a hard time understanding what Americans are talking about among themselves? Do you want to know why? The answer is, Americans are crazy about using slang. They tend to overdo it, though.

Otherwise, slang is fun to use. You should try it. And some slang is easy to understand. For example, if someone is "off the hook," it means that he is no longer in trouble. The "hook" is a fish hook. If a fish is on the hook, of course, it is in trouble. If it is "off the hook," then it is out of danger. Didn't we tell you slang is fun? Besides, it should at least help you feel more at home and not like a fish out of water when you speak to Americans.

你是否有時難以了解美國人彼此之間在說些什麼？你想要知道為什麼嗎？答案是美國人非常喜歡使用俚語。然而，他們往往會用得過火。

否則的話，使用俚語是很有趣的。你應該試試看。而有些俚語很容易了解。例如，如果說某人『脫離魚鉤』，那表示他已脫離困境。『鉤』在這裡指的是魚鉤。如果魚兒上鉤，牠就當然有了麻煩；若魚兒脫離了魚鉤，那牠就脫離了危險。我們不是告訴過你俚語很有趣嗎？此外，當你和美國佬交談時，用俚語至少會讓你感到比較自在而不覺得彆扭。

Vocabulary & Idioms 單字 & 片語註解

1. **Don't be a fish out of water.**　　不要覺得彆扭。

= Don't be embarrassingly different from everyone else.

* be / feel like　a fish out of water

像魚兒離水般不知所措/很不自在/侷促不安

* embarrassingly [ɪm'bærəsɪŋlɪ] adv. 彆扭地, 不自在地

例: Jane felt like a fish out of water when she wore jeans to the party but all the other girls wore skirts.
(當珍穿著牛仔褲參加派對而其他女孩子都穿裙子時，她覺得很不自在。)

2. **crazy** ['krezɪ] a. 狂熱的; 瘋狂的

be crazy about...　　非常喜歡……; 對……狂熱

go crazy　　抓狂

例: Dave is crazy about basketball.
(戴夫非常迷籃球。)

Tony went crazy when his girlfriend went out with another man.
(當湯尼的女友和別的男人約會時，他氣瘋了。)

3. **slang** [slæŋ] n. 俚語 (不可數)

例: People don't usually use slang on formal occasions.
(在正式場合中人們不常使用俚語。)

* occasion [əˈkeʒən] n. 場合

注意:

若表『一個俚語』則應說"a slang expression"。

4. **tend to + 原形動詞** 往往會……; 易於……; 有……傾向

= be apt to + 原形動詞

= be liable to + 原形動詞

例: Frank tends to get nervous when speaking to girls.
(法蘭克和女孩子講話時很容易緊張。)

5. **overdo** [ˌovəˌdu] vt. 過度使用

動詞三態: overdo、overdid [ˌovəˈdɪd]、overdone [ˌovəˈdʌn]。

例: It's good to work hard but don't overdo it.
(勤奮努力很好，但不可過度。)

6. **otherwise** [ˈʌðəˌwaɪz] adv. 否則 (的話)

例: Don't take drugs. Otherwise, you'll regret it one day.
(不要吸毒。否則，將來有一天你會後悔的。)

7. **be off the hook** 脫離困境/危險

hook [hʊk] n. 魚鉤; 鉤, 陷阱

例: Now that the real murderer confessed to the murder, the original suspect is off the hook.
(既然真正的凶手承認犯下了那樁謀殺案，原嫌疑犯便消白了。)

* suspect [ˈsʌspɛkt] n. 嫌疑犯

The Cantonese restaurant hangs the cooked chickens and ducks on hooks.
(那家廣式餐廳把煮好的雞鴨掛在鉤子上。)

8. **feel at home** 感到自在/不拘束
= feel relaxed

例: Make yourself feel at home; don't stand on ceremony.
(放輕鬆；不要拘束。)

* stand on ceremony 講究禮節; 拘於形式
ceremony [ˈsɛrə͵monɪ] n. 儀式

Grammar Notes 文法重點

本課複習"have a hard time + 動名詞" (做……有困難/麻煩) 的用法, 另介紹 "tend to + 原形動詞" (有……傾向) 的用法。

1. **Do you sometimes have a hard time understanding what Americans are talking about among themselves?**
你是否有時難以了解美國人彼此之間在說些什麼？
上列句中使用了"have a hard time + 動名詞" (做……有困難/麻煩) 的用法, 在此句型中, a hard time 後理論上有一介詞 in, 故其後須接動名詞作其受詞, 而不可接不定詞片語 (to + 原形動詞), 但實際使用時, in 一律不可寫出, 而直接接動名詞。

have	a hard time trouble difficulty problems	+ 動名詞	做/在……(方面) 有困難/麻煩

例: James has trouble getting along with others.
(詹姆士跟別人處不太來。)

Mr. Chen has problems communicating with his stubborn son.
(陳先生很難跟他固執的兒子溝通。)

注意:
下列句型亦採相同結構:

have fun / a good time + 動名詞 從事……很愉快/有趣

2. **They tend to overdo it, though.**
然而, 他們往往會用得過火。
tend to + 原形動詞 有……傾向, 易於……; 往往會……
= be apt to + 原形動詞
= be inclined to + 原形動詞
= be liable to + 原形動詞
= be prone to + 原形動詞
tend [tɛnd] vi. 有……傾向, 易於……
apt [æpt] a. 有……傾向的, 易於……
inclined [ɪnˈklaɪnd] a. 有……傾向的
liable [ˈlaɪəbl̩] a. 易於……的
prone [pron] a. 有……傾向的, 易於……的

例: Mothers tend to exaggerate about their children.
(做母親的往往會過份誇耀自己的孩子。)

Anna is inclined to believe whatever her husband says.
(安娜很容易相信丈夫說的話。)

The naughty kid is prone to get into trouble.
(那個調皮搗蛋的小子很容易闖禍。)

Substitution
代　　換

1. **Do you sometimes have a hard time understanding what Americans are talking about among themselves?**
   The students have trouble pronouncing "r" and "l".
   Do you have any difficulty understanding your teacher?
   你是否有時難以了解美國人彼此之間在說什麼？
   那些學生很難發出 r 和 l 的音。
   你有沒有任何困難聽懂你老師的話？

2. **They tend to overdo it, though.**
   The dishonest man is apt to lie.
   Henry is inclined to treat his students too leniently.
   然而，他們往往會用得過火。
   那名不誠實的男子常會說謊。
   亨利往往對其學生太寬厚了。

Lesson 72

Get with It, Bob

別土了，鮑勃

Dialogue 實用會話

Bob, who is Chinese, is speaking to his American classmate, Jill.

(J= Jill; B= Bob)

J: Hi, Bob. What's up?

B: I don't see anything up in the sky. Do you?

J: No, Bob. "What's up?" is slang for "What's happening?"

B: Well, why didn't you just ask me that in the first place?

J: Get with it, Bob. Everyone uses slang in America. It makes speech more colorful.

B: I'm having enough trouble learning English.

J: But you should give it your best shot, Bob.

B: Why?

J: How else can you get to meet American chicks?

B: What chicks? I don't like eggs.

J: "Chicks" means "girls," you fool.

B: Oh, I give up!

鮑勃是中國人，他正和美籍同學吉兒講話。
吉兒：嗨，鮑勃，怎麼樣啊？(字面意思為：天上有什麼？)
鮑勃：我沒看到天上有什麼東西。妳有嗎？
吉兒：不是，鮑勃。"What's up?"是"What's happening?"(怎麼樣啊？)的俚語用法。
鮑勃：嗯，那妳為什麼不一開始就那樣問我？
吉兒：別土了，鮑勃。美國每個人都用俚語，俚語使得說話更多采多姿。
鮑勃：我學英文就已經困難重重了。
吉兒：但是你應該盡力試試看。
鮑勃：為什麼？
吉兒：要不然你怎麼能夠認識美國馬子？(chick 字面意思為『小雞』)
鮑勃：什麼小雞？我不喜歡吃雞蛋。
吉兒："Chicks"指的是"girls"(女孩)，你這個笨蛋。
鮑勃：哦，我放棄了。

Key Points 重點提示

1. **get with it** 跟上時代潮流, 別土了

注意:
本片語是用在看到他人思想上或作風上落伍, 因而勸其要跟上時代潮流所用的慣用語。其中 it 乃指時代潮流。

例: Nobody wears that kind of tie anymore; get with it, Bruce.
(再也沒有人打那種領帶了，跟上潮流吧，布魯斯。)

2. **What's up**? 怎麼樣啊？/最近怎麼樣？/怎麼啦？

= What's happening?

= What's going on?

例: Andy, I haven't seen you for a long time; what's up?
(安迪，好久不見了，你最近怎麼樣？)

Vivian, you're crying. What's up?
(薇薇安，妳哭了。怎麼啦？)

3. **sky** [skaɪ] n. 天空

4. **in the first place** 一開始, 首先

例: Why are you so angry with me? In the first place, I wasn't criticizing you. I was talking about someone else.
(你為什麼生我的氣呢？首先，我不是在批評你，我在談論別人。)

5. **colorful** [ˈkʌlɚfəl] a. 多彩多姿的; 鮮豔的

例: The playboy leads a colorful life.
(那名花花公子過著多彩多姿的生活。)

I feel young when I wear colorful clothes.
(我穿著鮮豔衣服時覺得年輕有朝氣。)

6. **give it one's best shot** 盡 (某人) 全力去做

give it a shot 試試某事

= give it a try

例: Whatever you do, you should always give it your best shot.
(不管你做什麼事都應該盡全力去做。)

I've never tried bungee jumping, but I don't mind giving it a shot.
(我從沒試過高空彈跳，但我不介意試試看。)

7. **chick** [tʃɪk] n. 本意為『小雞』, 本文意指『女孩子』, 相當於年輕人口中的『馬子』

8. **give up** 放棄

give up... 放棄……

例: I can't guess how old you are. I give up.
(我猜不出來你幾歲，我放棄。)

It's not as difficult to give up smoking as you think.
(戒煙不如你想像中的難。)

請選出下列各句中正確的一項

1. A: Why don't you be quiet?
   B: Who asked for your opinion in the first ______?
   (A) step (B) place (C) sky (D) slang

2. Mrs. Chen is ______ to exaggerate things.
   (A) tend (B) apt (C) easy (D) hard

3. Rick has a hard time ______ to life in France.
   (A) adapt (B) to adapt (C) adapting (D) adapted

4. I don't know how difficult the job may be, but I'm willing to give it a ______.
   (A) play (B) shot (C) leg (D) head

5. Clark ______ learning Greek because he found it too difficult.
   (A) took up (B) took off (C) got up (D) gave up

解答:

1. (B) 2. (B) 3. (C) 4. (B) 5. (D)

Lesson 73

The Amish

亞米希人

Reading 閱讀

In the heart of America, in the states of Pennsylvania, Ohio and Indiana, live some people who are not your typical Americans. In order to lead simple lives, they don't use cars. Instead, they drive horse-drawn buggies. They don't use electric lights, either, not to mention telephones. They make their own clothing which looks ancient. And, to make matters worse, they don't speak English but German among themselves.

These people are the Amish. They settled in America almost 300 years ago. Most of them are farmers who stay away from the temptations of the city. As modern life becomes more and more complicated, the Amish way of life seems to make more and more sense.

在美國的心臟地帶，也就是在賓夕凡尼亞州、俄亥俄州和印第安納州，住著一些非典型的美國人。為了過簡樸的生活，他們不開車，反而駕駛馬車。他們也不使用電燈，更別說是電話了。他們自己做樣式古老的衣服。更糟的是，他們彼此之間不用英文交談，而是用德文。

這些人是亞米希人。他們在近三百年前來到美國定居。他們大部分都是遠離城市誘惑的農民。在現代生活變得愈來愈複雜的同時，亞米希人的生活方式似乎越來越有道理了。

Vocabulary & Idioms 單字 & 片語註解

1. **the Amish** 亞米希人
= Amish people
Amish [ˈɑmɪʃ] a. 亞米希 (人) 的

2. **in the heart of...** 在……的心臟地帶
例: Anna's apartment is in the heart of the city.
(安娜的公寓在市中心。)

3. **state** [stet] n. (美國) 州
例: Bill lived in the state of New York during his childhood.
(比爾年幼時住在紐約州。)

4. **typical** [ˈtɪpɪkḷ] a. 典型的
例: Charles has a typical Boston accent.
(查爾斯操著一口典型的波士頓口音。)

5. **in order to + 原形動詞** 為了……

例: Doris cooks every day in order to make her husband happy.
(桃樂絲為了取悅老公每天都下廚。)

6. **lead / live (a/an)...life** 過著……的生活/日子

注意:
上述片語係屬於同系名詞作及物動詞受詞的用法, 常見的尚有:
dream a/an...dream 做一個……的夢
sigh a/an...sigh 嘆了一口……的氣

例: Eric prefers to live a quiet life in the country.
(艾瑞克寧願在鄉下過著寧靜的生活。)

John dreamed a sweet dream of his girlfriend last night.
(約翰昨天晚上做了一個美夢，夢到他的女朋友。)

7. **horse-drawn** [ˈhɔrsˌdrɔn] a. 馬拉的

例: The bride arrived in a horse-drawn carriage for the wedding ceremony.
(新娘乘坐一輛馬車到達婚禮現場。)

8. **buggies** [ˈbʌgɪz] n. 四輪馬車 (複數形)
buggy [ˈbʌgɪ] n. 四輪馬車 (單數形)

9. 本文:
Instead, they drive horse-drawn buggies.
= Instead, they drive buggies which are drawn by horses.
他們反而駕駛馬車。

10. **electric light** [əˌlɛktrɪk ˈlaɪt] n. 電燈

例: Before the electric light was invented, people used lamps.
(電燈發明之前，人們都使用油燈。)
＊ lamp [læmp] n. 油燈

11. **not to mention...** 更別說是……

例: Mr. Wang can afford to buy a villa, not to mention an apartment.
(王先生買得起別墅，更別說是公寓了。)
* villa [ˈvɪlə] n. 別墅

12. **clothing** [ˈkloðɪŋ] n. 衣服 (集合名詞, 不可數)
clothes [kloz] n. 衣服 (恒為複數, 亦不可數)

例: The poor beggar needs food and clothing.
(那個可憐的乞丐需要吃的和穿的。)

Jane only wears brand-name clothes.
(珍只穿名牌衣服。)
* brand-name [ˈbrændˌnem] a. 著名品牌的

13. **ancient** [ˈenʃənt] a. 古老的

例: There's an ancient temple in the middle of the city.
(城中心有座古廟。)

14. **to make matters worse, 主詞 + 動詞** 更糟的是,……
= what is/was even worse, 主詞 + 動詞

例: Sara's divorced. To make matters worse, her husband got custody of the children.
(莎拉離婚了；更糟的是，她老公得到孩子的監護權。)
* custody [ˈkʌstədɪ] n. 監護權

15. **settle** [ˈsɛtl̩] vi. 定居; 安頓 & vt. 解決 (紛爭)
settle down 安定下來

例: It's about time for Fred to get married and settle down.
(是弗瑞德結婚安定下來的時候了。)

I'm busy now, but I'll surely settle the matter with you later.
(我現在很忙，但我待會兒一定會和你一起解決這件事。)

16. **farmer** [ˈfɑrmɚ] n. 農夫

17. **stay away from...** 遠離……

例: Be smart and stay away from bad friends.
(放聰明點，遠離損友。)

18. **temptation** [tɛmp'teʃən] n. 誘惑

例: The official couldn't resist the temptation and took the bribe.
(那個政府官員禁不住誘惑而接受了賄賂。)
∗ bribe [braɪb] n. 賄賂

19. **complicated** ['kɑmplə,ketɪd] a. 複雜的

例: This is a complicated world we live in.
(我們生活在一個複雜的世界中。)

20. **way of life** 生活方式

例: The farmer's way of life is very simple.
(那個農夫的生活方式非常簡樸。)

21. **make sense** 有意義, 有道理

sense [sɛns] n. 意義

例: It makes sense to plan your future carefully.
(仔細計畫未來是合情合理的。)

Grammar Notes 文法重點

本課介紹地方副詞 (片語) 置於句首時, 其後須採倒裝句構的用法, 並介紹 "not to mention" (更不用說) 的用法, 另介紹獨立不定詞片語"to make matters worse" (更糟的是) 的用法。

1. **In the heart of America, in the states of Pennsylvania, Ohio and Indiana, live some people who are not your typical Americans.**

= Some people who are not your typical Americans live in the heart of America, in the states of Pennsylvania, Ohio and Indiana.

在美國的心臟地帶,也就是賓夕凡尼亞州、俄亥俄州和印第安納州,住著一些非典型的美國人。

上列句中的 some people who...Americans 是主詞, live 是不及物動詞, in the heart of...Indiana 是地方副詞片語。

本句使用了倒裝句構, 因地方副詞或地方副詞片語若置於句首時, 其後的句子須倒裝。倒裝原則如下:

a. 主詞 + 不及物動詞 + 地方副詞 (片語)

→ 地方副詞 (片語) + 不及物動詞 + 主詞

＊本句即屬此用法。

例: Bill (主詞) stood (不及物動詞) there (地方副詞).

→ There (地方副詞) stood (不及物動詞) Bill (主詞).

(比爾站在那兒。)

An old monk (主詞) lives (不及物動詞) in that old temple (地方副詞片語).

→ In that old temple (地方副詞片語) lives (不及物動詞) an old monk (主詞).

(那座古剎裡住了一位老和尚。)

b. 主詞 + be 動詞 + 過去分詞 + 地方副詞 (片語)

→ 地方副詞 (片語) + be 動詞 + 過去分詞 + 主詞

例: A small village (主詞) is (be 動詞) located (過去分詞) on the top of the mountain (地方副詞片語).

→ On the top of the mountain (地方副詞片語) is (be 動詞) located (過去分詞) a small village (主詞).

(山頂上座落著一個小村莊。)

c. 主詞 + be 動詞 + 現在分詞 + 地方副詞 (片語)

→ 現在分詞 + 地方副詞 (片語) + be 動詞 + 主詞

例: My classmates　are　playing baseball　over there.
　　主詞　be 動詞　現在分詞　地方副詞片語

→ Playing baseball　over there　are　my classmates.
　　現在分詞　地方副詞片語　be 動詞　主詞

(在那兒打棒球的是我的同學。)

注意:

1) 上述句型中, 若主詞為代名詞 (it、he、she...) 時, 則不可採倒裝句; 換言之, 地方副詞仍可放在句首, 但其後句子不倒裝, 而地方副詞片語則不宜放在句首。

例: She sat there.

→ There she sat.
(她坐在那兒。)

In front of our house stood he. (×)

→ In front of our house he stood. (劣)

→ He stood in front of our house. (○)
(他站在我們家面前。)

2) 地方副詞 (片語) 置於句首的倒裝句構其好處在於:
由於倒裝句的主詞在句尾, 之後可接形容詞子句、分詞片語或介詞片語, 用以修飾主詞, 擴大主詞的內容, 並可避免主詞過大的毛病。

例: John, who came here to visit me the other day, is standing by the window. (可)

→ Standing by the window is John, who came here to visit me the other day. (佳)
(站在窗邊的那個人是約翰，他前幾天來這裡看過我。)

A boy with a dog behind him sat over there. (可)

→ Over there sat a boy with a dog behind him. (佳)
(有個男孩坐在那邊，後面跟著一條狗。)

2. **They don't use electric lights, either, not to mention telephones.**
他們也不使用電燈, 更別說是電話了。

not to mention...　更不用說……(用於肯定句與否定句中)
= not to speak of...
= to say nothing of...
let alone...　更不用說……(用於否定句中)
= much less...

注意:
在上列用法中, not to mention、not to speak of 及 to say nothing of 在肯定句與否定句中均可使用, 且因分別含有及物動詞 mention 及介詞 of, 故其後須接名詞或動名詞作受詞; 而 let alone 及 much less 則只能用於否定句中, 且因其有連接詞的作用, 故其後應置與其前相同的詞類。

例: I love apple pies, | not to mention / not to speak of / to say nothing of | apples.
(我喜歡蘋果派，更不用說蘋果了。)

John can't sing, | not to mention / not to speak of / to say nothing of | dancing.
= John can't sing (原形動詞), | let alone / much less | dance (原形動詞).
(約翰不會唱歌，更別說是跳舞了。)

Peter doesn't enjoy singing, | not to mention / to say nothing of / not to speak of | dancing.
= Peter doesn't enjoy singing (動名詞), | let alone / much less | dancing (動名詞).
(彼得不喜歡唱歌，更別說是跳舞了。)

3. **And, to make matters worse, they don't speak English but German among themselves.**
更糟的是, 他們彼此之間不用英文交談, 而是用德文。

上列句中的 to make matters worse (更糟的是) 為不定詞片語, 用於修飾整個主要子句, 使用時, 通常置於句首, 後加逗點, 再接主要子句。

to make matters worse, 主要子句　　更糟的是,……(用於壞的方面)

= what's (even/far) worse, 主要子句

what's (even/far) better, 主要子句　　更棒的是,……(用於好的方面)

what's more, 主要子句　　而且/此外,……(好、壞方面均可使用)

= moreover, 主要子句

= furthermore, 主要子句

例: Jerry has a bad headache. To make matters worse, he has an important interview this morning.

= Jerry has a bad headache. What's even worse, he has an important interview this morning.
(傑瑞頭痛得厲害；更糟的是，他今早有個重要的面試。)

James finally found the woman he wants to marry. What's better, she is rich.
(詹姆士終於找到了結婚對象；更棒的是，她很有錢。)

The man knew that it was a stolen watch. Moreover, he knew who had stolen it.
(那名男子知道這是只贓錶；而且他還知道是誰偷的。)

1. **In the heart of America, in the states of Pennsylvania, Ohio and Indiana, live some people who are not your typical Americans.**

   By the door stood a little boy.

   On this mountain roam several fierce lions.

   在美國的心臟地帶, 也就是賓夕凡尼亞州、俄亥俄州和印第安納州, 住著一些非典型的美國人。

   門邊站著一位小男孩。

   有好幾隻凶猛的獅子在這座山上出沒。

2. **They don't use electric lights, either, not to mention telephones.**

   The miser won't even lend you one dollar, not to speak of NT$1,000.

   The boy can't even write Chinese, let alone English.

   他們也不使用電燈, 更別說是電話了。

   那個吝嗇鬼連一元都不會借給你, 更不用說是一千元台幣了。

   那個男孩連中文都不會寫, 更別說是英文了。

Lesson 74

Live and Let Live

自己活也讓別人活

Dialogue
實用會話

Paul and Wendy are talking about the Amish.

(P=Paul; W=Wendy)

P: What do you plan to do in the summer, Wendy?

W: To be frank, I haven't made any plans. What about you?

P: I'm thinking of going to Indiana.

W: What on earth for?

P: To tell the truth, I want to see how the Amish people live.

W: What for? From what I hear, they're boring people. To be honest, I think they're kind of weird.

P: Nonsense! In fact, their simple way of life is quite appealing to me.

W: Well, to each their own, I guess.

P: Exactly, I wish more people would just live and let live.

保羅和溫蒂正在談論有關亞米希人的事。
保羅：夏天妳打算做什麼，溫蒂？
溫蒂：坦白說，我還沒做任何打算。你呢？
保羅：我想要去印第安納州。
溫蒂：究竟是為了什麼？
保羅：坦白說，我想要看看亞米希人是怎麼過日子的。
溫蒂：幹嘛？我聽說他們這些人很無聊。老實說，我認為他們有點怪異。
保羅：亂講！其實他們簡樸的生活方式令我非常嚮往。
溫蒂：嗯，我想是人各有所好吧。
保羅：正是，我希望有更多人能自己活也讓別人活。

Key Points 重點提示

1. 本文:

Live and let live. 自已活也讓別人活。

= You live your life the way you want and let others live theirs the way they want.

2. **To be frank (with you), 主詞 + 動詞** 坦白 (對你) 說,……

= Frankly speaking, 主詞 + 動詞

= To tell (you) the truth, 主詞 + 動詞

frank [fræŋk] a. 坦白的, 直言無諱的

注意:

上述用法中, to be frank (with you) 及 to tell (you) the truth 均為不定詞片語, 作副詞用, 修飾逗點之後的主要子句。

例: To be frank with you, I think the poor are more sincere than the rich.
(坦白說，我認為窮人比有錢人真誠。)
＊ sincere [sɪn'sɪr] a. 真誠的

To tell you the truth, I'm broke.
(坦白對你說，我破產了。)

I had a frank conversation with my parents last night.
(我昨晚和父母有番開誠佈公的談話。)

3. **What <u>on earth</u> for?** 究竟是為了什麼？

注意:

on earth 在句中為強調性副詞片語, 通常置於疑問詞 (what、who、where...) 之後, 中文譯為『到底、究竟』。

例: What are you doing?
(你在做什麼？)

→ What <u>on earth</u> are you doing?
= What <u>in the world</u> are you doing?
(你到底在做什麼？)

Who is he?
(他是誰？)

→ Who <u>on earth</u> is he?
= Who <u>in the world</u> is he?
(他究竟是誰？)

Where did she go?
(她去了哪兒？)

→ Where <u>on earth</u> did she go?
= Where <u>in the world</u> did she go?
(她究竟去了哪兒？)

4. **What for?** 為什麼？
= Why?

例: A: Should I give Bill a call?
B: What for?
(甲：我是不是該撥個電話給比爾？)
(乙：為什麼？)

5. **boring** [ˈbɔrɪŋ] a. 令人厭煩的

bored [bɔrd] a. 感到厭煩的

be bored with...　　對……感到厭煩, 厭煩……

= be fed up with...

= be sick of...

= be tired of...

例: Doing the same thing day in and day out can be boring.
(日復一日做相同的事會很無趣。)

Mr. Lin is bored with his monotonous lifestyle.
(林先生對他一成不變的生活方式感到厭煩。)

∗ monotonous [məˈnɑtn̩əs] a. 單調的, 無變化的

6. **To be honest, 主詞 + 動詞**　　老實說,……

注意:

to be honest 亦為不定詞片語, 置於句首作副詞用, 修飾之後的主要子句。使用時加逗點, 再接主要子句。

例: To be honest, I wouldn't mind being single all my life.
(老實說，我不介意終生單身。)

7. **kind of...**　　有點……

注意:

本片語和 sort of、somewhat 皆表『有點』, 作副詞用, 常用來修飾形容詞 (如本文)、副詞或動詞, 且皆放在其修飾的詞類之前。

例: Everyone thinks Andy is kind of nice.
(每個人都認為安迪還不錯。)

Sometimes, Sara behaves kind of foolishly.
(有時候，莎拉的行為有些愚蠢。)

I kind of think Nancy likes Alex.
(我認為南西有點喜歡艾歷克斯。)

8. **weird** [wɪrd] a. 怪異的

例: Young Jack likes to wear weird clothes.
(年輕的傑克喜歡穿著奇裝異服。)

9. **nonsense** [ˈnɑnsɛns] n. 無意義的話或文章; 胡扯 (不可數)

talk nonsense　　胡說八道

例: No one listens to him because he always talks nonsense.
(沒有人聽信他的話，因為他總是胡說八道。)

10. **appealing** [əˈpilɪŋ] a. 令人嚮往的, 動人的

appeal [əˈpil] vi. 吸引

注意:

appeal 常與介詞 to 並用, 形成下列用法:

appeal to + 人　　吸引某人

= attract + 人

* attract [əˈtrækt] vt. 吸引

例: The well-paying job is very appealing.
(那份高薪工作非常吸引人。)

Only well-educated women appeal to Mr. Chen.
(只有受過良好教育的女人才能讓陳先生心動。)

11. **To each one's own.**　　人各有所好。

例: A: I don't understand why Jim would marry such a woman.
B: To each his own.
(甲：我不懂為什麼吉姆會娶那種女人。)
(乙：人各有所好。)

12. **exactly** [ɪgˈzæktlɪ] adv. 正是; 正確地

例: You talk exactly like my grandmother.
(你說話的口氣就和我奶奶一模一樣。)

請選出下列各句中正確的一項

1. Alan doesn't _____ getting married till he's forty.
   (A) plan (B) plan on (C) plan to (D) plan of

2. _____, I don't care what people think of me.
   (A) To be frankly (B) Truly speaking
   (C) To tell the truth (D) Frank speaking

3. I love _____ Sara dances.
   (A) that (B) which (C) as (D) how

4. I'm _____ the way he handles things.
   (A) tired with (B) sick with (C) fed up with (D) bored of

解答

1. (B) 2. (C) 3. (D) 4. (C)

Lesson 75

Think before You Speak

三思而後言

Reading 閱讀

Sometimes we say things without thinking. Very often a thoughtless remark may hurt others' feelings or cause a misunderstanding or an embarrassment. We must, therefore, always think before we speak.

Once I told an old friend how beautiful his girlfriend looked when I saw them together at a movie theater the other day. Unfortunately, I made a mistake. It happened that she wasn't with my friend. She was with someone else. I had let the cat out of the bag, so to speak. I'd never been so embarrassed in my life. I certainly learned my lesson, but at a very high price. His girlfriend never spoke to me again! And to make matters worse, it is rumored that they eventually broke up.

有時候我們說話沒有經過思考。一段欠缺考慮的話往往會傷害到別人的感情，或造成誤會甚至尷尬的情況。因此，我們說話前必須先思考。

有一次我告訴一位老朋友我前幾天在電影院看到他們在一塊兒，而他女朋友看起來美極了。很不幸地，我弄錯了。恰巧她不是跟我朋友在一起；她是跟別人。我可以說是無意中洩漏了祕密。我這一輩子從來沒有那麼尷尬過。我的確學到了教訓，但是付出了很大的代價。他的女朋友再也沒有跟我講過話！更糟的是，謠傳他們最終分手了。

Vocabulary & Idioms 單字 & 片語註解

1. **Think before you speak.**
   說話前先想想/三思而後言。(本句源自下列諺語)
   Look before you leap.　　看清楚再跳; 喻: 三思而後行。(諺語)

* leap [lip] vi. 跳; 躍
   動詞三態: leap、leapt [lɛpt]/leaped [lipt]、leapt/leaped。
   例: Andy: Should I take the job he offered me?
   Donna: Look before you leap.
   (安迪：我該不該接受他提供我的那份工作呢？)
   (多娜：三思而後行。)

2. **thoughtless** [ˈθɔtlɪs] a. 欠考慮的; 粗心的
   thoughtful [ˈθɔtfəl] a. 考慮周詳的; 體貼的
   It is thoughtless of + 人 + to + 原形動詞　　某人做……欠考慮/太粗心
   It is thoughtful of + 人 + to + 原形動詞　　某人做……很體貼

例: It was thoughtless of me to forget my friend's birthday.
(我忘了朋友的生日，真是太粗心了。)

It is thoughtful of you to send me a get-well card.
(你真是體貼，寄給我一張早日康復的卡片。)

3. **remark** [rɪ'mɑrk] n. 言論

make a remark　　發表意見, 評論

例: Wendy made an unnecessary remark about the secretary's incompetence.
(對於祕書的不適任，溫蒂說了些不必要說的話。)
∗ incompetence [ɪn'kɑmpətəns] n. 不勝任, 無能力

4. **misunderstanding** [ˌmɪsʌndɚ'stændɪŋ] n. 誤解

例: Don't be angry; what happened was just a misunderstanding.
(不要生氣，所發生的事只是個誤會罷了。)

5. **embarrassment** [ɪm'bærəsmənt] n. 困窘

embarrass [ɪm'bærəs] vt. 使困窘

embarrassing [ɪm'bærəsɪŋ] a. 令人困窘的

embarrassed [ɪm'bærəst] a. 感到困窘的

例: The couple's divorce caused some embarrassment to the family.
(那對夫妻的離婚使該家族有點難堪。)

It's embarrassing to forget to bring money on a date.
(約會時忘了帶錢很令人難為情。)

Kent was embarrassed to meet his ex-wife at the party.
(肯特在派對裡遇見前妻，覺得很尷尬。)

6. **It happened + that 引導的過去式子句**　　當時恰巧……

例: It happened that I was there when it happened.
= I happened to be there when it happened.
(事情發生時，我恰巧在那裡。)

7. **let the cat out of the bag**　　無意中洩露了秘密

例: Our surprise party was not a surprise because Linda had let the cat out of the bag.
(我們的驚喜派對不成驚喜，因為琳達無意中洩露了秘密。)

8. **..., so to speak** 可以這樣說,……

例: John knows many words. He is, so to speak, a walking dictionary.
(約翰單字懂得很多。可以說他是個活字典。)

9. **learn one's lesson** 學了一課, 學得教訓

teach + 人 + a lesson 給某人一個教訓

例: I hope you have learned your lesson from the mistake you've caused.
(我希望你已從你造成的錯誤中學到教訓。)

That man is too proud; someone should teach him a lesson.
(那個人太驕傲了，該有人給他一個教訓。)

10. **at a high price** 以很高/大的代價

at a price of... 以……的代價

例: Jeff bought the house at a price of US$10,000 per square foot.
(傑夫以每平方呎美金一萬元買了這幢房子。)

11. **to make matters worse, 主詞 + 動詞** 更糟的是,……

= what's (even/far) worse, 主詞 + 動詞

例: The singer was late for his concert. To make matters worse, he lost his voice.
(那名歌手在演唱會中遲到了；更糟的是，他失聲了。)

12. **rumor** [ˈrumɚ] vt. & n. 謠傳

It is rumored + that 子句 謠傳……

= Rumor has it + that 子句

= Word has it + that 子句

例: It is rumored that the man is, in fact, a woman.
(謠傳那名男子實際上是個女人。)

13. **break up** 分手

break up with + 人 和某人分手

break [brek] vi. 結束; 破裂

動詞三態: break、broke [brok]、broken [ˈbrokən]。

例: Betty broke up with her boyfriend because he was two-timing her.
(貝蒂和男友分手，因為他對她不忠實。)

＊ two-time [ˈtuˌtaɪm] vt. 對 (女友、男友) 不忠實; 腳踏兩條船

Grammar Notes 文法重點

本課介紹使用過去完成式的時機, 並復習"so to speak" (可以這麼說) 的用法。

1. 使用過去完成式的時機:

過去完成式乃表截至過去某時為止所完成的動作、經驗, 且過去完成式不能單獨存在, 而要與另一過去式子句或表過去之副詞片語並用, 即在過去不同時間所發生的兩種動作。

先發生的→用過去完成式

後發生的→用過去式

例: I lost the book which my father had given me.
(我弄丟了父親給我的書。)

He had studied Japanese for ten years before he left for Japan.
(他赴日之前已學過十年日文。)

She had already left when I came.
(我來時她已離開了。)

My friend told me that he had seen the movie twice.
(我朋友告訴我說，那部電影他已經看過兩次了。)

注意:

但在文章中, 因承接上下文時態的關係, 故過去完成式可單獨存在。因此本文的"I had let the cat out of the bag, so to speak."與"I'd never been so embarrassed in my life."為過去完成式, 因承接上下文的時態, 故可單獨存在。

2. **I had let the cat out of the bag, <u>so to speak</u>.**
我可以說是無意中洩漏了祕密。
上列句中使用了 so to speak (可以這麼說) 置於句尾的用法, 但 so to speak 亦常作插入語使用, 尤其是置於句中 be 動詞之後。

例: Aaron can swim like a fish, so to speak.
(艾倫游泳可以說是游得和魚一樣好。)

It seems David never does anything wrong. He is, so to speak, a saint.
(大衛似乎從未做錯過事，他可以說是個聖人。)

Substitution 代換

1. **I had let the cat out of the bag, so to speak.**
Patty works like a dog, so to speak.
Mr. Lin has money to burn, so to speak.
我可以說是無意中洩露了秘密。
佩蒂可以說是工作得像條狗一樣辛苦。
林先生可以說是有錢得不得了。

2. **To make matters worse, it is rumored that they eventually broke up.**
John's very sick. What's worse, he can't afford to see a doctor.
Nick crashed his car. What's even worse, it wasn't insured.
更糟的是，謠傳他們最終分手了。
約翰病得很重；更糟的是，他負擔不起去看醫生。
尼克撞毀了他的車子；更糟的是，車子沒有投保。

Lesson 76

Believe It or Not

信不信由你

Dialogue
實用會話

My friend, Andy, is talking to his girlfriend, Jenny, about what I said in the previous lesson.

(A=Andy; J=Jenny)

A: So who did you go to the movies with?

J: Nobody.

A: What do you mean NOBODY?

J: Don't shout at me. Allow me to explain.

A: I'm waiting.

J: Uh...that was my uh...brother.

A: Do you expect me to believe that?

J: You can believe what you want.

A: I'll never get you to tell me the truth, I guess.

J: Why don't you believe me?

A: Because I had dinner with your brother last night!

我的朋友安迪正在和他的女朋友珍妮討論我前一課說的事情。
安迪：妳究竟陪誰去看電影？
珍妮：沒有啊。
安迪：妳說『沒有啊』是什麼意思？
珍妮：別對我大吼大叫。讓我解釋嘛。
安迪：我在等啊。
珍妮：呃……那是我呃……哥哥。
安迪：妳以為我會相信嗎？
珍妮：隨便你要相信什麼。
安迪：我想我永遠也沒辦法叫妳對我說實話了。
珍妮：你為什麼不相信我？
安迪：因為我昨天晚上是和妳哥哥一起吃晚飯的！

Key Points 重點提示

1. **Believe it or not.** 信不信由你。

Believe it or not, 主詞 + 動詞 信不信由你,……

= Whether you believe it or not, 主詞 + 動詞

注意:

"Believe it or not, 主詞 + 動詞"乃由"Whether you believe it or not, 主詞 + 動詞"化簡而來, 但因經常使用, 已成固定用法。

例: Believe it or not, this ten-year-old boy can solve math problems designed for university students.
(信不信由你，這個十歲大的男孩會解答為大學生出的數學題。)

2. **previous** [ˈprivɪəs] a. 先前的

例: We dealt with this problem at the previous meeting.
(我們在先前會議上討論過這個問題了。)

3. 本文:

So <u>who</u> did you go to the movies <u>with</u>?

你究竟陪誰去看電影？

注意:

根據嚴謹的文法, 此處 who 為介詞 with 的受詞, 按理應該用受格 whom 而非主格 who, 但在現代口語中往往用 who 取代 whom, 主因在於 who 較 whom 容易發音。

例: <u>Who</u> shall I speak <u>to</u>?
(我該和誰談？)

<u>Who</u> do you want to <u>see</u>?
(你想見誰呢？)

4. **shout** [ʃaʊt] vi. 呼喊, 吼叫

shout at... 對……大叫/吼叫

例: Children should never shout at their parents.
(做孩子的永遠不應該對他們的父母吼叫。)

5. 本文:

I'll never <u>get you to tell</u> the me truth, I guess.

我想我永遠也沒辦法叫妳對我說實話了。

get + 受詞 + to + 原形動詞 使/叫……

= make + 受詞 + 原形動詞

get + 受詞 + 過去分詞 把……

注意:

在上述用法中, get為使役動詞, 加受詞後, 可接不定詞片語 (to + 原形動詞) 作受詞補語, 表主動的概念, 此時 get 譯為『使/叫……』; 亦可接過去分詞作受詞補語, 表被動概念, 此時 get 譯成『把……』。

例: Let's get Eric to treat us to lunch.
(咱們叫艾瑞克請我們吃午餐。)

Dick tries to get his homework done before going to bed every day.
(狄克每天都設法在睡覺前把功課做好。)

請選出下列各句中正確的一項

1. The lady was _____ to tell us how old she was.
   (A) embarrass (B) embarrassing
   (C) embarrassed (D) embarrassment

2. These eggs are selling _____ a price of US$2 a dozen.
   (A) in (B) at (C) with (D) by

3. We _____ at him, but he didn't hear us because he's quite deaf.
   (A) shouted (B) shot (C) looked (D) pointed

4. _____ that a big earthquake is going to hit us sometime this year.
   (A) Rumor has it (B) Rumors have
   (C) A rumor has it (D) Rumors have it

5. If we work faster, we can still get the job _____ on time.
   (A) do (B) done (C) doing (D) to do

解答：

1. (C) 2. (B) 3. (A) 4. (A) 5. (B)

Lesson 77

The Weaker Sex?

女人是弱者？

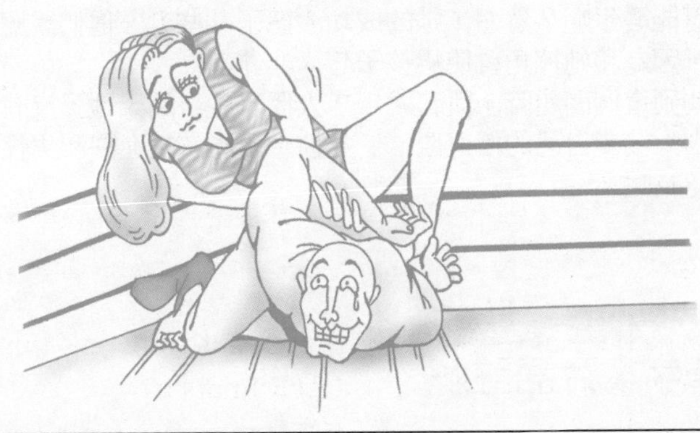

Reading 閱 讀

Who says that women are the weaker sex? Sixteen-year-old Kelly Williams from St. Petersburg, Florida is the first female wrestler to fight against boys and beat them. Who would have thought that possible not so very long ago? Her success, though, has angered some people. They say she should have been banned from wrestling because it will cause the boys to think impure thoughts.

When asked about this, Kelly said, "People live in their own worlds and nobody has the right to force their values on others."

Should women be allowed to wrestle with men in competition? What do you think?

誰說女人是弱者？來自佛羅里達州聖彼得堡十六歲的凱莉・威廉斯是第一位和男孩子摔角並擊敗他們的女摔角手。不久前，誰會認為那種事可能發生呢？然而，她的成功激怒了某些人。他們說應該禁止她摔角，因為和她摔角會使男孩子想入非非。

被問到這個問題時，凱莉說：『人們有各自的天地，沒有人有權利強迫別人接受自己的價值觀。』女性應不應該被允許和男性比賽摔角？你認為呢？

Vocabulary & Idioms 單字 & 片語註解

1. **St. Petersburg** [sent ˈpitɚz͵bɝg] n. 聖彼得堡 (地名)

2. **Florida** [ˈflɔrədə] n. 佛羅里達 (美國東南端的一州)

3. **female** [ˈfimel] n. & a. 女/雌性 (的)

   male [mel] n. & a. 男/雄性 (的)

   例: Males are not allowed in the women's dormitory.
   (男性不允許進入女生宿舍。)
   * dormitory [ˈdɔrmə͵tɔrɪ] n. 學生宿舍

   I prefer to have a female dog rather than a male dog.
   (我比較喜歡養母狗而不喜歡養公狗。)

4. **wrestler** [ˈrɛslɚ] n. 摔角手

   wrestle [ˈrɛsl̩] vi. (與……) 角力/摔角

   例: The wrestler is three times my size.
   (那個摔角手的塊頭是我的三倍大。)

When I was a kid, I loved to wrestle with my older brother.
(我小時候喜歡和哥哥玩摔角。)

5. **beat** [bit] vt. 擊敗
= defeat [dɪ'fit]

動詞三態: beat、beat、beaten。

例: I bet you can't win me in tennis. (×)
→ I bet you can't beat me in tennis. (○)
= I bet you can't defeat me in tennis.
(我打賭你無法在網球上打敗我。)

* win [wɪn] vt. 贏得 (不能接人作受詞, 而須用『比賽』、『獎品』作受詞)

6. **anger** ['æŋgɚ] vt. 觸怒, 使生氣 & n. 怒氣, 怒火

angry ['æŋgrɪ] a. 生氣的

be angry at + 事　　對某事生氣

be angry with + 人　　生某人的氣

例: It angered Andy's wife to see him get drunk.
(安迪的太太看到他喝醉酒很生氣。)

The boss left the meeting in anger.
(老闆怒氣沖沖地離開會議。)

The mayor was angry at the news report about him.
(市長對報上那則關於他的報導很生氣。)

Dan is angry with his wife for scolding him in front of others.
(丹很氣他太太在別人面前指責他。)

7. **ban** [bæn] vt. 下令禁止, 查禁

人 + be banned / barred / prohibited from + 動名詞　　某人被禁止……

主動用法為:

ban bar prohibit	+ 人 + from + 動名詞	禁止某人……

例: The player was banned from competing for two years.
(那個選手被禁賽兩年。)

The law prohibits people from taking drugs.
(法律禁止人們吸毒。)

8. **think + 形容詞 + thoughts** 有……的想法

laugh a/an + 形容詞 + laugh 笑了一個……的笑

注意:

上述片語為『及物動詞接同系名詞作受詞』的用法,特別注意無"laugh a/an...laughter"的用法。

例: War movies make Sean think ugly thoughts about the time he was in a war.
(戰爭片使夏恩想到他打仗時所發生的醜陋事情。)

Connie laughed a hearty laugh at Brad's joke.
(布萊德的笑話使康妮開懷大笑。)

9. **impure** [ɪm'pjʊr] a. 淫猥的; 污穢不潔的

pure [pjʊr] a. 純潔的

例: This impure water is not fit for human consumption.
(這種不潔的水不適合人們飲用。)

It is hard to remain pure with so much sex and violence on TV nowadays.
(現今電視上有著這麼多色情和暴力，要保持純潔是很難的。)

10. **have the right to + 原形動詞** 有權利……

例: Children have the right to be educated.
(孩子有受教育的權利。)

11. **force** [fɔrs] vt. 強迫, 迫使

force + 事 + on + 人　　強加某事在某人身上

例: We shouldn't force our ideas on others.
(我們不應該強迫別人接受我們的看法。)

12. **value** [ˈvæljʊ] n. 價值觀 (恆為複數); 價值 & vt. 珍惜, 重視

例: Our family live by high moral values.
(我們家本著崇高的道德價值觀做人處世。)

What's the value of this painting?
(這幅畫的價值在哪兒？)

I value my teacher's advice on whether to go abroad to study or not.
(對於我要不要出國唸書這個問題，我很看重老師的建議。)

13. **competition** [ˌkɑmpəˈtɪʃən] n. 競爭, 比賽

compete [kəmˈpit] vi. 競爭, 比賽

competitive [kəmˈpɛtətɪv] a. 競爭 (性) 的

compete with + 人 + for + 事物　　與某人競爭某事物

例: Competition encourages improvement.
(競爭使人進步。)

The two teams competed with each other for the championship.
(那兩支隊伍為冠軍而賽。)

Business is so competitive nowadays that we must improve our efficiency.
(現在生意非常競爭，所以我們必須改進我們的效率。)

Grammar Notes 文法重點

本課介紹複合形容詞的用法,以及複習副詞子句變成副詞片語的方法。

1. **Sixteen-year-old Kelly Williams from St. Petersburg, Florida is the first female wrestler to fight against boys and beat them.**
來自佛羅里達州聖彼得堡十六歲的凱莉・威廉斯是第一位和男孩子摔角並擊敗他們的女摔角手。
上列句中的 sixteen-year-old (十六歲的) 為一複合字形成的形容詞, 且其中的名詞 year 不可用複數形 years。此種可數名詞與數字詞用連字號"-"連接形成的複合形容詞中, 可數名詞一律用單數形而不可用複數形。

例: Carl has a son who is twenty years old.
→ Carl has a twenty-years-old son. (×)
→ Carl has a twenty-year-old son. (○)
(卡爾有個二十歲的兒子。)

Helen lives in a ten-stories building. (×)
→ Helen lives in a ten-story building. (○)
(海倫住在一棟十層樓的大廈裡。)

Paul is six feet tall.
→ Paul is a six-feet-tall boy. (×)
→ Paul is a six-foot-tall boy. (○)
(保羅是個六呎高的男孩子。)

2. **When asked about this, Kelly said, "People live in their own worlds and nobody has the right to force their values on others."**
= When she was asked about this, Kelly said, "People live in their own worlds and nobody has the right to force their values on others."
被問到這個問題時, 凱莉說:『人們有各自的天地, 沒有人有權利強迫別人接受自己的價值觀。』

上列第一句中劃線部分為副詞連接詞 when 引導的副詞片語, 用來修飾其後整個主要子句。

副詞連接詞 when (當) 和 while (在……的時候) 引導副詞子句時, 若此副詞子句之主詞與主要子句中之主詞相同時, 則此副詞子句可化簡為副詞片語。其化簡法則如下:

a. 去掉副詞子句之主詞;
b. 其後動詞化為現在分詞;
c. 若動詞為 be 動詞 (如: is、am、was...) 時, 則在變成現在分詞 being 後通常予以省略。

例: When I am rich, I will buy a car.
being
→ When being rich, I will buy a car.
→ When rich, I will buy a car.
(我有錢時會買部車子。)

When I swim, I never stay in the water for too long.
swimming
→ When swimming, I never stay in the water for too long.
(游泳時，我從不會在水中待太久。)

While I was in Paris, I had a great time.
being
→ While being in Paris, I had a great time.
→ While in Paris, I had a great time.
(我在巴黎時玩得很愉快。)

While you drive, you should never drink.
driving
→ While driving, you should never drink.
(開車時你絕不可喝酒。)

注意:

if (如果)、unless (除非)、once (一……就……) 及(al)though (雖然) 等

四個副詞連接詞引導的副詞子句中,其主詞若與主要子句中之主詞相同,且主詞後為『be 動詞 + 形容詞/過去分詞』時,則此副詞子句亦可化簡為副詞片語,且 be 動詞在化為現在分詞 being 後一律予以省略。

例: If ~~it~~ ~~is~~ too greasy, it can't be called health food.
(being)

→ If too greasy, it can't be called health food.
(如果太油膩的話,就不能叫作健康食品。)

Unless ~~you~~ ~~are~~ instructed, you should not try this experiment
(being)
by yourself.

→ Unless instructed, you should not try this experiment by yourself.
(除非有人指導,否則你不應該自己嘗試這項實驗。)

Once ~~he~~ ~~was~~ rejected by the girl, Willie decided never to ask
(being)
her out again.

→ Once rejected by the girl, Willie decided never to ask her out again.
(威利一被那個女孩拒絕就決定永遠不再邀她外出。)

Though ~~he~~ ~~was~~ reluctant, he still went to the party.
(being)

→ Though reluctant, he still went to the party.
(雖然不情願,他還是去了那個派對。)

Substitution 代　換

1. **Sixteen-year-old Kelly Williams from St. Petersburg, Florida is the first female wrestler to fight against boys and beat them.**

   The seven-foot-tall boy can be a basketball player.

   I live on the sixth floor of the ten-story building.

   來自佛羅里達州聖彼得堡十六歲的凱莉・威廉斯是第一位和男孩子摔角並擊敗他們的女摔角手。

   那個七呎高的男孩可以成為籃球球員。

   我住在這棟十層高的大樓第六層。

2. **When asked about this, Kelly said, "People live in their own worlds and nobody has the right to force their values on others."**

   While studying, I never listen to music.

   Unless asked, Mr. Lin would never give you any information.

   被問到這個問題時, 凱莉說:『人們有各自的天地, 沒有人有權利強迫別人接受自己的價值觀。』

   讀書時, 我從不聽音樂。

   除非被問到, 否則林先生不會給你任何訊息。

Lesson 78

Girls versus Boys

女孩對男孩

Dialogue 實用會話

Daisy is talking with Samson about Kelly Williams, the female wrestler.

(D=Daisy; S=Samson)

D: What do you think, Samson? Should girls be allowed to wrestle with boys?

S: I don't see anything wrong with that.

D: Well, wrestling is a contact sport. It's very physical.

S: So? I thought you women always wanted to be equal to men.

D: Yes. But this is different. They'll be grabbing each other. And to win, one wrestler has to lie on top of his or her opponent.

S: So what?

D: It's disgusting. Girls just shouldn't wrestle with boys.

S: Gee, Daisy! Maybe you ought to be a nun.

D: That's not funny! You sex maniac!

黛絲和山姆森正在討論女摔角手凱莉・威廉斯。
黛　絲：山姆森，你認為呢？應該讓女生去和男生摔角嗎？
山姆森：這也沒什麼不好的呀。
黛　絲：不過，摔角是一項接觸的運動，經常有身體上的接觸。
山姆森：那怎樣？我還以為妳們女人一直都想要和男人爭平等呢。
黛　絲：對，但這不一樣。他們要彼此抓住對方，而且為了求勝，一方必須把他或她的對手壓在底下。
山姆森：那又怎麼樣？
黛　絲：那樣很噁心。女孩子就是不應該和男孩子摔角。
山姆森：乖乖，黛絲！也許妳應該去當尼姑。
黛　絲：一點也不好笑！你這色狼！

1. **versus** [ˈvɝsəs] prep. 對⋯⋯; 對抗⋯⋯

例: This basketball game features the Chicago Bulls versus the New York Knicks.
(這場籃球賽由芝加哥公牛隊對抗紐約尼克隊。)

2. **contact** [ˈkɑntækt] a. 接觸的 & n. & vt. 接觸; 聯絡

get in contact with + 人　　和某人聯絡

例: Ice hockey is a rough contact sport.
(冰上曲棍球是一項激烈的身體接觸運動。)

You should get in contact with our office as soon as you arrive.
(你一到就應和我們辦公室聯絡。)

Sue contacted her boyfriend as soon as she arrived from England.
(蘇一從英國抵達此地就立即和她的男朋友聯絡。)

3. **physical** [ˈfɪzɪkḷ] a. 身體的; 體能的

例: Jeff needs more physical exercise.
(傑夫需要多做運動。)

4. **equal** [ˈikwəl] a. 平等的; 相等的; 勝任的 & vt. 匹敵, 比得上

be equal to...　　和……平等; 相等於……; 勝任……

例: Do you really think men are equal to women?
(你真的認為男女平等嗎？)

Ten plus ten is equal to twenty.
(十加十等於二十。)

＊ plus [plʌs] prep. 加

The applicant you recommended was not equal to / competent for the job.
(你推薦的人選無法勝任這份工作。)

＊ competent [ˈkɑmpətənt] a. 勝任的

The swimmer equaled the world record in the Olympic Games.
(那位泳者在奧林匹克比賽中平了世界紀錄。)

5. **grab** [græb] vt. 抓, 攫取

例: The shoplifter grabbed the diamond ring and ran.
(那個商店扒手抓起那只鑽戒後拔腿就跑。)

6. **lie on top of...**　　把……壓在下面, 躺在……上面

例: My cat likes to lie on top of the washing machine.
(我的貓喜歡趴在洗衣機上面。)

7. **So what?**　　那又怎麼樣？

例: Jessica: I can type twice as fast as you.
Carlos: So what?
(傑西卡：我打字可以比你快一倍。)
(卡洛士：那又怎麼樣？)

8. **disgusting** [dɪs'gʌstɪŋ] a. (令人) 噁心/厭惡的

disgusted [dɪs'gʌstɪd] a. 感到噁心/厭惡的

disgust [dɪs'gʌst] vt. 使厭惡; 使嫌惡

例: Picking your nose is a disgusting habit.
(挖鼻孔是個令人噁心的習慣。)

Fred's friends are disgusted at how badly he treats his wife.
(弗瑞德的朋友都對他不善待老婆而感到厭惡。)

Your bad behavior disgusts me.
(你惡劣的行為表現令我厭惡。)

9. **nun** [nʌn] n. 尼姑; 修女

10. **sex maniac** 色情狂

maniac ['menɪ,æk] n. 熱中者

注意:

maniac 表示『熱中某事物到了幾乎變態』的地步, 使用時常以"名詞 + maniac"表示之。

例: The soccer maniac never misses a game.
(那個足球狂從未錯過一場球賽。)

請選出下列各句中正確的一項

1. John refuses ______ with his best friend for Sara's love.
   (A) to compete　　(B) competing
   (C) to complete　　(D) competitive

2. The ______ kitchen knife turned out to be the murder weapon.
   (A) ten-inches　(B) ten-inch　(C) ten-inched　(D) ten-inching

3. The computer ______ takes his personal computer with him wherever he goes.
   (A) sport　(B) wrestler　(C) opponent　(D) maniac

4. ______, you should concentrate on what you're doing.
   (A) Working　　(B) When work
   (C) When working　　(D) When worked

5. Bob has a ______ way of eating his soup.
   (A) disgust　(B) disgusted　(C) disgusting　(D) disgustedly

解答

1. (A)　2. (B)　3. (D)　4. (C)　5. (C)

Lesson 79

Stop to Smell the Flowers

駐足片刻聞花香

Reading
閱　讀

In the hustle and bustle of modern-day life, people seldom stop to enjoy the beauty of nature. Ask yourself how many times you have listened to the birds sing. And when was the last time you looked at the sparkling stars twinkle in the sky? Time flies and life is short. So don't forget to stop and smell the flowers.

In our eagerness to make a living, we often forget about our quality of life. Too often you hear people say, "I'm too busy," for this or that. What a shame! One day, when they do find time to stop to smell the flowers, it might be too late.

在繁忙擾攘的現代生活中，人們鮮少停下來欣賞大自然之美。問問你自己你曾傾聽過幾次鳥兒啁啾，而你上次看天上亮晶晶的星星閃爍又是什麼時候？光陰似箭而人生短暫，所以別忘了停下來聞聞花香。

在我們迫切謀生的同時，我們往往遺忘了我們生活的品質。你常常會聽到人們因為要做這個或那個的說：『我太忙了。』真是令人遺憾！有一天，當他們真的找出時間停下來聞聞花香時，或許那時已經太遲了。

Vocabulary & Idioms 單字 & 片語註解

1. **the hustle and bustle** 繁忙擾攘

   hustle [ˈhʌsl̩] n. 熱鬧; 擁擠

   bustle [ˈbʌsl̩] n. 喧嘩; 忙亂

   例: It's stressful to live in the hustle and bustle of city life.
   (生活在繁忙擾攘的都市生活中壓力很大。)

2. **seldom** [ˈsɛldəm] adv. 不常, 鮮少

   例: Brad seldom comes to work late.
   (布萊德很少上班遲到。)

3. **nature** [ˈnetʃɚ] n. 大自然 (不可數, 之前不可置冠詞)

   例: The old man likes to walk in the hills to be with nature.
   (那位老先生喜歡在山間行走接觸大自然。)

4. **sparkling** [ˈspɑrklɪŋ] a. 閃爍的, 閃閃發光的

   sparkle [ˈspɑrkl̩] vi. 閃爍

   例: Every time Sue sees Nick, her eyes sparkle.
   (每次蘇看到尼克，她的眼睛都會為之一亮。)

5. **twinkle** [ˈtwɪŋkl̩] vi. 閃爍, 明滅不定

in the twinkling of an eye　　一眨眼功夫, 轉眼間

例: We saw the light twinkle in the distance.
(我們看到遠處有燈光閃爍。)

The magician made the rabbit disappear in the twinkling of an eye.
(眨眼間那名魔術師就把兔子變不見了。)

6. **Time flies.**　　光陰似箭。(諺語)

例: Brad: Tom will be back from his vacation tomorrow.
Grant: Time flies, doesn't it?
(布萊德：湯姆明天就度假回來了。)
(葛蘭特：時光過得真快，不是嗎？)

7. **eagerness** [ˈigɚnɪs] n. 渴望, 熱心

eager [ˈigɚ] a. 渴望的, 急切的

in one's eagerness to + 原形動詞　　某人迫切要……

be eager to + 原形動詞　　渴望/迫切……

例: In his eagerness to give his family a good life, Mr. Chen overworked and got sick.
(陳先生想儘快讓家人過好日子，於是乎他工作過度而病倒了。)

Some workers are too eager to please their bosses.
(有些員工太急切想取悅他們的老闆。)

8. **make a living**　　謀生

例: Dave makes a living by selling insurance.
(戴夫賣保險謀生。)

* insurance [ɪnˈʃurəns] n. 保險

9. **quality** [ˈkwɑlətɪ] n. 品質

例: Quality matters more than quantity.
(質比量重要。)

* quantity [ˈkwɑntətɪ] n. 量

10. **shame** [ʃem] n. 憾事; 羞愧

What a shame!　　真是遺憾 (啊) !

= What a pity!

It is a shame + that 子句　　很遺憾……

= It is a pity + that 子句

例: A: James broke up with his girlfriend again.
B: What a shame!
(甲：詹姆士又和他女朋友分手了。)
(乙：真是遺憾！)

It's a shame that Mark can't get along with his colleagues.
(很遺憾馬克無法和他的同事相處。)
* colleague [ˈkɑlig] n. 同事; 同僚

William: I failed the test again.
George: Shame on you!
(威廉：我又考不及格了。)
(喬治：你真丟臉！)

Grammar Notes 文法重點

本課複習及物動詞 stop 以及表『看』、『聽』、『感覺』三類知覺動詞的用法, 並介紹名詞 nature 表『大自然』的用法。

1. **In the hustle and bustle of modern-day life, people seldom stop to enjoy the beauty of nature.**
在繁忙擾攘的現代生活中, 人們鮮少停下來欣賞大自然之美。
So don't forget to stop to smell the flowers.
所以別忘了停下來聞聞花香。

One day, when they do find time to stop to smell the flowers, it might be too late.

有一天, 當他們真的找出時間停下來聞聞花香時, 或許那時已經太遲了。

上列句中使用了 stop 接不定詞片語 (to + 原形動詞) 的用法, 表『停下某事, 而改做另一件事』之意。

stop 後除可接不定詞片語之外, 亦可接動名詞作受詞, 但意思不同於前, 而是表『停止做……』或『不做……』之意, 此時亦可等於"cease + 動名詞"或"cease to + 原形動詞"。

注意:

cease 後可接不定詞片語或動名詞作受詞, 但兩者意思相同, 均表『停止做……』或『不做……』之意。

stop to + 原形動詞　　停下某事去做……

stop + 動名詞　　停止做……, 不做……

= cease + 動名詞

= cease to + 原形動詞 (少用)

例: Never stop to talk to strangers.
(絕對不可以停下來和陌生人說話。)

The students stopped playing as soon as the school bell rang.
= The students ceased playing as soon as the school bell rang.
= The students ceased to play as soon as the school bell rang. (少用)
(學生們一聽到校鐘響就停止了玩耍。)

2. **nature** [ˈnetʃɚ] 表『大自然』時, 為不可數名詞, 且其前不可置定冠詞 the。但 nature 亦可表『性質』、『特性』, 此時則為可數名詞, 其前可加定冠詞 the。

例: I love the nature. (×)
→ I love nature. (○)
(我愛大自然。)

Being loyal to its master is the nature of a dog.
(對主人忠實是狗的天性。)

3. **Ask yourself how many times you have listened to the birds sing.**
問問你自己你曾傾聽過幾次鳥兒啁啾。
And when was the last time you looked at the sparkling stars twinkle in the sky?
而你上次看天上亮晶晶的星星閃爍又是什麼時候？
Too often you hear people say, "I'm too busy," for this or that.
你常常會聽到人們因為要做這個或那個的說:『我太忙了。』
上列句中, 片語及物動詞 listened to (傾聽)、looked at (注視) 和及物動詞 hear (聽) 接了受詞後, 分別用原形動詞 sing、twinkle 及 say 作受詞補語。由於表『看』、『聽』、『感覺』三類知覺動詞的用法非常重要, 因此我們不厭其煩再復習一次其用法。
知覺動詞接受詞後, 可用原形動詞作受詞補語 (如本文用法), 表已發生的事實; 或用現在分詞作受詞補語, 表進行的狀態; 亦可用過去分詞作受詞補語, 表被動的概念。常見的知覺動詞如下:
看: see、watch、look at
聽: hear、listen to
感覺: feel。
a. 原形動詞作受詞補語, 旨在強調確有事情發生。

例: Everyone was looking at Jill dance.
(每個人都注視著吉兒跳舞。)

b. 以現在分詞作受詞補語, 旨在強調事情正在發生。

例: I could hear my neighbors quarreling last night.
(我可以聽到我的鄰居昨晚在吵架。)

c. 以過去分詞作受詞補語, 旨在強調被動的狀態:

例: I saw a dog run over by a bus.
(我看到一隻狗被公車輾過。)

Substitution 代換

1. **In the hustle and bustle of modern-day life, people seldom stop to enjoy the beauty of nature.**

   Once you stop working, you'll be bored.

   Have you ever stopped to think why you are in this world?

   在繁忙擾攘的現代生活中, 人們鮮少停下來欣賞大自然之美。

   你一旦不再工作, 會覺得無聊的。

   你有沒有停下來想過你為什麼會在這個世上呢？

2. **Ask yourself how many times you have listened to the birds sing.**

   Dan just sat there looking at the girls walk by.

   Can you hear roosters crow in the city?

   問問你自己你曾傾聽過幾次鳥兒啁啾。

   丹只是坐在那兒看著女孩子經過。

   在城市裡, 你可以聽到公雞啼叫嗎？

Lesson 80

Being around Nature

投入大自然的懷抱

Dialogue 實用會話

Ruby is trying to get her friend, Tony, to go bird-watching with her.

(R= Ruby; T=Tony)

R: You really should get some exercise, Tony. Why don't you come bird-watching with me this weekend?

T: That sounds boring. What's bird-watching all about anyway?

R: Bird watchers study birds in their natural surroundings. It's a great hobby.

T: What's the fun in that?

R: We enjoy listening to different birds sing, looking at them fly and watching how they behave.

T: What else?

R: Well, it's also relaxing to be around nature. And walking in the mountains helps keep you fit.

T: Nothing's more relaxing than watching TV in my air-conditioned room.

R: You're hopeless!

T: And you're birdbrained!

露比正設法說動她的朋友東尼陪她一起去賞鳥。

露比：你真的應該運動一下，東尼。這個週末你何不和我一起去賞鳥？

東尼：聽起來真無聊。賞鳥究竟是什麼玩意兒？

露比：賞鳥人士在鳥類棲息的自然環境中觀察牠們。是一項不錯的休閒活動哦。

東尼：那當中有何樂趣呢？

露比：我們樂於聆聽各種鳥鳴、觀看牠們飛翔和觀察牠們的行為。

東尼：還有什麼？

露比：嗯，投入大自然的懷抱也令人心曠神怡，還有在山間徒步有助於保持身體健康。

東尼：沒有什麼事比待在我房間吹冷氣看電視更令人心曠神怡的了。

露比：你無可救藥！

東尼：妳笨得可以！

Key Points 重點提示

1. **go bird-watching** 去賞鳥

注意:

『go + 現在分詞』的句型常見的如下:

go dancing 去跳舞

go shopping 去購物

go picnicking 去野餐

go swimming 去游泳

go bungee jumping 去高空彈跳

例: Thousands of people go bird-watching just to be around nature.
(數以千計的人去賞鳥只為了要接近大自然。)

Most men hate to go shopping.
(大多數的男人都討厭去購物。)

Even if you paid me to go bungee jumping, I wouldn't.
(即使你付錢叫我去高空彈跳，我也不會去。)

2. **exercise** [ˈɛksɚˌsaɪz] n. 運動 (通常為不可數名詞, 表種類時可數); 練習 (可數)

do exercise　　做運動 (美式用法)

take exercise　　做運動 (英式用法)

do exercises　　做練習/功課

例: Fat Freddy needs to do more exercise.
(肥仔弗瑞德需要多做些運動。)

Our basketball coach makes us do exercise for twenty minutes before a game.
(我們的籃球教練叫我們賽前做二十分鐘的暖身運動。)

As a senior high school student, he needs to do exercises almost every day.
(身為高中生，他幾乎每天都必須做功課。)

3. **What is + 事物 + all about?**　　某事物是關於什麼的？

例: Can you tell me what this book is all about?
(你能告訴我這本書寫些什麼嗎？)

4. **anyway** [ˈɛnɪˌwe] adv. (置於疑問句句尾) 到底; 究竟

例: Who invited you to my party anyway?
(到底是誰邀請你來參加我的派對呢？)

5. 本文:

What's bird-watching all about anyway?

= What on earth is bird-watching all about?

= What in the world is bird-watching all about?

賞鳥到底什麼玩意？

* 疑問詞 (what、who、where、when、how...等) 之後可置 on earth 或 in the world, 表『到底』, 用以強調該形容詞。

6. **surroundings** [sə'raʊndɪŋz] n. 周圍, 周遭, 環境 (恒用複數)

environment [ɪn'vaɪrənmənt] n. 環境

circumstances ['sɝkəm,stænsɪz] n. 情況, 情形; 環境 (常用複數)

注意:

surroundings 指個人生活周遭的小環境; environment 指生態上的大環境; circumstances 則為抽象的環境。

例: Mr. Rich lives in very beautiful surroundings.
(瑞奇先生住在非常優美的環境裡。)

It's everyone's duty to protect our environment.
(環保是每個人的責任。)

Our circumstances are such that we can't afford to spend any money on luxuries.
(我們所處的這種環境使我們無法花任何金錢在奢侈品上。)

7. **What's the fun in...?** ……的樂趣在哪裡？

例: What's the fun in taking drugs anyway?
(吸毒的樂趣到底在哪裡呢？)

8. **behave** [bɪ'hev] vi. 舉止, 行為

behavior [bɪ'hevjɚ] n. 行為 (不可數)

注意:

behave 亦可作及物動詞, 以反身代名詞作受詞, 形成下列用法:

behave + 反身代名詞 行為表現; 守規矩

例: Our children know how to behave in any circumstances.
(我們的小孩在任何場合中都知道要如何應對。)

Students in my class behave themselves very well.
(我班上的學生行為表現都很好。)

You'd better watch your behavior at the boss's party.
(你在老闆的派對上最好注意你的行為舉止。)

9. **keep + 人 + fit** 保持某人身體健康

= keep fit

fit [fɪt] a. 健康的

例: I jog every day to keep myself fit.
(我每天慢跑保持身體健康。)

10. **air-conditioned** [ˈɛrkənˌdɪʃənd] a. 有空調的; 有冷氣設施的

air conditioner [ˈɛrkənˌdɪʃənɚ] n. 空調裝置; 冷氣機

例: In summer, I can only sleep in an air-conditioned room.
(夏天時，我只有在有冷氣的房間才睡得著。)

Mr. Li has an air conditioner in every room of his house.
(李先生家裡每個房間都有一台冷氣機。)

11. **hopeless** [ˈhoplɪs] a. 無望的, 沒有希望的

例: When things look hopeless, we should try harder.
(事情看起來無望時，我們應該更努力。)

12. **birdbrained** [ˈbɝdˌbrend] a. 笨的, 愚蠢的

例: Everyone thought Joe was birdbrained, but he proved them wrong when he passed the exam.
(每個人都認為喬很笨，但當他通過考試時，他證明他們錯了。)

請選出下列各句中正確的一項

1. Look _____ the horse run!
   (A) for (B) at (C) after (D) down

2. This is perfect weather to _____.
   (A) hiking (B) go to hike (C) go hike (D) go hiking

3. The passersby stopped _____ at the street dancers.
   (A) to look (B) and looking
   (C) to watch (D) and watching

4. John goes to the gym every day to _____ himself fit.
   (A) remain (B) keep (C) watch (D) see

5. The man wants to give up all his possessions and return to _____.
   (A) nature (B) the nature (C) natures (D) the natures

解答：

1. (B) 2. (D) 3. (A) 4. (B) 5. (A)

Lesson 81

Man's Best Friend

人類最好的朋友

Reading 閱 讀

Of all the animals of the Chinese horoscope, the dog really stands out. Which other animal can compare to the dog? The horse? No, he's always horsing around. The monkey? No, he's always monkeying around.

The dog is a loyal companion. He makes us feel safe. He helps us keep thieves out of our homes. The dog has also helped us with our English. For example, if there were no dogs, how could people complain about leading a dog's life? And how could the weatherman say, "It's raining cats and dogs?"

The dog is truly man's best friend. So the next time a dog lifts a leg to your car, don't get angry. Just let it obey the call of nature.

在所有中國的十二生肖當中，狗真的是最突出的。其他有哪種動物能和狗狗一較長短的？馬嗎？不行，牠老是在鬼混。猴子嗎？也不行，牠老是在瞎搞。

狗是一個忠實的夥伴。牠使我們感到安全，牠幫助我們防止小偷闖進家裡。狗也幫了我們英文上的忙。例如，如果沒有狗的話，人們怎麼能說生活過得連狗都不如？而氣象播報員又怎麼能說：『現在正下著傾盆大雨』？

狗的確是人類最好的朋友。所以下次有狗對你的車抬起腿時，別生氣。就讓牠方便一下吧。

Vocabulary & Idioms 單字 & 片語註解

1. **the animals of the Chinese horoscope**
   中國的 (十二) 生肖
   horoscope [ˈhɔrəˌskop] n.天宮圖; 占星術; 天象觀測
   例: Only superstitious people believe in horoscopes.
   (只有迷信的人才會相信占卜。)
   ＊ superstitious [ˌsupɚˈstɪʃəs] a. 迷信的

2. **stand out** 突出
   outstanding [aʊtˈstændɪŋ] a. 傑出的, 優秀的
   例: Of all the students in my class, Sally really stands out.
   (在我所有的學生中，莎莉真的很傑出。)

The actors' performance was outstanding.
(那些演員的演出非常精彩。)

3. **compare** [kəm′pɛr] vi. & vt. 比較; 比喻

compare to...　　和……一較長短
= compare with...

compare A to B
比較 A 與 B (= compare A with B); 把 A 比喻成 B

compare A with B　　比較 A 與 B

例: John cannot compare to / with you as a writer.
(約翰在寫作方面無法跟你比。)

My parents always compare me to / with my cousins.
(我父母老是拿我和我的堂表兄弟姊妹相比。)

Life can be compared to a play.
(人生可以被比喻成一齣戲。)

If you compare mules with donkeys, you can't find much difference.
(如果你把騾和驢做個比較，會發現沒什麼不同。)

＊ mule [mjul] n. 騾
donkey [′dɑŋkɪ] n. 驢

4. **horse around**　　閒混, 鬼混
= goof around
= monkey around
= fool around
＊ goof [guf] vi. 閒混

例: Sam horses around only after he's done all his homework.
(山姆只有在做完所有的家庭作業後才會去混。)

5. **loyal** [ˈlɔɪəl] a. 忠實的, 忠心的

be loyal to...　　對……忠心

例: A dog will not always be loyal to a mean master.
(狗不會永遠對一個凶惡的主人忠心。)

* mean [min] a. 凶惡的

6. **companion** [kəmˈpænjən] n. 朋友, 夥伴

例: In his old age, he only wanted his wife as his companion.
(他年老時只想要太太為伴。)

7. **thieves** [θivz] n. 小偷, 竊賊 (複數形)

thief [θif] n. 小偷, 竊賊 (單數形)

8. **complain** [kəmˈplen] vi. 抱怨, 不滿 & vt. 抱怨 (以 that 子句作受詞)

complain about / of + 名詞/動名詞　　抱怨/不滿……

complain + that 子句　　抱怨……

例: The grumpy old man always complains about the smallest things.
(那個性情乖戾的老頭子總是抱怨雞毛蒜皮的小事。)

* grumpy [ˈgrʌmpɪ] a. 脾氣壞的, 性情乖戾的

The workers complained that they didn't get enough break time.
(那些工人抱怨他們的休息時間不夠。)

9. **weatherman** [ˈwɛðɚˌmæn] n. 氣象預報員

10. **It's raining cats and dogs.**　　下著傾盆大雨。

= It's pouring.

= It's raining heavily.

* pour [pɔr] vi. 下傾盆大雨

= drizzle [ˈdrɪzḷ] vi. 下毛毛雨

注意:

"rain cats and dogs" (雨下得很大) 據說是十七世紀時, 英國的下水道設施

建得不怎麼好，因此大雨過後總會發現很多貓狗的屍體到處漂浮；另外還有兩種說法，一是源自希臘字 catadupa [ˌkɑtəˈdupə] (瀑布)，那時候的人在下大雨時常常會聯想到瀑布，而 catadupa 發音聽起來像"cat and dog"『貓和狗』；另一說法則源自古代的天氣預報者，他們相信雨是由貓和狗的邪靈所引起的。

例: The children continued their basketball game although it was pouring.
(雖然下著傾盆大雨，那些小孩還是繼續他們的籃球比賽。)

It's only drizzling; why should we cancel the outing?
(只不過是下著毛毛雨，為什麼我們要取消遠足呢？)

11. **lift** [lɪft] vt. 抬起, 舉起

例: Clad lifted his son up onto his shoulders.
(克雷德把他的兒子舉到肩膀上。)

12. **obey** [əˈbe] vt. 遵守

例: Children should obey their parents.
(小孩子應該聽父母的話。)

13. **call of nature** (委婉的說法) 內急

例: Excuse me. Where's the washroom? I have to obey the call of nature.
(對不起，請問洗手間在哪兒？我必須去方便一下。)

Grammar Notes 文法重點

本課介紹"of all + 名詞" (在所有……之中) 的用法，以及複習使役動詞 make 及 let 和動詞 help 的用法。

1. **<u>Of all</u> the animals of the Chinese horoscope, the dog really stands out.**

= <u>Among (all)</u> the animals of the Chinese horoscope, the dog really stands out.

在所有中國的十二生肖中, 狗真的是最突出的。

"of all + 名詞"表『在所有……之中』, of all 可用 among 取代, 其後名詞表示的數量一定是三者或三者以上, 且使用此句型時, 其主要子句中通常含有最高級修飾語, 句型如下:

Of all + 名詞, 含最高級修飾語的主要子句

= Among (all) + 名詞, 含最高級修飾語的主要子句

在所有……之中,……最……

例: <u>Of all</u> the students in my class, Jane is <u>the prettiest.</u>

= <u>Among (all)</u> the students in my class, Jane is <u>the prettiest.</u>

(在我班上所有學生之中，珍是最漂亮的。)

注意:

"of the two + 名詞"則要使用比較級, 句型如下:

Of the two + 名詞, 含比較級修飾語的主要子句

在兩個……之中, ……比較……

例: <u>Of</u> the two brothers, Gary is (the) <u>smarter</u>.

(在這兩兄弟之中，蓋瑞比較聰明。)

2. **He <u>makes</u> us <u>feel</u> safe.**

牠使我們感到安全。

Just <u>let</u> it <u>obey</u> the call of nature.

就讓牠方便一下吧。

上列句中的 makes 及 let 均為使役動詞, 加受詞後, 分別接原形動詞 feel 及 obey 作受詞補語。

a. make 作使役動詞時, 譯成『使/令/叫……』, 此種意義的使役動詞尚有 have 及 get, have 後接原形動詞作受詞補語, 但 get 之後則要接不定詞片語 (to + 原形動詞) 作受詞補語。句型如下:

make/have + 人 + 原形動詞　　叫某人從事……
get + 人 + to + 原形動詞

例: Mom <u>makes</u> me <u>do</u> the laundry on weekends.
(媽媽周末時都會叫我洗衣服。)

Can you <u>have</u> the repairman <u>fix</u> the lock this afternoon?
(你可以叫修理工人今天下午來修鎖嗎?)

Let's <u>get</u> Mandy <u>to give</u> us a ride home.
(咱們叫曼蒂讓我們搭便車回家吧。)

b. have 及 get 加受詞後, 其後亦可接過去分詞作受詞補語, 此時的 have 及 get 譯成『把……』。句型如下:

have/get + 受詞 + 過去分詞　　把……(被)……

例: Sandy <u>had</u> her hair <u>cut</u> on the weekend.
(珊蒂周末時把頭髮理了。)

If you don't stop complaining about me, you'll <u>get</u> me <u>fired</u>.
(如果你對我抱怨個不停，會使我被開除的。)

c. let 亦為使役動詞, 表『讓……』, 其後亦接原形動詞作受詞補語。句型如下:

let + 受詞 + 原形動詞

例: Don't wake the baby up; <u>let</u> him <u>sleep</u>.
(別吵醒寶寶，讓他睡吧。)

3. **He <u>helps</u> us <u>keep</u> thieves out of our homes.**

= He helps us (to) keep thieves out of our homes.
牠幫助我們防止小偷闖到我們家裡。

The dog has also <u>helped</u> us <u>with</u> our English.
狗也幫了我們英文上的忙。

有關動詞 help 的重要用法我們複習如下:

a. help + 人 + (to) + 原形動詞　　幫助/忙某人……

例: These pills help me (to) sleep.
(這些藥丸幫助我入睡。)

b. help + (to) + 原形動詞　　幫助/忙……

例: This jacket will help (to) keep you warm.
(這件夾克可以幫助你保暖。)

c. help + (人) + with + 名詞　　幫助/忙 (某人) ……

例: Janet's boyfriend helps (her) with her homework.
(珍妮特的男友幫忙（她）做功課。)

d. help with + 名詞　　幫助/忙……

例: Can you help with the police inquiry?
(你可以協助警方調查嗎？)

Substitution 代換

1. **Of all the animals of the Chinese horoscope, the dog really stands out.**

   Of all the people in the world, I admire Mother Theresa the most.

   Of all the movies ever made, *Gone With the Wind* is the best.

   在所有中國的十二生肖中, 狗真的是最突出的。

   在所有世人中, 我最敬仰泰瑞莎修女。

   在所有拍過的電影中,『亂世佳人』是最棒的。

2. **He makes us feel safe.**

   My father lets me drive his car sometimes.

   Mom has me clean my room at least once a week.

   牠使我們感到安全。

   我爸爸偶爾會讓我開他的車子。

   老媽叫我一個禮拜最少清理我的房間一次。

Lesson 82

Oh My God!

我的天啊！

Dialogue
實用會話

Two animals, Porky the pig and Donald the duck, see something strange to them.

(P=Porky; D=Donald)

P: What's that four-legged furry thing?

D: Beats me. Why don't you get him to tell us who he is?

P: OK. Let me try. Hey! Hi, idiot!

D: Hey, Porky! Look at the tag hanging around its neck. It says G-O-D, God! You're in big trouble.

P: Oh, please forgive me. I didn't mean to call you an idiot, God.

D: Wait a minute! I read the tag backwards. It says D-O-G. Dog?

P: Oh, my God! What a relief! By the way, where did you learn to read English?

D: Uh...I'd better not say.

兩隻動物，波奇豬和唐老鴨，看到很奇怪的東西。
波奇豬：那個四隻腳毛絨絨的東西是什麼啊？
唐老鴨：問倒我了。你為什麼不叫他跟我們講他是誰？
波奇豬：好吧。我試試看。嘿！嗨，白痴！
唐老鴨：嘿，波奇！看看他脖子上掛的牌子。上面寫著『老天爺』，老天爺！你麻煩大囉！
波奇豬：哦，請你原諒我。我不是有意叫你白痴的，老天爺。
唐老鴨：等一下！我把牌子看反了。上面寫的是狗。狗？
波奇豬：我的天啊！真是鬆了口氣！哦，對了，你在哪裡學會看英文的？
唐老鴨：呃……我還是不說的好。

1. **Porky** [ˈpɔrkɪ] n. 波奇豬
   Donald [ˈdɑnəld] n. 唐老鴨

＊ Porky 和 Donald 是迪士尼卡通中的兩個要角。

2. **duck** [dʌk] n. 鴨 (子)

3. **four-legged** [ˌfɔrˈlɛgɪd] a. 四足的

注意:

身體部位如: leg (腿)、arm (手臂)、eye (眼睛)、hair (頭髮) 等, 變成過去分詞後, 其前加數字或其他形容詞形成複合形容詞, 之後再接名詞。

例: How many four-legged animals can you name?
(你可以說出多少種四隻腳動物的名字？)

The brown-haired boy over there is my English teacher's son.
(在那邊那個棕髮的男孩是我英文老師的兒子。)

4. **furry** [ˈfɝɪ] a. 毛絨絨的; 長毛的

fur [fɝ] n. 軟毛; 毛皮

例: A bear is a furry animal.
(熊是身上長毛的動物。)

People used to kill bears for their fur.
(人們過去曾為了熊皮而殺害熊。)

5. **Beats me.** 問倒我了/難倒我了。

= It beats me.

beat [bit] vt. 難倒, 使困惑; 打 & a. 疲乏的

例: Jennifer: What's the matter with Jenny?
Andrew: Beats me.
(珍妮佛：珍妮怎麼了？)
(安德魯：問倒我了。)

Mr. White never beats his children.
(懷特先生從來沒打過他的小孩。)

After a hard day's work, I'm really beat.
(辛苦工作了一天後，我真的累慘了。)

6. **tag** [tæg] n. 牌子, 標籤

例: Don't forget to put a tag on your luggage.
(別忘了在你的行李上掛個牌子。)

7. **hang** [hæŋ] vi. & vt. 掛

動詞三態: hang、hung [hʌŋ]、hung。

例: The wet clothes are hanging on the clothesline.
(那些濕衣服正掛在曬衣繩上。)

Dad hangs his suits in the closet.
(老爸把他的西裝掛在衣櫥裡。)

注意:

hang [hæŋ] vt. 吊死

動詞三態: hang、hanged、hanged。

例: In some countries, you can be hanged for committing a serious crime.
(在有些國家裡，犯重罪會被吊死。)

8. **neck** [nɛk] n. 脖子

9. **be in trouble** 陷入麻煩

例: If you go home drunk, you'll be in trouble.
(如果你喝醉酒回家，會有麻煩的。)

10. **forgive** [fɚˈgɪv] vt. 原諒

動詞三態: forgive、forgave [fɚˈgev]、forgiven [fɚˈgɪvən]。

例: I'll never forgive you for flirting with my boyfriend.
(我將永遠不會原諒妳和我男朋友調情的事。)
＊ flirt [flɝt] vi. 調情, 打情罵俏

11. **backward(s)** [ˈbækwɚd(z)] adv. 向後地, 倒向地

forward(s) [ˈfɔrwɚd(z)] adv. 向前地

例: John was in a rush and put his T-shirt on backwards.
(約翰趕時間而把 T 恤前後穿反了。)

Those who agree with me, please step forward.
(同意我的人，請往前站。)

12. **relief** [rɪˈlif] n. 安心, (痛苦、憂慮等) 解除

relieve [rɪˈliv] vt. 使減輕, 使抒緩

relieve the pain 減輕痛苦

What a relief! 真是鬆了一口氣！

例: It relieves me to know my son has returned from the war safely.
(知道我兒子已從戰爭中安全返回令我鬆了口氣。)

請選出下列各句中正確的一項

1. _____ all the teachers I've had, I think Mr. Chen is the best.
   (A) Between (B) Of (C) With (D) For

2. The _____ Japanese swordsman is a famous movie actor.
   (A) one arm (B) one-arm (C) one-armed (D) one-arming

3. Most students _____ having too much homework and too many tests.
   (A) complain about (B) complain
   (C) complain to (D) complain that

4. The robber was _____ by the villagers before the police arrived.
   (A) hang (B) hanging (C) hanged (D) hung

5. We always help Mom _____ the housework on weekends.
   (A) doing (B) with (C) by (D) about

解答：

1. (B) 2. (C) 3. (A) 4. (C) 5. (B)

Lesson 83

Beauty Is Only Skin-Deep

美色是膚淺的

It is natural for people to be attracted to beautiful things. It follows, therefore, that most women desire nothing but to look beautiful. That is why they cannot help but spend vast sums of money on cosmetics and fashionable clothing. They are interested in nothing but their looks. However, they should be reminded that beauty is only skin-deep.

Instead, they should pay more attention to their character because when you have character, you have class. And that is what gives one inner beauty.

人被美麗的事物所吸引是很自然的事情。因此，大部分的女性只想要看起來漂亮，這是有其道理的。那就是為何她們會忍不住將大筆金錢花在化粧品和流行服飾上的原因。她們只關心她們的容貌。然而，我們應該提醒她們美色是膚淺的。

相反地，她們應該多注意她們的品格，因為有了品格才會有水準。而那才能給予一個人內在美。

Vocabulary & Idioms 單字 & 片語註解

1. **skin-deep** [ˌskɪnˈdip] a. 膚淺的, 外表上的

例: His sorrow is only skin-deep; soon he'll be laughing again.
(他的悲傷只是表面的；過不了多久他就會再度露出笑顏。)
* sorrow [ˈsɑro] n. 悲傷; 愁苦

2. **attract** [əˈtrækt] vt. 吸引
attractive [əˈtræktɪv] a. 吸引人的, 引人注目的
be attracted to/by...　　被……所吸引

例: Children are easily attracted to toys.
(小孩很容易被玩具吸引。)
Jane has an attractive hairdo.
(珍的髮型很好看。)
* hairdo [ˈhɛrˌdu] n. 髮型

3. **It follows + that 子句**　　……是有道理的; 由此可見……

例: Thomas drives a BMW. It follows that he must be very rich.
(湯瑪士開了一輛寶馬車；由此可見他一定很有錢。)

4. **vast** [væst] a. 廣大的, 巨額的

例: A vast amount of money was missing from the safe.
(有一大筆錢從保險櫃中不翼而飛。)

5. **sum** [sʌm] n. (錢) 數目

例: You can start this business with a small sum of money.
(你用一小筆金錢就可以做這種生意。)

6. **cosmetics** [kɑzˈmɛtɪks] n. 化妝品 (常用複數)

makeup [ˈmekˌʌp] n. 化妝 (不可數)

put on makeup　　上妝

例: Mary's purse is full of cosmetics.
(瑪麗的皮包裝滿了化妝品。)

Young girls shouldn't put on too much makeup.
(年輕女孩不應該在臉上上太多的妝。)

7. **fashionable** [ˈfæʃənəbḷ] a. 流行的, 時髦的

例: Miniskirts are becoming fashionable again.
(迷你裙又再度流行了。)

8. **interested** [ˈɪntrɪstɪd] a. 感興趣的

interesting [ˈɪntrɪstɪŋ] a. (令人) 有趣的

be interested in + 事物/ 動名詞　　對……感興趣

例: Little Johnny is interested in computers.
(小強尼對電腦感興趣。)

Ann thinks history is very interesting.
(安認為歷史很有趣。)

9. **looks** [lʊks] n. 外貌 (恆用複數)

例: Tina has good looks but a lousy personality.
(蒂娜外表好看但個性很差。)

10. **remind** [rɪˈmaɪnd] vt. 提醒, 使想到

remind + 人 + that 子句　　提醒某人……

remind + 人 + to + 原形動詞　　提醒某人……

remind + 人 + of + 名詞/代名詞　　使某人想到……

例: My secretary reminded me that I have a meeting in an hour.
(我的秘書提醒我一個小時之後我要開會。)

Please remind me to send my mom a birthday card.
(請提醒我寄給我媽媽一張生日卡。)

This picture reminds me of my days in school.
(這張照片使我想起我在學校的日子。)

11. **pay attention to...** 注意……

例: Nobody was paying attention to what the principal was saying.
(沒有人注意聽校長在說什麼。)

12. **character** [ˈkærɪktɚ] n. 品格 (不可數)

characteristic [ˌkærɪktəˈrɪstɪk] a. 本性的; 特色的

例: John is a man of noble character.
(約翰是個品格高尚的人。)

It's characteristic of Ken to give his friends a helping hand.
(幫助朋友是肯恩的特色。)

13. **class** [klæs] n. 格調, 水準

例: Some people are rich but they have no class.
(有些人很有錢但沒格調。)

14. **inner beauty** 內在美

outer beauty 外在美

inner [ˈɪnɚ] a. 內在的

outer [ˈaʊtɚ] a. 外在的

Grammar Notes
文法重點

本課介紹"表示意願的及物動詞 (desire、expect、want、choose 等) + nothing but to + 原形動詞" (除了……外, 什麼都不……) 的用法, 以及"cannot help but + 原形動詞" (忍不住/禁不住……) 的用法, 另介紹 instead 的用法。

1. **It follows, therefore, that most women desire nothing but to look beautiful.**

因此, 大部分的女性只想要看起來漂亮, 這是有其道理的。

上列句中, 使用表示意願的動詞 desire 加 nothing but to 接原形動詞 (look) 的用法。茲將此句型的造句法分析如下:

desire expect want choose	nothing but to + 原形動詞

例: He desired nothing but to sleep.
(他什麼都不想，只想睡覺。)

解說:

第一步:

句中 but 可視為對等連接詞, 連接對等的動詞 desired, 即:

He desired nothing but desired...

第二步:

由於 desire、expect、want 及 choose 等均為表示意願的及物動詞, 其後通常要用不定詞片語 (to + 原形動詞) 作受詞。

例: He desired to sleep.
(他想要睡覺。)

第三步:

因此, 在 He desired nothing but desired...中, desired 之後要接『to + 原

形動詞』, 即成:

He desired nothing but desired to sleep.

第四步:

由於本句中第二個 desired 與其前的 desired 為相同的字, 故第二個 desired 可予以省略, 即成:

He desired nothing but to sleep.

同理, 本文中的:

They are interested in nothing but their looks.

= They are interested in nothing but (are interested in) their looks.

她們除了自己的容貌外，什麼都不感興趣。

本句中, but 之後即省略了與其前相同的詞類 are interested in。

又例:

I expect nothing but to be able to provide a decent living for my family.

(我什麼都不想，只想能夠提供家人一個過得去的生活。)

＊ decent [ˈdisənt] a. 尚佳的, 還不錯的

Being depressed, Ken wants nothing but to be left alone.

(肯恩很沮喪，因此什麼都不想，只想獨處。)

Fat Freddy enjoys nothing but eating.

= Fat Freddy enjoys nothing but (enjoys) eating.

(胖子弗萊迪除了喜歡吃以外什麼都不喜歡。)

注意:

do nothing but + 原形動詞　　除了……以外, 什麼都不做

例: He did nothing but play all day.

(他整天除了玩以外，什麼都沒做。)

解說:

第一步:

句中 but 可視為對等連接詞, 連接對等且形態相同的字 did, 即:

He did nothing but did...

第二步:

我們知道 do、does、did 在肯定句中, 可視為強調性的助動詞, 之後要接原形動詞。

例: 未強調前:

He studies hard.
(他用功。)

強調後:

He does study hard.
(他的確用功。)

未強調前:

He studied hard.

強調後:

He did study hard.

第三步:

因此, 在 He did nothing but did...中, did 之後要接原形動詞, 即成:

He did nothing but did play all day.

第四步:

對等連接詞 but 之後相同的字可予以省略。本句中第一個 did 為及物動詞的過去式, 而第二個 did 則為強調性的助動詞, 雖性質不一, 但外形相同, 故第二個 did 可予以省略, 即成:

He did nothing but play all day.

例: Grandpa did nothing but watch TV all day.
(爺爺整天除了看電視外，什麼都沒做。)

2. **That is why they cannot help but spend vast sums of money on cosmetics and fashionable clothing.**

那就是為何她們會忍不住將大筆金錢花在化妝品和流行服飾上的原因。

上列句中, 使用了"cannot help but + 原形動詞" (忍不住/禁不住……) 的句型。

表『忍不住/禁不住……』的用法尚有下列:

cannot help but + 原形動詞　　忍不住/禁不住……

= cannot help + 動名詞
= cannot but + 原形動詞

注意:

a. 在上列用法中, 以第一及第二句型較常見。

b. 在第二句型中, help 不譯成『幫助』, 而是等於 resist (抗拒) 或 avoid (避免) 的意思。故其後要接動名詞, 而不可接不定詞片語 (to + 原形動詞)。

例: Little Johnny couldn't help but take the cute stray dog home.
= Little Johnny couldn't help taking the cute stray dog home.
= Little Johnny couldn't but take the cute stray dog home.
(小強尼禁不住將那隻可愛的流浪狗帶回家。)

* stray dog 流浪狗
stray [stre] a. 迷路的, 走失的

3. **Instead, they should pay more attention to their character because when you have character, you have class.**
相反地, 她們應該多注意她們的品格, 因為有了品格, 才會有水準。
instead [ɪn'stɛd] adv. 相反地; (反) 而, 改以

注意:

instead 單獨使用, 作副詞用, 表『相反地』 時, 即等於 on the contrary; instead 亦可與介詞 of 並用, 其後接名詞或動名詞作受詞, 所形成的介詞片語作副詞用, 可置於句首或句尾, 表『(非但) 不……(反) 而……』。

例: Don't sleep all day. Instead, try to do something useful.
= Don't sleep all day. On the contrary, try to do something useful.
(別整天光是睡覺。相反地，設法做些有用的事情吧。)

Since there are only four people here, let's play bridge instead.
(既然這裡只有四個人，那咱們改打橋牌吧。)

Instead of working, the salesman went home to sleep.
= The salesman went home to sleep instead of working.
(那個業務員非但不工作，反而還跑回家睡覺。)

Substitution 代換

1. **It follows, therefore, that most women desire nothing but to look beautiful.**

Joan expects nothing but to get married, have children and be a simple housewife.

The sick old man does nothing but stare at the ceiling all day long.

因此，大部分的女性只想要看起來漂亮，這是有其道理的。

瓊安只想要結婚、生養小孩，做個單純的家庭主婦。

那個生病的老先生整天除了瞪著天花板看以外什麼都沒做。

2. **That is why they cannot help but spend vast sums of money on cosmetics and fashionable clothing.**

The businessman can't help thinking of ways to make money.

I cannot but feel sorry for those poor orphans.

那就是為何她們會忍不住將大筆金錢花在化妝品和流行服飾上的原因。

那個生意人沒辦法不想生財之道。

我忍不住會同情那些可憐的孤兒。

Lesson 84

Me and My Big Mouth

都怪我多嘴

Dialogue 實用會話

Duke is out shopping with his wife, Angel.

(D=Duke; A=Angel)

D: How come every time I'm out shopping with you, you buy nothing but cosmetics?

A: Don't you want me to look pretty?

D: Yes. But do you really need that much?

A: Well, since you put it that way, I guess I don't. Do I?

D: Of course, you don't.

A: Do you really think I look pretty enough without cosmetics?

D: Uh...sure. Besides, you're spending a fortune.

A: Oh, I see! You're interested in nothing but money. You don't really care how I look.

D: Come on. Be reasonable. You're married. Who's going to look at you anyway?

A: (She gets angry.) Make your own dinner tonight.

D: Me and my big mouth!

杜克在外面陪他太太安琪兒購物。
杜　克：為什麼每次我和妳出來逛街，妳就光買化粧品？
安琪兒：你不想要我看起來很漂亮嗎？
杜　克：要。可是妳真的需要那麼多嗎？
安琪兒：嗯，既然你那麼說的話，我想我不需要。我要嗎？
杜　克：妳當然不需要。
安琪兒：你真的認為我沒化粧看起來夠漂亮嗎？
杜　克：呃……當然。而且妳花了好多錢。
安琪兒：哦，我懂了！你只對錢有興趣，你並不是真正關心我的容貌。
杜　克：別這樣嘛。妳要講理。妳已經結婚了，誰要看妳啊？
安琪兒：(她生氣了。) 晚飯你自己做。
杜　克：都怪我多嘴！

Key Points 重點提示

1. **shop** [ʃɑp] vi. 購物

   shop for + 物　　購買某物

   do the/some shopping　　購物

   例: I'm shopping for a birthday present for my dad.
   (我正要買一份生日禮物給我爸。)

   Mom does the shopping once a week.
   (老媽一個禮拜購物一次。)

2. **put it that/this way**　　那/這樣敘述/表達

   例: If you put it that way, I think everyone will understand what you mean.
   (如果你那樣敘述的話，我想每個人都會聽懂你的意思。)

3. **fortune** [ˈfɔrtʃən] n. 財富

spend a fortune 花大錢

make a fortune 發了一筆大財

例: Mr. Brown made a fortune on the stocks.
(布朗先生玩股票賺了一筆錢。)

4. **reasonable** [ˈrizənəbl̩] a. 講道理的; 合理的

例: We bought the house at a reasonable price.
(我們以合理的價錢買了這幢房子。)

請選出下列各句中正確的一項

1. The boys couldn't help but ______ at the pretty girl.
   (A) to stare (B) staring (C) stared (D) stare

2. It would be ______ to work as a lifeguard.
   (A) interest (B) interesting (C) interested (D) interests

3. The old man ______ a lot of attention to what he eats.
   (A) makes (B) pays (C) has (D) takes

4. Bob is ______ a tie to match his suit.
   (A) shopping (B) shopping for
   (C) shopped (D) shopped for

解答：

1. (D) 2. (B) 3. (B) 4. (B)

Lesson 85

Traveling by Plane

搭乘飛機旅行

Reading 閱讀

Traveling by plane is exciting, but it can also be very tiring. There are so many things to be done. You have to pay the airport tax, check in your bags and then get to the departure gate. So it's best to arrive at the airport at least two hours before your plane is scheduled to take off.

When you check in, the attendant will ask you to show her your passport, ticket and airport-tax receipt. After you have done that, she will weigh your luggage. If it's overweight, you'll have to pay an extra fee. Then she will give you your boarding pass. On

your way to the gate, don't pass up the chance to buy something at the duty-free shop. Things are a lot cheaper there. The key is to give yourself plenty of time and everything should run as smooth as clockwork.

搭乘飛機旅行很刺激，但也可能很累人，因為有一大堆事情要辦。你得付機場稅、辦理行李登機，然後前往登機門。因此，你最好在你的班機預定起飛前兩個小時到達機場。

辦理登機手續時，櫃台服務人員會要求你出示護照、機票和機場稅收據。辦完這之後，她會將你的行李秤重過磅。如果超重的話，你就必須額外付費。然後，她會把登機證交給你。在你往登機門的途中，別錯過了在免稅商店買東西的機會，那裡賣的東西比外面便宜多了。其中的要訣是給自己充分的時間，那麼事事都會非常順利。

Vocabulary & Idioms 單字 & 片語註解

1. **exciting** [ɪk'saɪtɪŋ] a. 令人刺激/興奮的 (修飾事物)
   excited [ɪk'saɪtɪd] a. 感到刺激/興奮的 (修飾人)
   例: It is exciting to go on a roller coaster ride.
   (乘坐雲霄飛車很刺激。)
   * roller coaster ['rolɚ ˌkostɚ] n. 雲霄飛車
   The children got excited when their father promised to take them to the zoo.
   (當孩子們的父親答應帶他們去動物園時，他們很興奮。)

2. **tiring** ['taɪrɪŋ] a. 令人疲累的 (修飾事物)
   tired [taɪrd] a. 感到疲累的 (修飾人)

例: The trip was tiring but enjoyable.
(這趟旅程很累人但很好玩。)
∗ enjoyable [ɪnˈdʒɔɪəbḷ] a. 令人感到愉快的

Mr. Wang was very tired after a hard day's work.
(王先生在辛苦工作一天後非常疲倦。)

3. **airport tax** [ˈɛrˌpɔrt ˌtæks] n. 機場稅

4. **check in (...)** 登記 (……)

例: We should check in at the hotel before 2 p.m.
(我們應該在下午兩點前到旅館辦理登記。)

5. **departure** [dɪˈpɑrtʃɚ] n. 離開

例: The president's departure was a well-kept secret.
(總統離境是個被嚴守的秘密。)

6. **be scheduled to + 原形動詞** 預定/預期……

schedule [ˈskɛdʒʊl] vt. 排定

例: Jane is scheduled to arrive in London next week.
(阿珍預定下個星期抵達倫敦。)

7. **take off** (飛機) 起飛

例: The plane took off an hour late.
(那架飛機延遲了一個小時起飛。)

8. **attendant** [əˈtɛndənt] n. 服務員

flight attendant 空服員

∗ flight [flaɪt] n. 班機

例: If you need anything on the plane, you can ask the flight attendant.
(在飛機上你如果需要任何東西，可以跟空服員要。)

9. **passport** [ˈpæsˌpɔrt] n. 護照

例: When does your passport expire?
(你的護照什麼時候到期？)
∗ expire [ɪkˈspaɪr] vi. 期滿

10. **receipt** [rɪ'sit] n. 收據

例: When you buy anything valuable, you should ask for a receipt.
(你買任何貴重物品時，應該索取收據。)
* valuable ['væljuəbl̩] a. 珍貴的, 值錢的

11. **weigh** [we] vt. 稱重量 & vi. 重達

weight [wet] n. 重量; 體重

例: Phillis weighs herself every night before going to bed.
(菲麗絲每晚睡前都會秤體重。)

Dick always complains that his schoolbag weighs a ton.
(狄克總是抱怨他的書包重得要命。)

Can you guess the weight of this watermelon?
(你能猜出這顆西瓜多重嗎？)

12. **luggage** ['lʌgɪdʒ] n. 行李

= baggage ['bægɪdʒ] n.

注意:

luggage 與 baggage 皆為不可數名詞, 字尾不能加 s。如表『一件行李』時, 則以"a piece of luggage/baggage"表示之。

例: How many luggages do you have with you? (×)
→ How many pieces of luggage do you have with you? (○)
(你隨身攜帶多少件行李？)

13. **overweight** ['ovɚˌwet] a. 超重的, 過胖的

例: An overweight man tires easily.
(過胖的人很容易疲倦。)

14. **extra** ['ɛkstrə] a. 額外的

例: It's so cold that I need an extra blanket.
(天氣很冷，我需要加一條毛毯。)
* blanket ['blæŋkɪt] n. 毛毯

15. **fee** [fi] n. 費用

16. **boarding pass** [ˈbɔrdɪŋ ˌpæs] n. 登機證

例: Without a boarding pass, the attendant won't let you board the plane.
(沒有登機證，空服人員不會讓你登機。)

17. **pass up the chance to + 原形動詞** 錯過……的機會

例: Sandy will never pass up the chance to see the singer's live concert.
(珊蒂絕不會錯過觀賞這位歌手的現場演唱會。)

18. **duty-free** [ˈdjutɪˌfri] a. 免稅的

例: Duty-free things are sold cheaper.
(免稅的東西都比較便宜。)

19. 本文:
Things are a lot cheaper there.
那裡的東西便宜多了。

cheap [tʃip] a. 便宜的

* 此處 cheaper 是 cheap 的比較級。

注意:
用來修飾比較級形容詞或副詞的副詞常見的有下列六個: a lot, much, even, still, a great deal, far。

例: My sick father is a lot better now.
(我生病的父親現在好多了。)

Jack is tall but his son is even taller.
(傑克個子很高，但他兒子比他還高。)

20. **plenty of...** 許多……

例: There's no rush; we have plenty of time.
(別急，我們有很多時間。)

21. **run/go as smooth as clockwork**
像鐘錶的機械裝置一樣運行順暢, 非常順利
clockwork [ˈklɑk͵wɝk] n. 鐘錶的機械裝置
例: The meeting went as smooth as clockwork.
(會議進行得非常順利。)

Grammar Notes 文法重點

本課介紹"by + 交通工具"的用法, 以及"表一段時間的名詞+ before..."的用法, 並介紹"on one's way (to) ..." (某人往……途中) 的用法, 以及"plenty of..." (很多/充分/豐富……) 的用法。

1. **Traveling <u>by plane</u> is exciting but it can also be very tiring.**
搭乘飛機旅行很刺激, 但也可能很累人。

注意:

a. 表『搭乘』某種交通工具時, 可用"by + 交通工具"來表示, 且此交通工具前不可置任何冠詞, 如: by plane (搭飛機)、by train (搭火車)、by bus (搭公車)、by ship/boat (搭船)、by taxi (搭計程車)、by bicycle (騎腳踏車) 等。

例: Traveling by plane is not the only way to get to America.
(搭飛機旅行並非是到美國去的唯一途徑。)

It's cheaper to go to work by train than by taxi.
(搭火車去上班比搭計程車便宜。)

My kids go to school by bicycle.
(我的小孩都騎腳踏車上學。)

b. 表『步行』時, 則要用 on foot 來表示。

例: The only way to get to the village is on foot.
(到那個村莊去的唯一途徑是步行。)

c. 若交通工具前有冠詞 (如 a/an、the) 或所有格 (my、your、his 等) 時, 則介詞不用 by, 而要用 on 或 in; 若交通工具較大, 人可在其上面站立或走動者, 介詞用 on; 若交通工具較小, 人無法在其上面站立或走動者, 則介詞用 in。

例: I first met my wife on a bus.
(我在公車上初次遇見我太太。)

Whatever you do, don't throw up in my car.
(不管你做什麼，就是別吐在我車上。)

2. **So it's best to arrive at the airport at least <u>two</u> hours <u>before</u> your plane is scheduled to take off.**
因此你最好在你的班機預定起飛前兩個小時到達機場。
注意:

a. before 或 after 均可作連接詞或介詞, 在其所引導的副詞子句或介詞片語之前, 可置表一段時間的名詞, 表『在……之前/後……(時間) 』。

例: <u>Two years after</u> the couple got married, they got divorced.
(那對夫妻結婚後兩年就離婚了。)

<u>Just one year before</u> graduating, Steve started his own company.
(畢業前一年，史蒂夫便自行創業了。)

b. 在 before 或 after 引導的副詞子句或介詞片語之前, 亦可置副詞 shortly、immediately、long 等字, 表『在……之前/後不久/很久』。

例: <u>Shortly before</u> Dan arrived, everyone left.
(在丹到達前不久每個人就都離開了。)

<u>Long after</u> we moved to Tokyo, we returned to our hometown but couldn't find any of our friends.
(搬到東京好一陣子之後，我們回到家鄉去，但卻找不到任何一位朋友了。)

3. **<u>On your way to the gate</u>, don't pass up the chance to buy something at the duty-free shop.**

在你往登機門的途中，別錯過了在免稅商店買東西的機會。

注意:

on one's way to + 地方名詞 (如: school、train station 等)

on one's way + 地方副詞 (如: home、here、there、downtown 等)

上列兩種句型均表『某人往某地的途中』; 在 on one's way 後接的若是 school、train station 等地方名詞時, 則此地方名詞前要置介詞 to; 若接的是 home、here、there、downtown (市中心) 等地方副詞時, 則不可再用介詞 to。

例: <u>On my way to</u> the office, I met the boss, who was also late.
(我在上班的途中遇見了也同樣遲到的老闆。)

<u>On his way home</u>, Billy stopped at the coffee shop for a while.
(比利在回家途中到咖啡廳待了一陣子。)

比較:

stand in one's way　　擋了某人的路; 妨礙某人

例: When I took the picture, somebody stood in my way.
(我拍照時，有人擋到了我。)

4. **The key is to give yourself <u>plenty of</u> time and everything should run as smooth as clockwork.**

其中的要訣就是給自己充分的時間, 這樣事事就會非常順利。

plenty of + 不可數名詞/複數可數名詞　　很多/充分/豐富的……

注意:

plenty of 表『很多/充分/豐富的』之意, 之後可接不可數名詞或複數可數名詞作受詞。

例: The poor man has plenty of <u>work</u> but very little pay.
(那個窮人工作做不少，但薪資卻很少。)

There are plenty of apples on my apple tree.
(我的蘋果樹上結了很多蘋果。)

1. **Traveling by plane is exciting, but it can also be very tiring.**

   Going to Macau by boat is fun, and it is also very cheap.

   Going to work by taxi every day is expensive, but it's convenient.

   搭乘飛機旅行很刺激, 但也可能很累人。
   搭船到澳門去很好玩, 也很便宜。
   每天搭乘計程車上班很花錢, 但卻很方便。

2. **On your way to the gate, don't pass up the chance to buy something at the duty-free shop.**

   On your way to the zoo, don't forget to buy some bananas.

   On his way home, Carl was robbed.

   在你往登機門的途中, 別錯過了在免稅商店買東西的機會。
   在你到動物園途中, 別忘了買些香蕉。
   卡爾在回家途中被搶了。

Lesson 86

Bon Voyage!

一路順風！

Joe is standing in the check-in line at the airport. He has two bags to check in and one carry-on.

(A=Attendant; J=Joe)

A: Hello, sir. May I have your passport and ticket, please?

J: Here you are. I'd like to have an aisle seat in the smoking section, please.

A: I'll see what I can do. I'm sorry. They've all been taken. How about a window seat?

J: Sure. It doesn't really matter. What gate does my flight depart from?

A: Gate two. Here's your boarding pass. We'll begin boarding in about an hour.

J: Good. That will give me time to take advantage of the duty-free shop.

A: Bon voyage!

J: Thank you!

喬正站在辦理登機手續的地方排隊。他有兩件行李要寄運，一件隨身攜帶。

服務員：先生，你好。請把護照和機票給我一下好嗎？

喬：在這裡。我想要抽煙區靠近走道的位子。

服務員：我看看。對不起。那些位子都有人了。靠近窗戶的座位如何？

喬：當然好。其實也沒關係。我要從幾號門登機？

服務員：二號門。這是您的登機證。我們大約一小時後開始登機。

喬：很好。那樣我就有時間去免稅商店看一看。

服務員：祝您一路順風！

喬：謝謝！

Key Points 重點提示

1. **bon voyage** [ˌbɑn vɔɪˈɑʒ] n. (法文) 祝一路平安/順風

2. **stand in line** 排隊

   例: People should stand in line when they're waiting for a bus.
   (等公車時，人們應該排隊。)

3. **check-in** [ˈtʃɛkˌɪn] n. 辦理登機或旅館投宿手續

   ＊ 此字於本文中為名詞作形容詞用。

   例: Can you tell me when the check-in time is, please?
   (能不能請你告訴我登機的時間是什麼時候呢？)

4. **carry-on** [ˈkærɪˌɑn] n. 隨身行李

   例: This bag is too big for a carry-on; you'll have to check it in.
   (這個袋子做為一件隨身行李太大了，你得登記寄運才行。)

5. **Here you are.** 在這兒/拿去吧。

   注意:

"Here you are."或"Here you go."為表示拿東西給對方時的說法, 中文譯為『在這兒』、『拿去吧』、『這個便是』之意。

例: A: Can you show me that shirt, please?
B: Here you are.
(甲：請拿那件襯衫給我看看好嗎？)
(乙：在這兒。)

6. **aisle seat** [ˈaɪl ˌsit] n. 靠走道的座位
window seat [ˈwɪndo ˌsit] n. 靠窗的座位
aisle [aɪl] n. 通道

例: Kids like window seats so that they can look outside the plane.
(小孩子喜歡靠窗的座位，這樣他們才能看到飛機外面的景物。)

7. **smoking section** [ˈsmokɪŋ ˌsɛkʃən] n. 抽煙區
non-smoking section 禁煙區
section [ˈsɛkʃən] n. 地區, 區域

例: If you smoke, you'd better ask for a seat in the smoking section.
(如果你抽煙的話，你最好要求抽煙區的座位。)

8. **depart** [dɪˈpɑrt] vi. 離開; 出發
depart for... 出發前往……
= leave for...
= set out for...
= head for...

例: A bus departs for the airport every fifteen minutes.
(開往機場的公車每十五分鐘一班。)

The weather is so beautiful; let's head for the beach.
(天氣這麼好，咱們到海灘去吧。)

9. **board** [bɔrd] vi. 登上 (飛機、船等); 寄宿; 寄膳

例: My friend boarded with me until he found an apartment to rent.
(我的朋友寄住在我這兒直到他租到了一間公寓。)

10. **take advantage of...** 利用……

advantage [əd'væntɪdʒ] n. 益處

例: We took advantage of the long weekend and went on a trip.
(我們利用那次長週末去度了個假。)

請選出下列各句中正確的一項

1. The plane _______ for England in an hour.
   (A) flies (B) goes (C) departs (D) sets

2. When you _______ Rome, give me a call.
   (A) reach (B) reach to (C) get (D) arrive

3. Although it was raining, the crowd stood _______ line for an hour to buy tickets for the concert.
   (A) at (B) among (C) in (D) between

4. One day Jason will be ______ successful than his father.
   (A) much (B) even more (C) even (D) more even

解答：

1. (C) 2. (A) 3. (C) 4. (B)

Lesson 87

AIDS

愛滋病

Each day, more than 6,000 people around the world fall victim to HIV. That's how serious the problem is. The World Health Organization has estimated that about 17 million people have already been infected with this disease. The news is that the virus is now spreading fastest in Asia. It's high time some steps were taken.

Two proven methods should be followed. One way is to teach people how to avoid catching the virus sexually through condom promotion. The other way is to encourage people to

stop having casual sex. A word to the wise is sufficient, so don't take this warning lightly.

每天，全世界有超過六千人成為愛滋病毒的受害者。問題就是那麼嚴重。世界衛生組織估計大約有一千七百萬人已經感染了這個疾病。消息是該病毒在亞洲蔓延得最為迅速。現在該是採取一些措施的時候了。

有兩個已經驗證的方法應該遵循。其中一個方法是藉由提倡使用保險套來教導人們避免從性行為而感染到該病毒。另外一個方法則是鼓勵人們停止性濫交。智者一點就通，所以不要忽視這項警告。

Vocabulary & Idioms 單字 & 片語註解

1. **AIDS** [edz] n. 愛滋病; 後天免疫不全徵候群

= acquired immune deficiency syndrome

acquired [əˈkwaɪrd] a. 後天得到的

immune [ɪˈmjun] a. (對病毒等) 免疫的

deficiency [dɪˈfɪʃənsɪ] n. 不足, 缺乏

syndrome [ˈsɪndrom] n. (醫) 徵候群

2. **victim** [ˈvɪktɪm] n. 受害者; 犧牲品

fall victim to... 成為……的受害者/犧牲品

= fall prey to...

* prey [pre] n. 犧牲者

注意:

以上片語中的 victim 及 prey 之前均不置任何冠詞, 亦無複數的用法。

例: Many people in tropical countries fall victim to malaria every year.

(在熱帶國家裡，每年有許多人感染瘧疾。)

＊ tropical [ˈtrɑpɪkl̩] a. 熱帶的
malaria [məˈlɛrɪə] n. 瘧疾

3. **HIV** [ˌetʃaɪˈvi] n. 人體免疫缺乏病毒, 愛滋病毒
= human immunodeficiency virus
human [ˈhjumən] a. 人體的
immunodeficiency [ɪˌmjunodɪˈfɪʃənsɪ] n. 免疫缺乏
virus [ˈvaɪrəs] n. 濾過性病毒

4. **serious** [ˈsɪrɪəs] a. 嚴重的
例: The common cold is not considered a serious illness.
(普通感冒不被視為一種嚴重的疾病。)

5. **World Health Organization** 世界衛生組織 (常縮寫成 WHO)
organization [ˌɔrgənəˈzeʃən] n. 組織, 團體
例: Only rich people can join that organization.
(只有富人才能參加那個組織。)

6. **infect** [ɪnˈfɛkt] vt. 使感染 (常用於被動語態中)
be infected with... 感染……
例: The doctor says Jim is infected with some kind of skin disease.
(醫生說吉姆感染了某種皮膚病。)

7. **disease** [dɪˈziz] n. 疾病
例: The dying patient has an incurable disease.
(那個垂死的病人得了不治之症。)
＊ incurable [ɪnˈkjʊrəbl̩] a. 無法醫治的

8. **spread** [sprɛd] vi. 蔓延
動詞三態均為 spread。
例: The fire spread very quickly to the upper stories.
(火勢迅速蔓延到上面的樓層。)

9. **step** [stɛp] n. 步驟, 措施

take steps to + 原形動詞　　採取措施……

例: The boss took steps to cut down on his losses.
(老闆採取措施以減少虧損。)
＊ cut down on...　　減少……
= reduce...

10. **proven** [ˈpruvən] a. 已證實的

prove [pruv] vt. 證明 & vi. 顯示

prove + that 子句　　證明……
　　　　名詞

prove (to be) + 名詞/形容詞　　顯示/結果是……

例: The manager is a man of proven ability.
(該名經理證實是位有能力的人。)

The lawyer is trying his best to prove that his client is innocent.
(那名律師正盡全力證明他的委託人是清白的。)
＊ client [ˈklaɪənt] n. 委託人

Tom's method of doing the experiment proved (to be) right.
(湯姆做那項實驗的方法結果是正確的。)

11. **method** [ˈmɛθəd] n. 方法

12. **follow** [ˈfɑlo] vt. 遵從; 跟隨

例: I always follow my parents' advice.
(我總是聽從我父母的忠告。)

The policeman followed the suspect to his home.
(警察跟蹤嫌疑犯到他的家裡去。)

13. **avoid + 名詞/動名詞**　　避免/避開……

例: The shy boy tried to avoid his classmates.
(那個羞怯的男孩想要避開他的同班同學。)

14. **sexually** [ˈsɛkʃuəlɪ] adv. 性愛地

15. **condom** [ˈkɑndəm] n. 保險套

例: One way to practice safe sex is to wear a condom.
(進行安全性行為的方法之一便是使用保險套。)

16. **promotion** [prəˈmoʃən] n. 提倡, 促進

例: Our public relations office is involved in the promotion of many new products.
(我們的公關部門正致力促銷多項新產品。)

17. **encourage** [ɪnˈkɝɪdʒ] vt. 鼓勵

encourage + 人 + to + 原形動詞　　鼓勵某人……

例: We should encourage young people to take part in more cultural activities.
(我們應該鼓勵年輕人多參與文化活動。)

18. **casual sex**　　性濫交

casual [ˈkæʒuəl] a. 偶然的; 非正式的

例: Dad always wears casual clothes on weekends.
(老爸週末時都穿休閒裝。)

19. **the wise**　　智者, 聰明人

= wise people

注意:

某些形容詞前置定冠詞 the 時, 視為複數名詞, 用來泛指某一階層人或某一類人全體的概念, 如:

the rich = rich people　　富人

the poor = poor people　　窮人

the sick = sick people　　病人

the homeless = homeless people　　無家可歸的人

20. **sufficient** [səˈfɪʃənt] a. 足夠的, 充足的

例: The students had sufficient time to finish writing the test.
(學生們有足夠的時間寫完試卷。)

21. **warning** [ˈwɔrnɪŋ] n. 警告

例: The boss gave Mr. Wang a warning instead of firing him.
(老闆警告了王先生，而沒有炒他魷魚。)

22. **lightly** [ˈlaɪtlɪ] adv. 輕率地; 輕蔑地

take...lightly 輕忽……
take...seriously 嚴肅/認真對待……

例: One should never take one's work lightly.
(每個人都不該輕忽自己的工作。)

You should take my words seriously. I'm not kidding.
(你應正視我的話。我不是在開玩笑。)

Grammar Notes 文法重點

本課介紹"It's high time + that 引導的過去式名詞子句" (現在該是……的時候了) 的用法, 以及"one...the other..." (一個……另一個……) 的用法。

1. **It's high time some steps were taken.**

= It's high time that some steps were taken.
現在該是採取一些措施的時候了。

上列句中, 使用了"It's high time + that (可省略) 引導的過去式名詞子句" (現在該是……的時候了) 的句型, It's 是 It is 的縮寫; 此句型乃表『現在該是……的時候了』,但卻尚未做, 故為一種表與現在事實相反的假設語氣, 因此其後的 that 子句中要用過去式動詞, 且若此動詞為 be 動詞時, 則一律用 were。句型如下:

It's (high/about) time + that 引導的過去式名詞子句　　現在該是……的時候了

例: "It's (high) time that you got a haircut," the teacher told the student.
(老師對那學生說：『你該理髮了』。)

It's (about) time that you got married.
(該是你結婚的時候了。)

2. **Two proven methods should be followed. One way is to teach people how to avoid catching the virus sexually through condom promotion. The other way is to encourage people to stop having casual sex.**

有兩個已經驗證的方法應該遵循。其中一個方法是藉由提倡使用保險套來教導人們避免從性行為感染到該病毒, 而另一個方法則是鼓勵人們停止性濫交。

上列句中, 使用了"one...the other..." (一個……另一個……) 的句型。使用本句型時, 通常前面置"two + 複數名詞", 表示在限定兩者中的一個及另一個。

one...the other...　　一個……另一個……

例: Two people came to see her today. One was an old man; the other was a pretty girl.
(今天有兩個人來看她；其中一個是位老先生，而另一個則是位漂亮姑娘。)

注意:

a. 若指限定的三者時, 則須使用"one...another...the other..." (一個……一個……另一個……)。

例: I have three cars. One is black, another is yellow, and the other is pink.
(我有三部車；其中一部是黑色的，一部是黃色的，而另一部則是粉紅色的。)

b. "one...the others..." (一個……其餘……) 為用於限定的三者以上時使用之句型。

例: The test this morning was really tough. Only one student passed it; the others all failed.
(今早的考試真難。只有一個學生考及格，其他則全都不及格。)

c. "one...another..." (一個……另一個……) 為用以指非限定的三者以上時使用之句型。

例: There are different ways to cook this dish. One way is to steam it, and another is to deep-fry it.
(這道菜有幾種不同的煮法。其中一種是用蒸的，另一種則是用油炸的。)

d. "some...others..." (一些……另一些……) 為用以指非限定的兩個群體時使用之句型。

例: Some dogs are friendly, but others are fierce.
(有些狗很友善，另一些則很凶。)

e. "some...others...still others..." (一些……一些……而另一些……) 為用以指非限定的三個群體時使用之句型。

例: It was so hot that some runners slowed down, others stopped, and still others fainted.
(天氣非常熱，因此有些跑者的速度便慢下來，有些則停下來，還有一些則昏倒了。)

f. "some...the others..." (一些……其餘……) 則為用以指限定的兩個群體時使用之句型。

例: Some of these grapes are sweet but the others are sour.
(這些葡萄中有些很甜，其餘的則很酸。)

1. **It's high time some steps were taken.**

   It's time that my son learned how to behave more maturely.

   It's about time that someone pointed out his mistakes to him.

   現在該是採取一些措施的時候了。
   現在該是我兒子學習怎麼表現更成熟的時候了。
   現在該是有人向他指出他的錯誤的時候了。

2. **Two proven methods should be followed. One way is to teach people how to avoid catching the virus sexually through condom promotion. The other way is to encourage people to stop having casual sex.**

   One car ran into a truck and the other hit a tree.

   One thief shot the shopkeeper and the other ran away.

   有兩個已經驗證的方法應該遵循。其中一個是藉由提倡使用保險套來教導人們避免從性行為感染到該病毒。而另外一個方法則是鼓勵人們停止性濫交。
   一輛車撞上了卡車而另一輛則撞上了樹。
   一個竊賊射殺了店主,而另一個竊賊則逃走了。

Lesson 88

What an Idiot!

真是個大笨蛋！

Dialogue 實用會話

Lucy is talking to her boyfriend, Vic, about their friend, Randy. (L=Lucy; V=Vic)

L: Did you hear that Randy's got AIDS?

V: Oh my God! Really? How come?

L: He became infected after having sex with a call girl.

V: What an idiot! Where's he now?

L: He's in a hospital. When I went to see him, I found him trembling in fear.

V: What did he say?

L: Not much. He seemed tired. He lay in bed with his eyes staring up at the ceiling.

V: Gee! Poor guy.

L: Let that be a lesson to you.

V: You're right. I'll never do that again.

L: What! So you've done it before!

V: Uh oh!

露西正和她的男朋友維克談論他們的朋友朗迪。
露西：你聽說朗迪得到愛滋病了嗎？
維克：我的天啊！真的嗎？怎麼會呢？
露西：他和一名應召女郎發生性行為後感染到的。
維克：真是個大笨蛋！他現在在哪裡？
露西：他在醫院。我去看他的時候，發現他害怕得一直發抖。
維克：他說了些什麼？
露西：沒說很多。他似乎很疲倦。他躺在床上兩眼直瞪著天花板。
維克：哎！可憐的傢伙。
露西：那會給你個警惕。
維克：妳說得對。我再也不做那種事了。
露西：什麼！那麼說來，你以前有做過囉！
維克：糟了！

Key Points 重點提示

1. **idiot** [ˈɪdɪət] n. 白痴
2. **have sex with + 人**　與某人性交
   例: It's a crime to have sex with a minor.
   (和未成年的人發生性關係是有罪的。)
   ＊ minor [ˈmaɪnɚ] n. 未成年者
3. **call girl**　應召女郎
   例: Some gangsters forced the young lady to be a call girl.
   (有些壞蛋強迫那名年輕女郎應召。)
   ＊ gangster [ˈgæŋstɚ] n. 歹徒
4. **hospital** [ˈhɑspɪtḷ] n. 醫院
5. **tremble** [ˈtrɛmbḷ] vi. 發抖, 顫抖

例: The sick old man can't write anything because his hands tremble.
(那個生病的老先生無法寫字，因為他兩手顫抖。)

6. **in fear** 害怕中, 恐懼中

fear [fɪr] n. 害怕, 恐懼

例: Some rich people live in fear of being kidnapped.
(一些富有的人活在被綁架的恐懼中。)
* kidnap [ˈkɪdnæp] vt. 綁架

7. **stare at...** 瞪視著……

stare [stɛr] vi. 凝視

例: Whenever his wife stares at him, he knows something is wrong.
(每當他的太太瞪他時，他便知道有壞事發生了。)

8. **ceiling** [ˈsilɪŋ] n. 天花板

例: My wife likes to live in a house with a high ceiling.
(我太太喜歡住在天花板高的房子裡。)

9. 本文:

He lay in bed with his eyes staring up at the ceiling.
他躺在床上兩眼直瞪著天花板。

注意:
此為『情狀介詞片語』的用法, 顧名思義, 情狀介詞片語是一種表示主詞所處的情形或狀況的介詞片語 (介詞 + 受詞), 這種片語由介詞 with 引導, 其結構有下列三種:

a. with + 受詞 + 介詞 + 受詞
(作受詞補語)

例: Jeff, do you know that tall girl with a hat on her head?
(傑夫，你認識那個頭上戴了頂帽子的高個子女孩嗎？)

b. with + 受詞 + 現在分詞(表示主動涵意)
(作受詞補語)

* 本文即屬此種用法。

例: He talked to the principal with his legs trembling.
(他跟校長講話時雙腿發抖。)

c. with + 受詞 + 過去分詞(表被動涵意)
(作受詞補語)

例: Little Johnny walked into the kitchen with his eyes closed.
(小強尼閉著眼睛走進廚房裡。)

請選出下列各句中正確的一項

1. You should avoid ______ out with friends who like to gamble.
(A) to go (B) going (C) gone (D) go

2. The kind man stopped ______ the old lady cross the street.
(A) to help (B) helping (C) to take (D) taking

3. The new worker proved very ______.
(A) efficient (B) efficiently (C) efficiency (D) effort

4. The arrogant man claims he can beat anyone at table tennis with his eyes ______.
(A) to close (B) closing (C) closed (D) to be closed

5. Are you ______ any steps to improve your English?
(A) making (B) taking (C) falling (D) spreading

解答：

1. (B) 2. (A) 3. (A) 4. (C) 5. (B)

Lesson 89

Kayaking

划獨木舟

Reading
閱　讀

If you are a little adventurous, like water sports, and enjoy being around nature, then kayaking is definitely for you. Floating, drifting and speeding down rivers is all part of kayaking. What better way is there to spend a boiling hot summer day? And if you think it is dangerous, you're dead wrong. It's so safe, you don't even need to know how to swim! Everyone wears a life jacket while kayaking. So, you see, it's not a sport for the brave only.

Kayaking may look difficult but it's really very easy. Sea

kayaking can be learned in 5 minutes! However, it takes about two days to learn river kayaking. And for an estimated US$1,500, you'll be able to own all the proper equipment, including the kayak. It's not cheap, but good things seldom are.

如果你稍為有點冒險精神，又喜歡水上運動和接近大自然的話，那麼划獨木舟就一定很適合你。漂浮、漂移和沖下河流都是划獨木舟的一部分。還有什麼比這樣度過炎炎夏日更好的方法呢？而且如果你認為這很危險的話，那你就大錯特錯了。它非常安全，以致於你甚至不需要會游泳！划獨木舟的時候，每個人都會穿一件救生衣。所以，你看，這並不只是項專屬勇者的運動。

划獨木舟看起來很難，其實很容易。海上獨木舟不用五分鐘就可以學會了！然而，河流獨木舟大約需要兩天的時間。大概花個一千五百塊美金，所有的裝備你就可以一應俱全，包括獨木舟。那並不便宜，可是一分錢一分貨。

Vocabulary & Idioms 單字 & 片語註解

1. **kayak** [ˈkaɪæk] vi. 划獨木舟 & n. 獨木舟

   canoe [kəˊnu] vi. 乘獨木舟 & n. 獨木舟

   注意:

   kayak 通常指的是位置固定於中央且一人乘坐的獨木舟,而 canoe 指的是位置不固定且不止一人乘坐的獨木舟。

   例: It's dangerous to go kayaking alone.
   (單獨一個人去划獨木舟很危險。)

   A kayak is actually one kind of canoe.
   ("kayak"實際上是獨木舟（canoe）的一種。)

We canoed down the river looking for a good place to camp.
(我們乘坐獨木舟沿著河流尋找一處露營的好場所。)

In the old days a canoe was used for transportation.
(過去獨木舟被用來當作運輸工具使用。)

2. **adventurous** [ədˈvɛntʃərəs] a. 愛冒險的; 膽大的

adventure [ədˈvɛntʃɚ] n. 冒險

例: An adventurous man is not afraid of taking risks.
(膽大的人不怕冒險。)

Going on a safari was a real adventure.
(去狩獵旅行真是一項冒險。)

* safari [səˈfɑrɪ] n. (狩獵、探險等) 遠征旅行

3. **definitely** [ˈdɛfənɪtlɪ] adv. 無疑地, 確切地

4. **float** [flot] vi. 漂浮

* floating 於本文為動名詞作主詞。

例: When you learn how to swim, the first thing you must do is learn how to float.
(學游泳時，你必須做的第一件事就是學習怎麼漂浮。)

5. **drift** [drɪft] vi. 漂流

* drifting 於本文為動名詞作主詞。

例: The boat was drifting out to the ocean.
(那條船正往海裡漂流而去。)

6. **speed** [spid] vi. 速進; 急行 & n. 速度

動詞三態: speed、sped [spɛd]、sped。

at the/a speed of...　　以……的速度

* speeding 於本文亦為動名詞作主詞。

例: The police car sped down the road.
(那輛警車沿著馬路疾駛而過。)

John was driving at the speed of 100 kilometers per hour when the accident happened.
(當事故發生時，約翰正以每小時一百公里的速度行駛。)

7. **life jacket** [ˈlaɪf ˌdʒækɪt] n. 救生衣

例: The life jacket saved Ted from drowning.
(救生衣救了泰德使他免於溺斃。)
* drown [draʊn] vi. 溺斃, 淹死

8. **estimated** [ˈɛstəˌmetɪd] a. 估計的

estimate [ˈɛstəˌmet] vt. 估計

an estimated + 數字　　估計有……

It is estimated + that 子句　　據估計……

例: An estimated fifty people died in the fire.
= It is estimated that fifty people died in the fire.
(那場火災估計造成五十人死亡。)

9. **proper** [ˈprɑpɚ] a. 適當的; 正確的

improper [ɪmˈprɑpɚ] a. 不當的, 錯誤的

例: Is there a proper way of studying English?
(有正確學習英文的方法嗎？)

The school will not tolerate improper behavior.
(學校將不會縱容不當的行為。)
* tolerate [ˈtɑləˌret] vt. 容忍; 縱容

10. **equipment** [ɪˈkwɪpmənt] n. 設備, 裝備 (集合名詞, 不可數)

例: Do you have all the proper equipments for camping? (✕)
→ Do you have all the proper equipment for camping? (○)
(你的露營裝備齊全嗎？)

Grammar Notes
文法重點

本課介紹少數現在分詞及形容詞作副詞的用法,並複習"so...that..." (如此……以致於……) 的用法。

1. **What better way is there to spend a boiling hot summer day?**
還有什麼比這樣度過炎炎夏日更好的方法呢?
And if you think it is dangerous, you're dead wrong.
而且如果你認為這很危險的話, 那你就大錯特錯了。
上列第一句中的boiling本為boil的現在分詞, 作形容詞用, 表『(正在)沸騰/滾開的』, 但在此處卻作副詞用, 修飾其後的形容詞 hot, 表『極炎熱地』之意; 而第二句中的 dead 亦本為形容詞, 表『(已) 死的』, 但在此處卻作副詞用, 表『全然地』之意, 修飾其後的形容詞 wrong。
注意:
a. 少數現在分詞有副詞 very 的意味, 可修飾其後的形容詞。
例: The coffee is boiling hot.
副詞 形容詞
(這咖啡很燙。)
It was | freezing / biting | cold yesterday.
副詞 形容詞
(昨天天氣非常冷。)
* freezing cold 冷得似乎要把人凍僵了
biting cold 冷得全身刺痛似被咬的樣子
Dad was hopping mad at Mom for playing mahjong all day long.
副詞 形容詞
(老爸因老媽整天打麻將而非常生氣。)

＊hopping ['hɑpɪŋ] adv. 非常(生氣)地(出自動詞hop, 指『跳躍』, 故hopping mad 可譯成『氣得跳腳』)

b. 少數形容詞亦有副詞的功能, 修飾之後的形容詞。常用的有兩個: dead 及awful (均譯成『非常地』)。

例: He is dead (副詞) | beat. / tired. | (形容詞)

(他累斃了。)

Jogging for an hour every morning is awful (副詞) tiring (形容詞).

(每天早上慢跑一個小時非常累人。)

＊此處awful 是副詞, 表示『非常』, 原為形容詞, 表『差勁的』。

His writing is awful.
(他的寫作很差勁。)

2. **It's so safe, you don't even need to know how to swim!**

= It's so safe that you don't even need to know how to swim!

它非常安全, 以致於你甚至不需要會游泳！

在Lesson 11 中, 我們已提過在現在美語中, "so...that..."句構中的that常予以省略, 而用逗號取代, 或甚至連逗號都不用; 相同用法的句型尚有"such... that..."。因這兩種句型均是常見的用法, 故我們再複習如下:

so + 形容詞/副詞 + that 子句　　如此……以致於……

such + 名詞 + that 子句　　如此……以致於……

例: The runner was so exhausted after the race that he almost fainted.

= The runner was so exhausted after the race (,) he almost fainted.
(那位跑者在跑完比賽後累得差點昏倒。)

Molly was so beautifully dressed that everyone was staring at her.

= Molly was so beautifully dressed (,) everyone was staring at her.
(茉莉穿得很漂亮，因而每個人都盯著她瞧。)

Rob is <u>such</u> a forgetful person <u>that</u> he often forgets to bring his books to school.

= Rob is <u>such</u> a forgetful person (,) he often forgets to bring his books to school.

(羅伯是個非常健忘的人，以致他上學經常忘了帶書本。)

It's so safe, you don't even need to know how to swim!

The water is so deep, I can't stand in the pool.

Mr. Chen is such a good teacher, all the students like him.

它非常安全,以致於你甚至不需要會游泳！

池水非常深,以致於我無法在游泳池裡站立著。

陳先生是個很棒的老師,所以所有的學生都喜歡他。

Lesson 90

Only the Good Die Young

好人不長命

Diana bumps into her friend, Steve.

(D= Diana; S= Steve)

D: Hi, Steve! It's awful hot today, isn't it?

S: You can say that again!

D: Let's go kayaking later.

S: Are you kidding? I can't even swim.

D: So what? You'll be safe with a life jacket and a helmet on.

S: What if the kayak capsizes?

D: I'll teach you to "Eskimo roll."

S: What's that?

D: Well, it's a special technique we use to get the kayak upright when it overturns.

S: I don't know...it sounds pretty dangerous.

D: Come on. Don't worry. Only the good die young.

S: What do you mean by that?

D: Just kidding. Let's go, OK?

S: OK. Anyway, if only the good die young, we'll both probably live to be a hundred.

黛安娜和她的朋友史蒂夫不期而遇。
黛安娜：嗨，史蒂夫。今天熱死人了，是不是？
史蒂夫：妳說的一點也沒錯！
黛安娜：我們待會兒去划獨木舟吧。
史蒂夫：妳在開玩笑嗎？我連游泳都不會。
黛安娜：那又怎麼樣？穿上救生衣和戴上安全帽你就萬無一失了。
史蒂夫：如果獨木舟翻過來怎麼辦？
黛安娜：我會教你『愛斯基摩翻滾』。
史蒂夫：那是什麼東西啊？
黛安娜：嗯，那是獨木舟翻覆時所用的一種使獨木舟翻正的特殊技巧。
史蒂夫：我不知道⋯⋯聽起來蠻危險的。
黛安娜：好了啦。別擔心，只有好人不長命。
史蒂夫：妳這話什麼意思？
黛安娜：只是開玩笑。我們走吧，好不好？
史蒂夫：好吧。反正如果只有好人不長命，那我們兩個大概都會活到一百歲。

1. **the good**　好人

= good people

2. **Only <u>the good</u> <u>die young</u>.**

= Only <u>good people</u> die young.
只有好人不長命。

注意:

die 之後可接形容詞或名詞作主詞補語。

例: The gambler died a poor man.
(那個賭徒死時一貧如洗。)

3. **bump into...**　　偶然遇到……

= run into...

bump [bʌmp] vi. 碰撞

例: Andy bumped into his father at the video game store.
(安迪在電動玩具店撞見他父親。)

4. **So what?**　　那又怎麼樣？

例: A: You forgot to do your homework again.
B: So what?
(甲：你又忘了做你的家庭作業了。)
(乙：那又怎麼樣？)

5. **with...on**　　身上穿/戴著……

例: With a life jacket on, you won't drown.
(身上穿著救生衣，你就不會溺水了。)

6. **helmet** [ˈhɛlmɪt] n. 頭盔, 安全帽

例: It's against the law to ride a motorcycle without a helmet on.
(騎機車不戴安全帽是違法的。)

7. **capsize** [kæpˈsaɪz] vi. & vt. (使) 傾覆/翻覆

例: If there are too many people on the canoe, it may capsize.
(如果太多人乘坐一艘獨木舟，它便可能會翻覆。)

The big waves capsized the boat.
(大浪把船弄翻了。)

8. **Eskimo** [ˈɛskəˌmo] a. 愛斯基摩的 & n. 愛斯基摩

9. **roll** [rol] n. & vi. 翻滾

例: With one quick roll, the wrestler got up on his feet.
(那名角力選手迅速翻滾了一下，便站了起來。)

My dog rolled over and over on the grass.
(我的狗兒在草地上不斷地翻滾。)

10. **technique** [tɛk'nik] n. 技術, 技巧

例: Mother has very good knitting technique.
(媽媽的編織技巧很好。)

＊ knitting ['nɪtɪŋ] n. 編織 (於本句作形容詞用)

11. **upright** ['ʌp,raɪt] a. 直立的

12. **overturn** [,ovɚ'tɝn] vi. 翻覆

= capsize

例: The car ran into a truck and overturned.
(那輛車撞上一部卡車而翻覆了。)

13. **mean** [min] vt. 意味

meaning ['minɪŋ] n. 意義, 意思

例: What do you mean by staring at me like that?
(你那樣看著我是什麼意思？)

It's no use reciting a composition if you don't know its meaning.
(如果你不知道文章的意思，光背誦它是沒有用的。)

14. **live to be + 年紀** 活到……的歲數

例: My grandpa lived to be a hundred years old.
(我爺爺活了一百歲。)

15. 本文:

...we'll both probably live to be a hundred.

= ...we'll both probably live to be a hundred years old.

……我們兩個大概都會活到一百歲。

請選出下列各句中正確的一項

1. He is ______ careless boy that he always makes mistakes in spelling.
   (A) so a (B) a so (C) a such (D) such a

2. Although he died young, he died ______.
   (A) happiness (B) happily (C) happy (D) to be happy

3. ______ try to survive the best they can.
   (A) Homeless (B) A homeless (C) The homeless (D) Homes

4. At one stage the race driver drove ______ a speed of 150 miles per hour.
   (A) with (B) at (C) for (D) by

5. Some people like to sleep ______ nothing on.
   (A) with (B) at (C) in (D) for

解答：

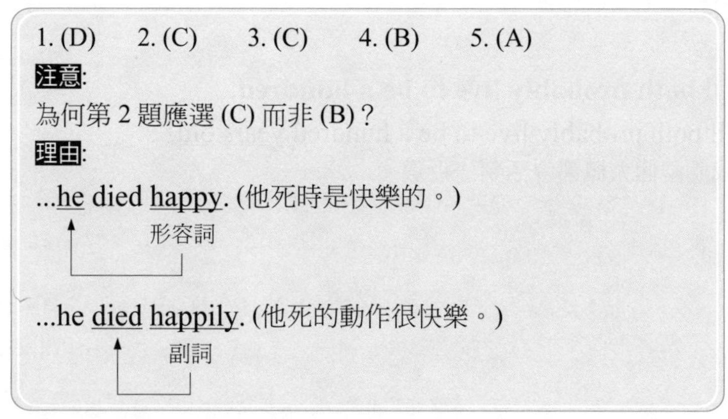

1. (D) 2. (C) 3. (C) 4. (B) 5. (A)

注意:

為何第 2 題應選 (C) 而非 (B)？

理由:

...he died happy. (他死時是快樂的。)

形容詞

...he died happily. (他死的動作很快樂。)

副詞

Lesson 91

One Good Turn Deserves Another

善有善報

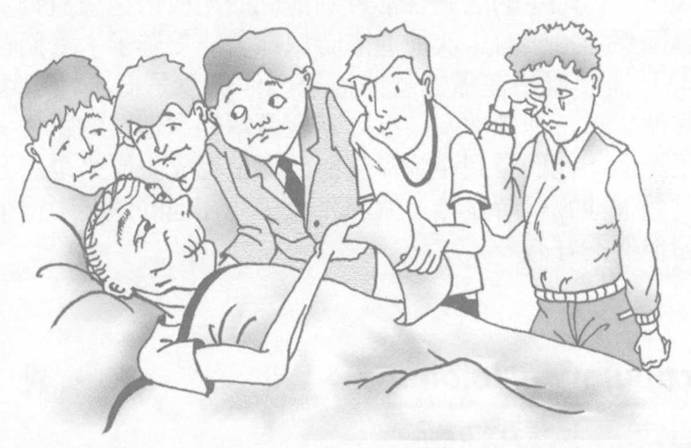

Reading 閱讀

One good turn deserves another. That's the lesson five store clerks learned recently.

Every day a strange old man came to their supermarket to buy groceries. "Once he came in wearing only one shoe," recalled one of the clerks. And although he grumbled a lot and they often had to stand there listening to him, he was a nice old man. The clerks befriended him and even helped him carry his groceries. One day when he fell ill with cancer, they even visited him in the hospital. The old man turned out to be a retired doctor.

And, of course, when he died, he didn't die a pauper. He left US $70,000 in his will to thank them for their kindness.

『善有善報』是五名店員最近學到的一課。

每天，一位陌生的老先生都會到他們的超級市場來買雜貨。其中一名店員回想道：『有一次他進來時只穿著一隻鞋子。』而雖然他常發牢騷並且他們得站在那裡聽他抱怨，他仍然是個心地不壞的老先生。那幾個店員待他像朋友一樣，甚至還幫他拿他買的雜貨。有一天他罹患了癌症，他們還到醫院探望他。那位老先生原來是一名退休的醫師。當然，他臨終時並非是個窮光蛋。他在他的遺囑中留下七萬美元來感謝他們的好心。

Vocabulary & Idioms 單字 & 片語註解

1. **One good turn deserves another.** 一報還一報/善有善報。

deserve [dɪ'zɝv] vt. 應得; 值得

例: Sean: Thanks for helping me fix my radio.
Leon: You helped me paint my house; one good turn deserves another.
(夏恩：謝謝你幫我修理我的收音機。)
(里昂：你幫我油漆房子，因此一報還一報。)

The diligent workers deserve a pay rise.
(那些勤勞的員工值得加薪。)

2. **store clerk** 店員

clerk [klɝk] n. (商店的) 售貨員, 店員

例: The clerk didn't know what to do, so he called the manager.
(售貨員不曉得該怎麼做，所以他便請來了經理。)

3. **recently** [ˈrisəntlɪ] adv. 最近, 近來

= lately [ˈletlɪ]

例: What happened to Ron? I haven't seen him recently.
(朗恩怎麼了？我最近都沒看到他。)

4. **grocery** [ˈgrosərɪ] n. 食品雜貨 (常用複數)

grocery store　　食品雜貨店

例: We buy our groceries once a week.
(我們一個禮拜購買一次食品雜貨。)

That grocery store has fresh meat.
(那家食品雜貨店販售新鮮肉類。)

5. **recall** [rɪˈkɔl] vt. 回憶, 回想起

例: I recognize him but I don't recall his name.
(我認得他，但我記不起來他的名字。)

6. **grumble** [ˈgrʌmbl̩] vi. 發牢騷, 抱怨

例: Every time Sara is frustrated, she grumbles.
(每當莎拉遇到挫折，她就會發牢騷。)

∗ frustrated [ˈfrʌstretɪd] a. 感到挫折/沮喪的

7. **befriend** [bɪˈfrɛnd] vt. 待之如友

例: The new employee is trying to befriend everyone at the office.
(這名新來的員工試圖對待辦公室內每個人有如朋友一樣。)

8. **fall ill with + 疾病**　　罹患某疾病

= come down with + 疾病

動詞三態: fall、fell [fɛl]、fallen [ˈfɔlən]。

此處 fall 相當於 become (變成) 之意。

例: Jack didn't go to school because he fell ill with a bad cold.
(傑克沒有去上學，因為他得了重感冒。)

9. **cancer** [ˈkænsɚ] n. 癌 (不可數)

例: Second-hand smoke can also cause cancer.
(二手煙也會致癌。)

10. **turn out (to be) ...** 結果 (竟然) 是……; 原來是……

例: The frog in the story turned out to be a prince.
(故事中的青蛙原來竟是個王子。)

11. **retired** [rɪˈtaɪrd] a. 退休的, 退職的

retire [rɪˈtaɪr] vi. 退休

例: The retired lawyer tells very interesting stories.
(那名退休律師講的故事都非常有趣。)

Dad intends to retire when he's sixty.
(爸爸想在六十歲時退休。)

12. **pauper** [ˈpɔpɚ] n. 貧民, 窮人

例: If you squander your money, you'll end up a pauper.
(如果你揮霍金錢，到頭來會成為窮光蛋。)

* squander [ˈskwɑndɚ] vt. 浪費, 揮霍

Grammar Notes 文法重點

本課主要介紹兩個動詞在一起而無連接詞連接時的變化方法。

1. 一句中有兩個動詞同時存在時, 彼此之間一定要有連接詞相連。

例: He studied hard and passed the exam.
(他很用功因而通過了考試。)

He rushed to the train station but failed to catch the train.
(他趕到火車站去，但未能趕上火車。)

2. 但若兩個動詞無連接詞相連時, 就要注意下列的變化原則:
   a. 若兩個動詞所代表的動作並非同時發生, 而是有先後次序時, 第二個動詞就要變成不定詞片語 (to + 原形動詞) , 以表示『目的』。

例: He went to America visited his best friend.
to visit

→ He went to America to visit his best friend.
(他到美國去看他最要好的朋友。)

理由:

他先到美國去, 再去看他最要好的朋友, 故 went 與 visited 並非同時發生, 因此第二個動詞就要變成不定詞 to visit。

例: He stood up asked a question.
to ask

→ He stood up to ask a question.
(他站起來發問。)

理由:

他先站起來, 再問問題, 故 stood up 與 asked 並非同時發生, 因此第二個動詞就要變成不定詞 to ask。

b. 若兩個動詞所代表的動作同時發生時, 第二個動詞一定要變成現在分詞, 若該動詞是 be 動詞時, 則變成現在分詞 being 之後要省略。

例: He stood there read a book.
reading

→ He stood there reading a book.
(他站在那裡看書。)

理由:

他一面站在那裡, 一面看書, 故 stood 與 read 兩個動作同時發生, 因此第二個動詞應變成現在分詞 reading。

例: He died was a nobody.
(being)

→ He died a nobody.
(他死時默默無聞。)

理由:

他死亡的同時是默默無聞, 故 died 與 was 同時發生, 因此 was 變成現在分詞 being 之後再予省略。

例: All people are born <u>are</u> free and equal.
(being)

→ All people are born free and equal.
(人皆生而自由平等。)

比較:

All people <u>are born</u> <u>freely and equally</u>. (×)

理由:

freely 和 equally 是副詞, 如此一來就修飾了句中動詞 are born, 形成『被自由平等地生下來』之荒謬語意。

c. 若兩個動詞有逗點相隔而無連接時, 則不必考慮動詞所代表的動作先後發生的次序, 第二個動詞一律變成現在分詞。

例: He left home early in the morning, <u>arrived</u> here at midnight.
arriving

→ He left home early in the morning, <u>arriving</u> here at midnight.
(他一大清早離開家，午夜時抵達此地。)

3. 根據上述, 可知本文的句構:

a. **Every day a strange old man <u>came</u> to their supermarket <u>to buy</u> groceries.**

每天, 一位陌生的老先生都會到他們的超級市場來買雜貨。

上列句中, 老先生先到他們的超級市場, 再買雜貨, 故兩個動詞所代表的動作並非同時發生, 因此第二個動詞就要變成不定詞片語 to buy。

b. **"Once he <u>came in</u> <u>wearing</u> only one shoe," recalled one of the clerks.**

其中一名店員回想道：『有一次他進來時只穿著一隻鞋子。』

上列句中, 他一面進來, 一面只穿著一隻鞋子, 故兩個動詞所代表的動作同時發生, 因此第二個動詞要變成現在分詞 wearing。

c. **And although he grumbled a lot and they had to <u>stand</u> there <u>listening</u> to him, he was a nice old man.**

而雖然他常發牢騷並且他們得站在那裡聽他抱怨，他仍然是個心地不壞的老先生。

上列句中，他們得一面站在那裡，一面聽他抱怨，故兩個動詞所代表的動作同時發生，因此第二個動詞要變成現在分詞 listening。

d. **And, of course, when he died, he didn't <u>die</u> <u>a</u> <u>pauper</u>.**

當然，他臨終時並非是個窮光蛋。

上列句中，他死去的同時並非是個窮光蛋 (was a pauper)，故兩個動詞所代表的動作同時發生，因此第二個動詞 was 要變成現在分詞 being 後，再予省略。

Substitution 代換

1. **Every day a strange old man came to their supermarket to buy groceries.**

Ted worked overtime to finish the project.

Jane sat there watching TV.

每天，一名陌生的老先生都會到他們的超級市場來買雜貨。

泰德加班來完成那項企劃案。

珍坐在那裡看電視。

2. **The old man turned out to be a retired doctor.**

The business deal turned out to be very profitable.

The party turned out to be a disaster.

那個老人原來是一名退休的醫師。

這筆生意結果非常賺錢。

派對結果成了一場災難。

Lesson 92

As Poor As a Church Mouse

一貧如洗

Dialogue 實用會話

Anna and Eric are talking about the previous lesson.

(E=Eric;A=Anna)

E: Wow! Those store clerks really got lucky.

A: You can say that again. Some people are born lucky.

E: There must be thousands of old men just like that doctor, I bet.

A: That's probably true. And they must be wanting to draw up a will to give their money away, too. So the next time you meet a lonely old man, you'd better treat him right.

E: Come on! What kind of person do you think I am?

A: Don't get so mad! I'm just kidding! Besides, you might not be so lucky and come across my old uncle, Jake.

E: What do you mean?

A: He's as poor as a church mouse!

安娜和艾瑞克正在討論前一課。

艾瑞克：哇！那些店員真是走運。

安　娜：我完全同意。有些人天生就是運氣好。

艾瑞克：我敢打賭一定有成千的老人跟那個醫生一樣。

安　娜：可能吧。而且他們一定也想要立遺囑把他們的錢給別人。所以下次你遇到孤獨的老人時最好要好好對待他。

艾瑞克：得了吧！妳以為我是那種人嗎？

安　娜：別那麼生氣嘛！我只是在開玩笑！而且你可能運氣很背去遇到我那老叔叔傑克。

艾瑞克：妳這話什麼意思？

安　娜：他是個窮光蛋！

Key Points 重點提示

1. **(be) as poor as a church mouse**
   窮得如教堂裡的老鼠一樣, (喻) 一貧如洗
   church [tʃɝtʃ] n. 教堂
   mouse [maʊs] n. 老鼠
   例: The dishonest businessman ended up as poor as a church mouse.
   (那名不老實的生意人最後一貧如洗。)

2. **previous** [ˈprivɪəs] a. 先前的
   例: Tim has forgotten what he learned in the previous chapter.
   (提姆已經忘了前一章節所學的。)

3. **lucky** [ˈlʌkɪ] a. 幸運的
   unlucky [ʌnˈlʌkɪ] a. 不幸的, 運氣不好的
   例: Some say it's unlucky to walk under a ladder.
   (有人說走在梯子下面運氣會不好。)

4. **draw up...** 草擬/寫……

draw [drɔ] vi. 草擬, 寫 & vt. 抽 (籤)

動詞三態: draw、drew [dru]、drawn [drɔn]。

例: The dying old man drew up a will.
(那名垂死的老人擬了一份遺囑。)

We drew lots to see who would foot the bill for lunch.
(我們抽籤決定誰付午餐錢。)

＊ lot [lɑt] n. 籤條
foot the bill 付帳
= pay the bill

5. **will** [wɪl] n. 遺囑; 意志

例: According to the will, the wife inherited everything.
(根據遺囑，那名遺孀繼承了一切。)

Where there is a will, there is a way.
(有志者事竟成。——諺語)

6. **treat** [trit] vt. 對待; 請客, 款待

treat + 人 + to + 三餐名稱 款待某人吃……(三餐名稱)

例: William treats his pet dog as if it were his son.
(威廉對待他的愛犬有如兒子一樣。)

If you treat me to dinner, I'll tell you a secret.
(如果你請我吃晚飯，我就告訴你一個祕密。)

7. **get mad** 生氣

get mad at + 人 生某人的氣
= get angry with + 人

mad [mæd] a. 生氣的

例: Mom got mad at Dad for coming back so late.
(老媽生老爸的氣，因為他晚歸。)

8. **come across...** 偶然遇到……

= run into...

= bump into...

= encounter...

∗ encounter [ɪnˈkaʊntɚ] vt. 偶遇, 邂逅

例: I came across my high school teacher on my way to the supermarket.
(我在到超級市場途中和我的高中老師不期而遇。)

請選出下列各句中正確的一項

1. The little boy ______ when he couldn't find his toy.
   (A) screamed and shouting (B) screamed and shouted
   (C) screaming and shouted (D) screaming and shouting

2. Mary ______ with the flu and didn't go to work.
   (A) felt ill (B) fell ill (C) fallen ill (D) fall ill

3. Jeff ______ into his uncle on his way home.
   (A) came (B) drew (C) encountered (D) ran

4. The man sat in the corner ______ a newspaper.
   (A) read (B) to read (C) reading (D) by reading

5. The novel turned ______ to be a bestseller.
   (A) out (B) up (C) on (D) off

解答：

1. (B) 2. (B) 3. (D) 4. (C) 5. (A)

Lesson 93

The Poor Man's Cure-all

窮人的萬靈丹

Reading
閱　讀

Having one of the world's largest garlic crops, Gilroy, California is known as the "garlic capital of the world." On a hot summer day, a pungent odor rises from this farming town which can be smelled miles away. All you have to do is roll down the window of your car and you know you're in Gilroy.

Believing that garlic helps the body fight many forms of diseases, people add garlic to their cooking in many parts of the world. Moreover, it's popularly used as the poor man's cure-all. During the First World War it was used as an antiseptic. And in

the Second World War it was known as "Russian penicillin." Nowadays, thinking that it kills bacteria, some people eat raw garlic as if it were candy.

由於擁有世界上最大的大蒜產量之一，加州的吉羅伊是著名的『世界大蒜之都』。在炎熱的夏天，一股刺鼻的味道從這個農業城鎮散發出來，數哩之外就聞得到。你所必須做的就是搖下車窗，那麼你就知道你是在吉羅伊了。

因為相信大蒜會幫人體抵抗許多疾病，世界上許多地方的人在烹調的時候會添加大蒜。此外，大蒜還被廣泛地用作窮人的萬靈丹。在第一次世界大戰期間，它被用來當作消炎藥。而在二次大戰期間它以『俄國人的盤尼西林』而聞名。如今，有些人認為它會殺菌而生吃大蒜就像它是糖果一樣。

Vocabulary & Idioms
單字 & 片語註解

1. **cure-all** [ˈkjʊrˌɔl] n. 萬靈丹

例: The cure-all cost a lot but did little.
(這種萬靈丹很貴但療效不彰。)

2. **garlic** [ˈgɑrlɪk] n. 大蒜

3. **crop** [krɑp] n. 農作物

4. **be known as + 身分**　以……身分聞名/為人所知

be known to + 人　為某人所熟知

be known for + 事情　以某事而聞名/為人所知

例: The writer is known as a satirist.
(那位作家是出名的諷刺文學作者。)
＊ satirist [ˈsætərɪst] n. 諷刺文學作者

Jackie Chan is known to audiences for his action films.
(成龍以演動作片為觀眾所熟知。)

5. **capital** [ˈkæpətl̩] n. 首都

6. **pungent** [ˈpʌndʒənt] a. 味道強烈的, 刺鼻的

例: A pungent smell is coming from the garbage dump.
(一股刺鼻的味道從那堆垃圾中散發出來。)

7. **odor** [ˈodɚ] n. (不好的) 氣味

fragrance [ˈfregrəns] n. 香味

smell [smɛl] n. (不分香臭的) 味道

例: Some people have very strong body odor.
(有些人身上有非常強烈的體味。)

The fragrance of the roses filled the room.
(玫瑰的香味充斥著這個房間。)

The chemical has a strange smell.
(這種化學藥品有很奇怪的氣味。)

* chemical [ˈkɛmɪkl̩] n. 化學藥品

8. **form** [fɔrm] n. 形式

例: There are many different forms of government in the world.
(世界上有許多種不同形式的政府。)

9. **add A to B** 添加 A 至 B 上

add [æd] vt. 添加

例: Please add some more sugar to my coffee.
(請再多加些糖到我的咖啡中。)

10. **cooking** [ˈkʊkɪŋ] n. 烹調

cook [kʊk] vt. & vi. 烹調

例: My mom's cooking is the best in the world.
(我媽媽的烹調是全世界最棒的。)

I can only cook eggs and instant noodles.
(我只會煮蛋和速食麵。)

Judy's husband likes to cook on weekends.
(茱蒂的丈夫喜歡在週末時作菜。)

11. **popularly** [ˈpɑpjələ˞lɪ] adv. 大眾化地, 一般地

popular [ˈpɑpjələ˞] a. 受歡迎的

be popular with/among... 受……歡迎

例: The mayor is popularly accepted by the citizens.
(市長廣被市民接受。)

Michael Jackson's music is very popular with young people.
(麥可・傑克森的音樂深受年輕人歡迎。)

12. **the First World War** 第一次世界大戰

= World War I (可縮寫成 WWI)

the Second World War 第二次世界大戰

= World War II (可縮寫成 WWII)

例: We hope people learned a big lesson from the Second World War.
(我們希望人們從第二次世界大戰中得到了一次重大的教訓。)

13. **be used as...** 被用作……

主動用法為:

use...as... 用……作為……

例: The poor man uses this block of wood as a table.
(那個貧窮的男子用這塊木頭作為桌子。)

14. **antiseptic** [ˌæntəˈsɛptɪk] n. (塗在傷口的) 消炎藥

例: Antiseptics help to kill germs.
(消炎藥有助殺菌。)

＊ germ [dʒɝm] n. 細菌

15. **Russian** [ˈrʌʃən] a. 俄羅斯 (人) 的 & n. 俄羅斯人

Russia [ˈrʌʃə] n. 俄羅斯

16. **penicillin** [ˌpɛnɪˈsɪlɪn] n. 盤尼西林, 青黴素

例: Penicillin is used to prevent or treat infections.
(盤尼西林被用來防止或治療感染。)
＊ infection [ɪnˈfɛkʃən] n. 感染

17. **bacteria** [bækˈtɪrɪə] n. 細菌 (複數形)

bacterium [bækˈtɪrɪəm] n. 細菌 (單數形)

例: Bacteria are often the cause of diseases.
(細菌常是疾病的肇因。)

18. **candy** [ˈkændɪ] n. 糖果

注意:

candy 表『糖果』時為不可數名詞, 所以『一顆糖果』、『一些糖果』, 應譯為"a piece of candy"、"some candy"; 但 candy 亦可表示『糖果的種類』, 此時則視為可數名詞。

例: Paul got sick after eating too much candy.
(保羅吃了太多糖果後身體不舒服。)

Candies from Holland are my favorite.
(荷蘭的糖果是我的最愛。)

Grammar Notes 文法重點

本課主要介紹兩句在一起無連接詞相連時的變化法則, 以及"all + 人 + have/has to do is + 原形動詞" (某人所必須做的就是⋯⋯) 的用法。

1. 兩句在一起若無連接詞相連時, 往往第一個句子要化簡, 變成分詞片語。其法則如下:
   a. 被化簡的句子中之主詞與主要子句的主詞相同時, 該主詞要被刪除, 若主詞不同時, 則要保留,

b. 之後的動詞要變成現在分詞;

c. 若該動詞為 be 動詞時，變成現在分詞 being 之後可予省略，但亦可不予省略，以強調『因為……』的意思。

例: He has nothing to do, he feels bored.
Having

→ Having nothing to do, he feels bored.
(他無事可做，覺得無聊。)

She walked along the street, she ran into her college classmate.
Walking

→ Walking along the street, she ran into her college classmate.
(她沿著街道走時，和她的大學同學不期而遇。)

He was sick of studying, he cut class.
(Being)

→ Being sick of studying, he cut class.

= Sick of studying, he cut class.
(他厭倦了唸書，便蹺課了。)

The school bell had rung, the students dashed out of the
having
classroom.

→ The school bell having rung, the students dashed out of the classroom.
(校鐘響了，學生們便衝出了教室。)

故本文:

Gilroy, California has one of the world's largest garlic crops,
Having

Gilroy, California is known as the "garlic capital of the world."

→ Having one of the world's largest garlic crops, Gilroy, California is known as the "garlic capital of the world."
(由於擁有世界上最大的大蒜產量之一，加州的吉羅伊是著名的『世界大蒜之都』。)

People believe that garlic helps the body fight many forms of
Believing
diseases, people add garlic to their cooking in many parts of the world.

→ Believing that garlic helps the body fight many forms of diseases, people add garlic to their cooking in many parts of the world.
(因為相信大蒜會幫人體抵抗許多疾病，世界上許多地方的人在烹調的時候會添加大蒜。)

Nowadays, some people think that it kills bacteria, some people
thinking
eat raw garlic as if it were candy.

→ Nowadays, thinking that it kills bacteria, some people eat raw garlic as if it were candy.
(如今，有些人認為它會殺菌而生吃大蒜就像它是糖果一樣。)

2. **All you have to do is roll down the window of your car and you know you're in Gilroy.**
你所必須做的就是搖下車窗, 那麼你就知道你是在吉羅伊了。

注意:

句中有"all/what + 人 + have/has to do" (某人所必須做的) 及"all/what + 人 + should/can do" (某人所應/能做的) 出現時, 其後的 be 動詞應接不定詞片語 (to + 原形動詞) 當主詞補語, 此時不定詞片語中的 to 通常均予以省略。

例: To borrow books, all you should do is (to) apply for a library card.
(要借書的話，你所應該做的就是申請一張借書證。)

If war breaks out, all we can do is (to) pray.
(如果戰爭爆發，我們就只能祈禱了。)

Substitution 代 換

1. **Having one of the world's largest garlic crops, Gilroy, California is known as the "garlic capital of the world."**

   Being only sixteen, the youngster couldn't get married without his parents' consent.

   Having spent all their money, the tourists decided to return home.

   由於擁有世界上最大的大蒜產量之一,加州的吉羅伊是著名的『世界大蒜之都』。

   因為只有十六歲,這個年輕人沒有他父母的同意就沒辦法結婚。

   因為花光了所有的錢,那些觀光客決定返家。

2. **All you have to do is roll down the window of your car and you know you're in Gilroy.**

   What more people should do is obey the traffic laws.

   All you can do is hope for the best.

   你所必須做的就是搖下車窗,那麼你就知道你是在吉羅伊了。

   更多人應該做的事便是遵守交通規則。

   你所能做的就是抱持樂觀的態度。

Lesson 94

What's the Point of Chewing Gum?

嚼口香糖有啥用？

Being an American, Donna wants to learn more about the Chinese. She's talking to her Chinese friend, Jeff.

(D=Donna; J=Jeff)

D: Hi, Jeff! What's up?

J: Nothing much. What about you?

D: Same as usual. Here, have a stick of gum.

J: No, thanks. I'll stick to my own brand.

D: And what brand's that?

J: Actually it's not gum. I eat raw garlic instead. Want a piece?

D: No way! So that's where the stinky smell is coming from.

J: Hey! Watch your tongue, OK? Garlic kills germs. It's good for you.

D: Says who?

J: Well, according to...

D: Never mind. Please stop talking. Your breath stinks. I'm out of here.

J: Boy! These Americans don't know what's good for them. Besides, what's the point of chewing gum anyway?

身為美國人，唐娜很想多了解中國人。她正在和她的中國朋友傑夫說話。

唐娜：嗨，傑夫！近來如何？
傑夫：沒什麼，妳呢？
唐娜：老樣子。喏，來一片口香糖吧。
傑夫：不，謝了。我還是用我的牌子好了。
唐娜：什麼牌子啊？
傑夫：其實不是口香糖。我是吃生的大蒜。要來一塊嗎？
唐娜：才不要呢！原來那股臭味就是從你那裡傳來的。
傑夫：嘿！說話當心點，好嗎？大蒜能殺菌，對妳身體有益。
唐娜：誰說的？
傑夫：嗯，根據……
唐娜：算了，請別再說了。你有口臭，我走了。
傑夫：天啊！這些美國人真不識貨。而且，嚼口香糖到底有什麼意思？

1. **point** [pɔɪnt] n. 重點

What's the point of + 動名詞?　　……有啥用？
There is no point in + 動名詞　　……是沒有用的。
= There is no sense in + 動名詞
= There is no use (in) + 動名詞

例: What's the point of spending such a lot of money on clothes?
(花這麼多錢在衣服上有啥用呢？)

There is no point in crying over spilt milk.
(為弄翻的牛奶而哭是沒有用的。喻：覆水難收。)

2. **chew** [tʃu] vt. & vi. 咀嚼

chewing gum ['tʃuɪŋ ˌgʌm] n. 口香糖 (不可數)

gum [gʌm] n. 樹脂; 口香糖 (= chewing gum)

注意:

chewing gum 為不可數名詞, 因此表『一片口香糖』應說"a stick of chewing gum"或"a piece of chewing gum", 而『一條/包口香糖』則說"a pack of chewing gum"。

例: Many American baseball players like to chew tobacco.
(許多美國棒球選手喜歡嚼煙草。)

Never bite off more than you can chew.
(貪多嚼不爛。喻：不要從事太多工作而超過自己的負荷力。)

Jeff never goes out without a pack of chewing gum in his pocket.
(傑夫每次外出時口袋內一定會有一條口香糖。)

3. **What's up?** 近來如何?/發生什麼事? (= What's the matter?)

例: Mike: Hi, Anna. What's up?
Anna: Nothing much. What about you?
(麥克：嗨，安娜。近來如何？)
(安娜：沒什麼特別的。你呢？)

James: What's up, Carlos?
Carlos: I just lost my false teeth.
(詹姆士：卡洛士，發生了什麼事？)
(卡洛士：我的假牙不見了。)

4. **Same as usual.** 老樣子。

as usual 和往常一樣

usual ['juʒuəl] a. 平常的, 通常的

例: Waiter: What are you having today?
Customer: Same as usual.
(侍者：您今天吃些什麼？)
(顧客：老樣子。)

As usual, Peter was late for work again.
(和往常一樣，彼得上班又遲到了。)

5. **stick** [stɪk] vi. & vt. 插; 黏貼

動詞三態: stick、stuck [stʌk]、stuck。

stick to + 名詞　　堅持/固守……

例: Whatever you do, you should stick to your principles.
(你不論做什麼事，都要把持原則。)

6. **brand** [brænd] n. 商標, 牌子

例: What brand of cigarettes do you smoke?
(你抽什麼牌子的香煙？)

7. **raw** [rɔ] a. 生的; 未處理過的

例: This steak is too raw for me.
(這塊牛排對我來說太生了。)

8. **No way!**　　才不要呢！

例: Jim: How about a kiss, Sue?
Sue: No way!
(吉姆：蘇，親一下，好嗎？)
(蘇：才不要呢！)

9. **stinky** [ˈstɪŋkɪ] a. 惡臭的

stink [stɪŋk] vi. 發臭味

例: Stinky tofu is my son's favorite snack.
(臭豆腐是我兒子最愛的小吃。)

The garbage in the kitchen stinks.
(廚房裡的垃圾發出臭味。)

10. **Watch your tongue, OK?**

= Watch your language, OK?
說話當心點, 好嗎？

tongue [tʌŋ] n. 語言 (原指『舌頭』)

例: His mother tongue is Chinese but he speaks English just like an American.
(他的母語是中文，但他英文講得就像美國人一樣。)

11. **germ** [dʒɝm] n. 細菌

例: This bandage will prevent germs from getting into the wound.
(這個繃帶將防止細菌侵入傷口。)
∗ bandage [ˈbændɪdʒ] n. 繃帶
wound [wund] n. 傷口

12. **according to...** 根據／依照……

例: According to the radio, the weather's going to be fine today.
(根據氣象報告，今天將是個好天氣。)

13. **Never mind.** 算了吧; 沒關係。

例: A: Should I tell you what he said?
B: Never mind.
(甲：我該不該告訴你他說了些什麼？)
(乙：算了，不用了。)

Tim: I'm sorry I'm late for the meeting.
Ann: Never mind.
(提姆：很抱歉會議我遲到了。)
(安：沒關係。)

14. **breath** [brɛθ] n. 氣息; 呼吸

breathtaking [ˈbrɛθˌtekɪŋ] a. 令人讚嘆的

catch one's breath 喘過氣來

hold one's breath 屏息 (靜氣)

例: Bacteria in the mouth cause bad breath.
(口中的細菌會引起口臭。)

I could hardly catch my breath after running up the flight of stairs.
(跑上了這層樓梯後，我差點喘不過氣來。)

How long can you hold your breath under water?
(你可以在水中彆氣多久？)

The tourists took pictures of the breathtaking scenery.
(遊客們拍下了這些令人讚嘆的美景。)

請選出下列各句中正確的一項

1. What Rob has to do ______ more attention to his pronunciation.
(A) are paying (B) are pay (C) is pay (D) is paying

2. Ian is known ______ his generous contributions to charity.
(A) as (B) to (C) for (D) of

3. The naughty boy ______ a piece of chewing gum on the teacher's chair.
(A) stick (B) stuck (C) strike (D) struck

4. What's that strange ______ coming from the kitchen?
(A) odor (B) order (C) smelling (D) smelled

5. Wife: I forgot the car key.
Husband: ______ I have an extra one with me.
(A) What's up? (B) No way.
(C) Watch your tongue. (D) Never mind.

解答：

1. (C) 2. (C) 3. (B) 4. (A) 5. (D)

Lesson 95

The Bronze Age

青銅器時代

Reading
閱 讀

While on an expedition in western China twenty years ago, some explorers discovered the mummies of a tall, red-haired people. Though estimated to be nearly 4,000 years old, the corpses were quite well preserved. Scientists are excited because these mummies are a link between the East and the West. What were redheads doing in China and who were they?

Though the answers to these questions may never be answered with certainty, these mummies provide new information about the Bronze Age, when men used tools and weapons made of bronze. This was the period between the Stone Age and the Iron Age. As the explorers continue their work, new mysteries are waiting to be discovered.

二十年前在中國西部探險時，一些探險家發現了身材高大的紅髮民族的木乃伊。雖然這些屍體據估計將近有四千年的歷史之久，但它們仍保存得相當好。科學家很興奮，因為這些木乃伊是東西方之間的一條連結線。這些紅髮人在中國做什麼而且他們是什麼人？

雖然我們可能永遠無法確實回答這些問題，然而這些木乃伊提供了有關青銅器時代的新資料，在當時人類使用青銅製成的工具和武器。此一時期介於石器時代與鐵器時代之間。在探險家繼續進行工作的同時，新的謎正等著被發現。

Vocabulary & Idioms 單字 & 片語註解

1. **the Bronze Age** 青銅器時代
   the Stone Age 石器時代
   the Iron Age 鐵器時代
   bronze [brɑnz] n. 青銅
   iron [ˈaɪɚn] n. 鐵
2. **expedition** [ˌɛkspɪˈdɪʃən] n. 遠征, 探險 (隊)
   例: The leader of the expedition disappeared in the jungle.
   (探險隊的領隊在叢林裡失蹤了。)
3. **explorer** [ɪkˈsplɔrɚ] n. 探險家
   explore [ɪkˈsplɔr] vt. 探險; 探究
   例: We explored several possible ways to solve the problem.
   (我們探究出幾種可以解決此問題的方法。)

4. **discover** [dɪ'skʌvɚ] vt. 發現

discovery [dɪ'skʌvərɪ] n. 發現 (物)

make a/the discovery of... 完成一項……的發現

例: The campers discovered a mysterious cave in the mountains.
(露營者在山中發現了一個神秘的洞穴。)

Dr. Fleming made the discovery of penicillin in 1928.
(佛萊明博士於一九二八年發現盤尼西林。)

＊ penicillin [ˌpɛnɪ'sɪlɪn] n. 盤尼西林

5. **mummy** ['mʌmɪ] n. 木乃伊

6. **corpse** [kɔrps] n. 屍體

例: The corpse at the mortuary began to stink.
(停屍間的屍體開始發臭。)

＊ mortuary ['mɔrtʃʊˌɛrɪ] n. 停屍間, 太平間

7. **preserve** [prɪ'zɝv] vt. 保存

例: Wax polish helps to preserve wood and leather.
(亮光蠟有助於保存木材和皮革。)

＊ polish ['pɑlɪʃ] n. 生光澤之物; 擦亮劑

8. **scientist** ['saɪəntɪst] n. 科學家

9. **excited** [ɪk'saɪtɪd] a. 感到興奮的

be excited about... 對……感到興奮

例: Jane is really excited about her forthcoming trip to Greece.
(珍對於即將到來的希臘之旅真的很興奮。)

10. **link** [lɪŋk] n. 環節, 使結合的人或物 & vt. 連接, 連繫

link A to B 將 A 與 B 連結在一起, 使 A 與 B 有關聯

例: Doctors say that there is a link between smoking and lung cancer.
(醫生說抽煙與肺癌有關聯。)

I would never have thought of linking Anna to Andy.
(我從未想過安娜和安迪之間有任何關係。)

11. **redhead** [ˈrɛd,hɛd] n. 紅髮的人

例: The redhead dyed her hair blond.
(那個紅頭髮的人把她的頭髮染成金髮。)

12. **answer** [ˈænsɚ] n. 答案 (與介詞 to 並用)

the answer to the question　　問題的答案

注意:

介詞 to 在此處表『針對』之意。類似用法有:

the key to success　　成功的要訣

the solution to the problem　　問題的解決方法

例: Everyone knew the answer to the question.
(每個人都知道這個問題的答案。)

Perseverance is the key to success.
(毅力是成功的要訣。)

＊ perseverance [,pɝsəˈvɪrəns] n. 堅忍, 毅力

13. **certainty** [ˈsɝtəntɪ] n. 確實, 確信 (不可數)

with certainty　　明確地

例: I can't say with any certainty when I will be back.
(我不很確定我何時會回來。)

14. **provide** [prəˈvaɪd] vt. 提供

provide + 人 + with + 東西　　提供某人某物

= supply + 人 + with + 東西

= provide + 東西 + for + 人

= supply + 東西 + for + 人

例: Jeff provided the poor stranger with food and clothing.
(傑夫提供食物和衣服給那個可憐的陌生人。)

15. **information** [ˌɪnfɚˈmeʃən] n. 資料, 消息

注意:

information、evidence (證據)、advice (忠告)、luggage/baggage (行李)、garbage/rubbish (垃圾) 等均為不可數名詞, 用 a lot of 或 a piece of 修飾。

例: We have collected <u>many</u> <u>informations</u> on the topic. (×)
→ We have collected <u>a lot of</u> <u>information</u> on the topic. (○)
(我們已經收集了許多有關這個題材的資料。)

16. **tool** [tul] n. 工具

例: A poor workman always blames his tools.
(工作做不好的人總是歸咎於工具不好。)

17. **weapon** [ˈwɛpən] n. 武器

例: Those gangsters carry weapons with them.
(那些歹徒隨身攜帶武器。)
* gangster [ˈgæŋstɚ] n. 歹徒

18. **a period of...** 一段 (時間)

period [ˈpɪrɪəd] n. 期間

例: The lost girl was finally found after a period of two days.
(失蹤的女孩終於在兩天後被找到了。)

19. **mystery** [ˈmɪstrɪ] n. 謎, 神祕

mysterious [mɪsˈtɪrɪəs] a. 神秘的

例: The boy's disappearance still remains a mystery.
(那個男孩的失蹤至今仍是個謎。)
The mysterious noise is coming from the basement.
(神秘的吵雜聲正從地下室裡傳來。)

Grammar Notes 文法重點

本課主要複習副詞子句化簡為副詞片語的用法, 並介紹一些表探險、旅遊、旅程的名詞與介詞on並用的用法, 和表身體組織的名詞可變成過去分詞作形容詞的用法, 以及名詞 people 的用法。

1. **While on an expedition in western China twenty years ago, some explorers discovered the mummies of a tall, red-haired people.**

= While they were on an expedition in western China twenty years ago, some explorers discovered the mummies of a tall, red-haired people.
二十年前在中國西部探險時, 一些探險家發現了身材高大的紅髮民族的木乃伊。

Though estimated to be nearly 4,000 years old, the corpses were quite well preserved.

= Though the corpses were estimated to be nearly 4,000 years old, the corpses were quite well preserved.
雖然這些屍體據估計將近有四千年歷史之久, 但它們仍保存得相當好。

上列句中, 劃線部分分別為副詞連接詞 while 及 though 引導的副詞片語, 用來修飾其後整個主要子句。

我們在 Lesson 77 已提過, 副詞連接詞 while (在……的時候) 和 when (當) 引導的副詞子句中之主詞與主要子句中之主詞相同時, 則此副詞子句可化簡為副詞片語; 而 though/although (雖然)、if (如果)、unless (除非) 及 once (一……就……) 等四個副詞連接詞引導的副詞子句中之主詞與主要子句之主詞相同, 且主詞後為『be 動詞 + 形容詞/過去分詞』時, 則此副詞子句亦可化簡為副詞片語。其化簡法則如下:

a. 去掉副詞子句之主詞;
b. 其後動詞化為現在分詞;

c. 若動詞為 be 動詞時, 則在變成現在分詞 being 後通常予以省略; 但在 though/although、if、nless、once 引導的句構中, 則 being 一律予以省略。

例: While I watch TV, I like to eat snacks.
watching
→ While watching TV, I like to eat snacks.
(我看電視時喜歡吃零食。)

When Dad works, Dad is always very serious.
working
→ When working, Dad is always very serious.
(工作時，老爸總是很認真。)

Though Aaron is young, Aaron is very mature.
(being)
→ Though young, Aaron is very mature.
(艾倫年紀雖輕卻很成熟。)

Once John is bored, John becomes very restless.
(being)
→ Once bored, John becomes very restless.
(約翰一無聊就會變得非常浮躁不安。)

2. **on an expedition** 探險

注意:

凡表『探險』、『旅遊』、『旅程』等名詞, 以及表持續性或時間性的任務或動作時, 通常均與介詞 on 並用。如:

on an expedition	探險
on an excursion	遠足
on a journey	旅行
on a trip	旅行
on an outing	出遊
on a picnic	野餐

on a mission 執行任務

on duty 值/上班

on errands/an errand [ˈɛrənd] 跑/辦差事

例: The Chens went on a trip to Guam.
(陳家人到關島旅行了。)

The secret agent almost got killed on a mission in that country.
(那名情報員在該國出任務時差點遇害身亡。)

The policeman never drinks on duty.
(那位警察值勤時從不喝酒。)

3. **red-haired** [ˌrɛdˈhɛrd] a. 紅髮的

注意:

表示身體組織的名詞可變成過去分詞作形容詞用, 如:

red-haired (紅髮的)、big-eyed (大眼睛的)、one-legged (獨腿的)、two-headed (雙頭的)、black-skinned (黑皮膚的)、barefooted (赤腳的)、brokenhearted (心碎的) 等。

例: When Cantonese people say you are a two-headed snake, they mean you are insincere.
(當廣東人說你是條雙頭蛇時，他們的意思就是你很不真誠。)

The performer walked barefooted on burning charcoal.
(那位表演者赤腳走在燃燒的木炭上。)

* charcoal [ˈtʃɑrˌkol] n. 木炭

4. **people** [ˈpipl̩] n. 種族, 民族; 人民, 人們

注意:

people 表『種族、民族』時, 為可數名詞, 其前可置 a 或用複數加-s, 表『一個或數個民族』; 但 people 表『人民、人們』時, 則視為複數, 其前不可置 a 或用複數加-s。

例: The Filipinos are a warm-hearted people.
(菲律賓人是個很熱情的民族。)

* Filipino [ˌfɪləˈpino] n. 菲律賓人

The people in my neighborhood are very friendly.
(我社區裡的人都很友善。)

Substitution 代換

While on an expedition in western China twenty years ago, some explorers discovered the mummies of a tall, red-haired people.

The boys enjoy going on long train journeys.

The secret agent is on a special mission in Europe.

二十年前在中國西部探險時，一些探險家發現了身材高大的紅髮民族的木乃伊。

那群男孩喜歡搭火車作長途旅行。

該情報員在歐洲執行特殊任務。

Lesson 96

Speaking from the Grave

地府之言

Dialogue 實用會話

Two students, Beth and Carl, are talking about the red-haired mummies.

(B=Beth; C=Carl)

B: Can you imagine what it was like 4,000 years ago?

C: That's hard to imagine. But if the mummies could speak, they could certainly tell us a great deal.

B: Well, that, of course, is impossible. But scientists can tell a lot from the things the explorers found.

C: I know. For example, they think the 4000-year-old mummies were Celts.

B: Who were the Celts?

C: They were an ancient European people who settled in Britain even before the Romans existed.

B: Wow! That's amazing!

C: So you see, although mummies don't really speak, they are "speaking" from their graves.

B: Stop it! You're giving me the creeps!

兩個學生貝絲和卡爾正在討論有關紅髮木乃伊的事。
貝絲：你能想像四千年前是什麼樣子嗎？
卡爾：很難想像。但是如果那些木乃伊能夠說話的話，他們一定能夠告訴我們很多事。
貝絲：不過，那當然是不可能的。但是科學家可以從探險家找到的東西告訴我們許多。
卡爾：我知道。比如說，他們認為有四千年歷史的木乃伊是塞爾特人。
貝絲：塞爾特人是誰啊？
卡爾：他們是古時候早在羅馬人出現前就定居於大不列顛島的歐洲民族。
貝絲：哇！真是令人驚異！
卡爾：所以妳看，雖然木乃伊不會真的說話，他們卻會從他們的墳墓『說話』。
貝絲：別說了！你害我毛骨悚然！

Key Points 重點提示

1. **grave** [grev] n. 墳墓
   graveyard [ˈgrev,jɑrd] n. 墓地, 墳場
   tomb [tum] n. (隆起的) 墓 (穴)
   from the cradle to the grave 從生到死, 一生中
   * cradle [ˈkredḷ] n. 搖籃

   例: From the cradle to the grave, Mr. Chen never uttered a dirty word.
   (陳先生一生中從未說過一句髒話。)
   * utter [ˈʌtɚ] vt. 說出

   Graveyards give me the creeps.
   (墓場使我毛骨悚然。)

   That rich man's tomb is bigger than my room.
   (那個有錢人的墓穴比我的房間大。)

2. **the Celts** [kɛlts/sɛlts] n. 塞爾特人 (為印歐語族的一派, 居住於愛爾蘭、威爾斯及蘇格蘭高地等處)

3. **ancient** [ˈenʃənt] a. 古代的

例: This ancient stamp is worth a fortune.
(這枚古老的郵票值不少錢。)

4. **exist** [ɪgˈzɪst] vi. 存在; 生存

existence [ɪgˈzɪstəns] n. 存在; 生存

come into existence　　產生, 出現

例: If we don't take care of some animals, they will soon cease to exist.
(如果我們不好好照料某些動物，牠們很快便會絕種了。)

The computer came into existence not very long ago.
(電腦在不久以前才問世。)

5. **amazing** [əˈmezɪŋ] a. 令人驚異的 (修飾事物)

amazed [əˈmezd] a. 感到驚異的 (修飾人)

amaze [əˈmez] vt. 使驚異

be amazed at...　　對……感到驚異

注意:

表『訝異』的形容詞大多與介詞 at 並用。

be surprised at...　　對……感到驚訝

be astonished at...　　對……感到驚嚇

be astounded at...　　對……感到震驚

例: It's amazing how Tom became so rich in such a short time.
(湯姆在如此短的時間內致富真令人驚異。)

Everyone was amazed at the acrobat's agility.
(每個人對該特技表演者的敏捷都很驚異。)

* acrobat [ˈækrə͵bæt] n. 表演特技者
agility [əˈdʒɪlətɪ] n. 敏捷

Lily never ceases to amaze me with her intelligence.
(莉莉的聰明才智總會令我驚異不已。)

6. **creep** [krip] n. 有如蟲爬肌膚的感覺 & vi. 爬行

動詞三態: creep、crept [krɛpt]、crept。

give + 人 + the creeps　　使某人毛骨悚然/不寒而慄

例: Snakes give me the creeps.
(蛇令我毛骨悚然。)

A cockroach crept under the child's blanket.
(一隻蟑螂爬到那個小孩的毛毯底下。)

＊ cockroach [ˈkɑk͵rotʃ] n. 蟑螂

請選出下列各句中正確的一項

1. Everyone in my family went ______ a picnic except me.
   (A) on　(B) to　(C) for　(D) by

2. The secretary was ______ at the boss's rudeness.
   (A) amazing　(B) astonished　(C) astound　(D) surprise

3. You'll have to find the solution ______ the problem by yourself.
   (A) among　(B) between　(C) with　(D) to

4. The school ______ the students with milk.
   (A) tells　(B) provides　(C) exists　(D) finds

5. The way Al looks at girls gives me the ______.
   (A) books　(B) cradles　(C) creeps　(D) graves

解答：

1. (A)　2. (B)　3. (D)　4. (B)　5. (C)

Lesson 97

Stop Swearing!

別罵髒話了！

Reading 閱讀

Everywhere in the world you can hear people swearing or using foul language. Even when learning a second language, many people know how to swear before they can speak the language properly. Indeed, it is a disease.

Recently, in New Jersey, the government decided to do something about the problem. It banned swearing. You could face a US$500 fine, including a three-month jail term for swearing. Considering the trivial nature of the crime, the punishment seemed quite harsh to some. Some say the law infringes on their rights. But others say it is a good law because people in New Jersey have really stopped swearing so much.

在世界各地你都可以聽到人們說髒話或使用粗俗的語言。甚至在學習第二語言時，許多人在能夠正確使用該語言之前就學會說髒話。這真是一種病態。

最近，在紐澤西州，政府決定針對這個問題有所行動。該政府禁止人們說髒話。你說髒話就可能被罰五百元美金，還包括三個月的徒刑。就這項罪行微不足道的性質而論，這樣的刑罰對有些人來說似乎相當嚴厲。有人說這項法律侵害到他們的權利。但是也有人卻說這是條好法律，因為紐澤西人真的已經不再那麼會說髒話了。

Vocabulary & Idioms 單字 & 片語註解

1. **swear** [swɛr] vi. 咒罵, 說髒話 & vt. 發誓

動詞三態: swear、swore [swɔr]、sworn [swɔrn]。

swear + that 子句　　發誓……

swear to + 原形動詞　　發誓……

例: Ted was so angry, he wanted to swear.
(泰德氣得想咒罵。)

I swear that I am telling the truth.
(我發誓我說的是真的。)

The witness swears to tell the truth, the whole truth and nothing but the truth.
(該證人發誓說真話，而且句句實話，絕無半句虛言。)

2. **foul** [faʊl] a. 粗俗的; 惡臭的

例: The meat smells foul.
(這塊肉聞起來好臭。)

3. **language** [ˈlæŋgwɪdʒ] n. 言辭 (不可數); 語言 (可數)

例: You'd better watch your language in front of the boss.
(在老闆面前最好注意你的措辭。)

How many languages do you speak?
(你會講幾種語言？)

4. **properly** [ˈprɑpɚlɪ] adv. 正確地; 適當地

5. **New Jersey** [nju ˈdʒɝzɪ] n. 紐澤西州 (美國東部的一州, 可縮寫為 N.J.或 NJ)

6. **do something about...** 對……採取行動

do nothing about... 不對……採取行動

例: Can you do something about your crying baby?
(你可不可以哄哄你那正在哭泣的嬰兒？)

Lazy Terry did nothing about getting a job.
(懶鬼賴瑞對找工作的事一點兒也沒進行。)

7. **ban** [bæn] vt. (下令) 禁止 & n. 禁令

ban (+ 人 + from) + 動名詞 禁止 (某人) ……

lift the ban on... 取消……禁令

impose a ban on... 對……施以禁令

* impose [ɪmˈpoz] vt. 施加

例: We should ban smoking in public places.
(在公眾場所我們應該禁煙。)

The law bans motorists from driving over 90 kilometers per hour.
(法令禁止汽車行駛時速超過九十公里。)

* motorist [ˈmotərɪst] n. 駕汽車者

Most countries impose a ban on the importation of drugs.
(大多數國家都實施禁止毒品輸入的法令。)

8. **fine** [faɪn] n. 罰鍰 & vt. 課以罰鍰, 處以罰金

例: You may have to pay a fine of US$50 for not flushing the public toilet in Singapore.
(在新加坡，你可能因上公廁未沖水而被罰五十元美金。)
* flush [flʌʃ] vt. 沖水

The police fined Greg for overstaying his tourist visa.
(警方因葛雷格逾期居留超過觀光簽證的時間而對他處以罰金。)

9. **jail** [dʒel] n. 監獄 & vt. 使下獄

go to jail　　入獄

put + 人 + in jail　　監禁某人, 使某人入獄

be jailed for...　　因……被監禁/入獄

例: Tom went to jail for stealing two ducks.
(湯姆因為偷了兩隻鴨子而入獄。)

The South African government put Nelson Mandela in jail in 1962.
(南非政府於一九六二年將尼爾森・曼德拉囚禁。)

You can be jailed for gambling in a public place.
(你可能因為在公共場所中賭博而入獄。)

10. **term** [tɝm] n. 期間, 期限

例: This plan will work in the short term.
(這個計畫短時間內就會奏效。)

11. **punishment** [ˈpʌnɪʃmənt] n. 處罰, 懲罰

例: The punishment was considered too light by the victim.
(受害者認為罪犯的懲罰太輕了。)

12. **harsh** [hɑrʃ] a. 嚴厲的

例: You should never use harsh words with your own parents.
(你絕對不應該對自己的父母說重話。)

13. **infringe** [ɪnˈfrɪndʒ] vi. 侵犯

infringe on...　　侵犯……

例: Some Americans claim that gun laws infringe on their rights.
(有一些美國人宣稱槍械管制條例侵犯了他們的權利。)

Grammar Notes 文法重點

本課主要介紹少數現在分詞可作介詞的用法。

You could face a US$500 fine, <u>including</u> a three-month jail term for swearing.

你說髒話就可能會被罰五百元美金, 還包括三個月的徒刑。

<u>Considering</u> the trivial nature of the crime, the punishment seemed quite harsh to some.

就這項罪行微不足道的性質而論, 這樣的刑罰對有些人來說似乎相當嚴厲。

上列句中, 分別使用了現在分詞 including (包括) 及 considering (就……而論) 作介系詞的用法。

少數現在分詞可當介詞使用, 常見者如下:

1. including (包括)、excluding (除外)

例: Everyone went to the party,	including excluding	Johnny.

→ Everyone went to the party, Johnny ~~was~~ (being)	included. excluded.

→ Everyone went to the party, Johnny	included. excluded.

= Everyone went to the party,	inclusive of exclusive of	Johnny.

(每個人都去參加了派對，包括／除了約翰。)

2. **considering** (就……而論; 鑒於……)

例: Considering Bill's age, he's still pretty fit.

→ Bill's age ~~is~~ considered, he's still pretty fit.
(being)

→ Bill's age considered, he's still pretty fit.
(就比爾的年紀而論，他的身體還算是相當健康。)

3. **regarding/concerning** (有關、關於)

例: The professor wrote a paper regarding / concerning / about / on computers.

The professor wrote a paper	regarding concerning about on	computers.

(該教授寫了一篇有關電腦的論文。)

Substitution 代換

1. **The government decided to do something about the problem.**
David did nothing about the project, which made the boss very angry.
The teacher warned me to do something about my long hair.
政府決定針對這個問題有所行動。
大衛對該企畫案沒採取行動使得老闆很生氣。
老師警告我要處理一下我的長頭髮。

2. **You could face a US$500 fine, including a three-month jail term for swearing.**
Considering his age, he did pretty well in the chess competition.
The boss talked with me regarding the new sales promotion campaign.
你說髒話就可能會被罰五百元美金, 還包括三個月的徒刑。
就他的年紀而論,他在西洋棋比賽中的表現相當優異。
老闆和我討論有關新的促銷活動。

Lesson 98

Stop Bullshitting!

別鬼扯了！

Dialogue 實用會話

Candy is asking her friend, Rudy, why guys swear so much. (C=Candy; R=Rudy)

C: Why do guys swear so much?

R: It adds color and emphasis to language.

C: Bullshit! People who swear don't have class.

R: See? You just said "bullshit."

C: "Bullshit" isn't swearing. It's even in the dictionary.

R: Sure, it's swearing.

C: It simply means, "male cow manure."

R: Then why don't you just say "shit?" It's in the dictionary as well.

C: We're just going round in circles. Tell you what. If you stop saying "shit," I'll stop saying "bullshit."

R: Since they both aren't very nice things to say anyway, it's a deal.

肯蒂正在問她的朋友魯迪為什麼男生都那麼會說髒話。
肯蒂：為什麼男生都那麼會說髒話？
魯迪：那樣可以使言語增加趣味和加強語氣。
肯蒂：鬼扯！說髒話的人最沒水準了。
魯迪：看吧！妳剛說了『鬼扯』。
肯蒂：『鬼扯』不是髒話。字典裡面有這個字呢。
魯迪：那當然是髒話囉。
肯蒂：它的意思只是『公牛的糞便』。
魯迪：那妳為什麼不說『狗屎』就好了？那個字字典裡也有。
肯蒂：我們只是在原地打轉。我跟你說吧。如果你不再說『狗屎』，我就不再說『鬼扯』了。
魯迪：既然兩者反正都不是好話，那就一言為定了。

Key Points 重點提示

1. **bullshit** [ˈbʊlˏʃɪt] vi. & n. 胡說, 瞎扯 (此字為不太文雅的用語, 最好避免使用)

   例: The arrogant guy likes to bullshit a lot.
   (那個傲慢的傢伙喜歡亂講話。)
   ＊ arrogant [ˈærəgənt] a. 傲慢的, 自大的

   What he just said is a lot of bullshit.
   (他剛剛所說的是一大堆廢話。)

2. **emphasis** [ˈɛmfəsɪs] n. 強調
   emphasize [ˈɛmfəˏsaɪz] vt. 強調
   stress [strɛs] n. & vt. 強調

put/lay	emphasis stress	on...	強調……

= emphasize/stress....

例: Sometimes people write a word in capital letters to put emphasis on it.
(有時人們會用大寫字母書寫文字來強調該字。)

3. **dictionary** [ˈdɪkʃəˌnɛrɪ] n. 字典

注意:

表示『查字典』應譯為"refer to/consult the dictionary", 而『查單字』則用"look up the/a word in the dictionary"表示之。

例: My teacher is so smart, he hardly ever needs to refer to the dictionary.
(我的老師非常聰明，他幾乎不用查字典。)

Don't be ashamed to look up words in the dictionary.
(不要恥於用字典查單字。)

4. **cow** [kaʊ] n. 母牛, 乳牛

5. **manure** [məˈnjʊr] n. 肥料, 糞肥

6. **go round in circles** 原地繞圈圈, 原地打轉

circle [ˈsɝkl̩] n. 圓圈

例: If everyone has a different opinion on how to solve the problem, we'll just be going round in circles.
(如果每個人對於如何解決這個問題都有不同意見的話，我們便會在原地打轉。)

7. **Tell you what.** 我跟你說吧。

= I'll tell you what.

例: A: Tell you what. I'll treat you to lunch if you treat me to a movie.
B: That's a deal.
(甲：我跟你說吧。如果你請我看電影，我就請你吃午飯。)
(乙：一言為定。)

8. **That's a deal.** 一言為定。

例: A: I'll foot the bill this time. You can get it next time.
B: That's a deal.
(甲：這次我付帳，下次再換你。)
(乙：一言為定。)

請選出下列各句中正確的一項

1. The government bans foreigners ______ working without a work permit.
(A) out (B) into (C) from (D) against

2. ______ his inexperience, we should give him another chance.
(A) To consider (B) Considered
(C) Consider (D) Considering

3. Everyone has to go to the school picnic, the teacher ______.
(A) included (B) including (C) includes (D) is included

4. Mother: If you get an "A" on the English exam, I'll buy you a bike.
Son: That's a ______.
(A) stress (B) circle (C) deal (D) swear

5. When you ______ a dictionary, pay attention to the example sentences.
(A) consult (B) consult to (C) look up (D) refer

解答：

1. (C) 2. (D) 3. (A) 4. (C) 5. (A)

Lesson 99

A Red-hot Cure

火辣辣的藥物

Reading
閱 讀

Have you ever had an operation? If you have, you'll know that surgical scars can leave you with a burning pain for months and sometimes even years. Frankly speaking, the pain is sometimes so unbearable it's hard to even stand the weight of your own clothes on the scars. Generally speaking, most ordinary painkillers won't work. Besides, they are so powerful that they may cause side effects.

Fortunately, according to a recent study, doctors say there is a red-hot cure: chili peppers. An ointment is made from the

ingredient that makes chili peppers hot. It kind of short-circuits the pain. The ointment is sold in a tube that lasts a month and costs only US$16. It's considered the newest, most creative and inexpensive way of dealing with the problem.

你曾經動過手術嗎？如果有的話，你就會曉得手術留下的疤痕會為你帶來好幾個月有時甚至幾年的灼熱疼痛。坦白說，這種疼痛難忍到有時連疤痕上衣服的重量也叫人無法忍受。一般說來，普通的止痛藥大多無效。此外，它們的藥效強到可能會產生副作用。

幸好，根據一項最近的研究，醫生表示現在有一種火辣辣的治療藥物：紅辣椒。有一種藥膏是由紅辣椒辛辣成分製成的。這種藥膏可以稍微縮短疼痛的時間。該藥膏以軟管包裝出售，可使用一個月而且一條只賣十六元美金。它被視為是處理這種問題最新、最富創意和便宜的方法。

Vocabulary & Idioms 單字 & 片語註解

1. **red-hot** [ˌrɛdˈhɑt] a. 熾熱的; 灼熱的

2. **cure** [kjʊr] n. 治療方法 & vt. 治療, 使痊癒

cure + 疾病　　治療……疾病

cure + 人 + of + 疾病　　治療/癒某人的疾病

例: My grandma says brandy is a good cure for a runny nose.
(我奶奶說白蘭地是治療流鼻水很好的療方。)

＊ have a runny nose　　流鼻水 (可別譯成『有一個流動的鼻子』)

Jerry says acupuncture cures rheumatism.
(傑瑞說針灸能治療風濕病。)

＊ acupuncture [ˈækjuˌpʌŋktʃɚ] n. 針灸
rheumatism [ˈruməˌtɪzm̩] n. 風濕病

Mom says a glass of warm milk before going to bed can cure you of insomnia.
(老媽說睡前一杯熱牛奶能治療失眠症。)
＊ insomnia [ɪnˈsɑmnɪə] n. 失眠症

3. **operation** [ˌɑpəˈreʃən] n. 手術
operate [ˈɑpəˌret] vi. 動手術 & vt. 操作; 經營
perform an operation on + 身體部位/人　　在身體某部位/為某人動手術
= operate on + 身體部位/人
例: The surgeon will perform an operation on Candy's knee next week.
= The surgeon will operate on Candy's knee next week.
(外科醫師將於下星期為肯蒂的膝蓋動手術。)
The new employee doesn't know how to operate these machines.
(新來的員工不知道如何操作這些機器。)

4. **surgical** [ˈsɝdʒɪkl̩] a. 外科的
surgery [ˈsɝdʒərɪ] n. 外科手術, 開刀 (不可數)
surgeon [ˈsɝdʒən] n. 外科醫師
例: A surgical instrument was left inside the patient's stomach.
(一支外科用的工具被留在那名病人的胃裡了。)
＊ instrument [ˈɪnstrəmənt] n. 工具, 儀器
Your serious illness requires surgery, I'm afraid.
(恐怕你的病嚴重到需要開刀。)

5. **scar** [skɑr] n. 疤, 傷痕
例: The operation left Jessica with a long scar.
(那次手術給潔西卡留下了一道很長的疤痕。)

6. **burning** [ˈbɝnɪŋ] a. 灼熱的
例: The ointment gave me a burning feeling.
(這種藥膏使我有股灼熱的疼痛。)

7. **pain** [pen] n. 痛苦 (不可數); 勞苦 (複數)

take pains 努力, 費力

例: The death of our loved ones gives us great pain.
(心愛的人去逝帶給我們極大的痛苦。)

Mary took great pains with her Chinese lessons and got high grades.
(瑪麗努力唸國文而考試得了高分。)

8. **Frankly speaking, 主詞 + 動詞** 坦白說,……

= To be frank, 主詞 + 動詞

= To tell you the truth, 主詞 + 動詞

= To tell the truth, 主詞 + 動詞

例: Frankly speaking, nobody wears that kind of clothes anymore.
(坦白說，再也沒有人穿那種衣服了。)

9. **unbearable** [ʌn'bɛrəbl̩] a. 不能忍受的

= intolerable [ɪn'tɑlərəbl̩] a.

例: Sometimes I get unbearable headaches.
(有時候我頭痛得受不了。)

10. **Generally speaking, 主詞 + 動詞** 一般說來,……

= In general, 主詞 + 動詞

= By and large, 主詞 + 動詞

= For the most part, 主詞 + 動詞

= On the whole, 主詞 + 動詞

例: Generally speaking, things are much cheaper in China than in Japan.
(一般說來，在中國東西要比日本便宜很多。)

11. **ordinary** ['ɔrdənɛrɪ] a. 普通的

例: Ordinary plants cannot grow in the ocean.
(普通的植物無法在海洋中生長。)

12. **painkiller** [ˈpen,kɪlɚ] n. 止痛藥

13. **work** [wɝk] vi. 有效, 奏效

例: I don't think your idea will work.
(我認為你的點子不管用。)

14. **side effect** [ˈsaɪd ɪ,fɛkt] n. 副作用

15. **chili pepper** [ˈtʃɪlɪ ,pɛpɚ] n. 紅辣椒

16. **ointment** [ˈɔɪntmənt] n. 藥膏

例: The ointment is made from many kinds of herbs.
(這種藥膏是由許多種藥草做成的。)
* herb [ɝb] n. 藥草

17. **be made from...** 由……製成/做成 (原料性質改變)

be made of... 由……製成/做成 (原料性質不變)

注意:

以上兩者用法原則上有所區別, 但在現代用法中, 老美常混用。

例: Cheese and butter are made from milk.
(乳酪和奶油是從牛奶中提煉出來的。)

The bank's safe is made of solid steel.
(該銀行的保險櫃是用純鋼打造的。)

18. **ingredient** [ɪnˈgridɪənt] n. 成分

例: Mom won't tell anyone what ingredients she uses for her stew.
(老媽不會告訴任何人她烹調燉肉使用的材料。)

19. **short-circuit** [,ʃɔrtˈsɝkɪt] vt. 使簡短

short circuit [,ʃɔrt ˈsɝkɪt] n. 短路, 漏電

例: This new system will short-circuit the office procedures and help get things done faster.
(這套新系統將會縮短辦公室作業流程且有助於工作早點完成。)

The fireman said that a short circuit caused the fire.
(那名消防隊員說電線走火引發這次火災。)

20. **tube** [tjub] n. (金屬、玻璃、塑膠等的) 管

21. **last** [læst] vi. 持續

例: These shoes cost more but they will last longer.
(這雙鞋子雖然比較貴但將會更耐久。)

22. **creative** [krɪˈetɪv] a. 富創意的

例: The playful student turned out to be a very creative writer.
(那個愛玩的學生最後竟成為一個非常有創意的作家。)

23. **deal with...** 處理⋯⋯; 和⋯⋯打交道

例: I find it hard to deal with selfish people.
(我覺得和自私的人打交道很難。)

Grammar Notes 文法重點

本課介紹獨立分詞片語的用法, 以及 kind of 作副詞, 表示『有一點』的用法, 另複習 consider (視⋯⋯為⋯⋯) 作不完全及物動詞的用法。

1. **<u>Frankly speaking</u>, the pain is sometimes so unbearable (that) it's hard to even stand the weight of your own clothes on the scars.**
坦白說, 這種疼痛難忍到有時連疤痕上衣服的重量也叫人無法忍受。
<u>Generally speaking</u>, most ordinary painkillers won't work.
一般說來, 一般的止痛藥大多無效。
上列句中, frankly speaking (坦白說) 及 generally speaking (一般說來) 均為獨立分詞片語, 作副詞用, 修飾整個句子。

這些獨立分詞片語有副詞的功能,使用時通常置於句首,其後加逗點,用以修飾整個句子。常見的獨立分詞片語如下:

frankly speaking　　坦白說
generally speaking　　一般說來
strictly speaking　　嚴格說來
judging from...　　從……看來
speaking of...　　說/談到……

例: Frankly speaking, I don't care if John doesn't come to my party.
(坦白說,我並不在乎約翰是否會來參加我的派對。)

Strictly speaking, you're not supposed to park here.
(嚴格說來,你不應該把車子停在這裡。)

Judging from the look on his face, the boss must have scolded him about his work.
(從他臉上的表情看來,老闆一定為了他的工作而責罵過他。)

Speaking of your brother, what's he doing now?
(說到你弟弟,他現在在做什麼呢?)

2. **It kind of short-circuits the pain.**
這種藥膏可以稍微縮短疼痛的時間。

上列句中, kind of 作副詞用, 表『有一點』、『有幾分』之意, 修飾其後的動詞 short-circuits。

kind of 作副詞用時, 即等於 sort of、a little 或 somewhat, 除可修飾動詞外, 亦可修飾形容詞和副詞。

例: Mr. Chen kind of takes things too seriously.
(陳先生看待事情有點太過認真。)

I was kind of sad to hear that my ex-girlfriend got married.
(聽到前任女友結婚的消息我有點難過。)

The boy from India spoke kind of strangely.
(那個印度男孩講話有點奇怪。)

比較:

a kind of...　　一種……
= a sort of...

注意:

a kind/sort of 其後可接單、複數名詞或不可數名詞, 且 a kind/sort of 之後接的是單數名詞時, 則此單數名詞前不可再置不定冠詞 a/an。

例: The villagers are suffering from a strange kind of a disease. (×)
→ The villagers are suffering from a strange kind of disease. (○)
(村民們罹患了一種怪病。)

There is a kind of plastic which is as strong as steel.
(有一種塑膠強度像鋼一樣。)

3. **It's considered the newest, most creative and inexpensive way of dealing with the problem.**
它被視為是處理這種問題最新、最富創意和便宜的方法。
上列句中, 使用了 consider 作不完全及物動詞的被動式用法, 其後接名詞 the newest, most creative and inexpensive way 作主詞補語。句型如下:
be considered + 名詞/形容詞 (作主詞補語)
被視為……, 被認為是……
主動用法:
consider + 受詞 + 名詞/形容詞 (作受詞補語)
視……為……, 認為……是……

例: It is considered rude to interrupt others when they're talking.
(打斷別人的談話被視為是不禮貌的。)

I consider it worthwhile to spend more time reading.
(我認為花多一點時間在閱讀上是值得的。)

Substitution 代 換

1. **Generally speaking, most ordinary painkillers won't work.**

   Strickly speaking, we should get the boss's permission before we do this.

   Speaking of Steve, did you know that he's getting married again?

   一般說來, 普通的止痛藥大多無效。

   嚴格說來, 我們應該在做這件事之前先得到老闆的允許。

   說到史提夫, 你知道他又要再婚了嗎？

2. **It kind of short-circuits the pain.**

   If you ask me, Mike is kind of weird.

   The old man still walks kind of fast for his age.

   這種藥膏可以稍微縮短疼痛的時間。

   如果你問我的話, 我會說麥克有點怪異。

   以他的年紀來看, 那位老人的步伐仍算有點快。

Lesson 100

Old Wives' Tales

無稽之談

Connie and Willy are talking about the previous lesson.

(C=Connie; W=Willy)

C: Do you believe what they say about chili peppers?

W: Frankly speaking, I don't. The last time I got hurt playing soccer, my mom told me not to eat anything spicy. She said it will irritate the wound.

C: My mom is the same. For example, according to her, eating fish eyes is good for the eyes.

W: If you think that's weird, listen to this. My mom says eating pigs' brains makes you smart.

C: Are you kidding? Frankly speaking, I don't believe in any of these old wives' tales.

W: I wish you would tell that to my mom. I'm sick of eating pigs' brains.

C: Poor guy!

W: Don't tell anyone, OK? Or I'll never hear the end of it.

C: OK. It doesn't work anyway.

W: What do you mean?

C: I'm only kidding. You're at least as smart as a pig.

康妮和威利正在談論先前那一課。

康妮：你相信他們所說有關紅辣椒的事嗎？

威利：坦白說，我不相信。上次我踢足球受傷時，我老媽告訴我別吃任何辛辣的東西。她說那會刺激傷口。

康妮：我媽也是這樣。舉個例子來說，根據她的說法，吃魚的眼睛對視力有益。

威利：如果妳認為那很怪異，聽聽這個。我老媽說吃豬腦能使人聰明。

康妮：你在開玩笑嗎？坦白說，我不相信任何這些無稽之談。

威利：我希望妳能這麼告訴我老媽。我對吃豬腦已經很厭煩了。

康妮：可憐的傢伙！

威利：別告訴任何人，好嗎？否則我的耳根就別想清淨了。

康妮：好吧。反正那也沒什麼用。

威利：妳這句話是什麼意思？

康妮：只是開玩笑罷了。你至少聰明得像隻豬。

Key Points 重點提示

1. **old wives' tale** [ˌold ˈwaɪvz ˌtel] n. (尤指老婦人所持的) 愚蠢的迷信, 無稽之談

例: Danny: You shouldn't wash your hair for one month after you give birth, Jenny.

Jenny: Come on. That's just an old wives' tale.

(丹尼：珍妮，妳生產後一個月內都不可以洗頭。)

(珍妮：得了吧。那只是無稽之談罷了。)

2. **hurt** [hɝt] vt. & vi. (使) 疼痛

動詞三態均為 hurt。

例: Maggie hurt her feet by wearing high heels all day.
(美琪穿了一整天的高跟鞋腳都痛了。)

Putting acupuncture needles in your body doesn't hurt.
(將針灸用的針插到你的身體裡是不會痛的。)

3. **play soccer** 踢足球

注意:

『play + 運動名稱』中間不能置任何冠詞 (the/a), 如: play soccer、play baseball (打棒球)、play basketball (打籃球)、play volleyball (打排球)、play badminton (打羽毛球)、play tennis (打網球) 等。

例: Billy always plays soccer with his friends on weekends.
(比利在週末時都會和朋友一起踢足球。)

4. **spicy** [ˈspaɪsɪ] a. 辛辣的; 加有香料的

例: Indian food is very spicy.
(印度料理非常辛辣。)

5. **irritate** [ˈɪrəˌtet] vt. 刺激, 使疼痛

例: This cheap lotion irritates the skin.
(這種廉價的乳液會刺激皮膚。)
∗ lotion [ˈloʃən] n. 護膚液, 乳液

6. **wound** [wund] n. 傷 (口)

例: You'd better clean that wound before it gets infected.
(你最好在傷口感染前清理一下。)

7. **weird** [wɪrd] a. 怪異的

例: Steve likes to wear weird clothes.
(史提夫喜歡穿著奇裝異服。)

Tom may not be very smart but he isn't dumb, either.
(湯姆也許不是很聰明，但他也不笨。)

＊ dumb [dʌm] a. 笨的

8. **believe in...** 相信……的真實性; 信仰……

例: I don't believe in feng shui.
(我不相信風水。)

＊ feng shui 是風水的羅馬拼音詞, 相當於英文的 geomancy [ˈdʒiə͵mænsɪ] n.

Mr. Lin is a Christian; he believes in Jesus.
(林先生是基督徒，他信仰耶穌。)

9. 本文:

Or I'll never hear the end of it.

= Or people will never stop teasing me about it.
否則我的耳根就別想清淨。

＊ tease [tiz] vt. 取笑, 揶揄

請選出下列各句中正確的一項

1. It's difficult to ______ badminton outdoors when it's windy.
(A) play with (B) play the (C) play a (D) play

2. The doctors ______ me after I had not eaten anything for twenty-four hours.
(A) operated (B) operated on
(C) performed (D) performed on

3. Jack ______ to make sure that there weren't any mistakes in his composition.
   (A) took pain (B) took pains (C) made pain (D) made pains

4. ______, women are more emotional than men.
   (A) Generally speak (B) General speaking
   (C) Generally speaking (D) General speak

5. This fine Chinese wine is made ______ rice.
   (A) from (B) into (C) to (D) by

解答：

1. (D) 2. (B) 3. (B) 4. (C) 5. (A)

Lesson 101

Seeing Is Believing

眼見為憑

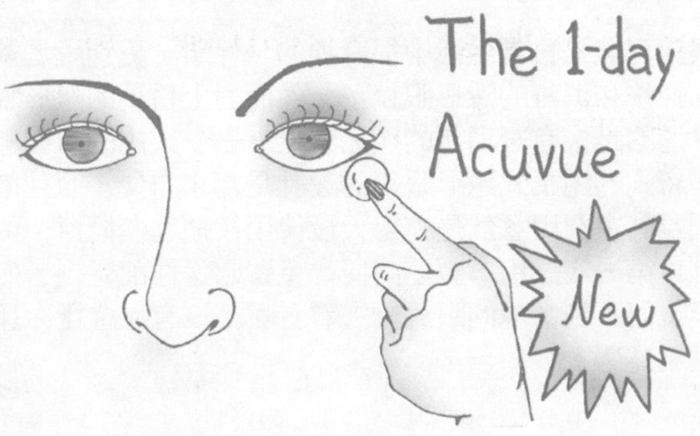

Wearing glasses can be a real day-to-day hassle, not to mention using contact lenses, which have to be cleaned, rinsed and disinfected every so often. Fortunately, however, for those millions of contact lens users, there's a new product out — the 1-day Acuvue.

These new disposable contact lenses are designed to be convenient and rather inexpensive because the idea is to throw them away after use at the end of each day. What's even better is if you are planning to give them a try for the first time, the manufacturers will give you your first five pairs for free. If you don't think that's possible, why not go down to your local optician and check it out? No one will blame you for doing that. After all, seeing is believing.

戴眼鏡可能是日常生活中很麻煩的一件事，更別說是戴常常必須要清潔、沖洗和消毒的隱形眼鏡了。然而對上百萬的隱形眼鏡使用者來說，幸運的是，有一項新的產品問世——一天用的阿袞維爾。

這些新式的拋棄式隱形眼鏡的設計是為求方便，而且價格也相當低廉，因為其主要用意就是在每天最後用後把它們扔掉。更棒的是，如果你打算第一次試用，製造商便會免費贈送你前五副。如果你認為那不可能，何不到當地的眼鏡行去看看呢？沒有人會怪你那麼做的。畢竟，眼見為憑。

Vocabulary & Idioms 單字 & 片語註解

1. 標題:

   Seeing is believing. 眼見為信。

   = To see is to believe.

   例: Mary: The boss is going to give you a big bonus this year.
   Paul: Seeing is believing.
   (瑪麗：老闆今年會發給你一大筆獎金。)
   (保羅：眼見為信。)

   * bonus ['bonəs] n. 獎金, 紅利

2. **wear** [wɛr] vt. 穿 (衣服); 戴 (眼鏡、帽子、耳環等)

   動詞三態: wear、wore、worn。

例: The strange guy wears sunglasses even at night.
(那個奇怪的傢伙甚至連晚上都戴著太陽眼鏡。)

Some teenagers like to wear earrings nowadays.
(時下一些十幾歲的青少年喜歡戴耳環。)
* teenager [ˈtinˌedʒɚ] n. (十三至十九歲的) 青少年

3. **glasses** [ˈglæsɪz] n. 眼鏡 (恆用複數)
glass [glæs] n. 玻璃 (不可數); 玻璃杯 (可數)
注意:
表『一副/二副眼鏡』應譯為"a pair/two pairs of glasses"。
a glass, two glasses 則表『一個玻璃杯』、『兩個玻璃杯』。
例: I can't see very well. I think I need (a pair of) glasses.
(我沒辦法看得很清楚，我想我需要 (一副) 眼鏡了。)

The necklace she's wearing is made of glass.
(她戴的那串項鍊是玻璃做的。)

4. **day-to-day** [ˌdetəˈde] a. 每天的, 日常生活的 (= daily)
例: My day-to-day living expenses are not very high.
(我的日常生活費用不是很高。)

5. **hassle** [ˈhæsl̩] n. 傷腦筋的事
例: It's a hassle to get to work in this traffic.
(在這種交通狀況之下要到達上班地點是件很傷腦筋的事。)

6. **contact lenses** 隱形眼鏡 (複數形, 因人有雙眼)
contact [ˈkɑntækt] n. 接觸
lens [lɛnz] n. 鏡片

7. **rinse** [rɪns] vt. 清洗
例: Don't forget to rinse the cup before you use it.
(在你使用這個杯子前，別忘了清洗一下。)

8. **disinfect** [ˌdɪsɪnˈfɛkt] vt. 消毒, 淨化
infect [ɪnˈfɛkt] vt. 使感染 (常用於被動語態)

be infected with...

例: The milk bottles should be disinfected before use.
(這些牛奶瓶在使用前應先消毒。)

You must disinfect the wound before you put a bandage over it.
(在你綁上繃帶前，必須先消毒傷口。)

* bandage [ˈbændɪdʒ] n. 繃帶

Peter <u>was infected with</u> a strange disease.
(彼得感染了一種怪病。)

9. **every so often** 常常, 經常

= quite often

例: Every so often Dad brings home flowers for Mom.
(老爸常常買花回家給老媽。)

10. **user** [ˈjuzɚ] n. 使用者

11. **disposable** [dɪˈspozəbl̩] a. 可丟棄的, 用後即丟的

dispose [dɪˈspoz] vi. 處置/理; 除去 (與介詞 of 並用)

dispose of... 處理/除去/收拾……

例: Disposable lunch boxes are a serious cause of pollution.
(用後即丟的便當盒是污染的一項重大肇因。)

Let's dispose of all this rubbish in the room.
(咱們收拾一下房間裡所有的垃圾吧。)

12. **design** [dɪˈzaɪn] vt. 設計

be designed to + 原形動詞 被設計來……; 目的是……

例: This plane isn't designed to fly; it's only a model.
(這架飛機不是被設計來飛行的，它只是架模型。)

13. **convenient** [kənˈvinjənt] a. 方便的

例: It's convenient to work near your home.
(在住家附近上班是挺方便的。)

14. **throw...away** 丟棄……

= throw away...

例: Mom threw all her old clothes away and bought new ones.
(老媽把她所有的舊衣服扔掉而買了新衣服。)

15. **at the end of...** 在……的最後

at the beginning of... 在……的最初/開始

例: At the end of the trip, everyone was exhausted.
(在旅途的最後，每個人都筋疲力竭了。)

At the beginning of the lecture, everyone was attentive.
(演講開始時，每個人都很專心聽。)

16. **give...a try** 試試看……

= give...a shot

例: Let's give bungee jumping a try.
(咱們去試試高空彈跳吧。)

17. **manufacturer** [ˌmænjəˈfæktʃərɚ] n. 製造商, 廠商

manufacture [ˌmænjəˈfæktʃɚ] n. 製造 & vt. (以機器大量) 製造, 生產

例: The manufacturer promises to return your money to you if you're not satisfied with the goods.
(如果你不滿意產品，廠商答應要退錢給你。)

Our company is engaged in the manufacture of plastic toys.
(我們公司從事塑膠玩具的製造。)

My father's factory manufactures shoes.
(我爸爸的工廠生產鞋子。)

18. **for free** 免費的

例: You can have these sample pens | for free / free |.

(你可以免費擁有這些樣品筆。)

19. **local** [ˈlokl̩] a. 當地的, 本地的 & n. 當地人, 本地人

例: The local barber knows everyone in the village.
(當地的理髮師認識村裡的每個人。)

The locals don't like to mix with outsiders.
(當地人不喜歡和外地人打交道。)

＊ mix with + 人　　與某人打交道

20. **optician** [ɑpˈtɪʃən] n. 眼鏡商, 眼鏡行

21. **check it out**　　查看看, 瞧瞧

= take a look at it

例: A: There's a new disco in town.
B: Let's go check it out.
(甲：鎮上新開了一家迪斯可舞廳。)
(乙：咱們去瞧瞧吧。)

Grammar Notes 文法重點

本課複習 not to mention 的用法, 並介紹"What's even better is + (that)子句"的用法, 以及動詞 blame 的用法。

1. **Wearing glasses can be a real day-to-day hassel, <u>not to mention</u> using contact lenses which have to be cleaned, rinsed and disinfected every so often.**

戴眼鏡可能是日常生活中很麻煩的一件事, 更別說是戴常常必須要清潔、沖洗和消毒的隱形眼鏡了。

本句中使用了 not to mention (更不用說) 的用法; 可用來表『更不用說……』的用法如下:

not to mention...　　更不用說……(用於肯定句與否定句中)

= not to speak of...

= to say nothing of...

let alone...　　更不用說……(用於否定句中)

= much less...

注意:

在上列用法中, not to mention、not to speak of 及 to say nothing of 在肯定句與否定句中均可使用, 且因分別含有及物動詞 mention 及介詞 of, 故其後須接名詞或動名詞作受詞; 而 let alone 及 much less 則只能用於否定句中, 且因其具有連接詞的作用, 故其後應置與其前相同的詞類。

例: The rich man can afford a house, | not to mention / not to speak of / to say nothing of | a car.

(那個有錢人買得起房子，更別說是車子了。)

The baby can't even walk, | not to mention / not to speak of / to say nothing of | running. (動名詞)

= The baby can't even walk, (原形動詞) | let alone / much less | run. (原形動詞)

(這嬰孩甚至連走路都不會，更不用說是跑了。)

2. **What's even better is (that) if you are planning to give them a try for the first time, the manufacturers will give you your first five pairs for free.**

= What's even better, if you are planning to give them a try for the first time,...

更棒的是, 如果你打算第一次試用, 廠商便會免費贈送你前五副。

上列句中, 使用了"What's even better is + (that) 子句" 的用法, 本句型由於經常使用, 故可化簡為"What's even better, 主詞 + 動詞", 且 even 亦可用 far 替代, 或兩者均不用亦可。

What's (even/far) better is + (that) 子句　　更棒的是,……(用於好的方面)

= What's (even/far) better, 主詞 + 動詞

類似用法:

What's (even/far) worse is + (that) 子句　　更糟的是, ……(用於壞的方面)

= What's (even/far) worse, 主詞 + 動詞

What's more is + (that) 子句　　而且/此外, ……(好、壞方面均可使用)

= What's more, 主詞 + 動詞

例: I was lucky enough to buy the last copy of this book. What's even better, I got it at a discount.
(我很幸運買到這本書的最後一本；更棒的是，還有打折。)

While traveling in France, I got lost. What's far worse, all my money was in my hotel room.
(在法國旅遊時，我迷了路；更糟的是，我所有的錢都留在旅館的房間裡。)

Jim is a good worker. What's more, he is very cooperative.
(吉姆是個好員工；此外，他還非常合作。)

Wendy comes to work late. What's more, she leaves the office early.
(溫蒂上班總是遲到；而且還提早下班。)

3. 有關動詞 blame [blem] 的重要用法如下:

a. blame + 人 + for + 名詞/動名詞　　將某事歸咎於某人

例: The students blamed the teacher for their failure.
(學生們把他們的失敗怪在老師頭上。)

b. blame + 事 + on + 人　　將某事歸咎於某人

例: Every time Little Bobby breaks something, he blames it on his little sister.
(每次小鮑比打破東西，他都會把它怪在他妹妹頭上。)

c. 人 + be to blame　　某人該受責備/負責任

注意:

"人 + be to blame"為習慣用法, 即等於"人 + should be blamed"之意。

例: Nobody <u>was to blame</u> for that car accident.
= Nobody <u>should be blamed</u> for that car accident.
(沒有人該為那樁車禍負責。)

Substitution 代　換

What's even better is if you're planning to give them a try for the first time, the manufacturers will give you your first five pairs for free.

Mandy got lost. What's even worse, she has no money with her.

Alan did very well on the exams. What's more, he was first in his class.

更棒的是, 如果你打算第一次試用, 廠商便會免費贈送你前五副。

曼蒂迷路了; 更糟的是, 她身上沒帶錢。

艾倫考試考得非常好; 而且他還是他班上第一名。

Lesson 102

No Free Lunch

沒有白吃的午餐

Hoping to get free contact lenses, Freddy goes to the optician.

(F=Freddy; O=Optician)

F: Could you help me check my eyes, please?

O: Sure. Please have a seat and put on these glasses. Now, tell me. Which letters seem clearer?

F: The ones on the right.

O: OK. Can you read these price tags?

F: Yes. They're as clear as daylight.

O: Fine. Read out the highest amount.

F: US$100.

O: Right. That's what it'll cost you.

F: But I thought the contact lenses are free.

O: Yes. But you'll have to pay for our service.

F: No wonder they say, "There's no such thing as a free lunch."

弗瑞德到眼鏡商那兒希望能得到免費的隱形眼鏡。
弗瑞德：可否麻煩你幫我做個視力檢查？
眼鏡商：當然。請坐下並戴上這副眼鏡。現在，告訴我。哪些字母看得比較清楚？
弗瑞德：右邊的那些。
眼鏡商：好的。你看得見這些價格標籤嗎？
弗瑞德：可以。清楚得很。
眼鏡商：很好。把價格最高的唸出來。
弗瑞德：美金一百元。
眼鏡商：沒錯。那就是你所要付的款數。
弗瑞德：但是我以為隱形眼鏡是免費的。
眼鏡商：是啊。不過你得付我們服務費。
弗瑞德：難怪人家說：『天底下沒有白吃的午餐。』

Key Points 重點提示

1. **have a seat** 請坐

= take a seat

seat [sit] n. 座位

例: Please have a seat; Mr. White will be with you in a minute.
(請坐，懷特先生馬上就來了。)

2. **clear** [klɪr] a. 清楚的, 清澈的

* 本文中 clearer [ˈklɪrɚ] 為 clear 的比較級。

例: The water in the lake is so clear that we can see the bottom.
(湖水清澈到可以見底。)

3. **be as clear as daylight** 非常清楚

daylight [ˈdeˌlaɪt] n. 白天, 日光

例: The boss's intentions are as clear as daylight.
(老闆的意圖非常清楚。)

4. **read out...** (大聲) 唸出……

例: The student was asked to read out his excellent composition to the class.
(那名學生被要求唸出他優異的作文給班上的人聽。)

5. **pay for...** 付……的錢

pay [pe] vi. 付 (款)

例: Who paid for the lunch we just had?
(誰付了我們剛吃的那份午餐錢呢？)

6. **no wonder** 難怪, 一點也不足為奇

注意:

no wonder 雖為名詞, 但使用時卻作副詞, 置於句首, 修飾其後全句。

例: No wonder he will marry the widow; she is a millionairess.
(難怪他願意娶那寡婦；她是個女富翁。)
* millionairess [ˌmɪljəˈnɛrɪs] n. 女富翁

7. **There is no such thing as a free lunch.** 天底下沒有白吃的午餐。

例: A: If you fly Cathay Pacific, you'll get free meals and free wine.
B: There is no such thing as a free lunch, you know. They're all included in the air fare.
(甲：如果你搭乘國泰航空，就可享用免費餐點和飲酒。)
(乙：天下沒有白吃的午餐，你知道的。它們全都包含在機票錢內了。)

請選出下列各句中正確的一項

1. Everyone in the office was ______ with the disease.
   (A) disposed (B) rinsed
   (C) disinfected (D) infected

2. Frank can afford a house, not to ______ a car.
   (A) mention (B) speak (C) say (D) tell

3. Why ______ Bob a call? He's pretty lonely these days.
   (A) give (B) not giving (C) not to give (D) not give

4. The lazy students blamed their poor exam results ______ their teacher.
   (A) for (B) to (C) on (D) with

5. The boss ______ our trip to Japan.
   (A) bought for (B) paid for (C) put on (D) paid

解答：

1. (D) 2. (A) 3. (D) 4. (C) 5. (B)

Lesson 103

Adorable Koalas in Danger

可愛的無尾熊有危險了

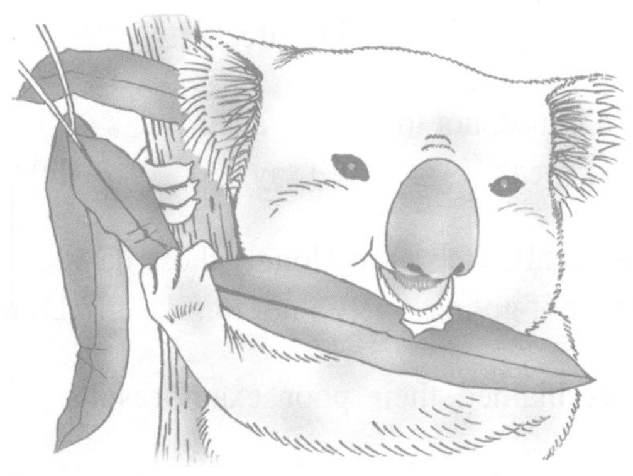

Reading 閱讀

Koalas are considered an Australian national icon. These adorable tree-hugging animals feed on eucalyptus tree leaves. The problem is on average a koala destroys 13 pounds of the leaves to eat 2 pounds a day. Because of this, 5,000 koalas soon face starvation on Kangaroo Island in the south of Australia.

The authorities are now considering shooting them to control the island's koala population explosion. However, animal activists suggest growing more trees. "There aren't too many koalas. There are too few trees," they argue. Neighboring

provinces have even recommended relocating some of the koalas to them. Most Australians feel that the authorities must do all they can to avoid killing the koalas for to do so would be a national disgrace.

　　無尾熊被視為是澳洲的國家象徵。這些可愛的抱樹動物以油加利樹的樹葉為食。問題是一隻無尾熊一天平均損毀十三磅的葉子來吃其中的兩磅。由於這個緣故，在澳洲南方的袋鼠島上，有五千隻無尾熊很快就面臨挨餓的問題。

　　當局現正考慮射殺牠們以便控制島上無尾熊數目的爆增。然而，保育動物人士則建議多種植一些樹。他們認為：『無尾熊並不會太多；是樹太少了。』鄰近的一些省甚至建議把其中的一些無尾熊遷移到他們那裡。大部分的澳洲人覺得政府當局必須竭力避免宰殺無尾熊，因為那麼做的話將是一項國恥。

Vocabulary & Idioms
單字 & 片語註解

1. **adorable** [əʹdorəbḷ] a. 可愛的, 迷人的
   adore [əʹdor] vt. 崇拜, 敬重
   例: We adore him for his brilliant academic accomplishment.
   (我們敬重他輝煌的學術成就。)

2. **koala** [koʹɑlə] n. 無尾熊

3. **(be) in danger** 處於危險之中
   danger [ʹdendʒɚ] n. 危險
   例: The storm put the fishermen in danger.
   (那場暴風雨使那些漁夫陷於危險中。)

4. **Australian** [ɔ'streljən] a. 澳洲 (人) 的 & n. 澳洲人

   Australia [ɔ'streljə] n. 澳洲

5. **icon** ['aɪkɑn] n. 象徵; 聖物

   例: The cow is a national icon in some countries.
   (牛是某些國家的神聖象徵。)

6. **tree-hugging** ['tri,hʌgɪŋ] a. 抱樹的

   hug [hʌg] vt. 擁抱

   例: The tree-hugging koalas are loved by everyone because they are so cute.
   (大家都喜愛抱樹的無尾熊，因為牠們非常可愛。)

   Sarah hugged her books to her chest.
   (莎拉把她的書抱在胸前。)

7. **動物 + feed on + 食物** 某動物以……為食

   例: Cows feed on grass.
   (牛以草為食。)

8. **eucalyptus** [,jukə'lɪptəs] n. 油加利樹 (澳洲原產的常綠喬木)

9. **average** ['ævərɪdʒ] n. 平均

   on average 平均而論

   例: On average, the restaurant makes US$1,000 a day.
   (這家餐廳平均一天賺一千元美金。)

10. **destroy** [dɪ'strɔɪ] vt. 毀壞

   例: The typhoon destroyed the crops.
   (那場颱風摧毀了農作物。)

11. **pound** [paʊnd] n. 磅

12. **starvation** [stɑr'veʃən] n. 飢餓

   starve [stɑrv] vi. 飢餓; 渴望 & vt. 使飢餓

starve to death　　餓得要死

例: These poor children suffer from starvation.
(這些可憐的小孩飽受飢餓之苦。)

The lost campers almost starved to death.
(那些迷路的露營者差點餓死。)

13. **Kangaroo Island**　　袋鼠島

kangaroo [ˌkæŋɡəˈru] n. 袋鼠 (產於澳洲的草食哺乳動物)

14. **authority** [əˈθɔrətɪ] n. 當局; 權威; 權威人士

注意:

a. authority 表『當局』時, 恆用複數形 authorities, 且其前需置定冠詞 the。

the authorities　　當局

the school authorities　　學校當局

the authorities concerned　　有關當局

例: The school authorities should consider revising the school curricula.
(學校當局應該考慮修訂課程。)

* revise [rɪˈvaɪz] vt. 修訂
curricula [kəˈrɪkjəlɪ] n. 課程 (複數)
curriculum [kəˈrɪkjələm] n. 課程 (單數)

b. 表『權威』時, 為不可數名詞。

例: Jeff doesn't belong to my department, so I have no authority over him.
(傑夫不屬於我的部門，因此我無權指揮他。)

c. 表『權威人士』時則為可數名詞。

例: Professor Clinton is an authority in chemistry.
(柯林頓教授是化學權威。)

15. **control** [kənˈtrol] vt. & n. 控制

under control　　在控制中

例: You should learn how to control your temper.
(你應該學習如何控制你的脾氣。)

Now that the boss is back, everything's under control.
(現在老闆回來了，一切都在控制之中。)

16. **population** [ˌpɑpjəˈleʃən] n. 人口

例: The world population is just growing and growing.
(世界人口正陸續不斷地增加。)

17. **explosion** [ɪkˈsploʒən] n. 突增; 爆炸

explode [ɪkˈsplod] vi. & vt. (使) 爆炸

例: The explosion of oil prices was the main cause of the economic depression.
(石油價格突增是經濟不景氣的主因。)

Everyone on the plane will die if the bomb explodes.
(如果這枚炸彈爆炸，機上所有人都會死的。)

The policemen exploded the bomb in safe surroundings.
(警察在安全的地方引爆了那枚炸彈。)

18. **activist** [ˈæktɪvɪst] n. 積極參與份子

例: The animal rights activists held a protest in front of the hospital.
(動物保育人士在那家醫院門前示威抗議。)

19. **argue** [ˈɑrgju] vt. 強烈認為 & vi. 爭論

argue + that 子句　　強烈認為……

argue with + 人 + over + 事　　和某人爭論某事

例: The murderer argued that he was unfairly tried.
(那名謀殺犯強烈認為他未獲公平審判。)

The customer argued with the waiter over the bill.
(那名顧客為了帳單和服務生爭論。)

20. **neighboring** [ˈnebərɪŋ] a. 鄰近的, 附近的

neighbor [ˈnebɚ] n. 鄰居

例: The neighboring countries are enjoying good relations.
(那些鄰近國家彼此關係良好。)

People don't care much about being good neighbors nowadays.
(現今人們對於做好鄰居並不是很在乎。)

21. **province** [ˈprɑvɪns] n. 省

22. **relocate** [riˈloket] vt. 重新安置

例: We intend to relocate our office by the end of the year.
(我們想在年底以前遷移辦公室。)

23. **do all one can to + 原形動詞** 某人盡全力……

= do one's best to + 原形動詞

= do one's utmost to + 原形動詞

= spare no effort to + 原形動詞

例: The generous old man did all he could to help his friend.
(那個慷慨的老人竭盡所能地幫助他的朋友。)

The police will spare no effort to find the kidnapper.
(警方將竭盡所能地抓到綁匪。)

24. **disgrace** [dɪsˈgres] n. 恥辱, 不名譽

national disgrace 國恥

例: The criminal was a disgrace to his family.
(那名罪犯是他家的恥辱。)

Grammar Notes
文法重點

本課介紹"feed on..."及"live on..."的區別, 以及表示地方的名詞與介詞 in、at、on 的用法。

1. **These adorable tree-hugging animals feed on eucalyptus tree leaves.**
   這些可愛的抱樹動物以油加利樹的樹葉為食。
   上列句中, 由於主詞是 animals (動物), 故其後要用 feed on, 表『以……為食』; 若主詞為『人』時, 則要用 live on, 表『以……為 (主) 食』或『依……為生』。
   feed on...　(動物) 以……為食
   live on...　(人) 以……為 (主) 食; 依……為生
   例: Rabbits feed on carrots.
   (兔子以胡蘿蔔為食。)
   The beggar lives only on bread and water.
   (那名乞丐只靠麵包和水過活。)
   How can you live on such a low salary?
   (你怎麼能靠如此微薄的薪水為生呢?)

2. **Because of this, 5,000 koalas soon face starvation on Kangaroo Island in the south of Australia.**
   由於這個緣故, 在澳洲南方的袋鼠島上, 有五千隻無尾熊很快就面臨挨餓的問題。
   有關表地方的名詞與介詞 in、at、on 的用法如下:
   a. 表示在『大地方』(如國家、城市、區域、範圍等), 或表『在……之內』時, 介詞要用 in。
      例: It's freezing all year round in Alaska.
      (阿拉斯加一年到頭都冷得要命。)

Mr. Wang has a restaurant in the heart of the city.
(王先生在該市的心臟地區開了一家餐廳。)

b. 表在『小地方』(如車站、商店、學校等建築物或機構), 或某特定地點時, 介詞要用 at。

例: I'll wait for you at the train station.
(我會在火車站那兒等你。)

We arrived at the airport just in time to catch our plane.
(我們到達機場時剛好及時趕上搭機。)

注意:

小地方如 station、post office、restaurant、supermarket、movie theater、school 等仍可與 in 並用, 只是 in 表示『在……裡面』, 而 at 則表示『在……那裡』, 也許是在外面, 也有可能在裡面。

例: It was really dark in the movie theater.
(電影院裡面真得很暗。)

We all met at the movie theater but we didn't see the movie.
(我們全都在電影院碰面，但並沒有看電影。)

c. 表示『在……上面』(如島嶼上、樓層上、街道上、海灘上、或任何東西的表面上等) 時, 則介詞要用 on。

例: We were stranded on a remote island.
(我們被困在一個遙遠的島上。)

＊ strand [strænd] vt. 使 (船) 擱淺; 使 (人) 束手無策/窘迫

Mary lives on the third floor of this building.
(瑪麗住在這棟大樓的三樓。)

There's a scratch on the surface of your new desk.
(你新書桌的表面上有道刮痕。)

Substitution
代 換

1. **Koalas are considered an Australian national icon.**
   Bill is viewed as an English grammar expert.
   I regard my father as a friend.
   無尾熊被視為是澳洲的國家象徵。
   比爾被視為英文文法專家。
   我視我父親為朋友。

2. **These adorable tree-hugging animals feed on eucalyptus tree leaves.**
   Vultures feed on carcasses.
   Snakes feed on frogs and rats.
   這些可愛的抱樹動物以油加利樹的樹葉為食。
   兀鷹以屍體為食。
   蛇以青蛙和老鼠為食。

＊ vulture [ˈvʌltʃɚ] n. 兀鷹
carcass [ˈkɑrkəs] n. 動物的屍體

Lesson 104

Killing Is No Solution

屠殺並非解決之道

Dialogue 實用會話

Two Australians, Mack and Jill, are camping on Kangaroo Island. (M=Mack; J=Jill)

M: Look! There's a koala hugging a tree. They're really so cute. Jill, why are you crying?

J: The government's planning on killing them because they may starve to death soon.

M: What a stupid idea! They should try saving them instead.

J: I agree. Let's start a campaign to save them. If we can find 5,000 people to each take one home, the problem will be solved.

M: That's a good idea. You know, there're about 18 million people in Australia. Five thousand is only 0.027 percent of the population.

J: Let's do it then.

M: Killing as a solution to a problem is just not right.

J: You can say that again.

兩名澳洲人，梅克和吉兒，正在袋鼠島上露營。

梅克：妳看！有隻無尾熊抱在樹上。它們真的好可愛。吉兒，妳怎麼哭了？

吉兒：政府正計畫宰殺牠們，因為牠們可能很快就會餓死了。

梅克：真是個愚蠢的主意！他們應當改而設法去拯救牠們才對。

吉兒：我同意。咱們發起一個活動來拯救牠們吧。如果我們能找到五千個人，讓每個人各帶一隻回家的話，問題就可以解決了。

梅克：好點子。妳是知道的，澳洲的人口大約有一千八百萬。五千只不過是總人口數的十萬分之二十七。

吉兒：那麼我們就這樣做。

梅克：用宰殺來當作問題的解決之道是不對的。

吉兒：你說的對極了。

Key Points 重點提示

1. **solution** [səˈluʃən] n. 解決方法 (與介詞 to 並用)

   a solution to the/a problem　　問題的解決方法

   例: Physical violence is not a solution to a problem.
   (肢體暴力不是解決問題的方法。)

2. **plan on + 動名詞**　　計畫……

   = plan to + 原形動詞

   例: I plan on studying abroad next year.
   (我計畫明年出國唸書。)

3. **try** [traɪ] vt. 嘗試, 試用 & vi. 設法, 努力

   try + 動名詞　　嘗試……

   try to + 原形動詞　　設法/試圖……

注意:

try 表『嘗試』時,用動名詞或名詞作受詞,旨在強調試試某種方法或某件事; try 若表『設法/試圖/努力』時,則用不定詞片語 (to +原形動詞) 作受詞,旨在強調企圖要做某件事。

例: Let's try asking the bank for a loan.
(咱們向銀行貸款試試看。)

Have you ever tried that fruit before?
(你曾嚐過那種水果嗎?)

We should try to be polite to others.
(我們應該設法對別人有禮貌。)

4. **instead** [ɪn'stɛd] adv. (反) 而; 相反地

注意:

instead 可置於句首使用, 譯成『相反地』, 等於 on the contrary; 亦可置於句尾 (如本文)。

例: I invited Lily for dinner. Instead, her brother Andy came over.
(我邀請莉莉共進晚餐;然而,來的卻是她的哥哥安迪。)

Dad sent Little Johnny to the store for some beer. He came home with milk instead.
(老爸叫小強尼去商店買些啤酒,他卻買了牛奶回來。)

5. **campaign** [kæm'pen] n. 活動

例: Mr. Doe's campaign to be the next president is going very well.
(杜先生競選下任總統的活動進行得很順利。)

6. **0.027 percent** 百分之零點零二七, 十萬分之二十七
= 0.027%

注意:

0.027 的英文唸法為"zero point zero two seven", 意即小數點後數字的讀音為逐字唸出, 因此 123.321 讀為"one hundred (and) twenty-three point three two one"。

7. **You can say that again.** 你說的對極了。

例: Sharon: Isn't Dave cute?

Diane: You can say that again.

(莎朗：戴夫很迷人，是不是呢？)

(黛安：妳說的對極了。)

請選出下列各句中正確的一項

1. This matter has been reported to the ______.
   (A) concerned authorities (B) authorities concerned
   (C) concerned authority (D) authority concerned

2. The Kremlin is located ______ central Moscow.
   (A) in (B) at (C) on (D) to

3. Many Asian peasants mainly ______ rice.
   (A) feed (B) live (C) feed on (D) live on

4. Rachel plans ______ suprising her husband on his birthday.
   (A) for (B) with (C) on (D) to

解答：

1. (B) 2. (A) 3. (D) 4. (C)

Lesson 105

I Want to Marry Your Wife

我想娶你老婆

Reading 閱讀

Strange people do strange things. Aging German millionaire Walter Thiele certainly fits the bill. Recently, he put advertisements in newspapers to find someone to "look after" his wife and his fortune after he dies. Needless to say, thousands of letters poured in from all over the world. Some young men even showed up at Walter's home. Once, when he opened the door, a young man said, "I want to marry your wife."

If you think that's funny, so does Walter. The problem is he isn't getting much sleep. So in order to get away for a while, he's taking his beautiful young wife on a round-the-world trip. Well, I guess it takes all kinds of people to make up the world.

奇怪的人做奇怪的事。逐漸年邁的德國百萬富翁華特・西里無疑正是這種人。最近，他在報紙上刊登廣告要找人在他死後來『照顧』他的妻子和財產。不用說，上千封的信件由世界各地如雪片般飛來。有些年輕男子甚至出現在華特家。有一次，當他開門時，有個年輕男子對他說：『我想娶你老婆。』

如果你認為這件事很好笑，華特也是這樣想。問題是，他現在連覺都睡不好。因此，為了要遠離這種困擾一陣子，他正帶他那年輕貌美的老婆環遊世界。呃，我看這世界真是什麼樣的人都有。

Vocabulary & Idioms 單字 & 片語註解

1. **aging** [ˈedʒɪŋ] a. 逐漸衰老的 (現在分詞作形容詞用) & n. 衰老, 老化
   aged [ˈedʒɪd] a. 年邁的; 老舊的
   例: My aging pet dog can hardly walk.
   (我那隻逐漸衰老的愛犬幾乎走不動了。)
   Can you stop the process of aging?
   (你能阻止衰老嗎？)
   The aged building is on the verge of collapsing.
   (那棟老舊的建築物快倒塌了。)
   * on the verge of.... 在……的邊緣
   verge [vɝdʒ] n. 邊緣

2. **millionaire** [ˌmɪljəˈnɛr] n. 百萬富翁
   billionaire [ˌbɪljəˈnɛr] n. 億萬富翁
   例: A millionaire is not considered to be very rich these days.
   (百萬富翁在現在不被認為很有錢了。)

3. **fit the bill**　完全符合情形、目的或要求

fit [fɪt] vt. 符合 & vi. 合適, 適宜 & a. 健康的

stay fit　保持健康

例: The interviewee fits the bill.
(那個應徵者符合條件。)

The plug won't fit into this socket.
(那個插頭和這個插座不合。)

Jeff jogs every day to stay fit.
(傑夫每天慢跑保持健康。)

4. **advertisement** [ˌædvɚˈtaɪzmənt] n. 廣告 (通常簡寫為 ad [æd])

put / place　an advertisement/ad　刊登廣告

例: Nancy put an ad in the newspaper looking for an apartment to rent.
(南西在報紙上刊登廣告，想要租一間公寓。)

5. **look after...**　照料/照顧……

take after...　長得像……

例: Mr. Williams looks after his dog as if it were his son.
(威廉斯先生照料他的狗兒就好像牠是他兒子一樣。)

Alan takes after his father and they are both lawyers.
(艾倫長得像他父親，而且他們兩個都是律師。)

6. **fortune** [ˈfɔrtʃən] n. 財產, 財富

make a fortune　發財

例: There's a fortune to be made in this kind of business.
(做這種生意可以賺錢。)

7. **pour in**　大量湧入, 蜂湧而至

pour [pɔr] vi. 蜂擁

例: Money began to pour in after he started his own business.
(自從他自創事業後，金錢便開始滾滾而來。)

8. **show up** 出現
= turn up
= appear [əˈpɪr] vi.
例: The singer didn't show up at his own concert.
(那名歌手沒有在自己的演唱會中出現。)

9. **If you think that's funny, so does Walter.**
= If you think that's funny, Walter also thinks that's funny.
如果你認為這件事很好笑, 華特也是這樣想。

10. **get away** 暫時離開工作以放鬆身心
例: After the project, I need to get away for a while.
(完成這項工作後，我需要拋開一切去輕鬆一陣子。)

11. **for a while** 一會兒, 一陣子
例: I guess I'm going to stay here for a while.
(我想我會在這裡待上一陣子。)

12. **round-the-world** [ˌraʊndðəˈwɝld] a. 環遊世界的
例: The big prize is a round-the-world airline ticket.
(大獎是一張環遊世界的機票。)

Grammar Notes 文法重點

本課介紹"Needless to say, 主詞 + 動詞" (不用說,……) 的用法, 及"make up..." (組成/構成……) 的用法, 並複習"thousands of + 複數名詞" (數以千計的……) 和"It takes + 表條件的名詞 (人或物均可) + to + 原形動詞" (從事……需要……條件) 的用法。

1. **Needless to say, thousands of letters poured in from all over the world.**

不用說, 上千封的信件由世界各地如雪片般飛來。

a. Needless to say, 主詞 + 動詞　　不用說,……

= It goes without saying + that 子句

注意:

"Needless to say, 主詞 + 動詞"乃由"It is needless to say + that 子句"化簡而來, 因經常使用, 已成固定用法。但使用"It goes without saying..."時, 則其後一定要接 that 引導的名詞子句, 而不可化簡。

例: Needless to say, every parent loves his or her own child.
(不用說，每個做父母的都愛自己的小孩。)

It goes without saying that a good son will always take care of his parents.
(不用說，好兒子會一直照顧他的雙親。)

b. thousands of + 複數名詞　　數以千計的……

dozens of + 複數名詞　　數十的……

hundreds of + 複數名詞　　數以百計的……

tens of thousands of + 複數名詞

數以萬計的……(係由 ten thousand『一萬』變化而成)

hundreds of thousands of + 複數名詞

數以十萬計的……(係由 one hundred thousand『十萬』變化而成)

millions of + 複數名詞　　數以百萬計的……

tens of millions of + 複數名詞

數以千萬計的……(係由 ten million『千萬』變化而成)

* 上列片語中的複數名詞前不可置定冠詞 the 或所有格 my、his、her...等, 即無"hundreds of the/his students"的用法。

例: Hundreds of the people demonstrated in front of the police station. (×)

→ Hundreds of people demonstrated in front of the police station.
(數好百人在警察局前示威。)

* demonstrate [ˈdɛmənˌstret] vi. 舉行示威運動

Hundreds of thousands of people died in the war.
(數十萬人死於那場戰爭中。)

Millions of dollars were wasted as a result of his carelessness.
(由於他的粗心，浪費了好幾百萬元。)

注意:

上列數量詞(hundred、thousand...)前若有明確數字，而其後有介詞of時，則此時其後的複數名詞前須置定冠詞the或所有格my、his、her...等。

例: Two hundred of the monkeys in the jungle were captured.
(叢林裡猴子中有兩百隻被捕了。)

A hundred of my friends came to my wedding.
(我的朋友中有一百個人來參加我的婚禮。)

2. **Well, I guess it takes all kinds of people to make up the world.**
呃，我看這世界真是什麼樣的人都有。

a. It takes + 表條件的名詞 (人或物均可) + to + 原形動詞
從事……需要……(條件)

注意:

在上列用法中，It 為虛主詞，代替其後的不定詞片語 (to + 原形動詞)，此不定詞片語才是真主詞。

例: It takes nine people to make up a baseball team.
(組成一支棒球隊需要九個人。)

It takes imagination to be a writer.
(要當作家需要有想像力。)

b. make up... 組成/構成……
= compose...
* compose [kəm'poz] vt. 組成，構成
被動用法:
be made up of... 由……組成/構成；包含……
= be composed of...

= consist of...

* consist [kən'sɪst] vi. (由……) 組成

例: We need one more player to make up a basketball team.

= We need one more player to compose a baseketball team.
(我們還差一位球員才能組成籃球隊。)

The small trading company is made up of the boss, a secretary and two clerks.

= The small trading company is composed of the boss, a secretary and two clerks.

= The small trading company consists of the boss, a secretary and two clerks.
(這家小貿易公司的成員包括老闆、秘書和兩位職員。)

1. **Thousands of letters poured in from all over the world.**
   Hundreds of fans waited for the pop singer's arrival at the airport.
   The mistake cost the boss hundreds of thousands of dollars.
   好幾千封信件由世界各地如雪片般飛來。
   數百名歌迷在機場等待那位流行歌手的抵達。
   那個錯誤讓老闆損失了數十萬元。

2. **I guess it takes all kinds of people to make up the world.**
   It takes courage to go skydiving.
   It takes patience to teach young children.
   我看這世界真是什麼樣的人都有。
   高空跳傘需要勇氣。
   教小孩子需要耐心。

Lesson 106

You've Got to Be Kidding!

愛說笑！

Walter answers the door at his home.

(S=stranger; W=Walter)

S: Hi! I'm from Russia. My name is Vodka. I want to marry your wife.

W: With a name like that, I'm not sure she'll want to marry you.

S: So, what kind of man does she like?

W: You need to be strong, handsome and have a good sense of humor.

S: No problem. I guess I qualify then.

W: You've got to be kidding! One look at you and my wife is bound to burst out laughing.

S: Where is she anyway? Can I meet her?

W: I'm afraid she might kick the bucket before me if she meets you. Goodbye!

S: What a jerk!

華特在他家門口應門。
陌生人：嗨！我來自俄國，我叫做伏特加 (俄羅斯一種烈酒亦稱『伏特加』)，我想娶你老婆。
華　特：你的名字那麼奇怪，我可沒把握她會嫁給你。
陌生人：那麼，她喜歡什麼樣的男人呢？
華　特：強壯、英俊而且具有幽默感的。
陌生人：沒問題，我想我符合這個條件。
華　特：愛說笑！我老婆只要看你一眼，一定會忍不住大笑起來。
陌生人：不管怎麼樣，她到底在哪裡？我可以見她嗎？
華　特：我怕她見到你會比我還早死呢。再見！
陌生人：真是個笨蛋！

Key Points 重點提示

1. **You've got to be kidding!**　　愛說笑！
= You must be kidding!
= You must be joking!

kid [kɪd] vi. & vt. 開玩笑

例: She is not crying; she's only kidding.
(她並沒有在哭，她不過是開玩笑而已。)
Don't kid me; are you really quitting your job?
(別開我玩笑了，你真地要辭掉工作嗎？)

2. **answer** [ˈænsɚ] vt. (對於敲門、電話等之) 回答

answer the door　　應門
answer one's call　　回應／接某人的電話

例: Could someone answer the door, please? I'm in the washroom.
(有沒有人可以應一下門，拜託？我在洗手間裡。)

My girlfriend is mad at me; she won't answer my calls.
(我女朋友在生我的氣，她不肯接我的電話。)

3. **人 + be from + 國名**　　某人來自某國, 某人是某國人

例: That pretty girl is from Canada.
(那個美女是加拿大人。)

4. **handsome** [ˈhænsəm] a. 英俊的

例: He thinks he's handsome, but in fact, he's not.
(他認為他很帥；但實際上，他並不帥。)

5. **humor** [ˈhjumɚ] n. 幽默

humorous [ˈhjumərəs] a. 幽默的, 風趣的

a sense of humor　　幽默感

例: Jim has a sense of humor; that's why people like him.
(吉姆有幽默感，那就是人們喜歡他的原因。)

You must be humorous to be a comedian.
(想成為一名喜劇演員得有幽默感。)

6. **qualify** [ˈkwɑləˌfaɪ] vi. 合格, 取得資格 & vt. 使有資格, 使合格

qualified [ˈkwɑləˌfaɪd] a. 有資格的

be qualified to + 原形動詞　　有資格……

be qualified for + 名詞　　有資格……

例: It's a very competitive competition; only the top ten will qualify.
(這是項非常競爭的比賽，只有前十名才能取得資格。)

Dan's not qualified to be an accountant.
(阿丹沒有資格成為一名會計師。)

Do you think I'm qualified for that job?
(你認為我有資格做那份工作嗎？)

7. 本文:

One look at you and my wife is...　　只要看你一眼, 我老婆就……

注意:

數量詞 + 名詞 (,) and + 主詞 + 動詞　　……, (那麼)……

例: One punch and the boxer was knocked out.
(一次重擊，那位拳擊手便被打倒在地，爬不起來了。)

One more step and the boy would have fallen over the cliff.
(再走一步的話，那個男孩當時就會跌落懸崖了。)

8. **be bound to + 原形動詞**　　必定會……

例: Lazy Tom is bound to fail the exam.
(懶鬼湯姆一定會考不及格的。)

9. **burst out laughing/crying**　　突然大笑/大哭

= burst into laughter/tears

burst [bɝst] vi. 爆炸; 脹滿

動詞三態均為 burst。

注意:

laughter [ˈlæftɚ] n. 笑聲 (不可數名詞)

例: When Jenny burst out laughing, everyone was shocked.
= When Jenny burst into laughter, everyone was shocked.
(珍妮突然放聲大笑時，每個人都嚇了一跳。)

On hearing the sad news, Mrs. Lin burst out crying.
= On hearing the sad news, Mrs. Lin burst into tears.
(一聽到那則壞消息，林太太便放聲大哭了起來。)

10. **kick the bucket**　　翹辮子, 死了

bucket [ˈbʌkɪt] n. 水桶

注意:

bucket 本意為『水桶』之意, kick the bucket 可能源於古人在上吊時常會站在水桶上, 把頭往繩索上一套, 然後用腳把水桶踢開, 便一命嗚呼, 上西天去了。

例: Many people kick the bucket from smoking cigarettes.
(有許多人因為抽煙而翹辮子。)

請選出下列各句中正確的一項

1. The jury ______ seven ordinary citizens.
   (A) composes of (B) consists of
   (C) makes up (D) makes up of

2. ______ to say, everyone must make a living.
   (A) Truly (B) Doubtless
   (C) Needless (D) Frankly

3. Two ______ the people in the riot were arrested.
   (A) hundred of (B) hundred
   (C) hundreds of (D) hundreds

4. The mother burst ______ tears when she learned that her son had died in the war.
   (A) into (B) out (C) out of (D) of

5. If you need a job, just ______ an ad in the newspaper.
   (A) make (B) print (C) throw (D) place

解答：

1. (B) 2. (C) 3. (A) 4. (A) 5. (D)

Lesson 107

Heavy and Chubby

胖嘟嘟

Watch out, all you chubby guys out there! If you continue to overeat, you might be just like Michael Hebrank.

He's 43 years old. He can't walk. He can stand up for no more than 30 seconds at a time. He has to use an oxygen mask to help him breathe. And he weighs 1,000 pounds (455 kilograms) . He once became seriously ill and couldn't get out of the house. In the end, he had to be forklifted out after the front wall of his house was torn down. Poor Michael says, "Once I start eating, I can't stop." So if you're on the heavy side, take care lest you become another Michael.

各位胖哥胖姐注意了！如果你們繼續暴飲暴食，可能就會變得和麥可・赫布蘭克一樣。

他今年才四十三歲就已寸步難行。他每次站立的時間沒辦法超過三十秒。他必須帶氧氣罩來幫助呼吸。此外，他體重高達一千磅 (四百五十五公斤)。有一次他病得很嚴重而且擠不出家門。最後，他房子正面的那道牆壁被拆掉後，他才被用堆高機搬出去。可憐的麥可說：『我一旦開始吃東西就停不下來。』所以如果你的體重偏高，那就要注意了，以免變成另一個麥可。

Vocabulary & Idioms 單字 & 片語註解

1. **heavy** [ˈhɛvɪ] a. 重的

例: These army boots are really heavy.
(這雙軍靴真地很重。)

2. **chubby** [ˈtʃʌbɪ] a. 圓胖的

例: The chubby little boy is the teacher's pet.
(那個胖嘟嘟的小男孩是老師的愛徒。)

3. **Watch out, all you chubby guys out there!**

= All you chubby guys out there, please watch out!
= Those who are fat should be careful!
各位胖哥胖姐注意了！

* 此處 guys 使用複數, 可表『眾男人』或『眾女人』, 或『眾男女』, 但若為單數時, 則一定指男人, 表某個傢伙。

4. **overeat** [ˌovəˈit] vi. 吃得過多, 飲食過量

動詞三態: overeat、overate [ˌovəˈet]、overeaten [ˌovəˈitən]。

例: John vomited because he overate.
(約翰因吃太多而吐了出來。)

5. **at a time** 一次

例: The man can play several musical instruments at a time.
(那個男子能一次彈奏數種樂器。)

6. **oxygen** [ˈɑksədʒən] n. 氧氣

7. **mask** [mæsk] n. 面罩; 面具

例: The bank robbers wore masks.
(那些銀行搶匪都戴面罩。)

8. **breathe** [brið] vi. 呼吸

例: It's hard to breathe in the polluted air of the city.
(要在這個空氣污染的城市中呼吸很困難。)

9. **pound** [paʊnd] n. 磅

10. **kilogram** [ˈkɪləˌgræm] n. 公斤

11. **seriously** [ˈsɪrɪəslɪ] adv. 嚴重地; 嚴肅地, 認真地

例: Fortunately, no one was seriously hurt in the accident.
(幸好，沒有人在這次事故中受到重傷。)

Anna takes her work very seriously.
(安娜非常認真看待她的工作。)

12. **in the end** 最後

in the beginning 起初, 剛開始
= at first

例: In the beginning, nobody liked the new student but in the end, he was popular with everyone.
(起初，沒有人喜歡那位新來的學生，但後來他很受大家歡迎。)

13. **forklift** [ˈfɔrkˌlɪft] vt. 用堆高機搬運

例: You'll have to forklift these rocks to clear the road.
(你們將得用堆高機搬運這些石塊以清除路面。)

＊ forklift truck 則為『堆高機』。

14. **tear down...**　　拆除……
= tear...down
tear [tɛr] vt. 拆, 卸
動詞三態: tear、tore [tɔr]、torn [tɔrn]。
例: The government tore down all the illegal sign boards in the city.
(政府拆除全市所有非法的看板。)

15. **lest** [lɛst] conj. 以免
例: We left early lest we should be late for our appointment.
(我們很早便出發了,以免約會遲到。)

Grammar Notes 文法重點

本課主要介紹 if 形成的假設語氣用法, 以及"lest...(should)..." (以免……) 的用法。

1. 假設語氣是一種表示假設狀態的句型, 乃由副詞連接詞 if 引導的副詞子句與主要子句構成, 整個句意相當於中文的『如果……的話,……就……』之意。一般而言, if 形成的假設語氣依時態的不同有下列四種句型:
   a. 表示純條件的假設語氣
   使用純條件的假設語氣時, if 子句的動詞用現在式, 主要子句中則要使用現在式助動詞。句型如下:
   If + 主詞 + 現在式動詞, 主詞 + 現在式助動詞 (will、can、may、should、must、ought to) + 原形動詞
   例: If you eat so much candy, you will get sick.
   (如果你吃下這麼多糖果,會生病的。)
   ＊由本例判斷, 我們並不知道你是否已經吃下這麼多糖果, 只知道你若吃了, 就會生病。

If Dan <u>is</u> broke, he <u>ought to</u> get a job.
(如果阿丹一文不名，他就該去找份工作。)

＊由本例判斷, 我們並不知道丹是否一文不名, 只知他若一文不名, 就該去找份工作。

本課閱讀部分中 if 形成的假設語氣即屬此用法:

If you <u>continue</u> to overeat, you <u>might</u> be just like Michael Hebrank.
(如果你們繼續暴飲暴食，可能就會像麥可・赫布蘭克一樣。)

＊本句主要子句中的 might 雖為過去式助動詞, 但乃表較小的可能性, 故屬正確用法, 若使用 may 時, 則表較高的可能性。

So if you<u>'re</u> on the heavy side, <u>(you should)</u> take care lest you become another Michael.
(所以如果你的體重偏重，那就要注意了，以免變成另一個麥可。)

＊本句的主要子句為一命令句, 其前省略了 you should, 故屬正確用法。

b. 表示與現在事實相反的假設語氣

使用本假設語氣時, if 子句的動詞用過去式, 主要子句中則要用過去式助動詞。句型如下:

If＋主詞＋過去式動詞, 主詞＋過去式助動詞 (would、could、might、should、ought to)＋原形動詞

例: If I <u>had</u> money, I <u>would</u> buy a house.
(如果我有錢，就會買棟房子。——但我現在沒錢。)

If I <u>could</u> help you, I certainly <u>would</u> do so.
(如果我能幫你，就一定會幫助你。——但我現在無法幫你。)

注意:

此用法中, if 引導的子句若有 be 動詞時, 則不論主詞為第幾人稱, 一律使用 were。

例: If I <u>were</u> you, I would get married as soon as possible.
(如果我是你，就會儘快結婚。)

c. 表示與過去事實相反的假設語氣

使用本假設語氣時, if 子句的動詞要用過去完成式, 主要子句則是用過去式助動詞, 再加『have + 過去分詞』。句型如下:

If + 主詞 + had + 過去分詞, 主詞 + 過去式助動詞 (would、could、might、should、ought to) + have + 過去分詞

例: If I had had time and money, I would have traveled around the world.
(如果我當時有時間和財力的話，早就去環遊世界了。——但我當時並沒有時間和財力，所以我也沒有去環遊世界)

If you had come earlier, you would have met her.
(如果你那時早點到的話，就可以見到她了。——但你那時並未早點到，所以你也沒有見到她)

d. 表示與未來狀況相反的假設語氣

表示與未來狀況相反的假設語氣中, if 子句要使用助動詞 should, 表示『萬一』或『如果真是』的意思,且由於未來狀況難以預料, 因此如果我們認為未來的狀況極可能發生時, 主要子句的助動詞可使用現在式, 以表極大的可能; 但我們若認為未來的狀況不太可能發生時, 則主要子句的助動詞可使用過去式, 以表示較低的可能性。

句型如下:

1) 高可能性

If + 主詞 + should + 原形動詞, 主詞 + 現在式助動詞 (will、can、may、should、ought to) + 原形動詞

例: If you should become bankrupt, I will give you some financial help.
(萬一你破產的話，我會給你一些財務上的幫助。——我想你有可能破產)

2) 低可能性

If + 主詞 + should + 原形動詞, 主詞 + 過去式助動詞 (would、could、might、should、ought to) + 原形動詞

例: If you should come to my hometown, I would throw a big party.

(如果你真來我家鄉的話，我會舉行一個盛大的派對。——我想你不太可能會來)

2. **So if you're on the heavy side, take care lest you become another Michael.**

= So if you're on the heavy side, take care lest you should become another Michael.

所以如果你的體重偏重, 那就要注意了, 以免變成另一個麥可。

上列句中, 使用了"lest... (should) ..." (以免……) 句型, lest為副詞連接詞, 引導副詞子句以修飾主要子句, 且該子句中只能用助動詞 should, 但 should 常予以省略, 而直接接原形動詞。

lest... (should) ...　　以免……; 唯恐……

例: If you're a workaholic, take care lest you (should) get sick.
(如果你是個工作狂，那就應保重身體以免病倒。)

注意:

表示『以免』涵義時, 亦可用"for fear that...may/might..."或"for fear of + 動名詞"表示; 主要子句為現在式時, may 或 might 均可使用, 但主要子句為過去式時, 則只能用 might, 且不論使用 may 或 might, 一律不可省略。

lest...(should)...　以免……;唯恐……
= for fear that...may/might...
= for fear of + 動名詞

例: If you go swimming, you should wear a safety jacket lest you (should) drown.
= If you go swimming, you should wear a safety jacket for fear that you may/might drown.
= If you go swimming, you should wear a safety jacket for fear of drowning.
(如果你去游泳，應該要穿救生衣以免溺水。)

Jason studied harder lest he (should) fail the exam again.

= Jason studied harder <u>for fear that</u> he <u>might fail</u> the exam again.
= Jason studied harder <u>for fear of failing</u> the exam again.
(傑生更加努力用功以免再次考不及格。)

Substitution 代換

1. **If you continue to overeat, you might be just like Michael Hebrank.**
   If I were you, I would not buy that apartment.
   If Dan had been more caring, his wife would not have left him.
   如果你們繼續暴飲暴食, 你們可能就會像麥可・赫布蘭克一樣。
   如果我是你的話, 我不會買那間公寓的。
   如果當時阿丹能更關心的話, 他老婆就不會離開他了。
2. **So if you're on the heavy side, take care lest you become another Michael.**
   Jeff gets up early lest he should be late for school.
   Sam washed his face lest he should fall asleep studying.
   所以如果你的體重偏重, 那就要注意了, 以免變成另一個麥可。
   傑夫總是早起, 以免上學遲到。
   山姆洗了把臉, 以免讀書時睡著了。

Lesson 108

Muscular My Foot!

強壯個頭！

Dialogue 實用會話

Jill is talking to her boyfriend, Mack.

(J=Jill; M=Mack)

J: You'd better watch your diet, Mack. You're getting really fat!

M: It's alright. I'm not fat. I'm muscular.

J: Muscular my foot! You're flabby. Do you want to be another Michael Hebrank?

M: Are you kidding? That guy weighed 1,000 pounds. He was a couch potato.

J: Well, you're not far from that.

M: Come on! I'm a big guy.

J: Well, either you lose weight or I'm out of here.

M: Gee, don't you know that the best way to a man's heart is through his stomach?

J: Yes. But in your case, there's so much fat around your stomach, I'll never make it to your heart.

吉兒正在和她的男友麥克談話。
吉兒：你最好注意你的飲食，麥克。你愈來愈胖了！
麥克：沒關係啦。我不是胖，我是強壯。
吉兒：強壯個頭！你是肌肉鬆軟。你想變成另一個麥可・赫布蘭克嗎？
麥克：開什麼玩笑？那傢伙有一千磅重。他整天都坐著看電視。
吉兒：這個嘛，你也好不到哪裡去。
麥克：拜託！我是個魁梧的男子漢。
吉兒：呃，你要是不減肥，我就走人。
麥克：天啊，難道妳不知道想抓住男人的心最好先抓住他的胃嗎？
吉兒：我知道。但是就你的情況來說，你胃的四周有那麼多脂肪，我永遠也別想抓到你的心。

Key Points 重點提示

1. **muscular** [ˈmʌskjələ˞] a. 肌肉發達的, 強壯的

例: Tom's wife is more muscular than he.
(湯姆的太太比他還強壯。)

2. **名詞/形容詞 + my foot!** ……才怪/個頭！(口語用法)

例: A: Your husband is really nice.
B: Nice my foot!
(甲：妳老公真好。)
(乙：好個頭！)

A: He is a real hero.
B: Hero my foot!
(甲：他真是個英雄。)
(乙：英雄個頭！)

3. **diet** [ˈdaɪət] n. 飲食; (為了治療、調節體重而吃的) 規定飲食

watch one's diet　　注意飲食

go on a diet　　節食, 按規定飲食

例: The doctor advised my mother to watch her diet.
(醫師勸告我媽媽要注意飲食。)

Tina is going on a diet because all her clothes don't fit her anymore.
(蒂娜正在節食，因為她的衣服都穿不下了。)

4. **alright** [ɔlˈraɪt] a. 沒關係的, 沒問題的
= all right

例: John thinks it's alright to be late for work once in a while.
(約翰認為上班偶爾遲到沒有關係。)

5. **fat** [fæt] a. 肥胖的 & n. 脂肪 (不可數)
fatty [ˈfætɪ] a. 油膩的, 脂肪過多的
fattening [ˈfætənɪŋ] a. 令人發胖的

例: Mike may be fat but he's in good health.
(麥克也許胖，但他健康狀況良好。)

James likes to eat the lean part of the meat whereas his wife likes to eat the fat.
(詹姆士喜歡吃瘦肉，他太太則喜歡吃肥肉。)
* lean [lin] a. 瘦的

Too much fatty food is really not good for anyone.
(脂肪過多的食品真的對任何人都不好。)

Hamburgers and hot dogs are fattening.
(漢堡和熱狗會令人發胖。)

6. **flabby** [ˈflæbɪ] a. 肌肉鬆軟的

例: The flabby man takes ten minutes to walk up this flight of steps.
(那個肌肉鬆軟的男子要花十分鐘走上這段樓梯。)

7. **couch potato** [ˈkautʃ pəˌteto] n. 整天坐著看電視的人, 電視迷

注意:

couch 原意為『長椅, 沙發』, potato 則為『馬鈴薯』, couch potato 乃指長期坐在沙發上看電視啥事也不做, 甚至變得肥胖的人, 也許因肥胖又坐在沙發上狀似馬鈴薯而有此稱呼。不過, 現今, 本字已被引申為『電視迷』。

例: Tim is a couch potato; he watches TV all day long.
(提姆是個電視迷，他整天都在看電視。)

8. **be far from + 名詞/形容詞**　　一點兒也不……, 遠非……

= be not + 名詞/形容詞 + at all

* 此處的 far from 視為副詞, 置於 be 動詞之後, 等於 not...at all (一點兒也不)。

例: What the man said is far from the truth.
= What the man said is not the truth at all.
(那個男子所說的絕不是實話。)

The couple are rich but far from happy.
= The couple are rich but not happy at all.
(那對夫妻很有錢，但一點也不快樂。)

9. **either + 主要子句 + or + 主要子句**　　要不……就是……

例: "Either you work harder or you're fired," shouted the boss.
(老闆大聲咆哮著：『你要不就更加努力工作，要不就走路。』)

10. **stomach** [ˈstʌmək] n. 胃

11. **make it to + 地方**　　到達某地

例: Rick overslept, so he had to take a taxi to make it to school on time.
(瑞克睡過頭了，所以他得搭計程車才能準時到校。)

請選出下列各句中正確的一項

1. Don't eat too much chocolate ______ you should get sick.
   (A) lest (B) if (C) unless (D) although

2. Dad turned down the music for fear ______ waking his children up.
   (A) into (B) about (C) off (D) of

3. If I ______ die before my wife, she will inherit everything I have.
   (A) should (B) would (C) might (D) could

4. Ken is far from ______; in fact, he's quite poor.
   (A) wealth (B) rich (C) richness (D) healthy

5. I ______ it home from my office today in less than ten minutes.
   (A) took (B) made (C) got (D) had

解答：

1. (A) 2. (D) 3. (A) 4. (B) 5. (B)

Lesson 109

A Very Special Juice

瓊漿玉液

Reading 閱讀

A Very Special Juice and *The Golden Fountain* are the titles of two books. They have sold hundreds of thousands of copies. Can you guess what they are about? They are guides to urine therapy. Don't laugh! Urine is big business these days. There's an annual market of US$500 million for products made from urine.

"It's a great aftershave," says one consumer. It's even used in many skin creams and perfumes. Besides, it is widely used as a kind of medicine. Believe it or not, a lady in America says she

drinks a glass of urine a day. At this point, you must excuse me; I have to go to the restroom.

《瓊漿玉液》和《黃金泉》是兩本書的書名。它們已經銷售了幾十萬本。你猜得出這兩本是什麼書嗎？它們是尿療法指南。別笑！尿液現今可是大行業，由尿提煉出來的產品每年有五億美元的市場。

有位消費者說：『尿液是很棒的刮鬍水。』它甚至被用在許多面霜和香水裡面。此外，它也被廣泛地當作一種藥品來使用。信不信由你，在美國有一位女士說她一天喝一杯尿。說到這裡，請恕我失陪一下，我得去一下洗手間。

Vocabulary & Idioms 單字&片語註解

1. **special** [ˈspɛʃəl] a. 特別的

   What's so special about...?　　……有什麼特別的？

   例: What's so special about owning a BMW?
   (擁有一輛寶馬車有啥特別呢？)

2. **juice** [dʒus] n. 果汁 (不可數)

   juicy [ˈdʒusɪ] a. 多汁的; 美味的

   例: I prefer apple juice to orange juice.
   (我比較喜歡蘋果汁而不喜歡柳橙汁。)

   My friend treated me to a juicy steak last night.
   (我朋友昨晚請我吃了塊多汁的牛排。)

3. **golden** [ˈgoldn̩] a. 黃金般的; 珍貴的

   gold [gold] n. 黃金 (不可數)

例: If you don't hurry up and call her, you will miss a golden opportunity to go out with her.
(如果你不快點打電話給她，就錯過了約她外出的好機會了。)

The ring I'm wearing is pure gold.
(我戴的這只戒指是純金的。)

4. **fountain** [ˈfaʊntn̩] n. 泉, 噴泉

例: The fountain spurts water according to the tempo of the music.
(那座噴泉依音樂的節拍噴出水來。)

* spurt [spɝt] vt. 噴出 (液體或氣體)
tempo [ˈtɛmpo] n. 節拍

5. **title** [ˈtaɪtl̩] n. 標題

6. **copy** [ˈkɑpɪ] n. 複本; 同類書的一本 (複數形為 copies)

例: One hundred thousand copies of the book were sold.
(這本書銷售了十萬本。)

7. **guide** [gaɪd] n. 指南, 手冊

be a guide to... 是……的指南

例: This booklet is a guide to child rearing.
(這本小冊子是育嬰指南。)

8. **urine** [ˈjʊrɪn] n. 小便, 尿

9. **therapy** [ˈθɛrəpɪ] n. 治療, (不需藥物或動手術的) 物理療法

例: After six months of therapy, the accident victim could walk again.
(在六個月的物理治療後，那名車禍受害人又能走路了。)

10. **business** [ˈbɪznɪs] n. 生意 (不可數); 商店; 工商企業 (可數)

do business 做生意

on business 出差

例: Our company does business with many European countries.
(我們公司和歐洲許多國家做生意。)

Mr. Li is in Rome on business.
(李先生正在羅馬出差。)
Many small businesses closed down during the recession.
(在不景氣時，許多小公司都倒閉了。)

11. **annual** [ˈænjuəl] a. 每年的

例: Most companies give their staff an annual pay raise.
(大部份的公司都會給予員工年度調薪。)

12. **aftershave** [ˈæftɚˌʃev] n. 刮鬍水

例: Aftershave not only smells good but also kills germs.
(刮鬍水不僅好聞而且還能殺菌。)

13. **consumer** [kənˈsumɚ] n. 消費者

例: Consumers have a right to get what they pay for.
(消費者有權利得到他們付費的東西。)

14. **skin cream** [ˈskɪn ˌkrim] n. 面霜

15. **perfume** [pɚˈfjum] n. 香水

注意:

skin cream 和 perfume 通常用作不可數名詞, 但若表『許多不同種類』的 skin cream 和 perfume, 則為可數名詞 (如本文)。

例: A bottle of perfume makes a good gift for a girlfriend.
(一瓶香水是送給女朋友很好的禮物。)

16. **widely** [ˈwaɪdlɪ] adv. 廣泛地

例: The tycoon is widely known for his generosity.
(那個大亨以其慷慨大方廣為人知。)

17. **Believe it or not,...** 信不信由你,……

例: Believe it or not, Bob became a millionaire at the age of twenty-five.
(信不信由你，鮑伯在二十五歲時成了百萬富翁。)

18. **At this point,...** 這個時候/說到這裡……

例: At this point, I think we should take a short break.
(說到這裡，我想我們應該休息一下。)

19. **restroom** ['rɛst,rum] n. (公共) 廁所

例: Molly used the restroom six times this morning because she has the runs.
(莫莉今早跑了六次廁所，因為她瀉肚子。)
* have the runs 拉肚子
拉肚子時會來回跑廁所, 故此處的 runs 應使用複數。

Grammar Notes 文法重點

本課複習一些名詞後習慣與介詞 to 並用的用法, 並介紹"Believe it or not, 主詞 + 動詞" (信不信由你,……)的用法, 以及分號 (;) 作連接詞的用法。

1. **They are guides to urine therapy.**
它們是尿療法指南。

注意:
在英文中, 凡表示『針對』某一問題或事件的解決方法、答案和要領等, 或表『通往……』之意時, 通常與介詞 to 並用; 此類常與介詞 to 並用的名詞常見的有下列:

a/the guide to + 名詞/動名詞 ……的指南
the key to the room 房間的鑰匙
the key to success 成功之鑰; 成功的要訣
the road to victory 勝利之路
an/the answer to the question 問題的答案
a/the solution to the problem 問題的解決方法

例: This booklet is a guide to household carpentry.
(這本小冊子是本家庭木工的指南。)
∗ carpentry [ˈkɑrpəntrɪ] n. 木工

The tenant needs a key to the room.
(那個房客需要一把房間的鑰匙。)
∗ tenant [ˈtɛnənt] n. 房客

Hard work is the key to success.
(努力是成功之鑰。)

Nobody knew the answer to the question.
(沒有人知道那個問題的答案。)

2. **Believe it or not, a lady in America says she drinks a glass of urine a day.**
信不信由你, 在美國有一位女士說她一天喝一杯尿。
Believe it or not, 主詞 + 動詞　　信不信由你,……
注意:
此用法乃由"Whether you believe it or not,..."變化而來, 因經常使用, 故將 Whether you believe it or not 簡化成 Believe it or not 之形式。使用時, 通常置於句首, 後加逗點, 再接主要子句。

例: Believe it or not, crime in my hometown is almost non-existant.
(信不信由你，在我的家鄉犯罪幾乎是不存在的。)

Whether you believe it or not, the ten-year-old boy is studying in the university.
(信不信由你，那個十歲男孩正在唸大學。)

3. **At this point, you must excuse me; I have to go to the restroom.**
說到這裡, 請恕我失陪一下, 我得去一下洗手間。
上列句中, 使用了分號 (;) 連接兩句的用法。
通常兩句在一起時, 中間須有連接詞相連, 若兩句間無連接詞連接時, 我們可用分號 (;) 連接兩句, 此時該分號 (;) 即等於 "逗點 (,) + 連接詞 (and、so、but...)"。

例: He is a man of principle; we all respect him.
= He is a man of principle, so we all respect him.
(他是個有原則的人，因此我們都尊敬他。)

He is a photographer; quite often he travels abroad to take pictures.
= He is a photographer, and quite often he travels abroad to take pictures.
(他是個攝影家，常常出國攝影。)

He is nice; no one likes him, though.
= He is nice, but no one likes him.
(他人很好，然而沒人喜歡他。)

注意:

我們在前面曾介紹過, 有些副詞如 however (然而)、therefore (因此) 等有連接詞的意味, 但卻不能作連接詞用, 此類副詞稱為連接性副詞, 故使用時, 前面要有分號 (;), 用以連接兩句。

例: He is nice, however, I don't like him. (×)
→ He is nice; however, I don't like him. (○)
= He is nice, but I don't like him.
(他人很好，然而我卻不喜歡他。)

She is kind, therefore, we all like her. (×)
→ She is kind; therefore, we all like her. (○)
= She is kind, so we all like her.
(她心腸好，因此我們全都喜歡她。)

Substitution 代換

1. **They are guides to urine therapy.**

   Hard work and honesty are the keys to success.

   After endeavoring for days, they finally found the solution to the problem.

   它們是尿療法指南。

   努力工作和誠實是成功的秘訣。

   在努力數日後, 他們終於找到問題的解決方法。

2. **Believe it or not, a lady in America says she drinks a glass of urine a day.**

   Believe it or not, some people say there's life on Mars.

   Believe it or not, Jeff says he saw a UFO last night.

   信不信由你, 在美國有一位女士說她一天喝一杯尿。

   信不信由你, 有人說火星上有生命。

   信不信由你, 傑夫說他昨晚看到了幽浮。

Lesson 110

I Prefer My Own Brand

我喜歡自己釀的

Dialogue
實用會話

Jenny and Frank are at a coffee shop.

(F=Frank; J=Jenny)

F: Did you read about the "special juice," Jenny?

J: Yeah. Isn't it disgusting?

F: Well, what gets me is how come so many people are using it.

J: It's incredible, isn't it?

F: Mind you, though, there might be some truth in the matter.

J: What? I can't believe what I'm hearing. Are you that naïve?

F: I'm not so sure. It might really work.

J: Gee, don't tell me you're interested in trying it.

F: Why not?

J: Tell you what, I've been drinking coffee all morning. I'll do you a favor...

F: Thanks, but I prefer my own brand.
(They break out laughing.)

珍妮和法蘭克在咖啡廳裡。
法蘭克：珍妮，妳讀過有關『瓊漿玉液』的報導嗎？
珍　妮：讀過啊。那不是很噁心嗎？
法蘭克：這個嘛，我搞不懂的是怎麼會有這麼多人在用這東西呢。
珍　妮：真是不可思議啊，不是嗎？
法蘭克：不過，告訴妳哦，這樣做也許有幾分道理。
珍　妮：什麼？我真不敢相信會聽到你這樣說。你就那麼天真嗎？
法蘭克：我並不是很有把握。那東西也許真的會有效。
珍　妮：天啊，你該不會也想試一試吧。
法蘭克：有何不可？
珍　妮：這樣好了，我喝了一早上的咖啡，就讓我來幫你個忙……。
法蘭克：謝了，不過我還是比較喜歡自己的品牌。
(兩人大笑起來。)

Key Points 重點提示

1. **prefer** [prɪ'fɝ] vt. 寧願, 較喜歡

prefer A to B　　喜歡 A 勝於喜歡 B

prefer + 動名詞 + to + 動名詞

= prefer to + 原形動詞 + rather than + 原形動詞

= prefer to + 原形動詞 + instead of + 動名詞

例: Saul prefers black coffee to tea.
(跟喝茶相比，蘇爾比較喜歡喝純咖啡。)

Jack prefers going to the beach to swimming in a pool.
(傑克比較喜歡到沙灘去而不喜歡在游泳池裡游泳。)

2. **disgusting** [dɪs'gʌstɪŋ] a. 令人作嘔/討厭的

disgusted [dɪs'gʌstɪd] a. 感到噁心/厭惡的

disgust [dɪs'gʌst] vt. 使作嘔, 使厭惡

例: Jim is in the habit of making disgusting sounds while eating.
(吉姆吃東西時習慣發出令人噁心的聲音。)

Anna is disgusted with her drunken husband.
(安娜非常厭惡她的酒鬼丈夫。)

Self-centered people disgust me.
(以自我為中心的人令我厭惡。)

3. **What gets + 人 + is...**

= What puzzles + 人 + is...
某人感到困惑/不明白的是……

* puzzle [ˈpʌzl̩] vt. 使困惑

例: What gets me is not what he did but how he did it.
(令我感到困惑的不是他做了什麼而是他怎麼做的。)

The speaker's remarks puzzled the audience.
(那個演說者的言論令聽眾一頭霧水。)

4. **Mind you,...** 告訴你,……(用作吸引對方的注意或提醒對方的開頭語)

例: Mind you, I don't mind being poor as long as I'm healthy.
(告訴你，只要我健康，我不介意貧窮。)

5. **naïve** [nɑˈiv] a. 天真的, 幼稚的

例: The naïve boy was easily led astray.
(那個天真的男孩很容易被別人帶壞。)

6. **be interested in...** 對……感到有興趣

例: My son is interested in social work.
(我兒子對社會工作有興趣。)

7. **favor** [ˈfevɚ] n. 好意, 善意; 贊成, 同意

do + 人 + a favor 幫某人一個忙

be in favor of... 贊同……

例: Sam did me a favor by babysitting for me last night.
(山姆昨晚幫了我一個忙，他幫我帶小孩。)

Many people are in favor of the death penalty.
(許多人都贊成死刑。)

8. **break out laughing/crying** 突然大笑/哭
= burst out laughing/crying
例: Whenever the teacher scolds Judy, she breaks out crying.
(每當老師責罵茱蒂，她總會嚎啕大哭。)

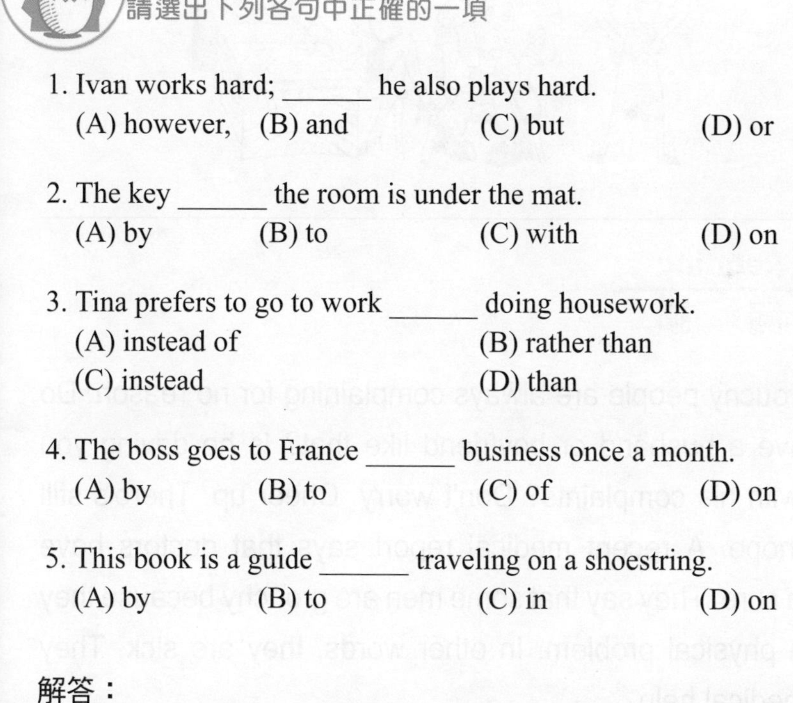

請選出下列各句中正確的一項

1. Ivan works hard; ______ he also plays hard.
(A) however, (B) and (C) but (D) or

2. The key ______ the room is under the mat.
(A) by (B) to (C) with (D) on

3. Tina prefers to go to work ______ doing housework.
(A) instead of (B) rather than
(C) instead (D) than

4. The boss goes to France ______ business once a month.
(A) by (B) to (C) of (D) on

5. This book is a guide ______ traveling on a shoestring.
(A) by (B) to (C) in (D) on

解答：

1. (A) 2. (B) 3. (A) 4. (D) 5. (B)

Lesson 111

Cheer Up!

高興點吧！

Reading 閱讀

Grouchy people are always complaining for no reason. Do you have a husband or boyfriend like that? Is he driving you crazy with his complaints? Don't worry. Cheer up. There's still some hope. A recent medical report says that doctors have found a cure. They say that some men are grouchy because they have a physical problem. In other words, they are sick. They need medical help.

So the next time your better half is grouchy, don't just sit there. Take him to the doctor's. There's one strange thing about the report, though. It doesn't say anything about grouchy girlfriends or wives.

滿腹牢騷的人總是毫無理由地抱怨。妳的老公或男友是否也是如此？他的那些抱怨是否逼得妳發瘋？別煩惱，高興點。還是有希望存在的。最近一項醫學報導指出，醫生們發現了一種療方。他們發現有些人愛發牢騷是因為身體上的毛病。換句話說，這些人有病了，他們需要醫治。

所以下次妳的另一半發牢騷時，別坐視不顧，帶他去看醫生。不過這項報導有一點怪，它對滿腹牢騷的女友或老婆隻字未提。

Vocabulary & Idioms
單字 & 片語註解

1. **cheer up** 高興/振作起來

例: Cheer up, Carlos! The worst is over.
(卡洛士，高興點！最糟的已過去了。)

2. **grouchy** [ˈgraʊtʃɪ] a. 滿腹牢騷的, 易怒的

grouch [graʊtʃ] n. 滿腹牢騷的人

例: A grouchy person will not have many friends.
(滿腹牢騷的人不會有許多朋友。)

Alice married a rich man who turned out to be a grouch.
(愛麗絲嫁給了一個有錢人，結果發現他是個滿腹牢騷的人。)

3. **complain** [kəmˈplen] vi. 抱怨, 發牢騷

complaint [kəmˈplent] n. 抱怨, 牢騷

例: Chris: Connie is complaining about her work again.
Claud: What's her complaint this time?

(克里斯：康妮又在抱怨她的工作了。)
(克勞德：這次是抱怨什麼呢？)

4. **for no reason** 毫無理由地, 無緣無故地

例: Jane burst out laughing for no reason at all.
(珍無緣無故突然大笑起來。)

5. **drive + 人 + crazy** 使某人發瘋

例: My mother-in-law is just driving me crazy.
(我岳母真是令我抓狂。)

6. **medical** [ˈmɛdɪkḷ] a. 醫學的

例: You need medical attention for that deep wound.
(你的傷口那麼深需要治療。)

7. **cure** [kjʊr] n. 治療方法 & vt. 治療, 治癒

cure + 人 + of + 疾病 治療/癒某人的疾病

例: There's no cure for AIDS as yet.
(目前愛滋病尚無療方。)

This Chinese medicine cured me of asthma.
(這種中藥治好了我的氣喘。)

8. **physical** [ˈfɪzɪkḷ] a. 身體的, 肉體的

mental [ˈmɛntḷ] a. 心理的, 精神的

例: The abbreviation for physical education is P.E.
(體育的縮寫為 P.E.。)

∗ abbreviation [əˌbrivɪˈeʃən] n. 縮寫

The paranoid woman is said to have a mental problem.
(聽說那個有妄想症的婦人精神上有問題。)

∗ paranoid [ˌpærəˈnɔɪd] a. 有妄想症的

9. **In other words, 主詞 + 動詞** 換言之,……

例: Willy is a loner; in other words, he's not very sociable.
(威利是個獨來獨往的人；換言之，他不喜歡和人交際。)

＊ loner [ˈlonɚ] n. 獨來獨往的人
sociable [ˈsoʃəbḷ] a. 好交際的

10. **better half** [ˈbɛtɚ ˌhæf] n. 另一半, 配偶

例: You'd better ask your better half if you can come for a drink with us.
(你最好問一下你的另一半看看你是否可以來和我們小酌一番。)

Grammar Notes 文法重點

本課介紹現在進行式的用法, 和動詞 complain 的用法, 以及"the＋所有格" 表示場所的用法, 並複習 though 作副詞表『不過、但是』的用法。

1. **Grouchy people are always complaining for no reason.**
滿腹牢騷的人總是毫無理由地抱怨。

Is he driving you crazy with his complaints?
他的那些抱怨是否逼得妳發瘋?

a. 一般使用現在進行式時, 通常用來表示現在正在做的動作。

例: Mary is doing her homework.
(瑪麗正在寫功課。)

He is watching TV.
(他正在看電視。)

She is reading the newspaper.
(她正在看報紙。)
但現在進行式亦可用來表示現在經常出現的常態情形, 如本文中的用法。

Whenever I go to visit Grandpa, he is sleeping.
(每次我去拜訪祖父時，他總是在睡覺。)

Joan is always <u>boasting about</u> how rich she is.
(瓊安總是誇耀自己有多富有。)
* boast [bost] vi. 自誇, 誇耀

b. complain [kəm′plen] vi. 抱怨, 不滿 & vt. 抱怨 (以 that 子句作受詞)
complaint [kəm′plent] n. 抱怨, 不滿; 控訴 (常與動詞 make 並用)

注意:

complain 是不及物動詞, 故其後不可直接加受詞, 而須先置介詞 about 或 of 後, 方可接受詞; 但 complain 亦可作及物動詞, 此時其後僅能接 that 引導的名詞子句作受詞。

complain about/of + 名詞/動名詞　　抱怨……

complain + that 子句　　抱怨……

make a complaint　　抱怨; 申訴

例: John complained about his neighbor's noisy children.
(約翰抱怨他鄰居吵鬧的小孩。)

The woman complained that her husband worked overtime every day.
(那位婦人抱怨她先生每天都加班。)

I'm going to make a complaint to the police if you don't stop playing loud music in the middle of the night.
(如果你還繼續在半夜大聲放音樂的話，我就要向警方申訴。)

2. **Take him to <u>the doctor's</u>.**
帶他去看醫生。

注意:

在英語中, 有定冠詞 the 引導的所有格若很清楚地表示出某人的職業時, 此時其後表示某人上班或工作場所的名詞可予以省略, 而直接用"the + 所有格"來表示該場所。此類"the + 所有格"常見的有下列數個:

the doctor's office/clinic → the doctor's　　醫生診療室/診所
the dentist's office → the dentist's　　牙醫診所
the grocery store → the grocer's　　食品雜貨店

the barber shop → the barber's　　　　　　理髮店
the butcher's shop → the butcher's　　　　　肉店

例: There are many patients waiting in line at the doctor's.
(有許多人在醫生診所裡排隊候診。)

Mom goes to the grocer's to buy food once a week.
(老媽一個禮拜到雜貨店去採購食品一次。)

David went to the barber's to have a haircut.
(大衛到理髮店去理髮。)

3. **There's one strange thing about the report, <u>though</u>.**
不過這項報導有一點很奇怪。

上列句中的though為副詞, 置於句尾, 表『不過、但是』, 即等於however之意, 但兩者用法不同; though 使用時可置於句中作插入語用, 兩旁置逗點, 亦可置於句尾, 其前加逗點; 而 however 使用時, 則可置於句首, 其後加逗點, 或置於兩子句中, 其前置分號, 其後加逗點, 亦可置於句中作插入語用, 兩旁以逗點相隔, 但較少置於句尾使用。

例: Helen is very pretty. I, though, don't like her.
= Helen is very pretty. I don't like her, though.
= Helen is very pretty. However, I don't like her.
= Helen is very pretty; however, I don't like her.
= Helen is very pretty. I, however, don't like her.
(海倫非常漂亮，但是我不喜歡她。)

I know you are angry with Jack. What can you do about it, though?
(我知道你很氣傑克，但是你又能怎樣呢？)

注意:

though 置於句首使用時, 則為副詞連接詞, 此時 though 可用 although 取代, 表『雖然』之意, 其所引導的副詞子句修飾句中的主要子句, 兩句中間以逗點相隔, 但此副詞子句亦可置於主要子句之後, 此時兩句間則不須用逗點。

例: Though Brad is old, he looks very young.
= Although Brad is old, he looks very young.
= Brad looks very young (al) though he is old.
(雖然布萊德年紀很大，但他看起來很年輕。)

Substitution 代　換

1. **Take him to the doctor's.**

   I went to the butcher's to buy a bone for my pet dog.

   If you have a toothache, you'd better go to the dentist's right away.

   帶他去看醫生。

   我到肉店去買了根骨頭給我的愛犬。

   如果你牙痛的話, 最好馬上去看牙醫。

2. **There's one strange thing about the report, though.**

   I want to go on vacation. I don't have any money, though.

   Helen is moody. She's honest, though.

   不過這項報導有一點很奇怪。

   我想去度假, 不過我沒錢。

   海倫雖然愛鬧情緒, 但她很誠實。

Lesson 112

What a Grouch!

好個抱怨鬼!

Barny and Sally are husband and wife. They're having dinner.
(B=Barny; S=Sally)

B: These water dumplings taste like tennis balls.

S: But they're your favorite dish!

B: Not the way you cook them.

S: Why are you so grouchy?

B: Why shouldn't I be? I've got a wife who can't cook, my kids are naughty and...

S: Hold it a minute. Maybe you are the problem!

B: Huh? How could that be?

S: There might be something wrong with you. You should see a doctor.

B: Huh? No way!

S: Why not?

B: Waiting in doctors' offices makes me grouchy.

巴尼和莎莉是夫妻，他們正在吃晚餐。
巴尼：這些水餃嚐起來像網球似的。
莎莉：可是這是你最愛吃的菜呀！
巴尼：可不是妳這種煮法。
莎莉：你怎麼會牢騷這麼多？
巴尼：怎麼不會？老婆不會做菜，孩子又頑皮而且……
莎莉：等一下，也許『你』才是問題所在！
巴尼：啊？那怎麼可能？
莎莉：你也許病了，應該去看醫生。
巴尼：啊？休想！
莎莉：為什麼不呢？
巴尼：在候診室等待會讓我火氣大。

Key Points 重點提示

1. **have dinner** 吃晚餐

注意:

表示『吃三餐/東西』的動詞, 可用 have 或 eat。

例: We have dinner at our grandparents' once a week.
= We eat dinner at our grandparents' once a week.
(我們一個禮拜一次在爺爺奶奶家吃晚餐。)

Have you had breakfast yet?
= Have you eaten breakfast yet?
(你吃過早餐了嗎？)

2. **dumpling** [ˈdʌmplɪŋ] n. 包餡的食品

例: Water dumplings are my favorite afternoon snack.
(水餃是我最喜歡的午後點心。)

3. **tennis ball** [ˈtɛnɪs ˌbɔl] n. 網球

4. **favorite** [ˈfevərɪt] a. 最喜愛的 & n. 最喜愛的人或物

例: Who is your favorite basketball player?
(誰是你最喜歡的籃球球員呢？)

5. **dish** [dɪʃ] n. 菜餚; 盤子

例: Mom made some special dishes on Dad's birthday.
(老媽在爸爸生日當天煮了幾道特別的菜餚。)

I always help my mom do the dishes after dinner.
(晚餐後，我都會幫我媽媽洗盤子。)

6. 本文:
Not the way you cook them.

= They're my favorite dish but I don't like them if you cook them the way you do.
它們是我喜愛吃的東西, 但如果按照你的煮法, 我就不會喜歡吃了。

＊ 此處 the way 有連接詞的功能, 譯成『按照』。

7. **naughty** [ˈnɔtɪ] a. 頑皮的

例: The teacher doesn't know how to deal with that naughty student.
(老師不知道要怎樣應付那位頑皮的學生。)

8. **Hold it a minute.** 等一下。慢著。

例: Emily: Let's go.
Clark: Hold it a minute. I'm not ready.
(愛蜜莉：咱們走吧。)
(克拉克：等一下，我還沒準備好。)

9. **No way!** 門兒都沒有! 休想!

例: Clerk: Can I get this done tomorrow?
Boss: No way!
(職員：我可以明天才做這件工作嗎？)
(老闆：休想！)

請選出下列各句中正確的一項

1. Her husband ______ his job day and night.
   (A) complains (B) complains about
   (C) complains with (D) complaints

2. The noise from the construction site is ______ me crazy.
   (A) putting (B) having (C) driving (D) helping

3. Stop ______ complaints of life.
   (A) taking (B) doing (C) making (D) planning

4. ______, Winnie! It's payday tomorrow!
   (A) Cheer up (B) I'm sorry (C) In other words (D) No wonder

5. Son: Can I use the car tonight?
   Father: ______
   (A) You're wrong. (B) Mind your own business!
   (C) Who cares anyway? (D) No way!

解答：

1. (B) 2. (C) 3. (C) 4. (A) 5. (D)

Lesson 113

Where's the Toilet?

廁所在哪兒？

Reading 閱讀

You're walking along the street. You need to go to the washroom desss...perately. What do you do? If you can't control yourself, you could be embarrassed to no end.

Don't worry. Someone in San Francisco has invented a self-cleaning public toilet. The toilet cleans itself. The seat goes back into the wall where it is washed and blow-dried. Even the floors are washed automatically. You must be quick, though. You've only got 20 minutes to "do your business." Then, there's a 2-minute warning before the door opens.When it does, you'd better be ready or your face will be red!

你正走在街上，非常非常想上洗手間。你該怎麼辦？如果你無法忍住，那麼你就糗大了。

別擔心，在舊金山有人已經發明了一種自我清洗的公廁。這種廁所會自動清洗乾淨。使用後馬桶會縮進牆裡，並在那裡洗淨吹乾。甚至連地板也會自動洗乾淨。但動作要快，你只有二十分鐘可以『辦事』。在門打開前兩分鐘會有一次警告，等門自動打開時，你最好已經辦完事，不然你可要臉紅了！

Vocabulary & Idioms 單字 & 片語註解

1. **toilet** [ˈtɔɪlɪt] n. 廁所
   washroom [ˈwɑʃˌrum] n. 盥洗室, 廁所
   restroom [ˈrɛstˌrum] n. (公共) 廁所
   lavatory [ˈlævəˌtorɪ] n. 洗手間, 廁所
   注意:
   toilet 本意為『馬桶』, 現今常用來表示『廁所』, restroom 則常用來表示一般的公共廁所, 但現今美國人表示『上廁所』時, 常見的有三種說法: "go to the toilet/the washroom/the restroom"; 而 lavatory 則常指飛機上的洗手間。此外, 英國人表示『上廁所』時, 一般都說"go to the lavatory"。

2. **desperately** [ˈdɛspərɪtlɪ] adv. 迫切地
   desperate [ˈdɛspərɪt] a. 走頭無路的
   例: I desperately need some financial help.
   (我急需一些財務上的援助。)
   When I'm desperate, I turn to my parents for help.
   (在我走頭無路時，會尋求父母的幫助。)

3. 本文:

You need to go to the washroom <u>desss...perately</u>.

你非常非常想上洗手間。

注意:

此為因緊張或內急的緣故, 所以講話結結巴巴, 可譯為『非、非常……常迫切』。

4. **embarrassed** [ɪmˈbærəst] a. 感到困窘/尷尬的

embarrass [ɪmˈbærəs] vt. 使困窘, 使尷尬

embarrassing [ɪmˈbærəsɪŋ] a. 令人困窘/尷尬的

例: James was embarrassed when his girlfriend beat him in ping-pong.
(詹姆士的女友打乒乓球打贏他時，他非常難堪。)

It's embarrassing to forget someone's name while talking to him.
(當你和某人講話卻忘了他的名字時很令人尷尬。)

5. **to no end** 無止境地, 無限地

= limitlessly [ˈlɪmɪtlɪslɪ] adv.

= without end

例: Mom scolded Dad to no end for leaving his briefcase in the taxi.
(老爸把他的手提箱留在計程車內，為此老媽一直責罵他。)

6. **invent** [ɪnˈvɛnt] vt. 發明, 創造; 杜撰, 捏造

invention [ɪnˈvɛnʃən] n. 發明 (物)

例: The boy is good at inventing sad stories to gain sympathy.
(那男孩擅於捏造令人傷心的故事來獲得同情。)

Mr. A.G. Bell is responsible for the invention of the telephone.
(發明電話的人是貝爾先生。)

The TV is indeed a great invention.
(電視的確是個偉大的發明。)

7. **self-cleaning** [ˏsɛlfˊklinɪŋ] a. 自動清洗的

clean [klin] vt. 使乾淨 & vi. 打掃, 清掃

clean up...　　將……清理乾淨, 徹底清理……

例: The maid cleans the house every day.
(那個女僕每天清理房子。)

It took us an hour to clean up the apartment after the party.
(派對後花了我們一個小時的時間才把公寓清理乾淨。)

8. **seat** [sit] n. 座位

take a seat　　請坐

例: Please take a seat; our discussion will take some time.
(請坐，我們的討論將花上一些時間。)

9. **blow-dry** [ˊbloˏdraɪ] vt. 吹乾

10. **automatically** [ˏɔtəˊmætɪklɪ] adv. 自動地; 不自覺地

automatic [ˏɔtəˊmætɪk] a. 自動的

例: When I meet someone, I almost automatically shake his hand.
(我和別人見面時，幾乎都會不自覺地和他握手。)

This car has an automatic transmission.
(這部車子是自動排檔。)

* transmission [trænsˊmɪʃən] n. 動力傳送器

11. **warning** [ˊwɔrnɪŋ] n. 警告

例: Thank you for your timely warning, or else I would have been in trouble.
(謝謝你及時的警告，否則我就有麻煩了。)

Grammar Notes 文法重點

本課複習關係副詞 where 的用法, 並介紹"had better + 原形動詞" (最好……) 的用法。

1. **The seat goes back into <u>the wall</u> <u>where</u> it is washed and blow-dried.**

使用後馬桶會縮進牆裡, 並在那裡洗淨吹乾。

上列句中的 where 為關係副詞, 即等於 in which, 修飾其前的名詞 the wall。

where 作關係副詞時, 其所引導的形容詞子句只用來修飾表地方的名詞, 此時 where 即等於"介詞 in/on/at + 關係代名詞 which", 若其前表地方的名詞為大地方 (如國家、城市、區域等) 或表內部 (在……之內) 時, 介詞用 in; 若表示在某物之上時, 介詞用 at; 若地方表外在 (在……上面) 時, 則介詞用 on。

例: That is the restaurant <u>where</u> Ted first met Paula.
= in which
(那就是泰德初次遇見寶拉的餐廳。)

I went to the station, <u>where</u> I ran into a good friend of mine.
= <u>at which</u>
(我到了車站去，在那兒我見到一位老友。)

That is the hilltop <u>where</u> our school is located.
= on which
(我們學校就是座落在那個山頂上。)

注意:

關係副詞除了 where 外, 尚有 when、why、how 三個:

a. when 用以修飾表時間的名詞。

例: The exam took place at 3 p.m., when all the students were
= at which
already very tired.
(考試在下午三點舉行, 那時所有的學生都已經很累了。)

b. why 只用以修飾 the reason (理由)。

例: I don't know the reason why Molly was fired.
= for which
(我不知道茉莉被開除的原因。)

c. how 只用以修飾 the way (方式、方法), 但使用時, the way 之後的 how 一定要省略, 如不省略反而會成為贅述, 但我們亦可省略 the way, 而使用 how。

例: Everyone likes | the way / how | he sings.
(每個人都喜歡他唱歌的方式。)

2. **When it does, you'd better be ready or your face will be red!**
當門自動打開時, 你最好已經辦完事, 不然你可要臉紅了！

a. 上列句中的 it 乃指前句中的 the door, 而 does 則代替前句中的動詞 opens, 此處用 it 和 does 乃為避免相同詞類的重複之故。

b. you'd better... 你最好……
= you had better...
had better + 原形動詞 最好……

注意:
使用此片語時, 若以代名詞作主詞時, 經常使用縮寫形, 如: you'd better (你最好)、I'd better (我最好)、he'd better (他最好)、she'd better (她最好)……等。

例: You'd better be on time for the meeting.
(你最好準時出席這次的會議。)

Henry had not better get drunk again or else his girlfriend would dump him. (×)

→ Henry <u>had better not</u> get drunk again or else his girlfriend would dump him. (○)
(亨利最好不要再喝醉，要不然他女友準會甩了他。)
＊ had better 與 not 並用時, not 須置於 better 之後, 而不可置於其前, 即無"had not better"的用法。

Substitution 代　換

1. **The seat goes back into the wall where it is washed and blow-dried.**
I put your glasses on the desk where your books are.
My son is playing in the park where I once played when I was his age.
使用後馬桶會縮進牆裡, 並在那裡洗淨吹乾。
我把你的眼鏡放在你放書的桌子上。
我兒子正在那座公園裡玩耍, 我在他這個年紀時, 也曾在那座公園裡玩過。

2. **You'd better be ready or your face will be red!**
I'd better leave or I'll be late for dinner.
You'd better not forget Mom's birthday this year.
你最好已經完事, 不然你可要臉紅了！
我最好走了, 要不然我會趕不上吃晚飯的時間。
你今年最好不要忘記老媽的生日。

Lesson 114

It's Too Late

來不及了

Dialogue
實用會話

A mother and child are walking along the street.

(C=child; M=mother; W=waiter in a restaurant)

C: Mom, I need to go to the washroom.

M: Uh-oh! Can't you wait?

C: I can't stand it anymore.

M: OK, let's go into this restaurant. Excuse me, but can my son use your toilet?

W: Of course not. This is a restaurant, not a public toilet.

M: You're so mean.

W: Oh, OK. But it'll cost you US$5.

M: What? That's highway robbery.

C: Mom, never mind. It's too late.

W: Hey, come back here and mop the floor.

有位媽媽和她的小孩正走在街上。
小　孩：媽，我需要上廁所。
媽　媽：糟糕！你難道不能等一等嗎？
小　孩：我不能再忍了。
媽　媽：好吧，我們到這家餐廳去上吧。抱歉，能不能讓我兒子用一下你們的廁所？
服務生：當然不行。這是餐廳，不是公廁。
媽　媽：你怎麼那麼小氣。
服務生：哦，好吧。不過要付五塊錢美金。
媽　媽：什麼？簡直是攔路打劫嘛。
小　孩：媽，算了吧。已經來不及了。
服務生：嘿，回來把地板擦乾淨。

Key Points 重點提示

1. **stand** [stænd] vt. 忍受, 忍耐

stand + 名詞/動名詞　　忍受……

cannot stand to + 原形動詞　　受不了……

= cannot stand + 動名詞

例: I can't stand nosy people.
(我不能忍受愛管閒事的人。)

＊ nosy [ˈnozɪ] a. 好管閒事的

Rosy can't stand waiting for a bus in the rain.
(羅絲無法忍受在雨中等公車。)

Daisy can't stand to see children cry.
(黛西受不了看到小孩子哭。)

2. **mean** [min] a. 小氣的; 很凶的

例: That rich woman is so mean that she hates to part with a single dollar.
(那個富婆很小氣，她連一塊錢都不願拿出來。)
* part with... 與……分離

That mean teacher loves to punish his students.
(那位凶巴巴的老師喜歡處罰學生。)

3. **highway robbery** 攔路打劫

highway [ˈhaɪˌwe] n. (高速) 公路

robbery [ˈrɑbərɪ] n. 搶劫, 掠奪

rob [rɑb] vt. 搶劫, 掠奪

注意:

本文中使用"highway robbery"乃誇張語, 因文中服務生的行為宛如『強盜在公路搶劫來往旅行者大量財物』, 故用來比喻『索價過高』, 和中文的『敲竹槓』很類似。

例: There's a robbery committed every day in that area.
(那個區域每天都有一樁搶案發生。)

The teenagers robbed a convenience store.
(那群青少年搶劫了一家便利商店。)

4. **Never mind.** 算了。沒關係。

= Forget it.

例: Tina: I'm sorry. I forgot to call you last night.
Jim: Never mind.
(蒂娜：對不起，我昨晚忘了打電話給你。)
(吉姆：沒關係。)

5. **mop** [mɑp] vt. 用拖把擦 (mop 亦可作名詞, 表『拖把』)

例: The janitor mops the staircase every day.
(那個大樓管理員每天都用拖把擦樓梯間。)
* staircase [ˈstɛrˌkes] n. 樓梯間

請選出下列各句中正確的一項

1. You'd ______ break your promise.
   (A) better to not (B) better not
   (C) not better (D) better not to

2. Mark still doesn't know the reason ______ he was fired.
   (A) how (B) where (C) when (D) why

3. I like ______ my girlfriend sings.
   (A) who (B) that (C) which (D) how

4. Please ______ anywhere you like.
   (A) seat yourself (B) seat
   (C) be sat (D) sit yourself

5. If you can't join us, ______; there will be many other opportunities to get together.
   (A) never mind (B) no way
   (C) excuse me (D) I'm sorry

解答：

1.(B) 2. (D) 3. (D) 4. (A) 5. (A)

Lesson 115

Kick the Habit

革除習慣

There are millions of people all over the world who smoke. Most of these smokers have tried to quit smoking at least once in their lives, but in vain. Make no mistake; smoking is addictive. And once you are addicted, it's very difficult to stop smoking. Many people have tried many different ways to kick the habit. None of them is easy.

Take a tip from me. I smoked for twenty-five years. Then one day, I decided to quit cold turkey after trying everything else. It worked. That was two years ago and I haven't smoked a single cigarette since then. Good luck!

全世界有數以百萬計的人吸煙。大多數的吸煙者一生中至少都有過一次嘗試戒煙的經驗，但卻徒勞無功。別搞錯哦，吸煙是會上癮的。而一旦你上了癮，就很難戒除。很多人試過很多不同的方法來擺脫這個習慣，但沒有一個方法是容易辦到的。

那麼聽我的忠告吧。我有二十五年的煙齡，在試過其它各種戒煙方法後，有一天我決定要斷然戒煙。結果這個方法奏效了。那是兩年前的事了，從那時起，我就再沒抽過一根煙。祝你好運！

Vocabulary & Idioms 單字 & 片語註解

1. **kick the habit** 擺脫/除去某習慣

kick the habit of... 擺脫/除去……的習慣

= get rid of the habit of...

例: Jeff is trying to kick the habit of going to work late.

= Jeff is trying to get rid of the habit of going to work late.

(傑夫正努力革除上班遲到的習慣。)

2. **in vain** 徒勞無功

注意:

in vain 作副詞片語, 修飾句中動詞。

例: Chad tried his best to get Molly to go out with him but all his efforts were in vain.

(查德盡全力想約茉莉和他外出，但他所有的努力都徒勞無功。)

3. **addictive** [əˈdɪktɪv] a. 使人上癮的

addicted [əˈdɪktɪd] a. 上癮的; 耽溺的 (與介詞 to 並用)

addict [ˈædɪkt] n. 上癮者

be addicted to... 有……的癮; 耽溺於……

例: There's no denying that cigarettes are addictive.

(無可否認香煙會使人上癮。)

The old man has been addicted to heroin for twenty years.
(這位老先生染上海洛因已有二十年之久。)

The drug addict lives a hard and lonely life.
(那毒癮者過著困苦孤單的生活。)

4. **Make no mistake.** 不要搞錯了／你要搞清楚。

例: Make no mistake. If you delay the project, you'll get in trouble.
(你要搞清楚，如果你延遲了這個企劃，會有麻煩的。)

5. **tip** [tɪp] n. 忠告; 小費 & vt. 給予忠告; 給予小費

take a tip from + 人　　聽從/接受某人的建議/忠告

tip + 人 + on...　　就……(方面) 給人建議/忠告

tip + 人 + 金錢　　給某人若干金錢當小費

例: Take a tip from me. Opium is addictive.
(聽我的忠告吧，鴉片是會使人上癮的。)

Mr. White tipped his students on how to learn English.
= Mr. White gave his students some tips on how to learn English.
(懷特先生給予他的學生一些如何學習英文的建議。)

The millionaire tipped the waiter US$100 for the service.
= The millionaire gave the waiter a tip of US$100 for the service.
(那百萬富翁給了侍者一百元美金的小費以酬謝謝他的服務。)

6. **single** [ˈsɪŋgḷ] a. 單一的; 單身的

例: Dan is single, but he has a steady girlfriend.
(阿丹還是個單身漢，但他有一位固定交往的女朋友。)

Grammar Notes 文法重點

本課介紹"all over the world" (全世界, 世界各地) 的用法, 以及現在完成式的用法。

1. **There are millions of people all over the world who smoke.**
全世界有數以百萬計的人吸煙。

all over the world　　全世界, 世界各地
= around the world
= the world over

注意:
上述片語可作形容詞用, 置於名詞後, 修飾該名詞; 亦可作副詞用, 修飾句中動詞; 且使用 the world over 時, 其前不可再置介詞 in, 即無"in the world over"的用法。

例: This brand of perfume can be bought all over the world.
= This brand of perfume can be bought around the world.
= This brand of perfume can be bought the world over.
(這種牌子的香水世界各地都可買到。)

2. **Most of these smokers have tried to quit smoking at least once in their lives, but in vain.**
大多數的吸煙者一生中至少都有過一次嘗試戒煙的經驗, 但卻徒勞無功。

Many people have tried many different ways to kick the habit.
很多人試過很多不同的方法來擺脫這個習慣。

That was two years ago and I haven't smoked a single cigarette since then.
那是兩年前的事了, 從那時起, 我就再沒抽過一根煙。

a. 現在完成式的句型:

主語 + have/has + 過去分詞　已經……

例: I have seen that movie.
(我已經看過那部電影了。)

He has finished writing the letter.
(他已經寫完那封信了。)

b. 現在完成式的功能:

1) 現在完成式可用以表示到現在為止完成的動作。

例: I have just finished the work.
(我剛把工作做完。)

= He has gone on vacation.
(他已經度假去了。)

2) 現在完成式可用以表示到現在為止的經驗。

例: I have read that book twice.
(那本書我已看過兩次了。)

= Tom has been to America before.
(湯姆以前曾去過美國。)

3) 現在完成式可用以表示從過去某時一直持續到現在的動作或狀態。

例: Carl has worked here for five years.
(卡爾已經在這裡工作五年了。)

= I have studied English since 1994.
(我從一九九四年就開始學英文。)

c. 使用現在完成式時, 因現在完成式並不強調時間的明確性, 只強調到現在為止已完成的動作, 故現在完成式不得與明確的過去時間副詞並用; 明確的過去時間副詞在句中出現時, 時態應採過去式。

例: I have finished my homework ten minutes ago. (×)
原因: 有明確的過去時間副詞。

→ I finished my homework ten minutes ago. (○)
(我十分鐘前把功課作完了。)

John has graduated from college last year.(×)
原因: 有明確的過去時間副詞。

→ John graduated from college last year. (○)
(約翰去年從大學畢業了。)

d. 現在完成式可單獨使用, 但過去完成式則不能單獨存在, 而要與另一過去式子句或表過去之副詞片語並用, 即在過去不同時間發生的兩種動作:
先發生的→用過去完成時
後發生的→用簡單過去式

例: He has finished painting the house. (○)
(他已經油漆完房子了。)

He had finished painting the house. (×)
→ He said (that) he had finished painting the house. (○)
(他說他已油漆完房子了。)

e. 瞬間動詞 (一瞬間動作便告完成的動詞) 使用完成式時, 不可與表持續性的時間副詞片語並用。但表示持續性動作的動詞則可與此類副詞片語並用。

例: He has lived here for five years. (○)
(他住在這裡已有五年。)

理由:

他每天都住在這裡, 如此持續了五年, 故 has lived 是表持續性的動作, 可與 for five years 並用。

He has died for five years. (×)
(他死了五年。)

理由:

他每天都死一次, 如此持續了五年不合邏輯, die 是瞬間動詞,不可能每天都發生, 故可用現在完成時, 但不得與 for five years 並用。
故我們可說:

He has died. (○)
但不得說:
He has died for five years. (×)
補救之道:

It is five years since he died. (○)
= Five years have passed since he died.
(自他死後已有五年。)
又例:

He has gone to Japan. (○)
(他已去了日本。)

He has gone to Japan for five years. (×)

理由:

go 是瞬間動詞, 故 has gone to Japan 表『已去了日本』, 不可能每天都去日本, 如此持續五年。

改正:

It is five years since he went to Japan. (○)

= Five years have passed since he went to Japan.

(自他去了日本後已過了五年。)

1. **There are millions of people all over the world who smoke.**

   There are many mountains around the world that nobody has climbed.

   This brand of bikes is well known the world over.

   全世界有數以百萬計的人吸煙。

   全世界有許多沒有人攀登過的山脈。

   這種廠牌的腳踏車舉世聞名。

2. **That was two years ago and I haven't smoked a single cigarette since then.**

   I've lived in Japan for the last ten years.

   Daren has traveled more than twenty countries so far.

   那是兩年前的事了, 從那時起, 我就再沒抽過一根煙。

   過去十年來, 我一直住在日本。

   戴倫到目前為止已旅遊過二十多個國家了。

Lesson 116

Candy Helps?

糖果有助戒煙嗎？

Dialogue
實用會話

Candy is trying to get her boyfriend Benny to stop smoking.
(C=Candy; B=Benny)

C: Benny, your breath smells like an ashtray. You've got to stop smoking!

B: I know. I want to, but it isn't easy.

C: Why don't you chew gum instead?

B: I can't. I've got false teeth. Remember?

C: Oh yeah. In that case, how about eating candies?

B: If they're as sweet as you, no problem.

C: Cut it out, will you? I'm serious.

B: Just kidding. Do I get a kiss if I really quit?

C: I don't like the taste of ashtrays. Maybe tomorrow if you quit right now.

B: OK, you've got a deal.

肯蒂設法要她的男朋友班尼戒煙。
肯蒂：班尼，你的口氣聞起來像煙灰缸。你必須要戒煙了！
班尼：我知道。我是想戒，但並不容易啊。
肯蒂：那你為什麼不嚼口香糖來代替呢？
班尼：沒辦法。我有假牙，記得嗎？
肯蒂：噢，是啊。那樣的話，改吃糖果如何？
班尼：如果糖果和妳一樣甜的話，那就沒問題。
肯蒂：少貧嘴，好嗎？我是說真的。
班尼：只是開開玩笑嘛。如果我真的戒了，妳會給我一個吻嗎？
肯蒂：我不喜歡煙灰缸的味道。如果你現在就戒，也許明天吧。
班尼：好，就這麼說定了。

Key Points 重點提示

1. **candy** [ˈkændɪ] n. 糖果

注意:

candy 本為不可數名詞 (如標題), 但若表『不同種類』時 (如本文), 則視為可數名詞。

例: Eating candy before a meal spoils my appetite.
(用餐前吃糖果會使我沒胃口。)

These local candies taste quite different.
(這些當地的糖果嚐起來相當不一樣。)

2. **ashtray** [ˈæʃˌtre] n. 煙灰缸

例: Put out the cigarette in the ashtray and not on the floor.
(在煙灰缸把香煙撚熄，而不要在地板上。)

3. **chew** [tʃu] vt. 咀嚼; 啃

chew + 人 + out　　把某人罵得狗血淋頭

例: When a dog is chewing its bone, don't disturb it.
(狗在啃骨頭時,別去干擾牠。)

Dad chewed me out for getting home so late.
(老爸因為我很晚回家而把我罵得狗血淋頭。)

4. **gum** [gʌm] n. 口香糖 (不可數)

a stick/piece of gum 一片/條口香糖

a pack of gum 一包口香糖 (通常有六至七片)

例: It's rude to chew gum at a job interview.
(在工作面試中嚼口香糖很沒禮貌。)

5. **false teeth** 假牙 (複數形)

false tooth 假牙 (單數形)

decayed tooth 蛀牙

false [fɔls] a. 假的

decayed [dɪ'ked] a. 腐敗的, 被蛀的

例: Ron's false tooth came off as he bit into his steak.
(朗恩一口咬下牛排時，他的一顆假牙掉了下來。)

You have a decayed tooth which needs to be pulled out.
(你有顆蛀牙得拔掉了。)

Can you tell a real diamond from a false one?
(你能分辨真假鑽石嗎？)

6. **in that case** 那樣的話, 如此一來

= in that situation

例: A: I've got to go now.
B: In that case, let's continue this meeting tomorrow.
(甲：我現在得走了。)
(乙：那樣的話，咱們明天再繼續這次的會議吧。)

7. **How about + 名詞/動名詞？** ……怎麼樣？

= What about + 名詞/動名詞？

例: Mom: Your dad and I are going to a movie.
Son: How about me?
(媽媽：你爸爸和我要去看電影。)
(兒子：那我呢？)

How about eating out today, Mom?
(媽，今天到外面吃飯好嗎？)

8. **cut it out** 停止; 住嘴
= knock it off

例: Jack: You're getting to be too fat, Sally.
Sally: Cut it out, will you?
(傑克：莎莉，妳越來越胖了。)
(莎莉：住嘴，行嗎？)

9. 本文:
Just kidding. 只是開開玩笑嘛。
= I'm just kidding.

10. **taste** [test] n. 味道

例: I love the taste of durian, but hate the smell.
(我喜歡榴槤的口感，但很討厭它的味道。)
＊ durian [ˈdjʊrɪən] n. 榴槤

11. **You've got a deal.** 一言為定。/成交。
= That's a deal.
= It's a deal.

例: Brother: Help me do the homework, and I won't tell anyone your secret.
Sister: You've got a deal!
(弟弟：幫我做家庭作業，我就不把妳的秘密告訴任何人。)
(姊姊：一言為定！)

請選出下列各句中正確的一項

1. Frank ______ in Paris since 1990.
   (A) lived (B) lives (C) has lived (D) is living

2. He ______ here ten years ago looking for a nice girl to marry.
   (A) comes (B) came (C) has come (D) is coming

3. You must ______ the habit of interrupting others while they're talking.
   (A) make (B) cut (C) knock (D) kick

4. This brand of clothing is known ______ the world.
   (A) across (B) over (C) cross (D) all

5. Whatever you do, don't become ______ to drugs.
   (A) addicted (B) addictive
   (C) interested (D) attractive

解答：

1. (C) 2. (B) 3. (D) 4. (A) 5. (A)

Lesson 117

Early to Bed, Early to Rise

早睡早起身體好

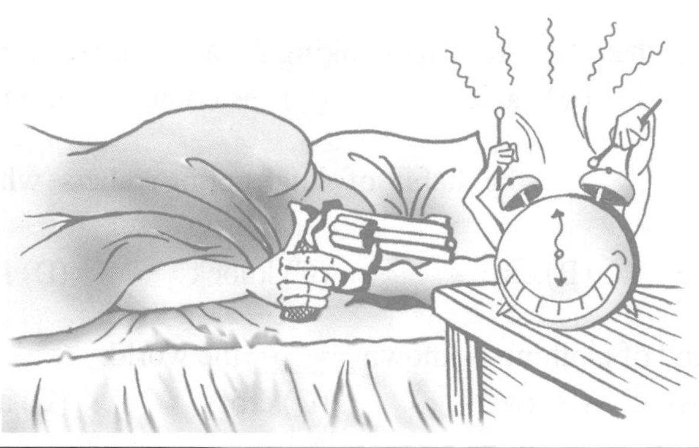

Reading 閱讀

"Early to bed, early to rise," so goes an old saying. But how many of us are in the habit of doing that? Not many, I bet. Most of us need an alarm clock to wake us up. But even that doesn't always work. It's too easy to punch the off button and fall asleep again.

The Lazybones Alarm Clock may be the solution to our problem. It's specially designed so that it cannot be switched off with a simple push of a button. The clock has several "protective shells." You must open these shells one by one before you can turn off the alarm. If you don't, it'll keep on saying, "Good morning...good morning..." So if any of you lazybones need a morning call that really gets you out of bed, this clock might be just the thing for you.

俗話說得好：『早睡早起身體好。』可是我們當中有多少人擁有這樣的習慣呢？我敢保證這樣的人並不多。我們大多數人都得靠鬧鐘來把我們叫醒。不過這個方法也並非永遠管用，因為我們可以輕易地按下停止鈕，然後倒頭再睡。

懶骨頭鬧鐘也許可以解決我們的問題。它經過了特殊設計，因此無法光靠按個鈕就可把它關掉。這種鬧鐘有好幾層『護殼』。你必須將這些護殼一層層地打開，才能讓鈴聲停止。如果你沒這樣做，它就會『早安，早安……』一直叫個不停。所以如果你們之中哪一個懶骨頭，需要靠晨呼才真正起得了床的話，這種鬧鐘可能正是你所需要的。

Vocabulary & Idioms 單字 & 片語註解

1. **saying** [ˈseɪŋ] n. 諺語, 俗語

例: As the saying goes, "Two heads are better than one."
 = As the saying puts it, "Two heads are better than one."
 = "Two heads are better than one," so goes the saying.
 (俗語說：『三個臭皮匠，勝過一個諸葛亮。』)

2. **be in the habit of + 名詞/動名詞**

有……的習慣

例: Joe's in the habit of having a snack before going to bed.
 (喬在睡前有吃點心的習慣。)

3. **bet** [bɛt] vt. 保證; 打賭 (三態均為 bet)

bet + 金錢 + on + 某事　　把錢賭在某事上面

例: I bet Jeff can't swim faster than I.
(我敢保證傑夫不可能游得比我快。)

Mr. Wang bet US$100 on the No.8 horse to win.
(王先生用一百元美金賭八號馬會贏。)

4. **alarm clock** [əˈlɑrm ˌklɑk] n. 鬧鐘

例: If it weren't for my alarm clock, I would be late for work every day.
(要不是有我的鬧鐘，我每天上班都會遲到。)

＊ if it weren't for + 名詞　　要不是因為……

5. **work** [wɝk] vi. 有效, 生效; 工作 & vt. 產生/造成 (奇蹟)

work miracles/wonders　　產生奇蹟

＊ miracle [ˈmɪrəkl̩] n. 奇蹟
wonder [ˈwʌndɚ] n. 奇蹟, 神奇

例: This medicine doesn't work at all; it doesn't help me fall asleep.
(這藥一點效果也沒有，無法助我入睡。)

Tony works for IBM as a computer programmer.
(湯尼在 IBM 公司擔任電腦程式設計師。)

The mystic claims he is able to work miracles.
(那個通靈者宣稱他能夠創造奇蹟。)

＊ mystic [ˈmɪstɪk] n. 通靈者

6. **punch** [pʌntʃ] vt. (以拳) 打, 擊

例: Nathan punched the bigger guy in the nose and ran for his life.
(耐森一拳打在那個塊頭比他大的傢伙的鼻子後便逃命去了。)

＊ run for one's life　　逃命

7. **button** [ˈbʌtn̩] n. 按鈕

the off button　　關掉的按鈕

the on button　　打開的按鈕

8. **lazybones** [′lezɪ͵bonz] n. 懶骨頭, 懶人 (單複數同形)

例: Everyone knows Chris is a lazybones.
(每個人都知道克里斯是個懶骨頭。)

The lazybones in the company were eventually fired.
(公司裡的那些懶人最後全被炒魷魚了。)

9. **design** [dɪ′zaɪn] vt. 設計

be designed to + 原形動詞　　被設計來……

例: This sofa is designed to serve as a bed as well.
(這張沙發同時也被設計來作為床使用。)

10. **switch** [swɪtʃ] vt. 扳動 (開關)

switch off...　　關掉……的開關

= turn off...

switch on...　　打開……的開關

= turn on...

例: Don't forget to switch off the air conditioner before you leave.
(離開前，別忘了關掉冷氣機。)

As soon as Larry gets home, he switches on the TV.
(賴瑞一回到家就打開電視機。)

11. **protective** [prə′tɛktɪv] a. 保護的, 有保護作用的

protect [prə′tɛkt] vt. 保護

protection [prə′tɛkʃən] n. 保護

be protective of...　　保護……

protect...from...　　保護……免於……

例: Mary's parents are extremely protective of her.
(瑪麗的父母非常保護她。)

This scarf will protect you from the cold.
(這條圍巾將能使你禦寒。)

The gangsters offered the store owner protection for a fee.
(那些幫派分子向店主要求保護費。)
＊ gangster [ˈgæŋstɚ] n. 歹徒, 幫派分子

12. **shell** [ʃɛl] n. (外) 殼; 貝殼

例: Thomas picked up these shells from the beach.
(湯瑪斯從沙灘撿來這些貝殼。)

13. **one by one** 一個接一個

例: The lazy workers got fired one by one.
(懶惰的員工一個接一個地被炒魷魚了。)

14. **a morning call** 早上叫醒人的電話

a wakeup call 叫醒人的電話 (不分早晚)

例: Let's ask the receptionist to give us a | morning call. / wakeup call. |
(咱們叫櫃檯接待員早上用電話叫醒我們。)
(咱們叫櫃檯接待員用電話叫醒我們。)
＊ receptionist [rɪˈsɛpʃənɪst] n. (櫃檯) 接待員

15. **be just the thing for + 人** 正是某人所需的東西

例: A long vacation may be just the thing for you right now.
(一個長假也許正是你目前所需要的。)

Grammar Notes 文法重點

本課介紹『俗話/諺語說 (得好) :……』的用法, 和"so that..." (以便……) 作連接詞的用法, 以及"keep on + 現在分詞" (繼續……) 的用法。

1. **"Early to bed, early to rise," so goes an old saying.**
俗話說得好:『早睡早起身體好。』

a. 本句"Early to bed, early to rise."乃諺語"Early to bed and early to rise makes one healthy, wealthy and wise." (早睡早起使人健康、致富又有智慧) 的縮寫。

原諺語中的"Early to bed"缺乏動詞是不合文法的, 應說"Early to go to bed"以與"early to rise"對稱, 但如此字數多了兩個, 反而不對稱, 為將就字數對稱, 便把 go to 犧牲了。

b. 表『俗話/諺語說 (得好) :……』有下列用法:

There is an old saying, "..."
= As an/the old saying goes, "..."
= As an/the old saying puts it, "..."
= "...," as an/the old saying goes.
= "...," so goes an/the old saying.

例: As an old saying goes, "A friend in need is a friend indeed."
(俗話說：『患難見真交。』)

Before you quit your job, you'd better think about it; "Look before you leap," as the old saying goes.
(你在辭職前最好考慮清楚；俗語說得好：『三思而後行。』)

Don't worry about that now. "We'll cross that bridge when we come to it," so goes the old saying.
(現在不要擔心那件事。俗話說得好：『船到橋頭自然直。』)

2. **It's specially designed so that it cannot be switched off with a simple push of a button.**

它經過了特殊設計, 因此無法光靠按個鈕就可把它關掉。

so that...　　如此/以便……
= in order that...

注意:

a. so that/in order that (如此, 以便) 為表示目的的副詞連接詞, 引導副詞子句, 修飾主要子句, 且 so that/in order that 所引導的副詞子句中通常要有助動詞 may、can 或 will。

例: I came | so that / in order that | I might see Helen.
(我來這樣便可見到海倫。)
John quickly finished his homework | so that / in order that | he could go out to play.
(約翰很快做完功課以便能夠出去玩。)
Tell me how to do it | so that / in order that | I will not make the same mistake again.
(告訴我怎麼做，這樣我才不會再犯同樣的錯誤。)

b. so that/in order that 所引導的副詞子句之主詞若與主要子句的主詞相同時, 則該主要子句可改為"so as to + 原形動詞"或"in order to + 原形動詞"; 而主詞不同時則不可採用此句法。故上列第一及第二例句亦可改寫成:

例: I came | so as to / in order to | see Helen.
John quickly finished his homework | so as to / in order to | go out to play.

3. **If you don't, it'll <u>keep on</u> saying, "Good morning ...good morning..."**
如果你沒這樣做, 它就會『早安, 早安……』一直叫個不停。
keep on + 動名詞　　繼續 (做) ……
= keep + 動名詞
= go on + 動名詞
例: If you <u>keep on gambling</u>, you'll end up a pauper.
= If you <u>keep gambling</u>, you'll end up a pauper.

= If you go on gambling, you'll end up a pauper.
(如果你繼續賭下去，到頭來你會變成窮鬼。)
∗ pauper ['pɔpɚ] n. 貧民, 窮人

1. **"Early to bed, early to rise," so goes an old saying.**
"Once bitten, twice shy," as an old saying goes.
There is an old saying, "Time and tide wait for no man."
俗話說得好:『早睡早起身體好。』
俗話說得好:『一朝被蛇咬, 十年怕草繩。』
俗話說得好:『歲月不饒人。』

2. **It's specially designed so that it cannot be switched off with a simple push of a button.**
We should leave now so that our host may get some rest.
You have to work hard in order to succeed.
它經過了特殊設計, 因此無法光靠按個鈕就可把它關掉。
我們現在該走了, 如此主人才能休息。
你必須努力工作才能成功。

Lesson 118

Don't Be a Lazybones

莫做懶骨頭

Daisy and Herbie are chatting.

(D=Daisy; H=Herbie)

D: How come you were late for school again this morning, Herbie? Didn't you just buy a Lazybones Alarm Clock?

H: Yes, I did.

D: Did you forget to set it?

H: No, I didn't.

D: Didn't it wake you up?

H: It sure did.

D: So what happened?

H: I had a hard time switching the alarm off, so I gave up.

D: What do you mean you gave up?

H: I threw it out the window and went back to sleep.

黛絲與郝畢正聊著天。

黛絲：郝畢，你怎麼早上上課又遲到了？你不是剛買了一個懶骨頭鬧鐘嗎？

郝畢：是啊，我是買了。

黛絲：你忘了設定時間嗎？

郝畢：不，我沒忘記。

黛絲：它沒把你鬧醒嗎？

郝畢：當然有。

黛絲：那到底是怎麼回事？

郝畢：我設法把鈴聲關掉，但是很難做到，所以我就放棄了。

黛絲：你說你放棄是什麼意思？

郝畢：我把它扔到窗外，回頭又睡著了。

1. **chat** [tʃæt] vi. & n. 聊天

   have a chat with...　　和……聊天/閒聊

   例: Let's chat about what happened.
   (咱們聊聊發生的事吧。)

   My sister has a chat with her boyfriend over the phone every night.
   (我妹妹每天晚上都和她男友在電話上聊天。)

2. 本文:

   <u>How come</u> <u>you were</u> late for school again this morning, Herbie?

   = <u>Why</u> <u>were you</u> late for...?

   你怎麼早上上課又遲到了, 郝畢？

   注意:

how come 的意思雖然等於 why, 但是 how come 引導的問句不用倒裝。

例: How come did you tell such a lie? (×)

→ How come you told such a lie? (○)

= Why did you tell such a lie?
(你為什麼撒這樣的謊？)

3. **forget** [fɚ'gɛt] vt. 忘記

動詞三態: forget、forgot [fɚ'gɑt]、forgotten [fɚ'gɑtn̩]。

forget to + 原形動詞　　忘了要……

forget + 動名詞　　忘了曾……

注意:

forget 接不定詞片語, 表示『忘了要去做某件事』; 若接動名詞, 則表示『忘了曾經做過某件事』。

類似用法尚有:

regret to + 原形動詞　　抱歉要去做……

regret + 動名詞　　後悔曾經……

remember to + 原形動詞　　記得要去做……

remember + 動名詞　　記得做過……

例: Don't forget to take your keys with you.
(別忘了要隨身攜帶你的鑰匙。)

I forgot having dinner with you two years ago.
(我忘了兩年前曾和你一起吃過晚飯。)

I regret to inform you that you didn't get the job.
(抱歉要通知你你沒有得到這份工作。)

John regrets not studying harder when he was young.
(約翰後悔年輕時不用功點。)

4. **set** [sɛt] vt. 設定 (時間) (三態同形)

注意:

set 通常與介詞 for 並用, 表示『對未來時間的設定』。

例: I set/made an appointment with the dentist <u>for</u> <u>ten</u> tomorrow morning.
(我跟牙醫約好明天早上十點見面。)
＊此處表『十點鐘』的 ten 之前不可置介詞 at, 因為 at ten 表示在十點鐘設定時間, 而 for ten 則表示設定未來的時間為十點鐘。

5. **have** | **a hard time** / difficulty / trouble / problems | **+ 動名詞**　　從事……很難

類似用法尚有:

have | a good time / a great time / a wonderful time / fun | + 動名詞　　從事……很愉快

例: Brad has a hard time making ends meet.
(布萊德很難讓收支平衡／入不敷出。)
＊ make ends meet　　使收支平衡
We had a good time dancing at the disco.
(我們在迪斯可舞廳跳舞，玩得很愉快。)

6. **give up**　　放棄
give up...　　放棄……
例: When things are tough, don't give up; try harder.
(遇到事情很棘手時，別放棄；應該更努力才是。)
You should try your best to give up smoking.
(你應該盡全力戒煙。)

7. **throw** [θro] vt. 丟, 擲 & vi. 嘔吐
動詞三態: throw、threw [θru]、thrown [θron]。
throw up　　嘔吐

例: The naughty kid threw a stone at the window.
(那個頑皮的小孩對著窗戶扔了顆石頭。)

Ken threw up because he drank too much.
(肯恩因為喝太多酒而吐了。)

請選出下列各句中正確的一項

1. As an old saying ______ it, "One good turn deserves another."
   (A) makes (B) writes (C) puts (D) goes

2. The stinky smell made me throw ______.
   (A) out (B) up (C) off (D) over

3. Fred works hard ______ his family can have a decent life.
   (A) in order (B) in that (C) so as (D) so that

4. Most parents are protective ______ their children.
   (A) against (B) on (C) to (D) of

5. You can't expect a teacher to ______ miracles with students who don't try.
   (A) throw (B) have (C) work (D) get

解答：

1. (C) 2. (B) 3. (D) 4. (D) 5. (C)

Lesson 119

Partying with Foreigners

與老外同樂

Reading 閱讀

Partying is fun. But have you ever been invited to a party by a foreigner? What should you wear? Should you bring anything? If so, what? Don't worry. Today we are going to give you some tips about partying with foreigners.

First, you should ask if it is a formal or casual party. Then you will know what to wear. It's as simple as that. At a casual party, it is customary to bring a bottle of wine or some other refreshment. It is not considered polite to bring someone along with you unless you first ask your host. At more formal parties like birthdays, a small gift will be sufficient. Giving money would cause some embarrassment. Finally, never overstay your welcome. When it's getting late, it's time to thank your host for a wonderful evening and say good night.

參加派對很有趣。可是，你曾被老外邀請去參加派對嗎？你該穿什麼樣的服裝？你該帶東西去嗎？如果要帶的話，帶什麼？別擔心，今天我們要給你一些提示，讓你知道和老外一起開派對該怎麼做。

首先，你得問清楚這是個正式或非正式的派對，那麼你就知道該穿著什麼服裝了。就是那麼簡單。若是非正式的派對，習慣上是要帶瓶酒或其他點心。除非事先問過主人，否則帶未經邀請的人參加是不禮貌的。若是較正式的派對，如生日派對等，送個小禮物就夠了，送錢會令人尷尬。最後要注意的是，千萬別逗留過久而惹人生厭。時候不早時，你就該向主人致謝告訴他你度過了一個美好的夜晚，然後說聲晚安告別。

Vocabulary & Idioms 單字 & 片語註解

1. **party** [ˈpɑrtɪ] vi. 開派對 & n. 派對

party with + 人　　與某人開派對同樂

throw / hold / have	a party	舉行派對

注意:

表『舉行派對』時, 動詞可用 throw/hold/have 來表示, 但若表『舉行會議』時, 動詞則用 hold/have 表示。

例: My new classmates are great people to party with.
(我新來的同班同學都是開派對同樂的極佳玩伴。)

Are you going to throw a party on your birthday this year?
(今年你生日當天會開派對嗎?)

Let's hold a meeting to discuss the problem.
(咱們來開個會討論這個問題吧。)

2. **If so,...** 果真如此的話,……

例: Should I go? If so, what should I wear?
(我應該去嗎?如果要的話,我該穿什麼衣服呢?)

3. **give + 人 + a tip/some tips + about/on...**
就……給某人建議/提示
tip [tɪp] n. 竅門, 祕訣

例: Eric can give you some good tips about budget traveling.
(艾瑞克可以給你一些有關自助旅行很好的建議。)
* budget [ˈbʌdʒɪt] n. 預算

4. **formal** [ˈfɔrml̩] a. 正式的

例: Mr. Chen hates to wear formal clothes.
(陳先生討厭穿著正式的穿著。)

5. **casual** [ˈkæʒuəl] a. 非正式的

例: It's a casual party, so just wear whatever you want.
(它是一個非正式的派對,所以只要隨便穿就可以了。)

6. **customary** [ˈkʌstəˌmɛrɪ] a. 慣例的, 習慣的
it is customary to + 原形動詞 ……是慣例/習俗

例: It's customary to give children money in red envelopes at Chinese New Year.
(過年時發給小孩子紅包是項習俗。)

7. **refreshment** [rɪˈfrɛʃmənt] n. 點心 (不可數)

例: Let's get some refreshment for the kids; they look exhausted.
(咱們拿點點心給孩子們吃吧，他們看起來累壞了。)

8. **polite** [pə'laɪt] a. 有禮貌的

例: We should be polite to our elders.
(我們應該對我們的長輩有禮貌。)

9. **host** [host] n. 主人 & vt. 主辦

hostess ['hostɪs] n. 女主人

例: If you host a party, you'll need to make sure there's enough food and drink.
(如果你主辦派對，必須確定有足夠的食物和飲料。)

The hostess made everyone feel at home.
(女主人使每個人賓至如歸。)

10. **sufficient** [sə'fɪʃənt] a. 充足的, 足夠的

例: I don't have sufficient money to treat you to dinner.
(我沒有足夠的錢請你吃晚餐。)

11. **embarrassment** [ɪm'bærəsmənt] n. 難堪, 尷尬

例: To avoid embarrassment, Judy prefers to stay home rather than go to the party with her drunken husband.
(為了避免難堪，茱蒂寧願待在家裡而不願和她酗酒的丈夫去參加派對。)

12. **overstay one's welcome** 逗留過久而惹人生厭

overstay [ˌovɚ'ste] vt. 停留過久

例: It's getting late. Let's go before we overstay our welcome.
(很晚了，咱們走吧免得逗留過久惹人生厭。)

Grammar Notes
文法重點

本課主要複習用 if 取代 whether 的用法。

First, you should ask <u>if</u> it is a formal or casual party.

= First, you should ask <u>whether</u> it is a formal or casual party.
首先,你得問清楚它是個正式或非正式的派對。

上列句中,if 引導的名詞子句作其前及物動詞 ask 的受詞。whether 引導的名詞子句若作及物動詞的受詞時,whether 可用 if 取代,此時 if 譯成『是否』,而非『如果』。

例: I don't know <u>whether</u> I'm right or not, but that's my opinion.
= I don't know <u>if</u> I'm right, but that's my opinion.
(我不知道自己對不對,但那是我的看法。)
＊用 if 取代 whether 時,通常不與 or not 並用。

注意:

1. whether 引導的名詞子句作主詞為虛詞 it 取代時,此時 whether 亦可用 if 代替。

例: Whether the jury's decision was right or not is still debatable.
= <u>It</u> is still debatable <u>whether</u> the jury's decision was right or not.
= <u>It</u> is still debatable <u>if</u> the jury's decision was right.
(陪審團的判決是否正確仍有待商榷。)

但: <u>If</u> the jury's decision was right is still debatable. (✕)

2. whether 引導的名詞子句若作介詞的受詞時,此時 whether 不可被 if 取代。

例: Our departure depends on <u>if</u> the weather will clear up tomorrow. (✕)
→ Our departure depends on <u>whether</u> the weather will clear up tomorrow. (〇)

(我們何時動身要看明天天氣是否會放晴而定。)

3. whether 引導的名詞子句若置於 be 動詞後作主詞補語時, 此時 whether 亦不可用 if 代替。

例: The question is if the boss will approve this idea. (×)
→ The question is whether the boss will approve this idea. (○)
(問題是老闆是否會同意這個點子。)

Substitution 代換

1. **First, you should ask if it is a formal or casual party.**
You can tell if the boss is angry just by looking at his face.
The doctor knows if you're sick by feeling your pulse.
首先, 你得問清楚它是個正式或非正式的派對。
只要看他的臉色, 你就會知道老闆是不是在生氣。
醫師藉由量脈膊知道你是不是生病了。

2. **At a casual party, it is customary to bring a bottle of wine or some other refreshment.**
It's customary to have a family reunion around Chinese New Year time.
It's customary to shake hands when you meet people for the first time.
若是非正式的派對, 習慣上是要帶瓶酒或其它點心。
過年時全家團圓是項習俗。
和別人第一次見面時, 握手是慣例。

Lesson 120

Wanna Dance?

想跳舞嗎？

Dialogue 實用會話

Candy goes to Dan's casual party. Dan's her American friend.

(C=Candy; D=Dan)

C: Hi, Dan!

D: Hi, Candy! Glad you could make it.

C: I wouldn't miss your party for the world.

D: Thanks for the compliment.

C: Here, I brought some beer and a bottle of wine.

D: That's great. Come on in. I want you to meet some of my friends.

C: OK.

D: Hey, everybody. This is Candy. Candy, uh...this is everybody.

(Everyone laughs as they continue to dance.)

C: Hey, don't let me interrupt.

D: Wanna dance?

C: Uh...how about some wine first? I need to get in the mood.

D: Sure thing.

肯蒂去參加阿丹的非正式派對。阿丹是她的美國朋友。
肯蒂：嗨，阿丹！
阿丹：嗨，肯蒂！真高興妳能來。
肯蒂：我絕不會錯過你的派對。
阿丹：謝謝妳的恭維。
肯蒂：喏，我帶了六罐啤酒和一瓶葡萄酒。
阿丹：太好了。請進。我想請妳會會我的一些朋友。
肯蒂：好的。
阿丹：嘿，大伙們，這是肯蒂。肯蒂，呃……這是大家。（大家邊跳舞邊笑。）
肯蒂：嘿，別讓我打斷你們。
阿丹：想跳舞嗎？
肯蒂：呃……先喝點酒怎麼樣？我需要培養一下情緒。
阿丹：當然好囉。

Key Points 重點提示

1. 標題:

Wanna dance? 想跳舞嗎？

= Do you want to dance?

注意:

在口語中"wanna"常可取代"want to"的說法, 一如"be gonna"即等於"be going to"一樣。

例: What do you wanna eat tonight?
= What do you want to eat tonight?
(你今晚想吃什麼？)

What are you gonna wear to tonight's party?
= What are you going to wear to tonight's party?
(你要穿什麼衣服參加今晚的派對？)

2. **人 + can make it** 某人可以參加 (某活動等)

例: We're going to Lily's party tonight. Can you make it?
(我們今晚要去參加莉莉的派對。你能去嗎？)

3. **not...for the world** 絕不可能……

= not...for anything

= not...no matter what

例: I wouldn't miss your wedding for the world.
= I wouldn't miss your wedding for anything.
= I wouldn't miss your wedding no matter what.
(我絕不會錯過你的婚禮的。)

4. **miss** [mɪs] vt. 錯過; 想念

例: If you don't leave now, you'll miss the train.
(如果你現在不走的話，會錯過火車的。)

Jenny misses her boyfriend, who is in the States.
(珍妮很想念她的男朋友，他人現在在美國。)

5. **compliment** [ˈkɑmpləmənt] n. & vt. 恭維, 稱讚

compliment + 人 + on + 事 稱讚某人某事

例: Be careful not to take flattery as a compliment.
(小心不要把諂媚的話當作是恭維。)
* flattery [ˈflætərɪ] n. 奉承; 拍馬屁

The boss complimented Jeff on a job well done.
(老闆稱讚傑夫某項工作表現優異。)

6. **beer** [bɪr] n. 啤酒

wine [waɪn] n. 葡萄酒

7. **Come on in.** 請進。

= Come in.

例: Don't stand at the door. Come (on) in.
(不要站在門口，請進。)

8. **interrupt** [ˌɪntəˈrʌpt] vi. & vt. 打斷, (使) 中斷

interruption [ˌɪntəˈrʌpʃən] n. 打斷, 打岔

例: I don't mean to interrupt, but I have something urgent to tell you.
(我並不想打岔，但我有要緊的事要告訴你。)

Don't interrupt me while I'm sleeping.
(我在睡覺時別來吵我。)

The interruption of the meeting was caused by an earthquake.
(一場地震打斷了會議進行。)

9. **mood** [mud] n. 心情, 情緒

moody [ˈmudɪ] a. 情緒不穩的

get in the mood　　培養情緒

be in the mood to + 原形動詞　　有心情做……(多用於疑問句或否定句中)

be in a good mood　　心情很好

be in a bad mood　　心情不好

例: Dan tried to get his girlfriend in the mood to dance with him.
(阿丹想辦法讓他女友有和他共舞的興緻。)

Are you in the mood to go for a ride?
(你有去兜風的興緻嗎？)

It looks like the boss is in a bad mood again.
(老闆好像心情又不好了。)

It's difficult to get along well with moody people.
(要和情緒化的人好好相處很難。)

10. **Sure thing.**　　當然 (可以) 囉。

= Of course.

例: Barry: Are you coming to dinner with us?
Sally: Sure thing.
(貝瑞：妳會來和我們共進晚餐嗎？)
(莎莉：當然。)

請選出下列各句中正確的一項

1. A: Are you going to get a job this summer?
   B: ______.
   (A) Never mind.　(B) Who cares?
   (C) Sure thing.　(D) It's alright.

2. Thank you ______ me a birthday card.
   (A) to send　(B) of sending　(C) for sending　(D) by sending

3. Mom ______ a big party on Dad's birthday.
   (A) made　(B) threw　(C) took　(D) brought

4. The beautician gave Anna some ______ on how to put on makeup.
   (A) tips　(B) suggests　(C) advices　(D) advise

5. It's hard to be ______ a good mood when you're among grouchy people.
   (A) with　(B) of　(C) as　(D) in

解答：

1. (C)　2. (C)　3. (B)　4. (A)　5. (D)

Lesson 121

A Shocking Experience

駭人的經驗

Reading 閱讀

Taking a taxi in Prague can be a "shocking" experience. Many Czech capital taxi drivers have metal wires stuck into the passenger seats. And when a button is pushed, the seat will give you an electric shock. These taxi drivers don't do this for fun. They do it to tourists who argue about the ridiculous fares they charge. Some drivers charge as much as ten times the legal fare. They have a secret switch which makes the meters run faster. If you refuse to pay, you are really in for a shock.

In one case, a German woman had no choice but to pay US

$120 for a US$20 ride from the airport. She said that she was "really taken for a ride," but what could she do? Besides the electric shock, she was verbally abused and threatened with physical violence. She has only one piece of advice to tourists: "Take the bus or stay at home."

在布拉格搭乘計程車可能會是個駭人的經驗。捷克首都裡有許多計程車司機會在乘客的座位裝上金屬電線，然後一按鈕，座位就會傳電使你受到電擊。這些計程車司機並不是為了好玩才這樣做，他們用這種方法對付那些與他們爭執車資不合理的觀光客。有些司機索取的車資高達原法定車資的十倍，他們車內有一個祕密開關，可以使計費錶轉速加快，如果你拒付的話，就鐵定會被電擊。

有一次，一位德國女士在機場搭車，坐了廿美元的路程卻不得不付出一百廿美元。她說她『確實是上當受騙了，』但又能怎麼辦呢？除了電擊之外，她還受到言詞辱罵和肢體暴力恐嚇，她對遊客只有一個忠告：『你要嘛坐公車要不然就待在家裡。』

Vocabulary & Idioms 單字 & 片語註解

1. **shocking** [ˈʃɑkɪŋ] a. 使人震驚的, 駭人的
   shocked [ʃɑkt] a. 感到震驚的
   shock [ʃɑk] vt. 使震驚; 給與衝擊 & n. 撞擊, 震驚
   例: Have you heard the shocking news about the plane crash?
   (你聽到有關這次令人震驚的墜機報導了嗎？)
   The guests were shocked | at / by | the host's rudeness.
   (來賓們對主人的無禮感到震驚。)

The shock of the blast shattered the windows in the neighborhood.
(那次爆炸的撞擊震碎了附近的窗戶。)

2. **Prague** [prɑg] n. 布拉格 (捷克的首都)

3. **Czech** [tʃɛk] a. 捷克 (人) 的, 捷克語的 & n. 捷克人, 捷克語

4. **capital** [ˈkæpətl̩] n. 首都

例: Paris is the capital of France.
(巴黎是法國的首都。)

5. **metal** [ˈmɛtl̩] a. 金屬的

例: This metal container won't break easily.
(這個金屬容器不容易打破。)

6. **wire** [waɪr] n. 電線, 鐵絲

例: The thief opened the car door with a piece of wire.
(竊賊用一根鐵絲打開了車門。)

7. **stick** [stɪk] vt. 插

動詞三態: stick、stuck [stʌk]、stuck。

stick A into B　　把 A 插到 B 裡面

例: He tried to stick the key into the keyhole but it didn't fit.
(他試圖把鑰匙插到鑰匙孔裡，但插不進去。)

8. **passenger** [ˈpæsəndʒɚ] n. 乘客, 旅客

例: The passengers got nervous when the plane began to shake.
(飛機開始震動時，旅客緊張起來了。)

9. **electric** [ɪˈlɛktrɪk] a. 電的

electricity [ɪˌlɛkˈtrɪsətɪ] n. 電, 電力

electric shock　　電擊

例: Don't touch the wire; you might get an electric shock.
(不要觸摸那條電線，你也許會觸電。)

After the flood, we didn't have electricity for a week.
(水災後，我們停電了一個禮拜。)

10. **for fun** 為了好玩/樂趣

例: We played cards for fun, not for money.
(我們打牌是為了好玩而不是為錢。)

11. **tourist** [ˈtʊrɪst] n. 觀光客

例: Some tourists got lost in the crowded city.
(有些觀光客在這個擁擠的城市裡迷路了。)

12. **argue** [ˈɑrgjʊ] vi. 爭論 & vt. 辯論; (堅持) 認為

argue about / over ... 爭論……

argue + that 子句 堅稱/強烈認為……

例: The couple are always arguing about how to bring up their children.
(那對夫婦老是為該怎麼撫養小孩而爭吵。)

The accused argued that the witness was lying.
(被告堅稱那位證人說謊。)

13. **ridiculous** [rɪˈdɪkjələs] a. 荒謬的, 怪誕的

例: That's the most ridiculous story I've ever heard.
(那是我所聽過最荒謬的故事了。)

14. **fare** [fɛr] n. (交通) 費用

fee [fi] n. (付給專業人員辦事的手續) 費用

例: Senior citizens need not pay the bus fare.
(年老的市民不需要付公車費用。)

The English tutor's fee is quite high.
(那位英文家教的收費很高。)

15. **charge** [tʃɑrdʒ] vt. 索價

例: The plumber charged me a lot of money to fix the toilet.
(那名水管工人修理馬桶向我收了很多錢。)
＊ plumber [ˈplʌmɚ] n. (修理水管、煤氣管等的) 鉛管工人

16. **legal** [ˈligl̩] a. 合法的; 法律上的
illegal [ɪˈligl̩] a. 非法的
例: If someone sues you, you should get legal advice.
(如果有人控告你，你應該尋求法律上的忠告。)
I'm afraid it's illegal to park here.
(恐怕在此處停車是不合法的。)

17. **refuse** [rɪˈfjuz] vt. 拒絕
refuse to + 原形動詞　　拒絕……
例: Tammy refused to tell the teacher who broke the window.
(黛咪不肯告訴老師是誰打破那塊窗戶。)

18. **be in for + 事**　　必定會遭遇到……
例: You're really in for a good time at Winnie's birthday party.
(你在溫妮的生日派對上一定會玩得很開心。)

19. **take + 人 + for a ride**
原指『開車載人兜風』, 此指『欺騙某人』、『把某人當凱子耍』。
＊ 本文中...she was "really taken for a ride,"...乃為被動用法。
例: A: You'll have to pay me US$100 an hour for my services.
B: Are you trying to take me for a ride?
(甲：你必須付我每小時美金一百元的服務費。)
(乙：你想騙我嗎？)

20. **verbally** [ˈvɝbəlɪ] adv. 口頭上地
verbal [ˈvɝbl̩] a. 口頭上的
例: The police asked Peter for a verbal statement of what he saw.
(警方要求彼得把他所見的說出來。)

21. **abuse** [əˈbjuz] vt. 虐待; 濫用

例: According to the report, some prisoners there are physically abused.
(根據報導，那兒的犯人有些受到肢體上的虐待。)

The policeman abused his power when he ate the vendor's apples and didn't pay for them.
(那個警察濫用他的職權，他吃了攤販的蘋果卻沒有付錢。)

22. **threaten** [ˈθrɛtn̩] vt. 恫嚇, 威脅
threat [θrɛt] n. 恫嚇, 威脅
pose a threat to... 對……構成威脅

例: The teacher threatened the student with severe punishment.
(老師威脅要嚴厲處罰那名學生。)

The typhoon poses a serious threat to the crops.
(颱風對農作物構成嚴重的威脅。)

23. **violence** [ˈvaɪələns] n. 暴力
violent [ˈvaɪələnt] a. 暴力的

例: When Mike lost the argument, he resorted to violence.
(當麥克爭輸時，他便訴諸暴力。)

The fight became violent after a while.
(打鬥過了一會兒後便變得很暴力。)

Grammar Notes 文法重點

本課複習 have 作使役動詞的用法, 並介紹倍數詞表『……的幾倍』的用法, 以及"have no choice but to + 原形動詞" (除了……外別無選擇) 的用法。

1. **Many Czech capital taxi drivers <u>have</u> metal wires <u>stuck</u> into the passenger seats.**

捷克首都裡有許多計程車司機會在乘客的座位裝上金屬電線。

上列句中, have 為使役動詞, 接受詞後, 再接 stick (將……插入) 的過去分詞 stuck 作受詞補語。

have 作使役動詞時, 加受詞後, 可接過去分詞作受詞補語, 此時 have 譯成『把……』; have 之後除可接過去分詞作受詞補語外, 亦可接原形動詞作受詞補語, 此時 have 譯成『叫/令……』。

have + 受詞 + 過去分詞　　把……

have + 受詞 + 原形動詞　　叫/令……

例: I <u>had</u> my radio <u>fixed</u> yesterday.
(我昨天把收音機拿去修理。)

Mom <u>has</u> us children <u>help</u> with the housework.
(媽媽叫我們這些小孩子幫忙做家事。)

2. **Some drivers charge as much as <u>ten times</u> <u>the</u> legal fare.**

有些司機索取的車資高達原法定車資的十倍。

有關倍數詞的用法如下:

* 倍數詞:

half (一半)、one-third (三分之一)、two-thirds (三分之二)、three-fourths (四分之三)、one-fifth (五分之一)、two-fifths (五分之二) ...twice (兩倍)、three times (三倍)……等。

a. 倍數詞 + as...as...　　是……的幾倍

例: He is <u>half</u> <u>as</u> rich <u>as</u> I.
(他的財富是我的一半。)

This car is <u>three times</u> <u>as</u> expensive <u>as</u> that one.
(這部車的價錢是那部車的三倍。)

b. more than + 倍數詞 + as...as...　　是……的幾倍還不止

例: I am <u>more than</u> <u>three times</u> <u>as</u> old <u>as</u> he.
(我的年齡是他的三倍還不止。)

Hugo is <u>more than</u> <u>twice</u> <u>as</u> heavy <u>as</u> his brother.
(雨果的體重是他弟弟的兩倍還不止。)

c. 倍數詞 + 定冠詞 the/所有格 (his、her、my...) /指示形容詞 (this、that、these、those) + 名詞 是……的幾倍

＊本文即屬"倍數詞 + 定冠詞 the + 名詞"之用法。

例: This river is ten times the length of the Tamsui River.

= This river is ten times as long as the Tamsui River.
(這條河的長度是淡水河的十倍長。)

The basketball player is twice my height.
(那個籃球員的身高是我的兩倍。)

d. more than + 倍數詞 + 定冠詞 the/所有格 (his、her、my...)/指示形容詞 (this、that、these、those) + 名詞 是……的幾倍還不止

例: This river is more than ten times the length of the Tamsui River.

= This river is ten times as long as the Tamsui River.
(這條河的長度是淡水河的十倍還不止。)

The basketball player is more than twice my height.
(那個籃球員身高是我的兩倍還不止。)

3. **In one case, a German woman had no choice but to pay US $120 for a US$20 ride from the airport.**

有一次，一位德國女士在機場搭車，坐了廿美元的路程卻不得不付出一百廿美元。

have no choice but to + 原形動詞
= have no alternative but to + 原形動詞
= have no option but to + 原形動詞
除了……外別無選擇; 不得不……

＊ alternative [ɔlˈtɝnətɪv] n. 選擇
option [ˈɑpʃən] n. 選擇

例: The bankrupt has no choice but to borrow more money from the bank.
(那個破產的人除了向銀行借更多錢外別無選擇。)

The plane had no alternative but to make an emergency landing.
(那架飛機除了緊急降落外別無選擇。)

The bank robber had no option but to surrender.
(那名銀行搶匪除了投降外別無選擇。)

Substitution 代換

1. **Some drivers charge as much as ten times the legal fare.**
   My house is three times as big as yours.
   I have two-thirds as many books as Jack.
   有些司機索取的車資高達原法定車資的十倍。
   我的房子是你的房子的三倍大。
   我擁有的書是傑克的三分之二。

2. **In one case, a German woman had no choice but to pay US $120 for a US$20 ride from the airport.**
   Because there was a blackout, the Lin family had no choice but to eat out.
   Jeff had no choice but to take a taxi to work because he got up late.
   有一次, 一位德國女士在機場搭車, 坐了廿美元的路程卻不得不付出一百廿美元。
   因為停電, 林家人不得不到外面用餐。
   傑夫因為晚起床, 所以不得不搭計程車去上班。

Lesson 122

A Long Ride

長路漫漫

Dialogue
實用會話

Florine is in a taxi.

(F=Florine; T=taxi driver)

F: Hey, driver, are we going the right way?

T: Of course. You think I'm cheating you?

F: Well, it seems like an awfully long ride. (after a while) Driver, how come your meter is running so fast? Is it out of order?

T: Hey, lady, if you think I'm cheating you, you can get out.

F: OK. I think I'll do just that. Stop the taxi.

T: Sorry, I can't. We're on the highway. You can get out if you like, but I can't stop.

F: I'm going to report you to the police.

T: Ha! Ha! That's what they all say. (They arrive.) See you.

F: I don't ever want to see you again.

T: Same here.

弗蘿蘭坐在計程車裡。
弗蘿蘭：嘿，司機，我們走的路線對嗎？
司　機：當然對，妳以為我在騙妳嗎？
弗蘿蘭：呃，好像走的時間太久了。（過了一會兒）司機先生，你的計費錶為什麼跑得這麼快？是不是壞了？
司　機：嘿，女士，如果妳以為我在騙妳的話，妳可以下車。
弗蘿蘭：好吧，我正想這樣做，停車。
司　機：抱歉，我不能停，我們現在正在高速公路上，如果妳想下車的話，請便，但是我不能停車。
弗蘿蘭：我會報警舉發你的。
司　機：哈！哈！誰都是這樣說的。(他們抵達後)再見。
弗蘿蘭：我再也不想見到你了。
司　機：我也是。

Key Points 重點提示

1. 本文:

...are we going the right way?

= ...are we going <u>in</u> the right direction?
……我們走的路線對嗎？

* direction [dəˈrɛkʃən] n. 方向

注意:

way 表『方向』時, 等於 direction, 之前與介詞 in 並用, 不過 way 之前的 in 通常可省略, direction 之前的 in 則不可省。

2. **cheat** [tʃit] vt. 欺騙 & vi. 不忠; 作弊

cheat + 人 + out of + 錢　　騙取某人若干錢

cheat on + 人　　(男女之間) 對某人 (感情) 不忠

例: Sam cheated Hedy out of one thousand dollars.
(山姆騙了海蒂一千塊錢。)

Tom cheated on his girlfriend; he went out with Jane.
(湯姆對他的女朋友不忠，他和珍約會。)

I don't know how Willy could cheat on the exam and still fail.
(我不知道為什麼威利會考試作弊卻仍考不及格。)

3. **awfully** [ˈɔfəlɪ] adv. 非常地 (正式用法)
= awful (限口語用法)
= very
* awful [ˈɔfl̩] adv. 非常地 & a. 可怕的, 糟透的

例: We've had | awfully / awful / very | bad weather all week.
(整個禮拜天氣都很糟。)

John made an awful mistake when counting money.
(約翰數錢時犯了一個嚴重的錯誤。)

4. **meter** [ˈmitɚ] n. 計費錶; 公尺

例: Besides paying what's on the meter, I usually give the taxi driver a small tip.
(除了付計費錶上的價錢外，我通常會給計程車司機一點小費。)

Joe ran the hundred-meter dash in 11.5 seconds.
(喬百米短跑跑了十一點五秒。)

5. **be out of order** (機器, 小零件等) 故障, 壞了
break down (車輛) 故障, 壞了

例: Please turn on the fan; the air conditioner is out of order.
(請打開電風扇，冷氣機壞了。)

The boss's car broke down on his way to work.
(老闆的車在上班途中拋錨了。)

6. **get** | **out of** / in (to) | ... | 下 / 上 | 轎車、計程車等交通工具

get	off on	...	下 上	公車、火車、船、飛機等交通工具

注意:

凡是交通工具較小, 不能在上面站立或走動者, 必須用 get in (to)/out of 來表示上、下此種交通工具; 若交通工具較大, 可任由人在其上站立或走動者, 表上、下這種交通工具時, 則用 get on/off。

例: The thief got into a taxi and escaped.
(小偷上了一輛計程車逃掉了。)

As soon as the movie star got off the plane, the fans started screaming.
(那位影星一下飛機，歌迷便開始尖叫起來。)

7. **report** [rɪ'pɔrt] vt. 告發; 報導, 報告 & n. 報導

report + 人/事 + to the police　　將某人/某事報警處理

例: The storekeeper reported the shoplifter to the police.
(店主報警處理那位商店扒手。)

* shoplifter ['ʃɑp,lɪftɚ] n. 商店扒手

The manager reported that the company made a huge profit last year.
(經理報告說公司去年賺了很多錢。)

According to the report, hundreds of people died as a result of the earthquake.
(根據報導，那場地震死了好幾百人。)

8. **Same here.**　　我也是。

= Me, too.

例: Jeff: I hate rainy days and Mondays.
Anna: Same here.
(傑夫：我討厭下雨天和星期一。)
(安娜：我也是。)

請選出下列各句中正確的一項

1. The woman divorced her husband because he ______ her.
   (A) was cheating (B) was cheating out of
   (C) cheated (D) cheated on

2. Ellen had no choice but ______ money to save her company from closing down.
   (A) to borrow (B) borrow (C) borrowing (D) borrowed

3. A: I'm sick and tired of working day and night.
   B: ______
   (A) Over here. (B) Same here.
   (C) Why not? (D) Here you are.

4. We played a trick on the teacher just for ______ , but he got very angry.
   (A) funny (B) fun (C) sure (D) free

5. The residents think that the nuclear power plant ______ a threat to their safety.
   (A) poses (B) imposes (C) lifts (D) throws

解答：

1. (D) 2. (A) 3. (B) 4. (B) 5. (A)

Lesson 123

Dog Days Off

愛犬假

Reading 閱讀

Have you ever made an excuse for not going to work? I guess most people have. But have you ever called in for a day off because your dog is sick? I bet you haven't. Most people wouldn't have the guts.

However, some companies in New Zealand find this as an acceptable reason for taking a day off. It is counted as paid sick leave. The reason, they say, is simple: "A sick dog is as much a dependant as a sick child." That makes plenty of sense, doesn't it? This is now known in New Zealand as "dog days off." I wonder

what the bosses in Taiwan will say if someone calls in for a dog day off.

你是否曾經找藉口不去上班？我猜大多數的人都曾這樣做過。不過，你是否曾因為你的狗生病而打電話到公司請一天假？我敢說你一定沒有這樣做過。大多數的人都沒有這個膽子。

然而，在紐西蘭有些公司認為以這樣的理由請一天假是可以接受的，而且還會把這種假視為薪水照付的病假。他們說這樣做的理由很簡單：『狗兒生病就像孩子生病一樣需要人照顧。』這很有道理吧，不是嗎？現在這種假在紐西蘭叫做『愛犬假』。我倒想知道如果在台灣有人打電話請愛犬假，老闆們會怎麼回答。

Vocabulary & Idioms
單字 & 片語註解

1. **call in for...** 為……而打電話到 (公司、單位) 來

例: The secretary called in for a day off because she wasn't feeling well.
(秘書打電話來請一天假，因為她覺得不太舒服。)

2. **a day off** 請一天假, 放一天假

ask for + 天數 + off 請幾天假

ask for leave 請假

例: Luke asked for a day off to visit his sick mother.
(路克請了一天假去看他生病的媽媽。)

Ruby wants to take a day off but she's afraid to ask for leave.
(露比想請一天假，但她不敢請假。)

3. **guts** [gʌts] n. 膽子, 勇氣

注意:

guts 表『膽子、勇氣』時, 恆用複數形, 其前須置定冠詞 the, 如"have the guts" (有膽子、有勇氣); 亦可以用 nerve 或 courage 取代, 但 nerve 及 courage 為不可數名詞, 故不可加 s。

have the guts / nerve / courage to + 原形動詞　有膽子/勇氣……

例: Do you have the guts / nerve / courage to go skydiving?
(你有勇氣去高空跳傘嗎？)

4. **acceptable** [ək'sɛptəbḷ] a. 可接受的, 尚可接受的

例: Your suggestion is quite acceptable.
(你的建議頗能令人接受。)

5. **New Zealand** [ˌnju'zilənd] n. 紐西蘭

6. **be counted as...**　被算為是……

例: Children are counted as half a person because they only pay half the price to take the bus.
(孩子被算作是半個人，因為他們坐公車只付半價。)

7. **paid** [ped] a. 有薪俸的; 已付清的

例: Jeff won an all-paid trip to Rome.
(傑夫贏得一趟到羅馬的全額免費旅行。)

8. **sick leave** ['sɪk ˌliv] n. 病假

be on sick leave　請病假

例: Ron is on sick leave but he isn't home.
(朗恩請病假但人卻不在家。)

9. **dependant** [dɪ'pɛndənt] n. 受撫養者, 眷屬

dependent [dɪ'pɛndənt] a. 依賴的, 離不開的

independent [ˌɪndɪˈpɛndənt] a. 獨立的

be dependent on...　　依賴……

be independent of...　　脫離……而獨立

例: Mr. Williams has many dependants to support.
(威廉斯先生有一大家子人要養。)

He's thirty, but he's still dependent on his parents.
(雖然他三十歲了，但他仍然依賴他的父母。)

Alan has been independent of his parents ever since he went to college.
(艾倫自從上了大學便不再依賴他的父母了。)

10. **plenty of + 不可數/複數名詞**　　許多……

例: Mr. Longman says he eats plenty of fish to keep healthy.
(朗文先生說他吃許多魚來保持健康。)

You can tell that he's a good guy because he has plenty of friends.
(你可以看得出來他是個好人，因為他有許多朋友。)

11. **make sense**　　有道理

例: Don't you think what he said makes sense?
(難道你不認為他說的話有道理嗎？)

Grammar Notes 文法重點

本課主要介紹"be as much + a/an + 名詞 + as..." (和……一樣是……) 的用法。

The reason, they say, is simple, "A sick dog is as much a dependant as a sick child."

他們說這樣做的理由很簡單:『狗兒生病就像孩子生病一樣需要人照顧。』

上列句子使用了"be as much + a/an + 名詞 + as..." (和……一樣是……) 的句

型, 此片語中的 much 為表程度的副詞, 修飾其前的 be 動詞。

be as much + a/an + 名詞 + as...　　和……一樣是……

＊ 在此用法中, 只可置入單數可數名詞, 而不可使用複數名詞。

例: Mr. Chen is as much a teacher as his father was.
(陳先生和他父親一樣是位老師。)

注意:

上述用法乃由"be as + 形容詞 + a/an + 單數可數名詞 + as..." (和……一樣地……) 演化而來; 此種只能與含有形容詞的單數可數名詞並用的句構有下列四種:

as...as...　　和……一樣地……

so...that...　　如此……以致於……

too...to...　　太……而不能……

how...　　多麼地……

在這四組片語中, 因 as (一樣地)、so (如此地)、too (太)、how (多麼地) 均為副詞, 故之後應先置形容詞以供修飾, 然後再置不定冠詞 (a/an) 及單數名詞。

1. as + 形容詞 + a/an + 名詞 + as...

   例: The young man is <u>as a successful businessman</u> as his father. (×)

   → The young man is <u>as successful a businessman</u> as his father. (○)
   (那個年輕人和他父親一樣是位成功的商人。)

2. so + 形容詞 + a/an + 名詞 + that...

   例: The woman is <u>so a popular singer</u> that people all over the world know who she is. (×)

   → The woman is <u>so popular a singer</u> that people all over the world know who she is. (○)
   (那位女士是個非常受歡迎的歌手，因此世界各地的人都知道她。)

   注意:

   使用"such...that..."時, 則 such 是之後可接任何名詞。

例: He is such an idiot that no one likes him.
單數名詞
(他很愚蠢，所以沒有人喜歡他。)

They are such idiots that no one likes them.
複數名詞
(他們是這麼的愚蠢，所以沒有人喜歡他們。)

It is such good music that everyone enjoys it.
不可數名詞
(這音樂這麼好聽，所以每個人很喜歡。)

3. too + 形容詞 + a/an + 名詞 + to...

例: Kenny is too a slow runner to compete in the race. (×)
→ Kenny is too slow a runner to compete in the race. (○)
(肯尼跑得太慢無法參賽。)

4. How + 形容詞 + a/an + 名詞!

例: How a considerate man he is! (×)
→ How considerate a man he is! (○)
(他真是個體貼的人！)

注意:

使用 what 時, 則之後可接任何名詞。

例: What a kind man he is!
單數名詞
(他人真好！)

What good boys they are!
複數名詞
(他們真是好孩子！)

What beautiful music it is!
不可數名詞
(真好聽的音樂！)

1. **Most people wouldn't have the guts.**

   The student had the guts to question the correctness of his teacher's explanation.

   James doesn't have the nerve to ask Alice out on a date.

   大多數的人都沒有這個膽子。

   那名學生有勇氣對他老師解說的正確性提出質疑。

   詹姆士沒有勇氣約愛麗絲出去。

2. **The reason, they say, is simple:"A sick dog is as much a dependant as a sick child."**

   The boy is as much a lazybones as his father.

   Fred is as much a hypocrite as his wife.

   他們說這樣做的理由很簡單：『狗兒生病就像孩子生病一樣需要人照顧』。

   那個男孩就像他父親一樣是個懶骨頭。

   弗瑞德就像他老婆一樣是個虛偽的人。

* lazybones [ˈlezɪˌbonz] n. 懶骨頭, 懶人 (單複數同形)

hypocrite [ˈhɪpəkrɪt] n. 偽君子

Lesson 124

An Inch Given, a Mile Taken

得寸進尺

Dialogue
實用會話

Karen calls the manager for a dog day off.

(K=Karen; M=manager)

K: Hello, Mr. Fu?

M: Yes. This is he.

K: Uh...I'm calling to ask for a day off.

M: What's the matter? Are you sick again?

K: No. Um...actually it's my dog. I think it's that time of the month. I've got to take her to the vet.

M: I guess it's OK. But I didn't know dogs had periods.

K: They sure do. By the way, if she gets pregnant, do I get two months off?

M: Do you want permanent leave?

K: Uh...what do you mean?

凱倫打電話向經理請『愛犬假』。
凱倫：哈囉，傅先生嗎？
經理：是的，我就是。
凱倫：呃……我是打電話來請假的。
經理：怎麼啦？妳又生病了嗎？
凱倫：不，呃……事實上，是我的狗生病了。我想牠這個月的生理期又到了。我得帶牠去獸醫那兒。
經理：好吧，不過，我不曉得狗也有生理期。
凱倫：牠們當然也有囉。哦，對了，如果牠懷孕了，我可以放兩個月的假嗎？
經理：妳想不想永遠放假？
凱倫：呃……什麼意思？

1. 標題:

An inch given, a mile taken. 得寸進尺。

= If we give him an inch, he will take a mile.

例: Lisa: I let my husband go out with his friends and he came home drunk.
Mom: If you give men an inch, they'll take a mile.
(莉莎：我讓我老公和他朋友出去，而他醉醺醺地回家。)
(媽媽：如果妳給男人方便，他們便會得寸進尺。)

2. **This is he/she.** 我就是。

注意:

接電話者正是被找的人時, 若為男的, 即可回答: "This is he./This is he speaking./Speaking.", 若為女的, 即可回答: "This is she./This is she speaking./Speaking.", 均可譯為『我就是』。

例: A: Hello? May I speak with Winnie?
B: This is she.
This is she speaking.
Speaking.
(甲：哈囉？我可以和溫妮說話嗎？)
(乙：我就是。)
若被找的人不在時, 即可回答: "Sorry, she's not in now. Can/Shall I take a message?" (對不起, 她現在不在, 要不要我留話呢?)

Sandy: Hello? Is Tim there?
Mike: Sorry, he's not in now. Can I take a message?
(珊蒂：喂？提姆在嗎？)
(麥可：很抱歉，他現在不在，要我留話嗎？)

3. **vet** [vɛt] n. 獸醫
= veterinarian [ˌvɛtrəˈnɛrɪən]

例: You'd better take your dog to see a vet; it doesn't look well.
(你最好帶你的狗去看獸醫，牠看起來不太對勁。)

4. **period** [ˈpɪrɪəd] n. 生理期, 月經

5. **By the way, ...** 哦, 對了 (順便一提) ,……

例: By the way, who told you that I was sick?
(哦，對了，誰告訴你我病了？)

6. **pregnant** [ˈprɛgnənt] a. 懷孕的

例: A pregnant woman gets tired very easily.
(孕婦很容易疲倦。)

7. **permanent** [ˈpɝmənənt] a. 永久的
temporary [ˈtɛmpəˌrɛrɪ] a. 短暫的, 暫時的

例: Mr. Wang is a permanent member of the school board.
(王先生是學校董事會的常任董事。)

Joe plans to look for a temporary job before he emigrates to the States.
(阿喬計畫在他移民到美國前先找一份臨時工。)

請選出下列各句中正確的一項

1. Students are dependent ______ their teacher for proper instruction.
   (A) of (B) against (C) on (D) for

2. Dave had the ______ to challenge the boxer to a fight.
   (A) gut (B) guts (C) nerves (D) courages

3. Can you help me ______ an excuse for my absence?
   (A) play (B) tell (C) do (D) make

4. Little Johnny is counted ______ an adult and has to pay the full fare because he is so tall.
   (A) as (B) on (C) into (D) like

5. Tommy is ______ much a teacher as you or I.
   (A) such (B) as (C) so (D) how

解答：

1. (C) 2. (B) 3. (D) 4. (A) 5. (B)

Lesson 125
Lost and Found
失物招領

Reading
閱　讀

In recent years, going abroad for a holiday has almost become a national pastime. Traveling is indeed fun. But those of you traveling for the first time beware! What should you do if you lose your luggage? Don't panic. Just go straight to the airline you're traveling with. They'll direct you to the Lost and Found department.

In most cases, they'll find your luggage. But you must not forget one thing when you're at the check-in counter. Make sure you get a baggage check stub. Without it, the airline will have great difficulty helping you. Worried about what to say at the Lost and Found? Well, read the next lesson and you'll know what to do.

最近幾年，到國外度假幾乎已成為一種全國性的休閒活動。旅遊的確很有趣，但是第一次出國旅遊的人可要小心了！萬一遺失了行李該怎麼辦？別驚慌。只要直接到你所搭乘的航空公司，他們會指引你到失物招領處。

在大多數情形下，他們會找到你的行李。但是千萬別忘了，在辦理登機手續時，一定要拿到寄運行李的存根。若沒有存根，航空公司要幫忙你就很困難了。擔心在失物招領處該說些什麼嗎？那麼，看下一課，你就會知道該怎麼辦了。

Vocabulary & Idioms 單字 & 片語註解

1. **lost and found** [ˈlɔst ænd ˈfaʊnd] n. & a. 失物招領 (的)

   the Lost and Found (department)　　失物招領處

* 此處 lost 和 found 分別為 lose [luz]及 find [faɪnd]的過去分詞。

   例: You might find your lost umbrella at the Lost and Found.
   (也許你可以在失物招領處找到你掉了的雨傘。)

2. **go abroad**　　到國外去, 出國

   abroad [əˈbrɔd] adv. 國外

   例: Michael goes abroad on vacation once every six months.
   (邁可每半年出國度假一次。)

3. **pastime** [ˈpæsˌtaɪm] n. 消遣, 娛樂

   例: My pastime is collecting stamps.
   (我的消遣是集郵。)

4. **travel** [ˈtrævḷ] vi. & vt. 旅行

例: Amy travels whenever she's bored.
(每當艾咪感到生活乏味時就去旅行。)

The tycoon traveled the world to look for a good woman to marry.
(那名大亨環遊世界各地想找個好女人結婚。)

* tycoon [taɪˈkun] n. 大亨, 工商鉅子

5. **indeed** [ɪnˈdid] adv. 的確

例: Jack is indeed a good friend; he's always willing to help me out.
(傑克的確是個很好的朋友，他總是樂意幫我解困。)

6. **But those of you traveling for the first time beware!**

= But those of you who are traveling for the first time should beware!
但第一次旅遊的人可要小心了。

* for the first time 首次, 第一次

例: I went bungee jumping for the first time this summer.
(今年夏天我第一次去玩高空彈跳。)

7. **beware** [bɪˈwɛr] vi. & vt. 注意, 小心 (有關用法請參考之後的『文法重點』)

8. **panic** [ˈpænɪk] vi. 驚慌

注意:

panic 的過去式動詞及過去分詞均為 panic<u>k</u>ed, 現在分詞及動名詞則為 panic<u>k</u>ing。

例: The thief panicked and threw the purse he stole into the sea.
(那名小偷很驚慌而把偷來的皮包丟進海裡去了。)

There's no use panicking in an earthquake.
(地震時驚慌是沒有用的。)

9. **straight** [stret] adv. 直接地

go straight to... 直接到……

例: Let's go straight to the boss and ask him about this matter.
(咱們直接到老闆那兒問他這件事。)

10. **airline** [ˈɛrˌlaɪn] n. 航空公司

11. **direct** [dəˈrɛkt] vt. 指引, 指示; 指揮

例: Two traffic cops direct traffic at this intersection.
(有兩個交通警察在這個十字路口指揮交通。)

12. **department** [dɪˈpɑrtmənt] n. 部門; 科系

例: Which department of the bank do you work for?
(你在銀行的哪個部門工作?)

Victor studies in the Department of Accounting.
(維克多就讀於會計系。)

13. **check-in counter** [ˈtʃɛkɪn ˌkaʊntɚ] n. 辦理登機的櫃台

例: The check-in counter opens two hours before the plane is scheduled to take off.
(辦理登機的櫃台在飛機預定起飛前兩個鐘頭開始作業。)

14. **Make sure + (that)子句** 確定/務必……

例: Make sure you mail the letter, Tom.
(湯姆,務必要把這封信寄出去。)

15. **stub** [stʌb] n. (票券等的) 存根, 票根

例: Julia likes to collect plane ticket stubs.
(茱莉亞喜歡收集機票存根。)

16. **have difficulty + 動名詞** 做/在……(方面) 有困難/麻煩

例: Since the accident, Connie has had difficulty walking.
(自從發生意外後,康妮走路一直都很困難。)

17. **Worried about what to say at the Lost and Found?**

= Are you worried about what to say at the Lost and Found?
擔心在失物招領處該說些什麼嗎?

* worried [ˈwɝɪd] a. 著急的, 憂慮的

be worried about... 擔憂……

例: Dad's worried about his weight.
(老爸很擔心他的體重。)

Grammar Notes 文法重點

本課介紹表示『最近』的副詞或副詞片語與時態的關係, 以及動詞 beware 的用法, 和"Make sure + (that) 子句" 的用法。

1. **In recent years, going abroad for a holiday has almost become a national pastime.**

   最近幾年, 到國外度假幾乎已成為一種全國性的休閒活動。

   上列句中, in recent years 為表『最近幾年』的時間副詞片語, 與現在完成式 has almost become 並用。

   凡句中有 in recent years/months (最近幾年/幾個月) 的時間副詞片語出現時, 常與現在完成式或現在完成進行式並用; 表示到現在為止仍在繼續的動作或狀態時, 使用現在完成式來表達; 表示一直持續到現在且可能仍將繼續下去的動作時, 則使用現在完成進行式來表達。

   例: In recent months there have been several demonstrations in that area.
   (最近幾個月那個地區有過數次的示威活動。)

   In recent years the economy has been getting worse.
   (最近幾年, 經濟愈來愈走下坡。)

   注意:

   a. 在英文中, 鮮少使用 in recent days, 而用 recently、lately、of late 來表示『最近』之意, 且亦與現在完成式或現在完成進行式並用; 而使用 recently 時, 亦可與過去式並用。

例: Recently business has been very good.
(最近的生意很好。)

Lately it has been getting colder.
(最近天氣愈變愈冷了。)

Recently John quit his job.
(最近約翰把工作辭了。)

b. 表未來的『最近』時, 則用 soon 或 in the near future 來表示, 此時時態須用未來式。

例: I will go to see you soon.
(我最近會去看你。)

The education system will change in the near future.
(教育制度在最近的未來將會有所改變。)

2. **But those of you traveling for the first time beware!**
但是第一次出國旅遊的人可要小心了！

beware [bɪˈwɛr] vi. 當心; 注意; 提防

beware of...　　當心/注意/提防……

注意:

"beware of..."通常只用於命令句 (即以原形動詞起首的句子) 或含有助動詞 should、must 的敘述句中。

例: Beware of people who say one thing and do another.
(要當心那些言行不一的人。)

You girls should beware of strangers.
(妳們女孩子應該要提防陌生人。)

You must beware of pickpockets in crowded places.
(在擁擠的地方你必須提防扒手。)

3. **Make sure you get a baggage check stub.**
= Make sure that you get a baggage check stub.
一定要拿到寄運行李的存根。

Make sure + (that) 子句　　確定/務必……

注意:

在"Make sure + (that) 子句"的句構中, that 子句的時態須為簡單現在式或現在完成式, 且不可加任何助動詞 should、must 等。

例: Make sure (that) you must come on time for the meeting. (×)

→ Make sure (that) you come on time for the meeting. (○)
(務必要準時來開會。)

Make sure (that) you have written your name on the exam paper before handing it in.
(你務必要把名字寫在考卷上，才交考卷。)

1. **In recent years, going abroad for a holiday has almost become a national pastime.**

   Lately Bob has paid more attention to his health.

   My teacher's going to start a cram school in the near future.

   最近幾年, 到國外度假幾乎已成為一種全國性的休閒活動。
   最近鮑伯比較注意自己的健康。
   我的老師最近要開設一間補習班。

2. **But those of you traveling for the first time beware!**

   Beware of cheap imitations when you buy watches.

   While walking on the street, you should beware of stray dogs.

   但是第一次出國旅遊的人可要小心了！
   當你購買手錶時, 小心別買到廉價的仿製品。
   在街上行走時, 你應該要小心流浪狗。

Lesson 126

What's in the Bag?

袋子裡裝了什麼？

Mr. White is at the Lost and Found. He's talking to one of the clerks there.

(W=Mr. White; C=Clerk)

W: Excuse me. I couldn't find my luggage at the carousel.

C: OK. Come with me, please. See if you can find it in this room.

W: (after a while) It doesn't seem to be here.

C: In that case, do you have your baggage check stub with you?

W: Yes. Here you are.

C: OK. I'm afraid you'll have to fill out this form.

W: OK... (He looks at the form.) Hey! Wait a minute. How can I remember every item I have in the bag?

C: Why not? It's your luggage, isn't it? You should know what's in it.

W: Can you tell me everything you have in your pockets right now?

C: Uh...Um...OK, smart aleck! Just write down what you can remember.

懷特先生正在失物招領處和那裡的一位職員談話。
懷特：抱歉，我在行李輸送帶那兒找不到我的行李。
職員：好吧，請跟我來，看看能不能在這個房間裡找到。
懷特：（過了一會兒）好像沒在這兒。
職員：這樣的話，你的行李寄運存根帶在身上了嗎？
懷特：帶了，就在這兒。
職員：好的。我想你得填妥這份表格。
懷特：好吧……（他看了表格。）嘿！等等，我怎麼可能記得我袋子裡的每樣東西？
職員：怎麼不可能？那是你的行李，不是嗎？你應該知道裡頭有些什麼東西。
懷特：你能馬上說出你口袋裡所有的東西嗎？
職員：呃……嗯……好吧，聰明的傢伙！只要把你記得的寫下來就好了。

1. **clerk** [klɝk] n. 職員, 店員

例: The clerk is always arguing with customers.
(那個店員老是和顧客起爭執。)

2. **carousel** [ˌkærəˈsɛl] n. 旋轉式行李輸送帶

例: If you can't find your luggage at the carousel, you'd better go to the Lost and Found.
(如果你在行李輸送帶上找不到你的行李，最好到失物招領處去。)

3. **after a while** 過了一會兒

例: After a while, the rain stopped and we all left for home.
(過了一會兒，雨停了，我們便都回家去了。)

4. **fill** [fɪl] vt. 填寫

fill out a form 填寫/填妥表格

5. **form** [fɔrm] n. 表格

例: There are numerous forms to be filled out if you want to open a bank account.
(如果你想在銀行開戶，就必須填寫許多表格。)

6. **item** [ˈaɪtəm] n. 項目

例: The first item on the list he bought was an alarm clock.
(這張單子上他買的第一項東西是一個鬧鐘。)

7. **pocket** [ˈpɑkɪt] n. 口袋

pocket money　　零用錢

例: It's easy to lose your wallet if you put it in the back pocket of your jeans.
(如果你把皮夾放在牛仔褲後面口袋裡的話，很容易就弄丟的。)

Judy's pocket money is more than my monthly pay.
(茱蒂的零用錢比我一個月的薪水還多。)

8. **smart aleck** [ˈsmɑrt ˌælɪk] n. 自作聰明者, 自以為了不起的人

smart [smɑrt] a. 聰明的

例: Brad is a smart aleck; he thinks he knows everything.
(布萊德是個自以為了不起的人，他認為他什麼都懂。)

Sam is too smart not to see the key point in this matter.
(山姆太聰明了，不會看不出這件事情的關鍵所在。)

9. **write down...**　　寫下/抄下……

= jot down...

= take down...

例: I'd better write / jot / take down your telephone number lest I forget it.
(我最好寫下你的電話號碼免得我忘了。)

請選出下列各句中正確的一項

1. Our company ______ expanding in the near future.
   (A) had been (B) was (C) will be (D) has been

2. The boy ______ and almost drowned.
   (A) panicking (B) panicked
   (C) was panicked (D) paniced

3. The salesman has ______ selling these useless goods.
   (A) trouble (B) hard time (C) a fun (D) problem

4. If you go to Eric's house, you'd better ______ his fierce dogs.
   (A) beware (B) beware on
   (C) beware of (D) beware that

5. Please make sure you ______ enough money for the trip.
   (A) will bring (B) bring
   (C) brought (D) must bring

解答：

1. (C) 2. (B) 3. (A) 4. (C) 5. (B)

Lesson 127

Smile, Everybody!

大家一起來微笑！

Reading 閱讀

"When you're smiling, the whole world smiles with you." These are the words taken from an old song. These words must have given Tomoji Kondo a bright idea. He started smiling classes. Now, they're all over Japan. People from all walks of life, aged 20 to 83, attend these classes.

As you enter the class, you must shout out, "Konbanwa!" (Good evening!) as loudly and cheerfully as possible. Then you're supposed to make direct eye contact and smile as you shake hands with your classmates. No bowing is necessary.

Laughing is not allowed, either. According to Kondo, smiling immediately makes you feel better. Sound like a good idea? Why not give it a try?

『如果你微笑，全世界的人都會和你一起微笑。』這是摘錄自一首老歌的歌詞。這句歌詞一定給了近藤有司一個很棒的點子。他開設起微笑補習班來，而這種補習班現在已經遍及全日本，上課的人來自各行各業，年齡從二十歲到八十三歲都有。

你踏進教室時，必須盡可能大聲而愉快地喊"Konbanwa!" (日語的『晚上好！』)。接著，你和同學握手時，應該面帶微笑地注視著對方。你不需要鞠躬，也不准笑出聲來。根據近藤先生的說法，微笑可以立即使你心情舒暢。這主意聽起來很不錯吧？何不試試看呢？

Vocabulary & Idioms 單字 & 片語註解

1. **smile** [smaɪl] vi. 微笑

smile at...　對……微笑

注意:

其它與介詞 at 並用的動詞片語, 常見的尚有:

laugh at...　嘲笑……

stare at...　凝視……

sneer at...　鄙夷/視……

peep at...　偷看……

point at...　(用手) 指著……

例: Jeff blushed when the pretty girl smiled at him.
(那位漂亮的女孩對著他笑時，傑夫臉紅了。)
＊ blush [blʌʃ] vi. 臉紅

Why are you staring at me? Is something wrong?
(你為什麼瞪著我看？我哪裏不對勁嗎？)

Some people consider it rude to point at others.
(有些人認為用手指著別人是很沒有禮貌的事。)

2. **bright** [braɪt] a. 聰明的

例: The bright student knew the answer to the question immediately.
(那個聰明的學生馬上就知道這個問題的答案了。)

3. **all over + 地方名詞** 某地到處

例: This cheap pen is for sale all over town.
(這種廉價筆在城市裡到處都有賣。)

4. **from all walks of life** 來自各行各業

注意:

使用本片語時, 其前須置與人有關的名詞。

例: People from all walks of life like the singer's songs.
(各行各業的人都喜歡聽那位歌手的歌。)

5. **aged** [edʒd] a. 有……歲數的 & [ˈedʒɪd] a. 年老的

例: Only those (who are) aged 3 to 5 can appear on the TV show.
(只有三到五歲的人可以參加那項電視節目表演。)

My aged grandma likes to exercise in the park in the morning.
(我那上了年紀的奶奶喜歡早上在公園運動。)

6. **attend** [əˈtɛnd] vt. 參加, 出席

例: If you don't attend the meeting, the boss will be angry.
(如果你不參加這次會議，老闆會生氣的。)

7. **shout out...** 大聲喊叫……

例: When you hear your name called, please shout out, "Here!"
(聽到叫到你的名字時，請大聲喊：『有！』)

8. **loudly** [ˈlaʊdlɪ] adv. 大聲地

loud [laʊd] a. 大聲的

例: Our neighbors were singing so loudly that we couldn't get to sleep.
(我們的鄰居唱歌唱得非常大聲，以致於我們沒辦法入睡。)

What's that loud noise coming from across the street?
(對街傳來那陣吵雜聲是什麼聲音？)

9. **cheerfully** [ˈtʃɪrfəlɪ] adv. 愉快地

cheerful [ˈtʃɪrfəl] a. 愉快的

例: We cheerfully sang and danced around the camp fire.
(我們圍著營火，愉快地唱歌跳舞。)

Janet always has a cheerful smile on her face.
(珍妮特臉上永遠帶著愉快的微笑。)

10. **be supposed to + 原形動詞** 應該……

例: What am I supposed to do with this rubbish?
(我應該怎麼處理這些垃圾呢？)

11. **contact** [ˈkɑntækt] n. 接觸, 聯繫

keep in contact with... 與……保持聯繫

例: I still keep in contact with my senior high school classmates although we haven't seen each other for years.
(我仍然和我的高中同班同學保持聯繫，雖然我們彼此已多年未見過面。)

12. **shake** [ʃek] vt. 搖擺, 搖動

動詞三態: shake、shook [ʃuk]、shaken [ˈʃekən]。

shake hands with + 人 與某人握手

例: It was a thrill to shake hands with my favorite singer.
(和我最喜歡的歌手握手令我很興奮。)

＊ thrill [θrɪl] n. 心情激動

13. **bowing** [ˈbauɪŋ] n. 鞠躬

bow [bau] vi. 鞠躬

bow to...　向……鞠躬; 屈服於……

例: Bowing is more common in East Asian countries than elsewhere.
(鞠躬在東亞國家比其它地方普遍。)

Japanese people bow to each other as a greeting.
(日本人互相鞠躬作為一種打招呼方式。)

The boss is modest enough to bow to his employees' opinion.
(老闆非常謙虛，願意接受員工的意見。)

14. **allow** [əˌlaʊ] vt. 允許

例: Swimming in the river is not allowed.
(這條河川禁止游泳。)

15. **immediately** [ɪˈmidɪətlɪ] adv. 立即, 馬上

例: "Please come here immediately!" the boss shouted.
(『請立刻來這裏！』老闆大聲喊道。)

Grammar Notes 文法重點

本課介紹表示年齡的用法, 和表示『盡可能地……』的用法, 以及委婉表示『應當』的用法。

1. **People from all walks of life, aged 20 to 83, attend these classes.**

= People from all walks of life, who <u>are aged</u> 20 to 83, attend these classes.

上課的人來自各行各業, 年齡從二十歲到八十三歲都有。

表示年齡的用法如下:

人 + be aged + 數字　　某人幾歲

= 人 + be + 數字 + year (s) + old

例: My grandfather is aged ninety-seven.
= My grandfather is ninety-seven years old.

(我爺爺已經九十七歲了。)

＊在"人 + be ＋數字 + year (s) + old"中, year (s) old 可一併省略。

My grandfather is ninety-seven years old.

→ My grandfather is ninety-seven years. (×)

→ My grandfather is ninety-seven. (○)

＊上述用法中的 old 亦可用 of age 取代。

My grandfather is ninety-seven years old.

= My grandfather is ninety-seven years of age.

2. **As you enter the class, you must shout out, "Konbanwa!" (Good evening!) as loudly and cheerfully as possible.**

你踏進教室時, 必須盡可能大聲而愉快地喊"Konbanwa!" (日語的『晚上好！』)。

表示『盡可能地……』的用法如下:

as + 形容詞/副詞 + as possible　　盡可能地……

= as + 形容詞/副詞 + as one can

注意:

在上述用法中, 第一個 as 為副詞, 表『一樣地』, 故其後須接形容詞或副詞以供修飾; 而第二個 as 則為副詞連接詞, 表『和』, 引導副詞子句, 修飾第一個 as, 故"as...as"譯成『和……一樣地』。

理論基礎:

a. as possible 係為 as it is/was possible 化簡而成, it 是代名詞, 代替其前述詞部分的概念, 實際使用時, it is/was 一定要省略, 已成固定用法。

例: He remained as quiet as possible.
(他盡可能地保持安靜。)

＊本句原為"He remained as quiet as it was possible.", it 即代替 remaining quiet (動名詞片語, 作主詞) 的概念。

You must study as hard as possible.
(你要盡可能地用功。)

＊本句原為"You must study as hard as it is possible.", it 即代替 studying hard (動名詞片語, 作主詞) 的概念。

b. as one can 之後即省略了與其前主要子句中相同的述詞部分, 以避免重覆。

例: He remained as quiet as he could.
→ He remained as quiet as he could (remain quiet) .
= He remained as quiet as possible.
＊本句 as he could 之後即省略了與其前相同的述詞部分 remain quiet。

You must study as hard as you can.
→ You must study as hard as you can (study hard) .
= You must study as hard as possible.
＊本句 as you can 之後即省略了與其前相同的述詞部分 study hard。

3. **Then you<u>'re supposed to</u> make direct eye contact and smile as you shake hands with your classmates.**
接著, 你和同學握手時, 應該面帶微笑地注視著對方。
本句中, 使用了"be supposed to ＋原形動詞"的句型, 此乃表『應當』之委婉說法。
表示『應當』、『應該』、『必須』時, 其語氣強弱的用法如下:

a. 用 must (必須)、have to (必須, 不得不) 的語氣最強。

例: You <u>must</u> finish your work before you leave.
(你必須做完工作才能離開。)

You <u>have to</u> finish your work before you leave.
(你得做完工作才能離開。)

b. should 的語氣稍弱。

例: You <u>should</u> finish your work before you leave.
(你應該做完工作才能離開。)

c. 使用"be supposed to + 原形動詞"時, 則語氣最弱, 為較委婉的說法。

例: You <u>are supposed to</u> finish your work before you leave.
(你應當做完工作才能離開。)

Substitution
代 換

1. **People from all walks of life, aged 20 to 83, attend these classes.**

   Kate, who is aged 20, has already graduated from college.

   Bob looks old, but he's only thirty years old.

   上課的人來自各行各業，年齡從二十歲到八十三歲都有。

   凱特今年二十歲，已經大學畢業了。

   鮑伯看起來很老但他卻只有三十歲。

2. **As you enter the class, you must shout out, "Konbanwa!" (Good evening!) as loudly and cheerfully as possible.**

   The workers worked as fast as possible but still couldn't meet the deadline.

   Please send me the information as soon as you can.

   你踏進教室時，必須儘量大聲愉快地喊"Konbanwa!"。

   那些工人盡可能快速趕工，但仍無法在期限內完成。

   請儘快地把那份資料寄給我。

Lesson 128

Konbanwa, Everybody!

各位晚上好！

Sato, a Japanese student, goes to a smiling class in Beijing.
(S=Sato; T=teacher)

S: Konbanwa, evali-badi! (everybody!) (The whole class laughs.) Ha! Ha! Ha!

T: What on earth is that?

S: Wow! You see. It works. My classmates are so happy they're laughing their heads off.

T: They're laughing at you, Mr. Shatou.

S: No, no, no. My name is Sato, not Shatou. (The class laughs again.) I think they're laughing at you.

T: Whatever! Anyway, try to just say, "Good evening!" in English next time. OK?

S: OK. Gud-e-va-ling! (Good evening!) How's that?

T: I haven't got a clue what you're saying.

S: Thank you. Ha! Ha! Ha!

日本學生佐藤在北京某微笑補習班上課。
佐藤：大家晚上好！（全班大笑）哈！哈！哈！
老師：你講的到底是什麼話？
佐藤：哇！你看。真的有效哦。我的同學都很快樂，他們都笑破肚皮了。
老師：殺頭先生，他們是在笑你。
佐藤：不，不，不。我叫佐藤，不叫殺頭。（全班再度大笑）我想他們是在笑你。
老師：隨你怎麼說！無論如何，下次請用英文練習說『晚上好！』，好嗎？
佐藤：好吧。狗打伊飯哩！（晚上好！）我說得如何？
老師：我一點都聽不懂你在說什麼。
佐藤：謝謝你。哈！哈！哈！

Key Points 重點提示

1. **What <u>on earth</u> is that?**

= What <u>the hell</u> is that?

= What <u>in the world</u> is that?

那到底是什麼意思？/你講的什麼鬼話？

注意:

疑問詞 (what、who、where...) 之後可加"the hell"、"on earth"、"in the world"作強調用法, 表『究竟』、『到底』之意,然 the hell 是比較粗俗的講法, 雖然常可在老美的電視影集及日常會話中聽到, 但是最好儘量避免使用。

2. **Whatever!** 隨便你怎麼說! 隨便!

例: Peggy: Shall we eat out today?
Garth: Whatever!

(佩琪：今天我們到外面吃，好嗎？)
(葛斯：隨便！)

4. **clue** [klu] n. 線索 (常與介詞 to 並用)
例: This fingerprint is the only clue to solving the murder.
(這枚指紋是解決這樁謀殺案唯一的線索。)

請選出下列各句中正確的一項

1. The boy tried to peep ______ his classmate's answer during the test.
   (A) to (B) at (C) upon (D) against

2. Mary is ______ 70 and still going strong.
   (A) of age (B) of aged (C) age (D) aged

3. Don walked up the stairs as ______ as possible so as not to wake his wife up.
   (A) quit (B) quite (C) quietly (D) quiet

4. You're ______ to take care of your little brother while I'm out.
   (A) supposed (B) have (C) must (D) should

5. The students laughed their ______ off when the teacher slipped and fell.
   (A) heads (B) teeth (C) hands (D) arms

解答：

1. (B) 2. (D) 3. (C) 4. (A) 5. (A)

國家圖書館出版品預行編目資料

中級美語 / 賴世雄著 -- 初版.
臺北市：常春藤有聲, 2004 [民 93]
冊： 公分. -- (常春藤進修系列；E06)

ISBN 986-7638-20-4 (下冊：平裝)

1. 英國語言 -- 讀本

805. 18 93000146

常春藤進修系列 E06

中級美語 (下)

編　　著：賴世雄
編　　審：Carlos Souza ・ Carl Anthony
張為麟・黃文玲・李橋・蔣宗君・張樹人
校　　對：常春藤中外編輯群
封面設計：羅容格・黃振倫・賴雅莉
插　　畫：張睿洋
電腦排版：朱瑪琍・劉濰崢・李宜芝
顧　　問：賴陳愉嫺
法律顧問：王存淦律師・蕭雄淋律師
發行日期：2005 年 9 月　初版/三刷

出 版 者：常春藤有聲出版有限公司
台北市忠孝西路一段 33 號 5 樓
行政院新聞局出版事業登記證
局版臺業字第肆捌貳陸號

服務電話：(02) 2331-7600　服務傳真：(02) 2381-0918
信　　箱：臺北郵政 8-18 號信箱
郵撥帳號：**19714777**　常春藤有聲出版有限公司
定　　價：360 元

*如有缺頁、裝訂錯誤或破損　請寄回本社更換

常春藤有聲出版有限公司

讀者回函卡

✍感謝您的填寫，您的建議將是公司重要的參考及修正指標！

我購買本書的書名是		編碼	
我購買本書的原因是	□老師、同學推薦 □家人推薦 □學校購買 □書店閱讀後感到喜歡 □其他		
我購得本書的管道是	□書攤 □業務人員推薦 □大型連鎖書店 □書店名稱＿＿＿＿＿ □其他		
我最滿意本書的三點依序是	□內容 □編排方式 □雙色印刷 □試題演鍊 □解析清楚 □封面 □售價 □促銷活動豐富 □信任品牌 □廣告 □其他		
我最不滿意本書的三點依序是	□內容 □編排方式 □雙色印刷 □試題演練 □解析不足 □封面 □售價 □促銷活動貧乏 □廣告 □其他		
我有一些其他想法與建議是			
我發現本書誤植的部份是	□書籍第__頁，第__行，有錯誤的部份是		
	□書籍第__頁，第__行，有錯誤的部份是		

✍我的基本資料

讀者姓名		生　日		性別	□男 □女
就讀學校		科系年級	科 年級	畢業	□已畢 □在學
聯絡電話		E-mail			
聯絡地址					

請您填寫完後寄至：

台北市忠孝西路一段 33 號 5 樓　常春藤有聲出版有限公司　出版部收

填寫日期：西元＿＿＿年＿＿＿月＿＿＿日

A Quick Note